Pioneer Love
Nellie and Platt's story

Cynthia Markham

CocoaMax—Fort Worth, TX
Paperback ISBN: 979-8-3305-9549-5
eBook ISBN: 979-8-3305-9582-2
Title: *Pioneer Love: Nellie and Platt's Story*
Author: Cynthia Markham
Digital distribution | 2024
Paperback | 2024

Published in the United States by New Book Authors Publishing

Dedication

I want to first of all dedicate this to my wonderful Mother my cheerleader and encourager.

It was from all the stories that she and my grandmother had told that inspired me to write this.

To my husband Daniel, my rock and soul mate.

To my amazing incredible intelligent Daughters Charity and Jessica who are always my encouragement.

And especially my Granddaughter Jordan who never stopped believing her Nana could do this she is my critic and editor.

My Sister Jeannie for the loan of Nellie's wedding dress for the photo.

My hope is that this book be enjoyed and that my Great, Great Grandparents would be honored for their incredible courage and enduring love they shared.

This is a historical fiction the names although some correct and most events historical the rest will remain fiction since no one but Platt and Nellie really knew what happened.

Chapter One
"The early years in Marshall Indiana"

It was early springtime in Marshall, Indiana and no place on earth could compare to the glory of the land. When the ground starts to resurrect from a long Winter's nap and burst into the promise of spring, where one can see whispers of green grass starting to peak through the crusty brown ground cover speckled with the last remnants of snow, giving hope that winter was finally over, and that Spring was ready to make her glorious debut. But the glories of spring were not the topic of conversation this morning in the Jefferson household, rather, there was a different scene altogether taking place this fine spring morning.

"Mama please hurry!" Nellie pleaded as she paced back and forth impatiently in the front parlor.

As she passed the divan covered in a rich gold and burgundy color with braid along the seams, she felt the material and traced the pattern with her fingers and found herself drifting off in deep thought. On the other side of the room was a wing backed chair covered in a burgundy with gold print in the corner. Nellie stopped tracing the pattern of the material, and for a moment looked around the room as if this was the first time she had really stopped and noticed. Her mother had exquisite taste and her father made sure she had exactly what she wanted in every room of the house. Each room was as tastefully decorated as the one before, adorned with pictures and lamps and a lovely pitcher and bowl set sitting on the table in the corner looked as if it could've come right out of one those catalogs they have at the general store. *This she thought, of all the rooms in the house, was her favorite. It was a place where she would relax and enjoy her favorite pastime reading and become lost in her thoughts.*

But this morning all she could do was pace back and forth waiting ever so impatiently for her mother to make an appearance. *Why today of all days would her mother, who was well known for her punctuality and prided herself on always being early, decide to break from tradition?* Normally Nellie would not give in to such impatience, but today was as far from a normal day as possible. She felt as if this was possibly the most important day of her life. The nerves were twisting her stomach every time she dared think about the day's events that awaited her, thus she certainly did not want to start it off by being tardy.

It was an honor to have been chosen to sit for this test. However, this was not just any test. Only the top-ranking students were invited to attend. If you scored well, you were given an opportunity at a spot at the university to study teaching. It was mind boggling to think she was even considered to sit for this exam. Although Nellie did not want to boast, she had studied very hard and was a good student, one of the top performing students in the school. She performed well for a girl, but there was a boy at her school who was older. A boy who always did just a little better and appeared just a little smarter than she, and he would never miss an opportunity to rub it in. He was always asking what she scored on a test just so he could boast that his grade was better. Even thinking about him made her get angry, but she was determined that even he would not distract her from her task at hand today.

Becoming briefly sidetracked from her current conundrum, Nellie looked out the front window; she noticed the first signs of spring after a dreadful winter. Spring was her favorite time of year. The wispy clouds dancing in a sky of blue, the sun had just begun its descent up the sides of the snowcapped mountains. Marshall, Indiana was a wonderful place to live and grow up, and it was the only home Nellie had ever known and she loved it! It was the perfect size town where all the people knew each other. Marshall had not grown so large as to lose the sense of community where one could walk down the street and be greeted by friends and neighbors who were always there for each other in hard times rejoiced with each other in good. What better place to live she thought! As she looked out at the hill side of the ranch that her father owned, she noticed more signs of springs as it began to paint the countryside in a breathtaking picture. The newly born sheep were playing in the lush green meadows where the flowers began to spring to life in vibrant colors and dot the hillside. *It looked too perfect! It looked as if it should be painted and hung above the fireplace to enjoy all year through.*

"Mama pleases hurry! I must not be late for this exam, or I will not be allowed admittance!" she pleaded.

The head instructor had given strict instructions that any students arriving late would not be allowed to take the exam.

Passing the large mirror, she stopped to check and see that she looked self-confident although truth be known she was feeling anything but confident. For such a special occasion, Nellie was determined to look her absolute best. She wanted to look just right so that she could do her very best. She retrieved one of her favorite dresses to wear. She had a difficult time trying to choose, but she decided on the blue one with tiny blue flowers. She knew she was very fortunate to own so many beautiful dresses, for there were many young girls who did not have the wardrobe and variety from which she had been so graciously blessed by her adoring parents.

Nellie Jefferson loved being the youngest child to her parents, Lester and Mary Jefferson. Her sisters Dora and Melissa were much older and had left home when she was very young, so she always felt as if she were an only child. There were times when it was lonely and she missed them terribly, but she had become close to her Mama and Papa in her sister's absence, and they had become her best friends. Mama and she would go on long walks and soak in the sweet aroma of the Cherry Blossom and Crepe Myrtle bushes beginning to bloom. She especially enjoyed walking along the pastures watching as the baby calves played in the meadow filled with wildflowers and witnessing the dead grass of winter gave way to a new carpet of green as far as the eye could see. Yes, spring was a wonderful time of year!

She did count her blessings and was grateful for what she had been given, being the youngest child, she knew her Papa and Mama loved to indulge her whenever possible. Being the younger sister to a very successful sister was not such a bad situation either. Her eldest Sister Mel was a printer at one of the only woman printers. She was quite successful in her chosen career, and Dora, her other sister, was a schoolteacher in California. She missed them terribly but always appreciated her visits to them.

The dress she was wearing was a gift from her sister Mel and she had such wonderful taste! The dress was comfortable, but she knew she looked stunning in it and that gave her more confidence. She combed her hair until it shined in the daylight, the deep mahogany color so deep and rich. She was wearing it half pulled up on top of her head and the rest hanging down her back. Although she was concerned that having any of her hair up might cause a headache, she decided to risk it.

This test was for all junior and senior students wanting to become teachers, journalists, doctors, or lawyers. If they had high enough scores, they could get a scholarship to university. Many of her fellow classmates wondered why she even wanted to take this exam. For after all, she was a girl and weren't girls supposed to get married and have children? But Nellie thought, why NOT a woman if they were as smart as a man and could score as well or better? She thought they deserved a chance to do something more with their lives than marry and bear children. Nellie knew that maybe, she thought that way in part due to her having strong independent spinster sisters, but Nellie studied hard to make very good marks in school. In fact, sometimes they were perfect scores; she just hoped she knew enough to do well on this exam.

"Are you ready to go?" Mary Jefferson said as she came down the stairs looking very poised and very attractive, perfectly groomed with every hair in place and clothes tastefully suited to her slim figure.

Nellie was always in awe of her mother's beauty and her poise. She knew what made Papa fall in love with her. Nellie hoped that one day when she found someone as perfect as Papa that he would look at her the way Papa looked at Momma. But not now and not today. The only thing she was thinking about right now was getting to town in time to take the exam.

As they headed to town, Nellie's attention was drawn once again to the countryside. It seemed everywhere she looked spring was beginning to explode into bloom, a welcome sign and after such a long hard winter. At times Nellie was sure it would be winter forever! Oh, how she loved spring! It was the promise of new life, baby animals, new blossoms on trees, and countless plants working their way to the surface of the Earth. One could certainly enjoy the change of seasons here in Marshall, Indiana. Nellie loved her home on the ranch. They had cattle, sheep, horses, wheat, and corn. She admired how her father was such a successful rancher and businessman.

Nellie was a bright young girl to say the least, but she had a beauty that was beyond compare. Deep brown eyes, dark mahogany hair, skin was a peaches and cream complexion, beautiful, tall, and slender. She would catch the eye of any young man and that concerned her Papa.

Nellie was so very thankful to have arrived at the examination with a few moments to spare to gather her thoughts and calm her down before the doors to the examination hall were opened.

While Nellie was waiting outside the room, she was pacing the floor and kept thinking about the test. *Would she be able to do it? Would she be smart enough? She knew she made good marks at school, but there was always that annoying boy in the grade ahead of her who had to do better than she. What if he made it and she didn't? She thought maybe he thought himself so smart just because his Father was the Circuit Court Judge and Attorney of Marshall County, Indiana.* She guessed that's what made him act the way he did, but today he would not take up any more of her thoughts. The doors opened to a massive room with great pillars appearing to be holding the room up in the air. The room was so large that it made her wonder just how many students were taking the exam. She was more than nervous than she had thought she would be but as she glanced around, she noticed that the room was filling quickly with many young men and woman who were taking this test. She only hoped that she was as smart as they were. She would certainly give it her best and dismiss the thoughts about that annoying young man, Platt. She had no more than seated herself and started to prepared her pencils for the exam when she heard someone sitting near her and recognized the voice immediately.

"Platt, well I see that you made it. I had my doubts about if you were going to make it, I thought you might be afraid that a girl might show you up," she said with a huff and turned to concentrate on getting her mind ready to concentrate.

"No need to worry that pretty head of yours, Nellie. I aim to beat your best grade by far," he said with a smile and tipped his head in her direction.

That boy was the most infuriating person she had ever met. But now she had to concentrate and forget Platt Corbaley! The test was about to start, and the room monitor was roaming around the massive room to ensure there was no cheating taking place. When they handed out the first test, Nellie was ecstatic. It was writing and the next part was math, which she excelled in. She was delighted that the test was much easier than she anticipated until she got to the history section. *Oh! Why did she not pay more attention in history?* She did the best she could and only hoped it was enough to win one of the coveted prizes of a scholarship to a university. At the end of the test, she felt exhausted, yet relieved that it was finally behind her, as she was preparing to leave the building, that was when she heard a familiar voice calling her name. She hurried along faster and faster, hoping to avoid the inevitable running into Mr. Platt Corbaley!

"Nellie," he called.

She continued to ignore him until the voice was getting closer and she knew she could not ignore him any longer on the verge of becoming rude. She turned and saw him walking ever so confidently towards her.

"Oh, Platt I did not see you. How do you think you did on the exam?" she managed to say as flippant but corrigible as she could muster.

He just walked right up to her and said, "May the best man, I mean student win," tipped his hat, kissed her hand, and walked off.

She was so grateful to see her mother and be on their way home.

"How was the test dear, do you think you scored well?" Her mother, being very sensitive to her daughter, knew that right now may not be the best time to engage in talk. Nellie appeared to be deep in thought.

Lunch

The next day at school was the big box lunch social where all the girls in the class had to pack their very best cooking and baked good and pack it in a box and no one is supposed to know who made which lunch and then who ever bid on your lunch got the lunch and the pleasure of your company for the lunch hour.

Of all the infuriating and selfish things, he had done, and she could remember more than a few, like the time he tied her braids in knots and when he had the nerve to bid on her lunch at the box lunch social. It wouldn't have been so bad but Matilda, her "best friend" had told him which one was hers. When the bidding had started, he just kept going and going until he paid a very embarrassing price for a box lunch! If it weren't for the school needing the new roof, she might have made a scene. The worst part came when you had to eat with whoever bought your lunch! She thought she would fix him, so she sat there and didn't speak to him the entire lunch. But it didn't appear to faze Platt at all. He ate lunch and relished every bite.

Nellie could stand it no longer and turned to him and said, "Platt Corbaley you are the boldest and self-absorbed boy I have ever met, and I will not sit here with you a minute longer!" and she got up to leave.

He said, "Suits me fine, but be sure and leave the lunch. After all, I did pay for it."

And with that Nellie turned and stormed off.

The next day at school was the worst; Platt acted as if nothing had happened. In fact, he went out of his way to be extra friendly. School came easy for him, but it seemed he was always showing off and that was the most frustrating of all. To get the best grade on a test or a project, and to be the first to always have his hand in the air and want to be called on in class, not wanting to give anyone else a chance to get it right! Or, she thought, maybe he was just very sure of himself, or maybe he was trying to impress her! She was just glad that he was graduating, and she would not have to constantly be harassed by this conceited person, and maybe the rest of the class could have a chance at learning and receiving some.

Chapter Two
The walk

The week after the lunch box social, Platt came over calling on Nellie. He asked Papa if he might have his permission to walk Nellie home. Papa looked at the young man with piercing dark eyes, and he respected the fact that he would ask permission from him to walk his youngest daughter home from school. He saw his hand twisting and his shifting from one foot to the other and for a moment enjoyed seeing him squirm.

But then he thought about the amount of courage he took for him to do this and before he could stop, he heard himself saying, "Maybe."

Nellie had seen Platt come by the house and request to speak to Papa, and curiosity got the better of her and she had to listen in.

"Maybe?" What was he thinking? She would never let him walk her home, or anywhere, for that matter. And Papa, he was so protective. What was he thinking? Nellie was perplexed. But she would show him where he stood with her once and for all.

When she arrived at school that day, she completely ignored Platt and went over to where the girls were. She started talking to her best friend Matilda, hoping to make a point with him. But he just seemed to be ignoring her! The nerve of that boy! Talking with Matilda proved fruitless, for all she and the other girls wanted to talk about was how "dreamy and handsome" Platt was, and how when he smiled and looked at you, you wanted to melt into a puddle.

"Well, here is one girl who won't be melting," Nellie replied.

"What?" gasped Matilda. "I thought that you and Platt were sweet on each other."

Nellie turned her head so quick and shouted, "NO! That is not true! I don't know where you got your information, but it is erroneous!"

"Well, then I hope he comes courting me," said Matilda.

"You are a little young to be thinking about courting, but when the time comes, he is all yours!" Nellie stated. "We are seniors in high school so why are you thinking about marrying when we have more important things to think about?"

"I mean, my Mama was married by our age," Matilda said.

"But don't you want more for yourself? Get more education, see the world, or be someone famous. We could be anything or anyone we wanted to be!" Nellie uttered.

"Nellie, all I want is to find a good man and settle down, that's enough for me," Matilda said with staunch determination.

"Well, it's not for me," Nellie responded just as the school bell rang and it was time for all the students to take their places.

Platt made a point of stopping by Nellie's desk to say "good morning" to her, which only infuriated her more, but she was not about to let him have any satisfaction. She acted polite and then quickly put her head in her book, trying not to make eye contact with him and let him see the blush on her cheeks. *Why did he have this effect on her? Oh, she couldn't think of it now!* She had to concentrate on her studies.

Today, Nellie was finding it difficult to concentrate. She didn't know if it was because of Platt or the beautiful spring day. After school, Nellie decided because she had so much on her mind, she would take the long way home. *Nellie knew she needed to clear her mind and a walk was the best way. She also knew that Mama would never approve of her walking in the woods by herself without an escort. She could hear her saying it now, "Nellie no proper young woman goes on a walk without an escort." Well, who said she was "proper" or wanted to be, although she knew it was her mama and papa's goal. What was she to do with all this free spirit? Maybe she was a lot like her sisters, Melissa and Dora. After all, and maybe that was what worried her parents. She knew she must figure this all out without breaking her parents' heart in the process.*

Nellie began walking and enjoying the sunshine, the birds singing, and she even saw a baby fawn and mother doe. The sun was warm and bright and felt so good on her face. She enjoyed the time alone with her thoughts. She hadn't realized how far she had gone and how late it was getting until she looked up and noticed that the sun was starting to set. She decided she had best turn around and start back home. But she had walked a long way and she needed to get home the quickest way. Nellie started looking for a short cut, but with all the spring rains the creek had risen above the banks in many areas. Nellie started to run up and down the riverbank looking for the shortest way to cross the river and to get home before dark. Everywhere she looked was covered by water. Surely there was a short cut along here so she would not have to retrace her steps.

Up the mountain side! As she was scouring the landscape Nellie came across a log that had fallen over in one of the recent storms. She tugged at it and was not able to budge it, so she felt sure it was secure. Nellie put her books in her bag and placed it over head and across her shoulder. Next, very carefully placing one foot in front of the other, Nellie began to carefully cross to the other side of the riverbanks. She was inching her feet very carefully and feeling more confident that the other side was looking closer. She took another step but hadn't realized that the log was so wet, and her foot slipped, causing her to slip off the log and crash into the freezing and rapidly moving water.

"HELP! HELP!" she yelled as loudly as she could.

As she was bobbing to stay afloat all the while the current was beckoning her under. She tried desperately to grasp onto something, but all she could do was try her best to stay afloat. She remembered her Papa telling her once when she was at the river that if she were ever to fall in, the best thing was not panic, but to try and relax and go with the current. When she did that, it seemed to help her, so she was not being pulled under as much. However, it didn't solve the problem of getting out of the river before it went into the falls. She knew if she were to go over the falls she would not survive. Nellie kept trying to look for something, anything, to hold on to. She looked up and saw a branch. She was so relieved! She reached up and grabbed it and held on for dear life, but the branch was too weak and could not hold her weight and broke. Nellie began to panic as the waves and current were getting stronger and dragging her under. She had to fight ever harder to try and stay afloat. She knew when the current was getting stronger that the falls were close.

"Oh God, help me!" she prayed as she felt her body being dragged deeper and deeper into the fast-moving current of the swelling river.

She was getting weary and felt as if her strength was nearly gone from fighting the water currents for so long. The waters were pulling her deeper and deeper. Nellie was just too weary to fight any longer when she came back up to the surface and with a sudden tug. Her book satchel that had been over her shoulders had become entangled in a tree branch and she was stuck. At least for now she was no longer headed down toward the falls. Now she needed a plan to detach her satchel and still manage to stay afloat and grab on to this tree. First, she decided to take off the satchel from around her shoulder, sounded simple enough, and would have been under any normal circumstance. But rushing waters are NOT NORMAL! Slowly, slowly and inch by inch, she moved the satchel strap off her shoulder. The moving current made this task more difficult, but at last, she was able to free herself from the satchel.

It felt like a hundred pounds had been lifted off her shoulders! Now for plan number two, she had to hang on to this tree branch with all the strength in her! Slowly, she made her way against the rushing current closer and closer to the other side of the bank until at last she was able to feel ground under feet and when she did, she collapsed in a heap onto the shore. When she regained coherency, she realized that when she slipped on the log, she had gashed her leg. She hadn't realized it in the water because the water was so cold, and she had been fighting to stay afloat. Now that she had a chance to see it, she realized it was quite large and gouged deeply. She bled profusely, but she had to do something. But what? She had nothing and there was no one around.

She yelled out, "HELP! HELP!" but no answer came.

Nellie knew she was losing a lot of blood, so she ripped off some of her petticoat and wrapped it as snuggly as she could. She remembered reading about that in a medical article she loved to read.

Nellie was getting very tired and decided to sit for a minute and get her bearings about where she was before heading home. She was so cold and wet from being in the river that she couldn't help but start to shiver. She walked sluggishly over and sat by a tree where there was a pile of leaves and brush. She covered herself with that and used it for warmth so she could sit for a few minutes. Nellie was so weak from the struggle, and now from the blood loss, that she felt like she needed to rest before heading home. Wherever that was, she thought as she drifted off to sleep.

Papa was pacing the floor. "Where is she? She is NEVER late and never goes to anyone's house without permission!" Papa was fuming and one could almost see smoke coming from his ears.

"Where is that girl?" he asked Mama.

She replied, "Lester why don't you go look for her, maybe something happened?"

That was all the encouragement he needed, and he headed for the door. He went to all of her friends' houses asking if they had seen her. He was getting worried when he went to Matilda's, and she told him Platt Corbaley was supposed to walk her home from school. Then Papa's worry turned to anger.

When he arrived at the Richard Corbaley ranch, Platt was home. Lester was so overcome with worry and grief, he blurted out, "You were to walk Nellie home after school. Have you seen her?"

"No Sir, Nellie turned down my offer to walk her home from school. She said she wanted to walk home and enjoy the spring day, why sir what's wrong?"

"Nellie never made it home from school."

"WHAT?! Where is she?" Platt blurted out.

"I don't know that Platt, that's why I am asking you."

"I am going to help you look for her sir, and Pa will get the ranch hands together and we will start a search party for her. We will send someone into town and get the sheriff and start a search party as well for it will be dark soon and it gets cold on these spring nights."

"Well young man, you are well organized I will give you that." But before he could finish his sentence, Platt was out the door saddling up his horse so he could look for Nellie.

Nellie, what a strange thought! Why did this young woman who argued with him over everything have such an effect on him? He could not get her out of his mind, he thought about her in the morning during school when he should be paying attention, especially since graduation was in a few months. But as hard as he tried, he could not shake her. But he may have to, he thought, especially since she doesn't seem to feel the same. What he needed to concentrate on now was finding her. Nellie, where would she go? Up the river? Yes, that's the way she would go, I just feel it. Off he raced on his horse, yelling her name, but no response. He was becoming really scared, where could she have gone? The flowers were in the most abundance in this west area, so he steered his horse in that direction, all the while yelling Nellie's name.

With only a deafening silence in return, it was getting dark, and he was about to give up and head out in another direction, when he noticed something along the river bank. He headed his horse in that direction as quickly as he could, all the while yelling her name. His heart was in his throat as he drew near and saw no movement. *NO,*

NO. Please God! Don't let Nellie be dead. When he got up to where Nellie was, he started yelling her name and she started moving.

"Why are you shouting?"

"Oh Nellie, I am so glad to find you!" Platt said as he scooped her up in his arms and held her close.

Nellie was so glad to be found, she melted into his arms, not even realizing how glad she was it was Platt's arm she was in.

"How did you find me Platt? How did you know I was missing, and after I was so rude to you?"

"It's okay Nellie, all that's important is you're found and safe. I was so worried. I didn't know if I would ever see you again." Platt's eyes quickly shifted to the pool of blood on the ground and located its source rather quickly. "Nellie you're hurt?" Platt said as he looked down at the blood-soaked bandage on her leg.

"I gashed my leg on a rock when I fell into the river," Nellie replied.

"It looks like it's bleeding pretty badly, may I look at it?"

"Certainly NOT," Nellie replied. "I appreciate your rescue, but don't be making any advances."

"My only concern right now is getting you home. Let's get going before it gets any later." Platt helped Nellie on his horse, but she was so weak she could hardly hang on. She was bleeding more freely now, and she knew it was more serious than she first realized. As they worked their way down the riverbank towards the Jefferson Ranch, Platt raced towards her house to get home quickly, but he knew he had to take it slow because she was having so much difficulty staying on the horse. He was worried about her leg, knowing she needed medical attention as soon as possible. He was also worried about her blood loss and going into shock. He had wrapped a blanket from his horse and his coat around her but could feel her shiver and shake against his body. Holding her close against his body was unnerving him, and it was making him have enough body heat for both. He couldn't explain the effect that having her body close to his had on him. It bothered him, when all he should be thinking about is getting her home and her leg looked at.

As they neared the Jefferson's, they met Papa coming in with his horse and rig. As he neared them, Platt yelled out to him that Nellie was injured, very weak, and would need a doctor. Papa said to go on up to the house and get Nellie inside, for by now she had started going in and out of consciousness. When they got her inside, Papa thanked

Platt and asked him to go for Doc. That was all Platt needed. He was out the door and headed for town as fast as his horse could go. He got to Doc's office, and he wasn't there, where could he be? He sped off downtown to try and find someone, anyone, who might know where Doc. was. The diner, he thought as he turned his horse in that direction.

Platt burst through the door of the diner yelling, "Has anyone seen Doc? Nellie Jefferson fell in the river and gashed her leg. She needs to see the Doc right away!"

Someone yelled out that Doc had gone to the Smithers ranch to deliver a baby. The door was swinging behind. They could hardly finish their sentence and Platt was on his way to find Doc. He headed his horse in the direction of the Smithers Ranch as fast as he could possibly go. On his way, he met up with Doc coming back to town. He tried to explain what had happened, but he could hardly talk. This was very odd for Platt, but soon the two of them were headed to the Jefferson ranch. When they arrived, Nellie was lying on the bed and had slipped into shock.

With the extreme temperature changes she experienced from falling in the river, she looked so pale and lifeless. It was very unnerving to Platt. *What if she didn't come out of this? He was thinking he would never have a chance to tell her how much she means to him, how she makes his life seem worth living, and more worthwhile. Would he ever have the chance? He shouldn't be thinking that now, what he needs to be concentrating on is Nellie and her recovery.* Platt was pacing the floor when Papa came out of the room. He crossed to where Platt was standing and stretched out his hand.

"Thank you, son, I don't know what we would have done if anything had happened to Nellie. Thank you for finding her and bringing her home safely."

"It was my privilege sir. I would risk my life for Nellie."

Papa knew that look, for it was the same way he looked at his sweet wife. He knew this was more than a mere infatuation, but he couldn't think about it right now.

Doc was in with Nellie for what seemed like an eternity, as Platt and Papa both continued to pace the floor. Papa had thought about sending him home, but knew he was much too like himself. As much as he would like for him to go home and get some rest, he also knew he would never leave until he knew Nellie was out of the woods. Doc was very worried because fever had begun to set in and although he did manage to get the bleeding stopped, the wound didn't look good. It should have been sutured if it had been tended to immediately but since it was left open to the elements and possible infection, he would just have to wait and see. He hoped he would not have to open it up and bleed out the infection. Time would tell. Mama kept a damp cloth on her head to control the fever and packed her in ice when it would go high, but she just wouldn't wake. Doc said this was what they called a coma.

Whatever it was, Platt wanted Nellie to wake up and be okay. He never left her bedside except when he was forced to leave to go to school, and even then, he rushed back to the Jefferson's as quickly as he could. He couldn't be away from Nellie, what if she woke up and needed him? He just knew he had to be there, and Papa seemed to understand. Doc made frequent visits to check on her and decided to put her on a new antibiotic medication called penicillin because she had developed blood poisoning. He had left the wound on her leg open to bleed out the poison from her system. But she still did not wake up.

The next day after school, Platt was on his way back to the Jefferson Ranch, which had become his regular routine, when he was greeted at the door by Mr. Jefferson. His heart stopped for a moment and his mind began to whirl, thinking the worst that something terrible had happened to Nellie.

"Come in, Platt," Mr. Jefferson said as he greeted Platt. He could see that the look on his face was not one of concern or sadness, but of joy.

"What has happened to Nellie?" he asked.

"Come see for yourself," Mr. Jefferson said as he motioned to the parlor.

Platt walked in the room, and he could see Nellie propped up on a settee, looking very thin and pale, but awake and alive! "I'm so glad to see you Nellie, and that you are alright!"

"Thanks to you Platt, how can I ever thank you? Papa says you have been here every day. Why?"

Platt didn't respond at first, he just stood there looking at her. *She was so beautiful, even in her weakened state. He was sure of it; he was in love with Nellie. But this was not the time or place to express his love for her.*

"I brought your schoolwork so you wouldn't fall behind. Mrs. Hastings is a very understanding teacher and said you could catch up on everything you missed, and I would be glad to come by and help you. Well, you know, so you don't get behind." He seemed to be searching for words to say. "And I think you did well on your test we took. You probably have a higher score than I do," he said.

"Thank you, Platt, I will look at them. I appreciate you bringing them, but Papa could have gotten them. Is that the reason you came every day was to bring my schoolwork?"

"Well yes, no, I mean, I brought your schoolwork, but that's not the reason I came every day. I was so worried about you, Nellie. I didn't know if you were going to make it, and I couldn't have stood it if anything happened to you. Nellie I really care for you."

Nellie didn't know what to say, but the blush that came into her pale cheeks might have said it all. Just then, Mama came into the parlor and asked if Platt would like some lemonade. The looks that went back and forth between the two of them said more than words could have said. It was the unspoken language between them that they did not at this time understand.

Mothers always seem to know, even before their daughters, and Mama's heart began to sink. She knew the look that had just passed between those two young lovers. Yes, she knew about this newfound affection, which was obviously more apparent to her than her daughter. She smiled to herself as she thought of herself and Lester, and when their love first blossomed. No, she would not say anything. If it were true love, it would continue to grow in time, only time would tell.

Chapter Three

Each day Nellie seemed to be gaining more strength. Although the progress was slower than she would have liked, no one really knew how closely she really came to looking death in the face. She longed for the day to return to school and back to her friends, and yes even Platt. Summer was fast approaching; spring and summer time on the ranch were always such busy times. Although Papa says ranch work was not for his little girl, there was still so much to do with gardening and helping with cooking chores. Although they did have a cook, with all the extra ranch hands it took everyone doing their parts to make the harvest a success. Nellie always felt if there was anything on a Ranch that a man could do, a girl could do it just as good. There goes that wild and free independent spirit again. Papa never had a son so she guessed he would have to make do with Nellie.

The day had finally arrived for her visit with Doc. When Doc agreed to release her to go back to school and back to her classmates, she was so excited she could hardly stand it.

"But you still must pace yourself, don't overdo it. If you begin to feel fatigued, then you must halt your activity and rest," Doc said.

I have been sitting around for weeks! I am ready to spread my wings and fly; she was thinking to herself.

"I know that look," said Papa. "I know you are as edgy as a cat on a hot tin roof and are going stir crazy from being sick, but you must heed the Doctor's advice."

"Oh, Papa, you know me so well. I will I promise," she said as she hugged his neck.

Even though school was almost out, it felt almost like the first day of school for Nellie. She had been gone for so long. It was good to be back with her friends and to feel NORMAL again, whatever that was. Platt was already in his seat when she walked through the door. She almost took his breath away with her dark mahogany hair, half pulled up and the rest spilled over her tiny shoulders. It glistened in the sunlight. The dress she had on made her appear even smaller and fragile, making him even more aware of just how sick she really had been. He didn't realize that he was still staring at her when she looked his way, causing him to feel weak in the knees. What had come of him? Why was he reacting this way? What was happening to him? The teacher announced that class would begin, and he was glad about the distraction, although his thoughts kept going back to Nellie and the way she looked when she walked into the room. At lunch that day, the teacher asked if both Platt and Nellie could stay after class because he had a matter he needed to discuss with them. They looked at each other and wondered what ever that could be Nellie had been out recovering and Platt had been faithful to turn her work into the teacher for her.

When they arrived at the teacher's desk, they were greeted with a, "Congratulations to you both. You have both scored high on the scholarship exam and were granted scholarships!"

They looked at each other in surprise and congratulated each other. Platt would be eligible to use his scholarship this coming fall and Nellie hers the next. The teacher was so excited that they had never had students from the same school win this much sought after scholarship. That evening they each shared the wonderful news with their families who also celebrated with them their great accomplishments.

Mel's Visit

With each passing day Nellie continued to gain more strength was returning and she was soon feeling more like her old self. Not soon enough for her as she was impatiently awaiting the arrival of her older sister Melissa, the one they called Mel. She moved to the city and went to work for a printing company as a printer. She was one of the only females who was ever hired in the company. Some called her an "old maid, a spinster," but Nellie called her an exciting woman of the world! It wasn't that Mel had not had her share of suitors; she had, for she was beautiful. Mel was tall, slender, but full bodied with dark brown eyes like Mama. She had jet black hair which she wore piled on top of her head, which made her look more sophisticated. That was probably why she never lacked an escort to a ball and had numerous wedding proposals, which she had turned down. Mel did have a beau when she was younger, Jeffrey Scott, and he was killed in a farming accident. She never seemed to get over him or find anyone else who measured up, so she just decided to stay single. Mel was also a self-proclaimed artist. She did several excellent pieces, one of a maiden in a field with a cow carrying some wheat on her shoulders, the others were portraits. She had so much talent.

Nellie was just finishing getting the room ready for her sister's arrival when Papa knocked on the door. "Are you ready to go to town with me and get your sister?" He didn't have to ask her twice, for she grabbed her bonnet and out the door, she flew.

"Slow down Nellie! Remember, it wasn't that long ago you were very ill."

"I am fine Papa, and I can't wait a minute longer to get to town and get Mel."

On the way to town, Nellie and Papa had a chance to talk about something they had not had much time to do. With all the turmoil of her injury and sickness, and then the recovery and with that Corbaley boy hanging around all the time, Papa realized how much he missed his time alone with his youngest daughter.

"I think Mel must be about the most famous person I know," Nellie announced.

"What makes you say that?" Papa asked.

"Well, just think about it how many women there are in the printing business? It is primarily a man's world, and then to have a young, and I might add bright and beautiful, woman to break into the business and succeed. I think when they first gave her they job they were expecting her fall flat on her face, but she really showed them didn't she Papa?"

"Yes Melissa has done very well for herself, but I still worry about her being in the city all by herself without a husband or a Papa to protect her. Yes Nellie, I do worry about my girls, even the gown ones."

"Even Dora, Papa?" Nellie asked.

"I have never stopped loving my daughters, not for a minute, even when they choose career paths overstaying on the ranch and near home. I know I seemed calloused, but the truth is I am just afraid for them. Not that they will succeed, because I know they will, but because they are strong intelligent and innovative. Because they won't need me anymore, and I guess that's the hardest of all to let go."

"Papa, I think that you and Mel are too much alike, that is way you always end up arguing."

Papa thought about it for a moment, then turned to Nellie and said, "I believe you have deep insight far beyond your young years. It's not that I don't love my daughter, because the Lord knows I do. When we are together sometimes it's like two rams locking horns with no hope of resolve. But NEVER for one moment have I ever stopped loving my daughters." The subjects began to change to school and the graduation dance and who would be her escort.

Although, they both knew the answer to that question.

All the sudden, a snake scooted across the road, startling the horse.

Frightened, the horse reared up on its back two legs, resulting in the wagon coming detached. Twisting from the left side of the road, then to the right and then turned repeatedly before finally landing with Papa pinned under it. Nellie was thrown from the wagon about 20 feet and was unconscious for several minutes before waking. She called out for Papa, but when she didn't get a response, she started to cry and fear the worst. She started looking frantically for him and was becoming more anxious as the moments passed. When she found him pinned under the wagon unconscious and bleeding, she knew she must get help and get it soon. *Where was everybody? She thought to herself, this is a busy road, where is someone when you need them? She must go for help and go now!* Nellie started running down the street. She didn't know how far she had gone, when she saw there was a wagon in the distance.

She called out, "Help please! Help me!"

As the wagon got closer, she could see it was Platt. She was so relieved.

"We have had a terrible accident and Papa is pinned under the wagon, please help me!"

"Nellie, are you alright? Let me help get you up here in the wagon. Now let's go get help." Platt turned the wagon around and they went off in a flash to his ranch where he recruited his father and hired hands. He sent one of the hired hands to get Doc and arrange for him to meet them. Platt just took charge of the situation as if it was second nature and in no time, they were back at the wagon.

Papa was still unconscious. It took Mr. Corbaley, Platt, and the hired men no time at all to lift the wagon off Papa and load Papa in the back of Platt's wagon and on his way to the Jefferson ranch. Doc was waiting for them when they arrived. They carefully moved Papa off the wagon, into the house and on into the parlor, bringing back memories of Nellie's own recent illness. She was so frightened for Papa. The wound on his head looked ominous and his left arm, with an obvious fracture, was so swollen and disfigured. But it was the abdominal swelling that worried Doc the most. He wanted to transfer him to a nearby city hospital, which had a new x-ray machine and more modern medical treatment. But for now, he must stabilize before being transported anywhere.

Nellie wondered, *Maybe Mel knew someone in the city who could help Papa. MEL! OH, MY GOODNESS MEL! She was still waiting at the stagecoach office.*

Platt could see the panic on Nellie face.

"What is it?" he asked.

"Mel, my sister, is waiting at the stage. We must get to her; we were on our way when we had the accident. Can you bring me?"

"Of course. Come on, let's go."

Mel was at the stagecoach office pacing back and forth, thinking to her, *I know I told him what time I would be here! He said it was a good time to come and that the past was all forgiven. Maybe it's not and he is making a statement by making me wait or forgetting to come get me all together. But it doesn't explain Mama or Nellie. They would never do this to me, and I know they knew about my visit. What was going on? If they don't show up here in the next 10 minutes, I will buy a ticket back to the city. I never should have come in the first place, silly me thinking things would be different between Papa and I.*

She was abruptly brought back from her thoughts when she heard someone calling her name. She looked up to see Nellie, but she was with a young man. Highly abnormal for Papa to allow such things! Nellie looked so tattered, dirty, and bloody. She knew right away that something catastrophic had taken place.

"Nellie! Where is Papa? What has happened?"

Platt brought the wagon to a halt and Nellie was off the wagon and in the arms of her sister, hugging with what seemed like an eternity. Nellie was relieved to have her.

My older sister is home now not only for a visit, but for support as well. Once they had Mel's trunk loaded, Nellie caught her up on the events of the day and accident. Nellie soon realized she had neglected to introduce her to Platt. *But how do you introduce someone that saved your life and now her father? Did she call him her hero, her classmate, her friend? She couldn't say boyfriend because he had never uttered such a thing. She guessed she should refer to him as her special friend, her kindred spirit, and leave it at that for now.* Mel looked at Nellie and then Platt and saw they had that look of love. *It was hard to imagine. Nellie! She was still so young!*

Trip to the City Hospital

In minutes the trio arrived at the Jefferson Ranch. Nellie and Mel rushed in to check on Papa. Doc was busy stitching the large gash on his forehead, but the biggest concern was Papa's abdomen and if he had internal injuries. There was just no way to know. His abdomen was swelling as if filling up with fluid, or worse yet blood, if only there was some way to see inside the body!

Doc silently walked out of the parlor, rolling down the cuffs of his shirt. He didn't have to say a word; Nellie could see it in his eyes. He was worried about Papa's condition as it was becoming increasingly clear that it was more serious than previously thought. Doc explained that Papa was still not conscious, but as soon as he regained consciousness and stabilized, they would need to move him to the city hospital.

"I have read that they just discovered a new machine called an X-Ray! It can see inside the human body, isn't that amazing? It is quite a phenomenon!"

Nellie loved to hear Doc talk about medical terminology and new medical advances.

"The X-ray was discovered accidently by William Copinn. He was working in his lab with cathode rays doing an experiment. To test the experiments, he covered the tube with black cardboard in a darkened room and supplied the electric current. He had forgotten to put a screen directly in front of the tube. Nonetheless a greenish yellow glow appeared on the cardboard that was lying on a chair several feet away from the tube. And that is this invention they call x-ray. I guess I am rambling on, but I felt if you knew what I was referring to then maybe you can feel better about your father."

"Doc, we appreciate everything you have done for Papa. Please know that he wouldn't even be alive now of it weren't for you."

Mama came out of the parlor about that time. "Doc. Papa, his stomach, the bloating appears to be getting worse. What are we to do?"

22

Doc excused himself to chec on Papa.

Nellie turned to Platt and burst into tears. She fell into his embrace as he just held her and let her cry.

"Platt it's my entire fault! I should not have been distracting him."

Platt held her back by her shoulders gently and looked into those red tear-filled eyes and spoke in a soft tender voice.

"Nellie you are not responsible for what happened. It was an accident. No one blames you and I don't want you to blame yourself," he said as he engulfed her in a tender embrace.

He held her close and let her cry until there were no more tears left to cry. He didn't want to admit it, even to himself, how wonderful it felt to have her in his arms, as if she belonged there forever. About that time, Mel appeared from the other room and Nellie was quick to move away from Platt's embrace. The two were trying to act as normally as they could, suddenly brought back to the seriousness of the situation at hand.

"Nellie, it was obvious to me when I first saw you and Platt together that you two have something special. Don't worry; it's not like me to run to Papa, to tell him his youngest daughter is in love. I won't tell when he regains consciousness. I had a love like that once and it was the most special thing."

Nellie was quick to argue with her sister that they were just good friends but deep in her heart, she knew the truth. It was much more. What she didn't realize was just how deep her feelings were. With each passing day, these emotions grew stronger, and she did not know how much longer she could ignore it.

Doc was desperately trying to stabilize papa so they could transfer him to the Indianapolis Hospital. That was the closest city, but it was still a full day's journey. Doc was uncertain if he could make the trip, but waiting could be his death sentence. The family had a decision to make a make soon. Mama was in no condition to make any decision. She was crying and emotionally distraught. Mel and Nellie were left to make the decision. Platt offered his wisdom when asked but didn't want to be too pushy and offend the Jefferson's. Platt could see that one of the biggest concerns was how to get Mr. Jefferson there safely and quickly. The stage was out and the wagon would be too uncomfortable for Papa to ride in. Platt offered their new buggy. It was covered and they could pad the back so Mr. Jefferson could lay down for the journey. Doc decided to accompany him on the journey and Nellie was grateful. She wondered if it was partly because of his curiosity, due to all the new medical equipment and techniques that they were using at the big hospital in Indianapolis. Despite the reasoning, the decision was made, and they would leave at sunup. It was decided that Platt would drive, and Nellie, Mel, and Doc would accompany. Mama was so emotional, and she wanted to go, but knew someone had to stay behind and make sure that the ranch was being run properly.

Yes, she had been raised as a proper young woman, but she could get out there and run cattle, ride a horse, and plant and harvest crops. She knew all about the inner workings of a farm. Some women work the farm alongside their husband, but most just care for the gardens and household chores. Some do look after the chickens; there was so much work to do on a farm, it was work from before sunup to late in the evening. Some women can sew, plant and harvest crops, and some can even milk cows, but Mama could ride, herd with the cowboys, and brand the cattle. She could do all this and still get cleaned up, bake fresh bread and the best apple pie one ever tasted. It won first place at the county fair. Not that she had to do all the cooking anymore, she had help in the kitchen, but she still liked to get in there and do it herself. She said it was satisfying work. Being out on the ranch in Marshall, Papa made sure that all his girls, Mama included, knew how to handle firearms. He wanted all his girls to be able to protect themselves. It made Nellie feel better knowing that her Mama was an excellent shot with a pistol. Papa used to say she could shoot a flea off the back side of a bear 50 feet away and never disturb it.

The Sun was just peaking its head up over the mountain tops as it gave promise of a beautiful spring, perfect for traveling if only under different circumstances. Nellie was up and getting things ready for the trip. Mama was up scurrying around making sure they would have enough food for the trip and second guessing her decision about accompanying her husband, but knowing in her heart she was doing what was needful. Just then, she heard a soft knock on the door, it was Platt.

"I didn't want to wake everyone if they weren't up yet," he said as Mama answered the door.

"Well, everyone better be up and ready or we won't be making very good time," Mel announced as she breezed into the room. They gently loaded Mr. Jefferson into the back of the well-padded wagon.

Doc. got settled with Papa in the back and Mel decided to ride in the back in one of the padded seats. Nellie rode up with Platt to keep him company and to keep him alert for the long trip ahead of them to Indianapolis. Mama put the food and water in the wagon and Doc had his medical bag. They were ready for their journey.

It was not yet daybreak, but Platt had no problem maneuvering the team and wagon. *He was very skilled with the wagon, she wondered if it was from driving on the ranch, but they had hired hands? It just didn't make sense.*

At any rate she was very grateful for his generosity and skill. *He was taking time away from school to do this for me and Papa, how can I ever repay him? What about his graduation!?*

"Platt, what about graduation? Are you going to be able to graduate? Are you going to be able to finish your work, taking this time off for us?"

"Nellie, I finished all my required assignments I have just been going to school every day in hopes of seeing you."

"Really, Platt you are already done? What about next year? I don't fancy you a boy to stay on the farm or to take up after your father's trade of preacher or attorney. What will you do?" Nellie asked.

"I want to stay in Marshall and wait for you to graduate Nellie. I want to wait and see what happens between us, but my Pa is really pushing for me to start college. He wants me to be a judge or something," Platt replied.

"What do you want to do with your life Platt?"

"Wow, that's a big question for first thing in the morning. It may take me all day to answer that one," Platt replied, and they both laughed.

Nellie checked on Papa to make sure he was making the trip okay. Doc said he was stable and appeared comfortable. The two up fronts seem enthralled with conversation, which seemed to help pass the time. Nellie was amazed with how easy it was for her to be herself and talk to Platt about anything and everything. She had never known anyone, not even Matilda, that she could talk to and feel the freedom to express her ideas. She could share all her dreams for making the world a better place and getting an education, and he didn't discourage it. It was really an amazing feeling.

Nellie was very grateful that they would soon be to the city and have Papa at the hospital so he could get the treatment he needed.

Deep in her heart, she hoped and prayed he had made it and didn't have any complications before he arrived. She was thankful for the skillful way in which Platt maneuvered the wagon along the roads to avoid as many bumps and potholes as possible, thus making the ride much safer and smoother for Papa.

As they drove into the city Nellie was wide-eyed amazed at everything she saw. But not soon enough they arrived in the city of Indianapolis. It was a much larger city compared to their little sleepy town of Marshall. It was a bustling place. Everywhere you looked you saw buggies and wagons, it bristled with excitement. It had music coming from saloons and cafes on every corner and stores! She had never seen so many clothing stores, hard good stores or even an ice cream parlor. She had never seen the likes of such a thing! She had sure never seen so many people, especially in one place! The city had a certain appeal to it with the bright lights and loud noises. She saw now what had attracted Mel and the draw it was for her away from the sleepy little town of Marshall. But for Nellie, she loved the wide-open spaces and the small town where you know everybody's name, where neighbor is always willing to help another neighbor. You just don't have that small town atmosphere in the city.

They finally arrived at Wishard Hospital. It was originally founded in response to a smallpox epidemic in the city. It was also used during the civil war by the union army to treat the soldiers. It is a teaching hospital where they train new physicians, so they have all the newest and latest in medical knowledge and technology. Nellie was amazed at the precision with which the medical staff moved her Papa from the wagon to the gurney, effortlessly as if he weighed nothing at all. The swiftness in response to his needs was truly incredible, and the way the doctors were shouting orders to the nurses and their interrupting them was almost more than Nellie could take in at one time. They whisked Papa off to be examined before she knew it and she was left standing in the corridor of the large hall looking around for someone, anyone, she knew.

Doc. had gone off with Papa. Mel was giving the ladies at the desk some information and Platt must be putting up the wagon. Never had she felt so small and all alone. She tried to be brave for Papa as she awaited news from the Doctor regarding his condition, but the tears began to form and spill over and before she knew it she was crying and shaking and she sat all alone waiting. Platt rounded the corner of the hospital looking for Doc. but what he found was Nellie. When he saw her sitting there all alone, he knew right away that she was crying. He knew how proud she was and would not want him to find her like this. He decided that his approach to the situation would be to head to the cafeteria and bring her a cup of hot chocolate. When he arrived with the hot chocolate, it was met by a sweet smile and red tear-filled eyes. Seeing her vulnerable side only made him fall more in love with her.

"They have been in there forever and still no word. What if we were too late?"

"Nellie, we got him here as quickly as we could, you know that, and they are doing everything humanly possible. The rest is left to God." Nellie was a woman of strong belief in God. She believed that now she really needed to depend on him to help her Papa. Nellie was up pacing the floor with Platt right beside her until he felt she needed her time to herself, and then he would back away and leave her alone for a while.

The Surgeon and Doc came out and they both looked grim. The surgeon spoke first.

"Mr. Jefferson has a ruptured bowel from the trauma of the accident. He will need immediate surgery, and it may have been too long already. We have a machine here that is new to the United States. It lets you look at the inside of a person! It's called x-ray. We used it on your father, and it showed fluid and hole in the bowel. This invasive surgery is new and very controversial, still under research, but I will tell you for certain that if your father does not have it, he most certainly will die. Without the surgery, he does run the risk of infection and most assuredly will not survive. With the invention of anesthesia, it is making surgery so much easier and safer. You and your sister will have a lot to talk over and with Doc's wisdom; I know you will come to the right decision regarding your father's health."

And just that quickly the surgeon was gone, leaving behind a pool of emotions and uncertainty. Mel and Nellie looked at each other and burst into tears as they fell into each other's arms. Mel gathered her emotions together.

"Look Nellie, we have a decision to make, and we must have a clear mind. Papa deserves the best medical attention he can get, so let's give that to him. This surgeon trained in Europe, he is one of the best in the country and one of the only ones who has ever attempted bowel surgery after a traumatic rupture. I say we do the surgery for without it, he will surely die."

Nellie agreed with her sister, and they quickly told the surgeon of their decision. Before they knew it, Papa was on his way to surgery. Now, the waiting. Patience was never one of Nellie's strong suits and every moment that passed seemed like an eternity. Platt was a silent strength for Nellie. She wanted a shoulder to cry on or someone to hold her, or just to listen to her. She didn't realize how much she was beginning to lean on him and just how much she was enjoying having him around. Nellie had finally drifted off to sleep laying her head on Platt's shoulder when the surgeon emerged to give them a report. Nellie was startled and jumped nearly three feet off the ground. The surgeon said that he was able to repair the bowel but there was some infection already setting in. Papa's condition would be touch and go for the next 24 hours. They had to leave the skin incision open due to the large amount of infection that was already present. He was able to lavage the area as best he could. The rest was up to Papa and to God. When they could see him was, of course, the next question on their minds. The surgeon informed them that as soon as the anesthesia wore off, they could see their darling Papa.

Nellie and Mel were pacing the floor, waiting for what seemed like forever, before the nurse came out and said that they could go back and see him. Neither was prepared for what they saw. Papa was still unconscious, and he had a large open wound in his abdomen with a very large bandage. He looked so pale, so unlike his ruddy tanned skin tone. It just didn't look like Papa at all!

"Oh, Platt what happens if he never wakes up and it was my fault entirely?!" she said as she melted into a mass of tears.

"Your fault? What are you talking about Nellie? Why would you ever think this was YOUR fault?" Mel questioned.

"Because I was talking to Papa when we on our way to town and I distracted him! That was why he didn't see the snake."

"That is the most ridiculous thing I have ever heard! You, nor Papa, can control how a horse will react to a snake crossing in front of it. I don't want you to blame yourself! Not now, not ever, regardless of what the outcome is with Papa. Do you understand me, Nellie?"

Nellie slowly nodded her head but, in her heart, she was not so sure.

As Nellie walked down that cold corridor of the hospital that smelled of antiseptic, it seemed indifferent, so uncaring. She just wanted things to be the way they were before the accident, oh how she wanted and needed her Papa back. As Nellie walked into the room, she was once again taken back at the sight of her Papa, unconscious with a very large dressing on his abdomen and a tube in his arm. She was unsure what that was all about, but decided it was a way of giving medicine. *Oh, why doesn't he wake up?* She sat down next to the bed and took his hand. It was cold and lifeless, so different from when he usually took her by the hand. But she held his hand and started talking to him, just as if he were awake and could answer her. She told him all about the accident and about how Platt saved him and brought him to the city. She must have talked for hours, for it seemed to wear her out and before she knew it, she had laid her head down on his hand. Nellie was awakened when she felt a stroking of her hair. It startled her. She jerked her head up to come face to face with eyes as dark blue as hers.

"Oh Papa, I thought you were never going to wake up! Are you in pain? I am going to go get the Doctor!" After hugging his neck, but not giving him a chance to reply, she was off down the corridor as fast as she could go. A nurse scolded her for running but she didn't care. Her Papa was awake! Platt and Mel saw her come running down the hall and were very concerned until they saw her face. They could see that she was elated and not saddened.

"Where is the Doctor? Papa is awake!"

Off they went to look for the Doctor and, in a flash, the nurse returned, accompanied by the Doctor. They explained what happened and he didn't seem overly anxious or excited, but maybe that was his professional bedside manner. Soon they were at Papa's side and the Doctor was able to examine him. He explained that he didn't understand what had caused him to take the turn for the better, but he certainly did. His vital signs were improved, the infection drain was becoming clearer, and all in all, he felt good about his recovery. Nellie knew it was nothing short of a miracle. The days that followed were slower progress for Papa as he wanted to go home and be with his beloved wife. He yearned to be back to work on the ranch, always worried it would fall apart without him. He continued to recover with the utmost of care and the day finally came when they could take him home. Nellie was so excited; she could hardly contain herself. Of course, Platt offered to drive the buggy to pick him up, but Mel had arranged for a few more days off from work. Mel wanted to make sure he was home and settled and doing well before heading back to work. She had a wonderful opportunity to visit with Mama this time, which was a rare gift.

Mama was an amazing woman! She knew why Papa worshipped her. She was smart, talented and wise beyond her years. Where did she get that from, growing up in such a sheltered environment? Nevertheless, she was amazing, and she was proud to be her daughter. She would really miss her time with Mama and Nellie when she went back to the city, but she knew she didn't belong in a small town. Once back home, she would be so busy and could drown herself in her work. But the task at hand now was to assist getting Papa home safe and sound.

When they arrived at the hospital, Papa was sitting in a chair; the rather large bandage over his abdomen had been replaced with a much smaller one. No more drains. He had recovered beautifully thanks to the wonderful surgeon he had and God's intervention. He was still very sore and weak, which was understandable, healing is a process which cannot be rushed. The nurses assisted Mr. Jefferson in the buggy and put him in so he would be as comfortable as possible for the long ride home. He was even amazed at how smooth the ride home was in Corbaley's new buggy. The trip home was uneventful and in what seemed like no time at all, they had arrived in Marshall. At the Jefferson Ranch, Platt assisted Mr. Jefferson into the house with the aid of Mel and Mrs. Jefferson. When he was all settled, Mr. Jefferson asked to speak to Platt alone. Platt started to get sweaty hands, wondering if he knew of his love for his youngest daughter. He walked into the parlor where Mr. Jefferson was laying, and he stuck out his hand.

"Platt, I don't know how to say thank you for saving my life. You helped get the wagon off of me and you took me all the way to Indianapolis. I just don't know what to say or how I could ever repay you."

"It was my privilege to be of assistance to you sir! Not to change the subject and I realize that my timing is poor, but I didn't know if I would even have the nerve to ask you. You are under no obligation to say yes, but…well…sir…"

"What boy? What do you want?"

"Your permission to take Nellie to the graduation dance sir, if that's alright. I mean you don't have to say yes, but the dance is this Saturday and if I don't ask your permission now, I just don't know when. I am rambling. I apologize, sir."

"Platt, Nellie would be insulted if you didn't ask her. So, I would give you, my permission. You are a fine young man and I know you care for my Nellie."

"Thank you, sir." Lester smiled to himself as he remembered asking permission to ask his own sweet Mary out to the dance. He still remembered how she looked and what she wore, she was still just as beautiful.

Platt emerged from the parlor looking pale, hands ringing with sweat. Nellie wondered what had transpired in the other room.

"What did Papa want to talk to you about?"

"He just wanted to thank me for taking him to Indianapolis and for my part in the rescue. But, Nellie, there is something else and if I don't ask you now, I may lose my nerve. Will you go to the graduation dance with me?" Nellie was totally caught off guard. She just stood there and looked at him, imagining the night of dancing and of being escorted by the most handsome boy in school.

"Nellie, will you go to the graduation dance with me? I have your father's permission."

"Yes! Of course, I will go with you." She lunged forward and into his arms right in front of Mama and Mel, but she didn't care. Nellie was going to the dance with Platt! The boy she thought was of her nightmares, had suddenly become the man of her dreams. She had a date, a real date, and Papa had given his permission. It just couldn't get any better than this!

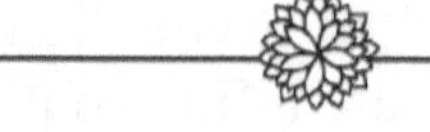

Chapter Four
The Dance

Nellie could not wait for the day of the dance to arrive. She had gone to town and she and Mama had picked out the most beautiful gown she is sure she had ever seen. She could sense that Mama understood her excitement about this special evening, or was it her special escort? The day of the dance arrived with a glorious sunrise after a spring rain overnight and it was turning everything green. The sunshine made the raindrops glisten like jewels. Nellie wondered what she was going to do all day to make the time pass until Platt came to escort her to the dance. Mama could sense her uneasiness and decided that idle hands are not good. She had Nellie busy with all sorts of chores, helping in the kitchen and helping her in the flower bed. Gardening was Mama's pride and joy. She loved it when Nellie helped her so they could have some undisturbed time to talk. Her baby Nellie was growing into a young woman, and she didn't know if she was ready for that. She saw the independent spirit in Nellie, the same one that was in her sisters. It saddened Mama knowing that sooner than she realized, she too would be gone. So, she must enjoy every minute they have together. After an afternoon of gardening, Nellie realized it was time to get ready for the dance. She bathed and got dressed in her new dress, she felt like a storybook princess! The dress was pale blue with a scoop neck and seed pearls around the neck. The bodice was fitted, and the waist had a thick ribbon sash with seed pearls adorning the front. It was the most exquisite gown she had ever seen! Nellie was sure if Mama had not bargained with Mr. Smithers, the local mercantile store owner, she would not be wearing it tonight. Mama was a shrewd businesswoman and for that, Nellie was very grateful. Nellie had Mama help put her hair up on top of her head, rolled at the sides. It made her look more grown up and sophisticated. She put a pearl broach that belonged to Mama around her neck.

"Well, what do you think?" she asked her Mama and Papa.

They just sat and stared at first. Mama took a moment then said how much she looked like her sister, Mel. Just then, they heard a knock at the door. Mama answered a very nervous looking Platt.

"Won't you come in?" Mama said.

"Good evening. I am here to escort your daughter to the graduation dance. Is she ready?" She noticed his hands were sweating and she decided not to make him wait with anticipation.

"I will go and get Nellie. Why don't you go to the parlor and visit Mr. Jefferson?"

Great! I must visit her father now before we go. If I weren't nervous before, I would be now.

"Good evening. Mr. Jefferson, how are you feeling?"

"I am feeling stronger every day. If I can just get back to ranching soon, I will be happy. I need to get started on the crops and the calving season is already under way. They need my help and supervision."

"Not until the Dr. releases you, Lester," Mrs. Jefferson interrupted when she and Nellie entered the room.

Platt turned and his mouth fell open. He knew she was beautiful, but she looked radiant tonight, glowing in that gown! He was speechless for a moment. Mama and Papa watched the looks that passed between the two of them.

"Nellie, you look exquisite. There are no words to describe how lovely you look tonight!"

"Why thank you, Platt. You look rather dashing yourself!" Mama scowled at her, for it was not proper for a young woman to comment on her escort, but she knew the maverick spirit of her child.

"I promise to take good care of her and have her home after the dance."

"Have a good time and be careful," Papa said, but they barely heard as they walked out the door and down the path to his father's best buggy.

The ride was very smooth in this buggy and Nellie felt like the bell of the ball with the most handsome boy in the graduating class as her date. Platt was very quiet at first and Nellie was concerned that maybe he didn't want to take her to the dance. She had to break the silence.

"Platt is everything all right? You haven't said anything. Do you not want to go to the dance, or have you changed your mind about asking to escort me!?" He burst out in laughter which at first surprised her and then it made her mad.

Why was he laughing, was he making fun of her?

"Nellie, where do you come up with this stuff? I am just nervous about being alone with you on our first official date. I don't want to make any mistakes! I feel like I am the luckiest man alive to be your escort tonight. And no! I would never change my mind about you!" He reached over and kissed her forehead. "Nellie, do you realize I was at your house an hour early? I was pacing back and forth on the porch, trying to get up the nerve to come in and call on you tonight. I want this night to be so special for you!"

"Oh, Platt! I had no idea you felt that way. I know it is going to be a special night just because we are together." She moved in closer to him and enjoyed the closeness and the feelings stirring in her.

When they arrived at the dance, Nellie was in awe at how they had transformed the meeting hall into a magical enchanted palace. It was like nothing Nellie had ever seen before. It was adorned with flowers, lanterns, and stars made of paper hung from the ceiling. There was punch and food, and a local band played the best music she had ever heard.

Nellie and Platt danced almost every dance in each other's arms. It was turning out to be a magical night! But not just for them. Nellie noticed that Matilda and Fred had come together and had not left each other's side all night. He was in Platt's graduating class and was going to work in town with his Father at the feed store. Nellie knew Matilda was smitten and only hoped she would finish her schooling before she married with only one more year. It was wonderful to see all her friends from school as she knew with summer coming; she wouldn't be seeing them as often.

The dance came to an end far too soon for Nellie and it was soon time to start walking back to the buggy and head for home. She didn't want this evening to end! It had been so perfect in every way; it just couldn't be over yet. They took the long way around to the buggy and when Platt reached for her hand to assist her on the curb he didn't let go and she didn't resist. It felt so perfect to have her hand in his, so safe and protected. She loved the heated sensation she was feeling just from holding his hand. They talked and laughed about the evening as they walked hand in hand. It seemed so natural and so right to be with him. When they arrived at the buggy and Platt went to help her up, he caught her by the waist and turned her, so they stood face to face. She was breathing a little quicker now and the moonlight was perfectly highlighting her face. He could resist no longer! His hand reached up and cupped the side of her face and smoothed back some loose hairs as he gazed into her eyes. He lowered his face toward hers and their lips met in a passionate kiss. With the heat that was pulsating through her veins, she was sure her heart was going to burst out of her chest! She felt heat from her head to her toes; she wanted more as he held her closer and pressed her body close to his. Platt kissed her again but this time he realized it was his body that was now awakening to feelings and sensations that he was not previously aware of. He knew at that moment he was undoubtedly in love.

"I think I better get you home before your parents worry," Nellie agreed, but not because she wanted to stop kissing him. She had never been kissed like that and especially by someone she was in love with. *Yes! She was in love with Platt, she knew it!* On the way home, Platt never let go of her hand. She was glad about that, but she didn't want the night to end. The ride home was over far too soon, and it was time to say good night. Neither of them wanted the wonderful night to end. It could go on forever, she thought. As he walked her to the door, the light was on, and Papa was most likely still awake. Platt walked her in and was about to say good night and steal another kiss when Mama came to the foyer.

"Won't you come in for a moment and tell us all about the dance Platt?"

His face blushed red and then turned a strange color of white. Mama looked at him strangely as if he might be getting sick. By this time, Nellie's attention was on him also. Realizing he was catching the attention of the women made him red in the face even more. He thought he had best to accept her invitation before she thought something inappropriate had taken place.

"Why yes, Mrs. Jefferson, I would love to come in but only for a moment due to the lateness of the hour. I would love to share with you all the wonders of our glorious evening."

Nellie was so excited, she could hardly contain herself when she was describing the decorations, food, and music. She went into detail about Fred and Matilda and what she thought their future would be.

Platt excused himself and expressed how he should be getting home as it was getting late. Nellie walked him to the door and told him how much she enjoyed the evening. Platt interrupted and reached down to kiss her softly with a kiss that was sure to be implanted in her memory.

It was so tender it made her feel like she was floating. Then he was gone, as if in a dream.

Nellie didn't think she would be able to sleep at all that night. She just kept replaying the events of the evening over and over in her head. Platt had certainly been there for her in the last few months. She had always thought of him as such a wonderful friend, her rescuer, her father's hero, but never in all that time had she realized that she was in love! Platt was the last thing she would think about before she went to bed and the first thing she thought about in the morning. She knew this summer was going to be busy now that school was out, and with Papa still healing from his surgery, he couldn't work the ranch as normal. The brunt of the work would fall on Mama and Nellie, and of course, George the hired hand. Mama had a list of things she wanted Nellie to do every day from working in the flower beds, to working in the fields, everyone had to do their part. This was a new experience for Nellie. She was raised as a young woman of refinement and the most strenuous activity usually included helping in the kitchen with baking or putting up preserves, which she adored doing.

But things had changed this year since the accident and Nellie could sense it. Papa was not getting stronger as they had hoped. He was recovering but truth be known, he may never run the ranch again and she knew it.

Platt came over every chance he could to see Nellie and to offer help, but there was such a big demand for his time on the Corbaley Ranch that he was equally busy there. One evening after supper, Platt came over to visit Nellie. It was a beautiful summer evening. The sun was beginning to go down and it had shades of orange and pink cascading across the sky, it was breath taking to behold. They were walking along the riverbank, hand in hand, talking about the events of the day and the last few weeks. Platt turned and looked at Nellie.

"I don't like seeing you working this hard. I wish there was something I could do to make it better for you and your father. You shouldn't have to be working in the fields, you should be gossiping with Matilda or whatever it is you girls do."

"What do you mean, gossip with the girls? I will let you know that I did a lot of worthwhile activities before I had to help, and I don't mind helping my family if they need me! What kind of daughter would I be if I just sat back and did nothing when they were in a state of financial crisis?! And…"

Before she could say another word, he covered her protest with a kiss.

"Now that's not fair!"

"I know, but it is sure a lot more fun than arguing. I didn't mean to say that you were a spoiled rich girl who didn't do anything. I am saying I want you to be. I don't like to see you so tired and working so hard."

"I know and I appreciate it, but for now, I have to help my family."

They continued to walk along the river, enjoying the sunset, but it was getting to be time to walk back. They walked to the house, and he asked if he might come in and speak to her father for a moment. Nellie thought this was an odd request, knowing how nervous he always was around her father, but she granted it less.

"Good evening, Mr. Jefferson."

"Come in. Platt, good to see you. I wanted to thank you for your help with the crops. We couldn't and wouldn't have done it without your help. I know you're splitting your time between here and your Ranch, so thank you."

"You're Welcome. Sir, it is always my privilege to help a neighbor."

"Maybe, the neighbor with a beautiful daughter."

"Nellie doesn't know about me working in the fields and sir, I would like to keep it that way. You know how proud she is."

"Yes, I do, a lot like her Mama."

"Sir, I do have a request for you. The county fair is this coming weekend."

"Why yes, it is. Mary always enters her pies and preserves and wins a blue ribbon!"

"Sir, I wanted your permission to ask Nellie if I might escort her to the fair."

"I appreciate you asking, but I do believe the one you need to ask permission of is not of me, but Nellie."

"Thank you for your permission! I shall ask her."

He was out of the parlor and raced out into the front room looking for Nellie. He went from room to room, and no Nellie to be found. He assumed she had gone up to bed, so with his head hanging down and feeling dejected, he started for the door. He was ready to call it a night. *There was always tomorrow but what about this enthusiasm he was feeling right now? Would it be there tomorrow?* He would have to wait and see. He was putting on his hat when he heard a voice calling.

"So, what was so important that you had to spend time with my Papa tonight instead of me?"

He whirled her around and grabbed her by the waist, before he realized where he was. "For your information, your majesty, I was asking your Papa's permission if I might escort you to the county fair this weekend."

"Why did you ask Papa? Why did you not ask me?"

"That's what he said. Also, what is your answer? Will you go with me to the county fair?"

She reached up, grabbed his neck, and she kissed him.

"That's your answer!" And with that, she said good night. All she heard as he walked out the door was a mumbling.

"Women, who can understand them?!" Then, he turned and called after her. "I will pick you up on Saturday morning at 11:00 A.M. Is that acceptable with you?"

"Why yes, Mr. Corbaley, I do believe it is."

He could resist her sassy attitude no longer. He turned and walked back up to the porch where she was standing with a smirk on her face. He grabbed her around the waist and pulled her into himself. Their bodies meshed into one. He lowered his face close to hers and could no longer resist. He left her with a kiss that was passionate and left her wanting more. He let go of her and said, "Good night, my love. I will see you on Saturday." He was off down the front path onto his horse and down the road.

Nellie stood there, watching him for some time, still dazed by his kiss. She knew that life with him was never going to be predictable and always adventurous. When Nellie was falling asleep that night, she kept thinking about the events of the evening. About the kiss and how it felt to be held so close to him. How could she fall in love with him? She still had another year of school to finish, and she was determined to do just that. Yet, at the same time, her heart kept crying out another message. One she could no longer ignore! She was in love with Platt. But she knew he planned to go away to school. If their love was real, it would last a year before they could wed. Wed? That sounded so strange and yet, at the same time, so right. Well, she was getting a little ahead of herself. He had not even asked her to be his gal, let alone his wife! Time would tell if that were to happen.

In the morning, Nellie arose and began to help Gertie with the morning chores. Gertie had been working for the Jefferson's since Dora was a baby. She was initially hired to assist Mary after the baby's birth, but as the ranch began to prosper, they were able keep her on permanently. Gertie was such a Godsend! She kept working and never even fussed when she did not get her salary at times. She thought of the Jefferson's as family and not as an employer.

She did miss her days of privilege when she didn't have to do so many chores. Before Papa was injured, but since that time, everyone had to pitch in and help. It wasn't that they were poor, by any means, but life as they had known it with Papa in his good health had certainly changed. It was now time for Nellie and Mama and to pitch in and help with the chores.

It was truly amazing how everything in her life had changed so drastically in the past few months. From the household to the ranch, to her Papa's health, and now her relationship with Platt, nothing would ever be the same! Why did she have to meet him now when she had so much to accomplish? Her dream of finishing school and working, or even possibly university, at the same time, she could not imagine doing any of these things now without Platt. But she was still young and had time on her side.

Chapter Five
Day at the Fair

The sweet aroma of pies baking awakened Nellie's senses on the day of the county fair. The whole household was buzzing with activity, making the last-minute preparations to ensure perfection all of Mama's baked goods and specialty preserves. She had made them with great care, and they were ready for judging. It was important to Mama to always win a blue ribbon. Papa said he was feeling up to attending the fair, although he was walking with the assistance of a walking stick. After helping Mama get the last-minute preparations ready for everything, it was time for Nellie to get ready before her escort arrived. She had chosen a red and white crisp cotton dress. It looked so fresh and perfect for summertime. She wished she could have gone to the city and bought a new dress, but their finances had to be watched more closely than in previous years. She had only worn the dress once to Betsy Snyders' birthday party and she was sure no one would remember. Even if they did, she didn't care. She was going to the fair with the most handsome boy in the whole county! When Nellie slipped the dress on and pulled the sash around her tiny waist, she made the dress! Mama came in to see how she was doing and looked at her in amazement. Her little girl was now a young woman, where did time go?

"Do you need any help with the buttons in the back?"

"Yes, thank you." Her Mama slipped a choker necklace on her with a broach.

"Oh, Mama it's beautiful! Where did you get it? I have never seen it before."

"My Mama gave it to me when I started dating your Papa. In fact, she gave it to me for our engagement. I want you to have this. It is of sentimental value to me and now I give it to you."

Nellie embraced her. She knew things were changing and would never be the same and she wanted to remember every special moment like this she had with her Mama.

A knock on the door interrupted their special moment and Nellie realized it was Platt. She quickly dried her face from the tears and finished her hair. She raced down the stairs to meet the man of her dreams. Platt was wearing dark slacks and a light blue shirt with a black string tie, and he looked very handsome indeed! Those dark, piercing eyes and that smile of confidence, she thought it was almost prideful. When he saw her his mouth almost feel open. Her beauty always had that effect on him.

"Good morning, Miss Nellie." He reached his hand forward to take hers and bring it to his mouth and kiss it gently.

"And a good morning to you, Mr. Corbaley." Platt made the rounds and visited Mr. Jefferson, Gertie and Mrs. Jefferson and then turned into a very impatient Nellie.

"Are you ready to go the fair my dear?"

"Why yes, I do believe I am."

They said their goodbyes and he escorted her down the walk and into the buggy. They were off to the fair. At the fair they had all sorts of booths, even had a pie eating contest which Platt had to enter and came in 2nd. They had the greased pig contest, which they both refrained from. They had booths where merchants sold their crafts and beautiful candles. They had the local band playing music and of course, they had the baked goods and preserves on display. Farmers took pride in displaying the cream of their crops. Mama was awarded a blue ribbon for her apple pie and strawberry preserves. She said she was happy with her wins, but underneath, she wished for a blue ribbon on ALL her entries. The ice cream was wonderful, and they made it fresh at the fair! Hand and hand, Platt and Nellie strolled all day, talking and talking. They never seemed to run out of things to talk about. As the day was ending, Platt asked Nellie if she would like to take a walk down by the river.

"Nellie, I have had such a tremendous day! I loved every moment with you. I only wish you would have done the pie eating contest also. But seriously, I know that harvest is just around the corner for your Pa. I know that since the accident, he has had to let some of the workers go. I want to offer myself to help. Will you talk to your Pa for me? I know he is prideful and won't ask, but I am offering."

"That's what you wanted to have a moonlight walk with me for to talk about the harvest?" He stopped walking; knowing that what he wanted to say was not coming out right. Now he had gone from helping to making her mad and he had best defuse the situation and do so quickly. Platt looked deep into her beautiful blue eyes and his heart stopped as it always did when he was near her. He pulled her close to himself, not caring if the whole town was watching. He reached up and tenderly pushed a piece of hair back from her face and his hand cupped her face gently as he brought his face close to hers. He lowered his mouth over hers in a deep kiss. It was so soft and tender that it left her breathless.

"What were you saying?" he asked her, visibly shaken from that last kiss.

"Nothing, nothing at all," she replied as he bent down and kissed her again.

He told her they had better be making their way towards her home or her folks would begin to worry where she was. They talked all the way home about the events of the day and enjoyed every minute of being together, knowing that corn and hay harvest would start. Soon she would not see as much of him as she would like. When they arrived at the house, Mr. and Mrs. Jefferson had just finished unloading all the baked goods Mrs. Jefferson had baked for the competition. They saw Platt and Nellie and invited them in for pie and Platt said he couldn't refuse a blue-ribbon pie. Mr. Jefferson visited for a while but excused himself to retire for the evening as it had been an exhausting day. Platt and Nellie could tell that there was something amiss with Papa that evening, something that she couldn't put her finger on. After Pie, Platt excused himself and said goodnight to Mrs. Jefferson and Nellie walked him out on the porch. He stole another kiss and said goodnight.

"Nellie, thank you for giving me a day to remember, please will you speak to your father about the harvest? Good night my love" He kissed her head this time.

"Thank you for making this a day of my dreams, and yes, I promise to speak to Father. Good night, my love." She had never called him "her love" before. He forgot himself for a moment and flew back up on the porch and embraced her in his arms. He tenderly and passionately kissed her, then released her turn and down from the porch he went. She stood there in a daze for a few moments, trying to sort through what had just occurred.

She went on up to bed, still going over the events of the day. *Had Mama and Papa ever had this kind of love? Had anyone else ever known this kind of love? It was the most amazing feeling she had ever experienced.* He was all she wanted to think about, although she knew she must tend to other affairs. Every spare moment was dedicated to Platt and him alone.

The next morning at breakfast, she could tell that Papa and Mama were both upset. Not knowing if they had had a disagreement which they seldom had, she was reluctant to say anything. After eating her breakfast, she was getting ready to help with the morning chores when Papa asked to have a word with her. For a minute, she thought that maybe he had seen Platt kiss her good night and he was going to scold her, but she could tell it was more serious.

"Nellie, I saw the Doctor last week. He thought I would be making more progress than I am. Although the infection is gone and I am alive, which I am grateful for, I just don't know if I will be able to continue farming any longer. We have decided to sell the ranch and move. You only have one more year left and then you will want to go to school or marry and we have a buyer for the ranch now. I know this is a shock."

"Shock That is putting it mildly. Why do you have to sell? Why not let me finish school here? I am almost done! Why now and where are we going?" she asked with tears streaming down her cheeks.

"We are moving to Oceanside California; it will be a much better environment there for your father. We will leave in two weeks, just as soon as we can pack up our personal items and we will sell the rest at auction."

"Two weeks why so soon, why not wait until harvest is over, I just don't understand, why do I have to go!"

She turned and went out of the kitchen and to the stables. She got her buggy with Fred's assistance, she was able to get it hooked up and off she went down the road, tears streaming down her cheeks. All she thought about was that she needed to see Platt and be in his arms. Papa was ready to go after her, but Mama said she needed time alone and that she had probably gone over to see Platt. Mama said that he needed to relax and trust his daughter. But she was so upset! He kept thinking that if anything happened to her, he would never forgive himself. *Why all the sudden does she needs to consult with a young man when she was upset? Had she not always come to him when she had a problem or was upset?* Letting go of his youngest daughter was indeed the most difficult.

When Nellie arrived at the Corbaley ranch, Platt was walking out to the stables to work with the horses. He was startled and alarmed to see Nellie, knowing the only reason she would be there in the middle of the day was if something was terribly wrong.

"What is it? What has happened?" he asked as she drove up and stopped her buggy rather abruptly. When he saw her and her tear-stained cheeks, he knew it was very serious.

"Oh Platt! Papa is selling the ranch, and we are moving in two weeks! No warning! We are moving! He saw the Doctor and his health is not improving and he is unable to ranch any longer. He found a buyer, so he is selling! Oh Platt, what will become of us?"

He just held her for the longest time and let her cry. He took her by the shoulders and pushed her back from himself so that he could look directly into her face.

"Nellie the answer is so simple this was not the way I wanted to ask you but you can marry me now instead of next year and you can finish school here." She looked into his eyes, searching them "You are leaving in a few weeks to go to college I can't have you change your plans and what about your scholarship and lose out on opportunities just for me, nor will I let you. If we are to be married it will work out but not like this, as much as I don't want to go I know I must they need me I can't leave Papa and Mama now and I need to finish this last year of school and then if we are supposed to be together we will be."

"Nellie, I have wanted to tell you something for some time and I have skirted around it. This wasn't how I planned it, but I love you, Nellie! I have for what seems like all my life and I want you to know that I am committed to you. Wherever you go, I will come and get you because we are soul mates for life."

Nellie stood silently with tears on her cheek. He looked at her curiously.

"Are you alright?"

"Platt, I have waited my whole life for someone to tell me they loved me, and I wouldn't want it to be anyone else because I love you too." She flew into his open arms, and he held her close to his chest and just breathed her in. He took in the smell of her skin, the smell of her hair, the softness of her body against his, and he embraced her tightly. He held her for the longest time, as they both seemed to understand that it would be a long time before they had an opportunity to be in one another's arms again.

"Why did the timing have to be so bad?"

"We will be together, Nellie! I promise you, we will."

"But how can you make promises like that? What happens if we move far away, and we never see each other again?"

"We will because we are joined together by our hearts. Our love is eternal, and no distance can keep or tear that away! I have never felt more strongly about something in my life, and I know you feel it too. We are destined to be together forever!"

He reached for her and pulled her to himself, looking down at those dark blue eyes that he would get so lost in. He pushed the wispy hair away from her face and tenderly pressed a kiss to her lips. He gently kissed away the tears that stained her cheeks. They knew they were soul mates, knit together for life.

Chapter Six
The Move

The next two weeks were a blur with busyness, everyone getting things ready for the auction and the move. *They were packing up an entire lifetime of belongings and moving across the country, it was absurd! Why did they have to go in the first place?* She knew the answer in her heart, but she kept her feelings hidden, so as not to put more burdens on Papa or Mama. Platt came over every evening to spend as much time with her as possible, but it did seem unfair that they had found love and now they had to say goodbye. The day of the auction had a similar atmosphere to that of a circus. They had people from the whole county come to bid on Lester Jefferson's Ranch equipment. There were so many people there! Mama baked some of her famous pies but there was not enough to go around, so the auctioneer decided to sell her pies to the highest bidder. She did very well and made $5 on one pie. Mama said she had never heard of such a thing. It was the banker who bought it, and everyone knew he was trying to help out. Everyone in town was so thoughtful and considerate, coming by to visit and help wherever they could.

After the auction was over, it was time for the task of loading everything that could be loaded on the wagons. Gertie and Hattie decided they wanted to accompany them to Oceanside, California.

Fred would drive the wagon with the Jeffersons belongings and accompany the ladies then he would return to Marshall to assist the new owner with the ranch. Nellie, Mama and Papa would take the train. It would be a more comfortable journey for Papa. After the last trunk was loaded, Fred and Gertie and Hattie said their goodbyes and they started on their journey.

Nellie walked back into the house, the big empty house, except for their suitcases. What a strange sensation! She was overwhelmed with the feeling of sadness. She was leaving part of her life behind.

Platt came over the evening before they were to board the train and gracefully volunteered to take them to the train station the next day. That evening they went for a stroll, Platt holding Nellie's tiny hand in his.

"I have so much I want to say to you! I feel like we were cheated out of time to get it all said."

"I know, I feel the same way, but we must be positive. Remember, we will be together again! Isn't that what you said?"

"Yes, yes, I know but when and where? I just don't know how I can stand it without you?!"

"This is beyond our control. We must stay focused and keep thinking of the day that we will finally be together forever."

He could resist no longer. He pulled her to himself, almost crushing her tiny frame, but she didn't care. She was in his arms, and she knew it was the right place to be. He gently pressed a kiss to her lips, and they kissed and kissed again. This time it was more urgent, more intense, leaving her feeling weak in the legs. She hoped that the time they were apart would go by quickly. She just didn't know how long she would survive without his love.

Early the next morning, Platt was there to drive them to the train station. He looked as if the world had come to an end, and maybe in a way, it had for the two of them. This period of separation would try their love in new ways and if their love was real, they would come out victorious. If not, then they knew this was the end of the most beautiful relationship that either one had ever experienced.

It started to rain as they got to the train station. Fitting in with her mood, Nellie thought all she wanted to do was get aboard the train and melt into a seat. She hoped and prayed that this was all a bad nightmare. She wanted to be sad and get the goodbye over with, but on the other hand, she wanted to cherish every minute she had with him because she didn't know if she would ever see him again. Platt could sense her conflict, as always, he seemed to know her better than she knew herself. He took her tiny hands in his.

"Nellie, remember, I will come for you. I give you my promise and you know I have never lied to you. I will write to you as soon as I get to college, and you will write to me just as soon as you have an address! I love you and want you to know that I always have, even when I was tying your braids in knots. I have never told another person that! Only you, Nellie." He reached down and tenderly kissed her. They didn't care if Papa or Mama saw them.

"I love you! Don't forget that, please, especially when you are at college with all those beautiful girls.”

“Like I said, there is no one for me but you.”

“ALL ABOARD!” the conductor’s voice boomed throughout the station.

“No! It can’t be time yet!” *It just hasn’t been long enough!*

Platt reached out and pulled her to himself for one last embrace. They held each other, as if they were each other’s lifeline.

“Nellie you must board now,” Mama said tenderly to her youngest daughter. She could see the love that they had and knew it was something extra special. “You will be together again. I can feel it. What the two of you have is a rare gift that few find. Let this separation make each of you stronger people, so when you come back together you will have an even deeper love. “

They looked at each other, shocked that Mama had uttered the word love. This only made the parting more difficult.

They both knew in their heads that this separation was something beyond their control, but their hearts did not seem to understand. Nellie felt so many emotions and it felt like they were about to burst right out of her chest. Platt could see the conflict that was waging war within Nellie. He grabbed her in his arms and held her tightly.

“My darling Nellie, I love you more than I could ever have thought possible. This year will go quickly! I will write to you daily and before you know it, spring will be here, and I will come for you. We will never have to say goodbye again, I promise my love.”

Nellie began to cry. Partly from the emotions she was feeling and partly because she never dreamed, she could be loved so passionately by someone. She was a blessed woman, and she must be strong for him.

“I love you, Platt! Spring can’t come soon enough for me. I will write you every day!”

She was, once again, interrupted by the conductor yelling, “LAST CALL, ALL ABOARD!”

“I must go now.”

After one last kiss, she stepped aboard the train headed for Oceanside, California. Nellie joined her parents in the car. The train took off as she waved to Platt, who became smaller and smaller until he was completely out of sight. Nellie waved and watched until she could see him no longer. She felt strangely alone, even though her parents were with her. She had a sense of loneliness she had never experienced before.

She asked to excuse herself from her parents and said she wanted to walk to the other car to be by herself for a while. They agreed and seemed to understand what she was going through. Nellie walked to an empty car and settled herself into a seat. The tears started to fall, and they began to fall harder and harder. She was very thankful that no one else was nearby so she could be alone with her thoughts. *How was she going to make it a year without him? What happens if he were to meet another girl at college?* These thoughts whirled around in her mind. She decided there was nothing she could do about the "what ifs?" She had enough reality to deal with. Moving to a new town and finishing her last year of school at a new school was overwhelming enough. *How was she going to settle in and have any time to make friends before school started?*

"Friends." She huffed to herself. *Maybe no one in California would like her? Maybe Indiana was too different from California!* She had never had a minute to even think about this aspect of the move. *Well, I will not worry about making friends this year. After all, it is my last year and all I want to do is get through it and get back together with my love. I shall be an encouragement to my parents and be there to help whenever needed. After all, this move is all about them and this is better for Papa.*

She did not resent her parents for moving her from the only home she ever knew. She understood and wanted to help wherever needed. But knowing that did not take away the ache she felt in her own heart. She had cried tears until there were no more left to cry. She reached in her bag for a handkerchief but couldn't find one. She left, quite drained, after purging herself of all those pent-up emotions and wanted to make her way back to the car where her parents were. When she stood up, she felt a little lightheaded, realizing it was dinner time and she had not eaten all day. As she made her way back to her parents' car, she realized she had been so upset that she had forgotten which direction she had come from. *Well, there are only two possibilities, to the right or to the left. The key here was to act as if you knew where you were going, that's what Platt had told her about big cities.*

When she felt steadier on her feet, she gathered her skirt and set out in the left direction. She held her head high, looking every bit the part of a seasoned traveler. She walked along the aisle looking for her parents, smiling at everyone and trying to remain calm while scanning the crowds for a familiar face. When she had made her way through the first car, she decided to find a seat for a moment as not to draw attention to herself as a lost traveler. After a few moments she proceeded to the right, knowing that she would see her parents within a few moments. As she walked, she saw her Mama coming towards her.

"Nellie! We were beginning to get worried about you. Why are you coming from this direction? Didn't I see you leave in the other direction?"

"It's a long story Mama. I think I need a little assistance with my directions."

Mama began to laugh. "You got lost."

"It's not as funny as one might think."

"Were you alright? Did anyone bother you?"

"No. No one else was in that part of the car, I was alone. It's just frightening when you realize you do not have your bearings."

"I understand, really, I do. We are not in our little town any longer. We must be conscious about what is happening around us. Now, let's go have dinner. I believe your Papa is waiting on us."

They had dinner in the dining car, which was very nice for a train. While at dinner, there was a young man who came over and introduced himself. His name was Fredrick Wickham, a nice enough person she guessed, but she had no interest in being friends with him. She had a love, but her parents were being so friendly to him. It was a little unnerving. *Did they not realize that she had just left the love of her life?* Fredrick was from Oceanside, California, so her parents had many questions about the schools, the weather, everything about the town, from the balls to the library. Nellie could take no more! She had to excuse herself. She was angry. *What were her parents thinking? Wasn't it enough that she had given up marrying the love of her life to assist them? This was too much. They were more polite and gracious to this stranger than they were to the very man who had saved her and Papa's life! Well, they could sit and visit and be polite, but she did not have to! In fact, all she wanted to do was to be by herself and with her thoughts of her love. She never thought that the ache she was feeling from separation would turn into physical pain. How would she ever survive this time of separation?* She decided to sit down in solitude and let herself be carried away with her thoughts and memories, for she decided that was her only outlet of sanity.

Before she knew it, Mama was softly tapping her shoulder to say it was time for her to return to their bunk. That first night on the train was restless. Nellie found it difficult to get comfortable. The next morning at breakfast, Nellie found it difficult to keep her eyes open, deciding that tea would be a good choice of breakfast beverage. The cuisine provided was appetizing and the service was impeccable, but none of it seemed to help ease the aching in her heart. Today would be more travel and she planned to start a letter to Platt about all the beautiful countryside she was seeing. She didn't want to let him know just how miserable and lonely she really was. She did not want him to worry or do something rash like decide not to go to school and come and rescue her. She would try and be as positive as possible under her circumstances. Her parents needed her, and she needed to always keep that in front of her thoughts. After all, her father had never known anything but being a farmer. Giving it up and selling the farm was an excruciating decision for him. Keeping that in perspective helped to make the transition more bearable for her.

What would this new area be like? Would the people be friendly? Would she be able to make new friends? Would they even accept an outsider? She decided to write out all her thoughts and concerns, carefully written so as not to let on about her true misery. Then again, this was Platt she was writing to. He would be able to read between the lines. Soon Nellie was so engrossed in her letter writing that she did not realize that it was dinnertime. She must have been writing for hours! It seemed so natural to tell everything to Platt. *Oh, how she missed him already! How would she ever survive? Would he miss her? Or would he find someone new to love?* These thoughts kept creeping in. She did trust him and their love for each other, but less, it was still so young and untested. She would have to have faith in Platt and their love that they pledged to each other. She knew in her heart, beyond any doubts, that it was real, and it would prove to be so. She was deeply engrossed in thoughts when she felt a hand on her shoulder.

"It's dinner time. Nellie, dear, won't you join us in the dining car?" She was startled until she realized it was her own sweet Mama.

"I will be along shortly. I just want to sign off this letter and get it in an envelope for mailing."

Mama returned to the dining car to meet Papa, who had already made friends with almost the entire train. What a friendly man he was, which made it even harder to leave their hometown and all their lifelong friends. Nellie joined her parents in the dining car for dinner, but not before she had stopped by the car to comb her hair and freshen up. As they were sitting down, Frederick interrupted the trio. He approached the table and extended his hand to Papa and reached for Mama's hand and gently kissed the back of it. He reached for Nellie's, trying to be the perfect gentleman, but she did not return the gesture. Instead, she completely ignored him, as if he did not exist. Mama gave her a glaring look, but she chose to ignore it. She had made enough sacrifices, and her heart would not be the next. Papa had the audacity to ask him to join them for dinner. Nellie's head spun around, and her eyes met Fredrick's.

"I will join you if that is alright with Ms. Jefferson."

"You are my father's guest. I have nothing to say about his decisions."

Papa looked long and hard at his youngest daughter. He wondered if this move was a wise decision. He had tried to convince himself it was right, and Nellie would come around in time, but now he wasn't so sure about anything.

Fredrick was a wealth of information about Oceanside, California and just about any other subject, but Nellie thought him conceited and too self-confident. She listened for as long as she could and then excused herself. She said she was tired after a long day and was going to retire. She really was not tired but wanted desperately to get away from Fredrick. *All she wanted was to be with Platt! Not anyone else, not now, not ever!* She knew she must be cordial, but how could she when he always looked at her that way? It made her skin crawl when he tried to kiss her hand. She knew her parents raised a proper young woman who was supposed to be polite in every circumstance, but she also was a bit more outspoken than most young women. She was determined not to embarrass her parents and it looked as if this challenge would take every ounce of self-control she could muster. She would call it a night and dream about being back in her own home with her love. She could still feel his last embrace, how it felt being in his arms, as if she would descend into a puddle at the very thought of him. He left her feeling weak in the knees. As she closed her eyes that night, she imagined she was back at the county fair and they were walking hand in hand as she drifted off to sleep.

Chapter Seven
Platts Next Step

It seemed as if a lifetime had already passed, and yet, it had only been 2 days since he last saw Nellie. He realized that his zeal for working seemed waning; in fact, his zeal for everything was gone! He didn't realize how much Nellie had affected his life! He knew he had told her to be strong and that this time would go quickly, but at this very moment, he was not fully convinced of that. Oh, how he needed her! The smile on her face, how she could light up a room just by walking into it, talking to her, even arguing, he missed it all! He knew he must prepare for school and do it as soon as possible. Everywhere he went in town reminded him of Nellie and that was too painful. He knew that this new chapter in his life was waiting to unfold, and he must walk forward toward it. He shared with his Father about his desire to get settled at school as soon as possible and he seemed to understand. So, the wheels of his future were about to be set in motion. As he began to pack up his room and prepare to leave, he saw a letter that Nellie had written to him. She made him promise not to read it until she had already left. He had been reluctant to read it. Even now he found it difficult but decided he needed this connection with her. But at the same time, he was leery that she might be breaking up with him in the letter. *Maybe she can't be in a long-distance relationship? Maybe our love isn't as strong as I thought? Alright, I must be a man! I will be strong and read it.* He opened it carefully, recognizing the scent of her perfume that she had dabbed on the paper. As he unfolded the paper, he was overwhelmed with the feeling of butterflies in his stomach. *What is wrong with you? This is just a letter from Nellie! But what if she thinks it would be best if we didn't see each other again? My heart could not take the rejection!* After he could stand the anxiety no longer, he decided that he had to read it.

"My Dearest Platt,

I know I have not yet embarked upon the door of the train, but it seems as if I have been separated from you for a lifetime. I know this is the right decision to leave with my parents, but why does it feel so difficult!? I love my parents so very much and feel obligated to assist them in any way that I can and yet, I am torn apart because I want to stay and be with my true love. I know that you say this year will pass quickly and my love, I am hoping and believing you're right! I don't know what I would do without you. I have waited my whole life to meet my soul mate and now we are separated. It just doesn't seem fair! Now nonetheless, it is my lot in life, and I must endure it and be strong for you, my love and for my parents. We will be together again. Please don't forget me! I love you so much it makes my heart ache and long for the next time that we are together. We will be strong together my love and before you know it, we will be united.

Your Nellie"

He was so relieved! After finally reading the letter, he felt exhausted, as if he had been working in the fields bucking hay all day. *How can reading a letter affect a person in such a way?* But everything about Nellie affected him, looking at her face when she walked into a room, the touch of her hand in his, and feeling her in his embrace. He knew he would never make it a year if he kept thinking about Nellie like this. *No! I must keep busy with the task at hand… getting ready to go to college!* As he finished packing the suitcase, he decided it wise to go and spend some quality time with his father. He really loved his Father and was thankful that like Nellie, he also had a close relationship with his parents.

Platt wanted to be sure that all the harvest was in before he departed for college. He went out to the fields looking for his father, knowing that he would be out there working the harvest. They had so many acres that he was not sure where he would be. He checked with the hired hands, and no one had seen him for hours. Platt decided to ride his horse so he could cover more ground and find him faster. He had looked everywhere and was running out of options but decided to ride back toward the south acres. As he was yelling for his father, he noticed something on the ground. At first it looked like a pile of brush, but as he got closer, he realized it was his father who had passed out on the ground. He quickly dismounted from his horse and rushed to his father's side, shaking him to see if he was responsive. He was barely responsive and gasping for air. Platt knew enough about asthma and that he had to move fast. He tried to lift his father, at first with no success, but he knew how imperative it was that his father got help. Platt conjured up strength beyond himself. He picked up his father, put him on his horse, and began the ride back to the ranch. It seemed to take an eternity to get there. He knew that every minute his father went without medical attention could result in death, if he was not too late already.

"Father! We are almost there! Wake up, speak to me! Don't leave me now!"

He knew if his father went out of consciousness completely and his breathing became more labored than he was in horrible trouble. He must reach home soon! His Father had a home breather that the Doctor had given him because his Asthma had become so much worse, and the harvesting always seemed to aggravate his symptoms. All his father would do is put the medication that Doc gave him in the ceramic pot and heat it up. Then he would breathe in the steam, and it would help him breathe. The device had saved his life on more than one occasion and Platt hoped this would be another.

Sam, a hired hand, saw Platt riding up with his father lying across his horse. He knew something was very wrong and sprang into action. He helped Platt lift him off the horse and into the house. His mother saw them coming and knew immediately there was a problem and went for his medicine. She put his medicine in the pot so he could begin to steam right away. She tried to give him his medicine, but it didn't seem to help. It had gone too far this time! He needed medical attention, and he needed it expeditiously. She looked at Platt with panic in her eyes and he understood all too well. She didn't even have to say a word and he was out the door and on his horse. He pushed his horse to its limits, rushing to get to Doc. *I hope I am not too late! Why hadn't I gone to look for him sooner? I was so wrapped up in my own affairs! I should have been out helping him.* What would Nellie say right now? *She would tell me that it was not my fault, and this could happen to him at any time. It was because of his asthma. But what will I do if father doesn't make it this time?* No, I must remain optimistic and positive.

His as well as all his brothers, the relationship with their father was a rare one. Most men choose to be stern with their sons, but not their father. They had a very special father-son relationship. It was nurturing and a genuine friendship. His father seemed genuinely interested in what was going on his in life and he felt comfortable talking to him about anything, even his Love for Nellie. Most of the boys he attended school with had stern fathers. They were more like employers than fathers.

As he came into town, he noticed Doc's buggy just pulling into his office. His horse galloped toward him as fast as it could go. Platt jumped off his horse, exasperated, explaining as quickly as he could that his father was in trouble. He could barely speak but he was able to muster out "asthmatic" and that was all he needed to say. Doc jumped back in his buggy and spun off to the Corbaley's as quickly as his horse could run with Platt right behind him.

They arrived at the Corbaley ranch and Doc flew off the buggy and into the house. Platt was not far behind him but had to tie up the horses. Sam rushed over so he could leave the horses and be with his father. Doc was with his father for a very long time, trying inhalation after inhalation to try and get him breathing again. Platt had never seen anyone receive so much medication before! He was fearful of over medicating, but he also knew without the medication his father would die. At last, Doc said he felt that his father was stable, but he had to have round the clock attention. He would try an inhalation treatment which had just recently been studied in France and was found to be very effective in the treatment of Asthma! It was called "sodium chloride" and was experimental.

Mama was worn out. Platt could tell but she refused to leave the vigil at his bedside.

"Let me take over for a while. I will let you know if there is any change."

His Mother was too tired to disagree. As Platt sat next to his bedside, he realized how thankful he was for his father. He didn't really know just how much he appreciated him until now. Platt administered his vapor treatments just as Doc had ordered and he could see the improvement, but his father was still not awake or alert.

Morning came but Platt had not closed his eyes to sleep, even for a minute. He was too concerned for his father's condition, and he knew keeping to a strict medication regime was crucial. Mama came down bright and early and she insisted that Platt have some breakfast and get some rest. He reluctantly agreed for he knew it would benefit him nothing to argue with her. He also knew how tired and emotionally drained he was from the whole ordeal of the previous day. He did not have much of an appetite and sleep seemed to be far more appealing now. On his way to his bedroom his thoughts turned to Nellie. He thought about little else these days and he began to wonder what she would say about the developments of the last few days. Oh! How he needed her, she always seemed to have the right words to say to encourage him. Exhaustion pulled at every muscle of his body and when he laid his head on the pillow, sleep followed soon behind. Before he knew it, his mother was gently nudging his shoulder, telling him it was morning. He needed to make sure that all the hired hands were organized in bringing in the corn harvest since his Father was incapacitated.

Platt knew that the farm responsibilities had now fallen on his shoulders. This brought up a new dilemma, what to do about college? He had been planning and dreaming about it for so long and had worked so hard in school, getting almost perfect scores in all his subjects. *Why now?* To even think such a thought, he felt deep remorse. He knew his responsibly to his family far outweighed his own hopes and dreams but letting go was more difficult than he first thought. Platt dressed and went out to the barn and met Sam. He had been with them for as far back as he could remember and had always proved to be a faithful employee. Sam had already organized the other hired hands and was mapping out which fields needed to be harvested first. When he arrived, Sam asked if the plan met with his approval. Platt was very wise, knowing that Sam's years of working the farm would be to his benefit. He agreed with the plan and told Sam he was in charge and to direct him with what to do and which field to go to. Sam wiped the sweat from his brow. He had been sweating, wondering if young Platt would ever take over. It was his farm, after all, he thought to himself. At the same time, he was relieved that Platt had let him continue to do his job. He knew his father would be proud of him for that decision and realized just what a fine young man he had turned out to be.

Sam was in his 40's now and not as young as he once was. The sun had made his skin weathered and brown. His large eyes were crystal blue and his hair that was bleached blonde from the sunshine was now graying around the temporal area. He was thought to be a handsome and dashing young man in his day, but those days had come and gone. Now he was left with wrinkles, gray hair, an aching back, and memories of those days. But he had a good woman to go home to every night. Mattie Mae was a beauty, just as beautiful as the day they met! He could remember it as if it were yesterday. He was new in town and eating at the café, going to inquire about any jobs in the area when he looked up from the table and saw her. She was working at the café. Her parents owned it and she was helping them by working there. When she came by the table to take his order, she, instead, stole his heart. She was tall and slender with the most beautiful long blonde hair. It looked of pure corn silk, it did. She has the biggest smile with lips the color of cherries and the sweetest disposition to match. Why she ever agreed to date and marry him, he would never know. He was thankful every day for his bride; for she was the reason he rose in the morning. He only wished that he could have given her more material things. She says that it doesn't matter and that she is grateful for the good life that they share, but his dream was to give her a place, a ranch of their own. Sam knew he was very blessed with his job as foreman and the Corbaley's had always been good to him, but his dream was to have his own farm. He yearned to be his own boss. He had been saving his money, but it seemed like it took so much just to live. He was grateful that Mattie Mae's parents had given them a small house as a wedding present. It was a fine house and they added on to it when the children came along. It had served them well, but he just wanted more! Someday, he knew it would happen but today he must attend to Mr. Corbaley's land and do the best job he could. He had always been taught that you must be faithful to the jobs at hand if you ever expect promotion.

That day of harvesting went much smoother than Sam or Platt had ever imagined. Since father had always been the organizer of the harvest, Platt had always worked where he was told but never really paid attention to the details of the harvest. He was finding out there were a lot more of them than he had ever imagined!

It had been a long and exhausting day. All Platt could think about was getting back to the house to check on his father and subsequently climbing into bed. Sam asked if he might have a few moments of his time. The last thing he wanted to do was talk "farm talk." He was exhausted but he knew that it was his responsibility until his father was well again, so he put aside his own needs and obliged. Sam said that they had done a lot today but that he and his father had been in negotiations with some immigrant workers to assist in getting the rest of the fields harvested before the bad weather hit. Platt was surprised his father had never used immigrant workers before and wanted to get his father's opinion before deciding, but time seemed to be of the essence. Sam had to give them an answer tonight or they would go to work at another neighboring farm.

"Sam, my father has trusted you to be foreman and run this ranch for over 20 years. You're like family to us and I know any decision you make will be in the best interest of this farm. I can speak for my father and my brothers. Whatever decision you come to; you will have my backing 100 percent."

Sam stood there, just looking at him, not knowing what to say. He was right. He did love the ranch like it was his own and the Corbaley's like they were his family. He would plan just as if Mr. Corbaley himself were here making it. They had worked together for so long; it was almost as if they thought of one anyway. But what amazed him was the maturity of young Platt. How he had grown into a fine young man and was wise beyond his years.

"Thank you for the confidence you have in me. I will take care of it right now."

Almost instantaneously, he was off to town to take care of business. Platt dragged himself back to the house, ridden with anxiety, not knowing what he would find. He knew his father's condition was very grave the day before, but after all day and night of giving the medications and inhalations, he hoped he would be better. As he entered the house he was met by his mother. She relayed to him the events of the day and how her husband remained unconscious most of the time.

"He has moments where he wakes but they are only moments. Then he is asleep again. The doctor said to continue the medication and the inhalations, but I feel like the Belladonna is making him so sleepy."

"Mother, do whatever the doctor says. It might expedite a speedy recovery."

She reluctantly agreed. She had questions about the course of treatment and due to not seeing any results, she was entertaining the idea of taking him to a specialist in the city. She would never offend Doc. or have him think that she did not have full confidence in his medical ability, but she had a nagging feeling that her husband needed more than he could offer here in this small town. For now, she would continue to do whatever was needed to get her husband well. That afternoon, Doc came out to the ranch to check on Richard's condition and from the look on his face, Jane could see that the news was grim.

"Tell me Doc. How is our patient today?" she said it was as cheerful and confident as she could muster. She put up a brave front, not wanting anyone to know just how scared she really was.

Richard had been sick with Asthma his whole life from childhood, but they had been able to control these attacks until this one. This was different, much more serious, and she knew it. The worst part of it was the man she loved was laying, fighting for every breath and she was helpless to make it better for him!

"Jane, I need to speak to you and Platt. Your other sons can arrange for a time to meet with me when I come out to check on Richard tomorrow. Can you arrange that?"

"Doc. What is it? Do I need to send them now? Tell me! I can't bear to wait. Is Richard dying?"

"No Jane. I just need to talk to all of you about his condition. So please, continue his medication as I have written it out for you, and I will be back tomorrow." He was out the door and off in his buggy to another house call. Doc had been around for a long time and had been there to help to save Nellie's life and her father's, so he was certainly a doctor to be trusted with sound medical advice.

It would be a feat to get all the children together at one time. Al and Platt were no problem, as were Mary who still lived at home. Franklin, William, and John had all gone off to start families of their own. Reuniting at the holidays was difficult enough with their demands and responsibility of family life, but they knew that this was important. The children were vastly different, but they did have one thing in common, a deep love and respect for their father and mother.

That night when Platt came in from the fields, he saw his mother sitting in the parlor and she looked as if she had been crying. For a moment, his heart stopped beating, thinking the worst had happened. He quickly realized that if some fatality had become his father, he would have been told before he reached the house.

"Mother what is it? Is father all right?"

"Yes. Platt, the Doctor was out today, and he wants to meet with you and I tomorrow when he makes his rounds to check on father. I don't suppose he is at all pleased with his progress and I am not at all sure what he intends to do. Platt, I wouldn't tell anyone this, but I am quite scared about his condition. I listen to him breathe and watch him struggle for air and I am very scared." Platt stood there, gazing over at his mother.

She was a strong woman who never acknowledged her weaknesses. He didn't know how to react to what she said. He always had a very close and loving relationship with his parents, his father more so than his mother. He went over and touched the top of her shoulder. She responded by covering his hand with hers. It was an unspoken language of the heart. This day was the embarking of a new relationship with a new understanding between mother and son, one that didn't always require a lot of words but sometimes only a look. A relationship between a mother and her son is as rare as a precious jewel. He didn't realize it now, but would soon, in the days to come, just how much he needed and respected his parents.

"Mother, I was able to contact all the brothers and I believe they will all be here tonight, if possible. You know how busy they are with their own farms and with the store, and Frank being such a successful attorney, but they will be here for they love you and father so dearly."

It was very quiet that night at dinner. Everyone was in their own thoughts. Jane was thinking only of Richard, his condition, and what was so serious that Doc. needed her, and the children present to discuss. Her appetite escaped her. She was too consumed with apprehension and worry to even eat. It seemed Platt sat in silence too, only playing with the food on his plate, even though he had been famished earlier after a long day of work. Now all his thoughts were toward his father, his condition, and the news they were to hear tomorrow. *If ever there was a time, I needed Nellie to help me sort things out and to see things the way they are. Why, of all times, are we separated when I need her the most?* He excused himself from the table and went to his room to write Nellie a letter. Maybe if he put it all down on paper it would make more sense. He began writing his letter, telling her about finding his father in the field and how him and Sam were running the farm and getting in the rest of the harvest with the assistance of the immigrant workers. He wrote about his mother and how their relationship seemed to be changing and about the big meeting with Doc scheduled for tomorrow that they were all a bit apprehensive about. He was very thankful for his brother and how their relationship seemed to have deepened during this time of family crisis. What was once sibling rivalry had become a friendship with a bond that was as thick as a horsehair rope. His Brothers had always been closer to his mother and AL and Platt to his Father but during this time, the family pulled together to become a symphony, each playing their own instrument but bringing forth a melodious sound. They would all need to lean on each other, especially with whatever news the Doctor was going to deliver tomorrow. Platt wrote every lingering thought and before he knew it, he had written several pages. He was weary after such a long day but found that sleep would not come easy that night.

He was awakened by the rooster crowing. It was time to get up and start the chores before the meeting with the doctor. He was on his way down to breakfast when he stopped to check in on his father and there was still no change! *When would he wake up from this coma? Would he wake up from this coma?* He knew he must not think negative thoughts, but he couldn't help it. It had been what seemed like an eternity waiting for him to wake up. Platt reached out and held his father's hand. He deeply missed talking to him.

"Oh, father! Please, would you wake up? I need you. There are too many things I still need to learn from you." He gently laid his hand back on the bed. He reached down and kissed his brow and went off to the kitchen for breakfast, then back to the fields to bring in the crop.

They had been very blessed this year and his father would be very pleased to see an abundant crop. He was very thankful for Sam being such a wonderful foreman. He knew that his heart was on this ranch and with his father because he worked just as hard when he was awake or laying in a bed comatose. Workers like that are few and far between and Platt was very thankful they had found him.

The sky was clear as crystal, with not a cloud anywhere in sight. Platt was so engrossed in his work cutting the crops that he hardly noticed when A.L. came to get him and tell him that Mama and Doc. We're waiting to meet with them. A.L. was a tremendous help on the ranch but Platt knew that he would not be able to run things by himself, even with Sam's assistance. He knew college would maybe have to wait for now. Platt and A.L. walked toward the house, not saying anything. They were both absorbed deep in their thoughts about this upcoming meeting. Platt excused himself so he could clean up before meeting with Doc. He felt as if he were going to the executioner and had such a sense of dread. He finished washing up and walked down the stairs toward the parlor. He heard voices, several voices, and one he was very familiar with. He quickened his pace. His heart was skipping a beat. *Could it possibly be? Yes! It was father, he was awake! But when? How??*

"Father, how long have you been awake? How are you?" Platt rushed to hug his father's neck.

"I woke up sometime last night. Your Mother has been doctoring me back to health."

Doc. stepped forward. "You're probably wondering why I requested this meeting. At the time, I had no idea your father would be awake, but I am glad that he is. His health is still very fragile, and he has some lung damage due to this last attack and near-death experience. Farming and ranching, unfortunately, are no longer going to be a viable option. It is my recommendation, and I feel it would be in your best interest, if you considered selling the ranch/farm and moving to a place where you can breathe more easily. What are your thoughts on that?"

Father sat in silence for a few minutes. "This Ranch has been in our family for generations, but if it is to the point that I can't farm, then I would rather sell. I know what I would want to do with the Ranch, and I will discuss it with you boys, Alvaro, Frank, William, Platt and Marie their sister since it is your inheritance."

Platt jumped to his feet. "What is this talk, sell the farm? It sounds like lunacy! So out of character for you! Father, are you just giving up?" He went out on the porch to get some air but was so upset; he just kept walking and soon found himself amidst the corn in the field. *Sell the ranch! What are they thinking? Move to California? What would they possibly do there?* He walked up and down the rows of corn, trying to make sense of everything that had transpired. *Then again, I would be closer to my Nellie than I am right now. Oh, how I miss her! She always seems to know the right things to say to make me feel calm and whole again. I feel like a part of me is missing with her gone.* He decided he had gathered his composure sufficiently to return to the conversation with his father. All eyes turned in Platt's direction as he entered the room.

"Have you had time to gather yourself so we might continue with our conversation?"

"Yes, I am ready to talk about this rather impulsive idea. I will attempt to have an open mind as I know, the most important thing is your health."

His father gave him a look that let him know he understood his frustration but did not approve of the harsh way his son had spoken.

His Father began to unfold his plan for the selling of the ranch. He didn't want the ranch to go to the person who was the highest bidder at auction. He had been thinking about this for some time as the boys were getting older. He knew they would be leaving and starting their own lives at some point and the possibility that they may not have an interest in pursuing ranching as a lifestyle was always there. He knew Platt and A.L. always seemed to enjoy ranching but he also knew his boys were destined for greatness. Staying on the ranch just wasn't part of that equation. John, Franklin, and William had other interests or investments and he did not foresee Marie running this ranch by herself. This was a very difficult decision for Richard and Jane. Their whole lives had been spent in this house, the early married years and their family was born and raised there. It was more than a house or ranch; it was a part of them. They built it up to what it was today, a thriving ranch farm with acres of rich soil that produced bountiful crops. No, this decision did not come easy.

As Richard told the family of his plan, Platt became more excited than anything. After he laid it all out, Richard called Sam in to tell him what was to be happening with the ranch. He gave Sam a detailed plan, no intricacy left to mystery. Sam left the Corbaley's house looking as if he had seen a ghost. He was visibly shaken. When he got to his house, he barely made it to the door when he was met by his sweet wife. She saw Sam's face and thought something dreadful had happened. She helped him inside to a chair and asked what left him so troubled. Sam sat and stared into space for a few minutes. He looked at his beautiful wife and took her face in his hands.

"Sam, you are worrying me. What happened today?" He looked deeply into her beautiful blue eyes and kissed her deeply and passionately. Now she was perplexed.

"Mattie Mae, Mr. Corbaley came out of his coma today." She smiled and sighed a sigh of relief but didn't understand his reaction to the news. Before she could say anything else, he continued, "He pulled me in for a conference with the family and Doc."

Now Mattie Mae was very confused! "Why would the ranch foreman be asked to be a part of a family conference with the Doctor? This is not making sense!"

"They are selling the ranch." He waited to see her response.

"Well, you have been a good foreman for a very long time, and I am sure that Mr. Corbaley will put in a good word for you to the new owner." She began pacing the floor.

"Well, that may not be necessary."

"And why would that be? Sam, we need the money. I guess I could take on an extra job to help, but we must pay for food and…"

Sam interrupted her. "Mattie Mae…I, well, I mean we are the new owners of the Corbaley estates!"

She stood there silently, not knowing what to say, trying to comprehend if what she heard was right.

"Did you just say WE are the new owners? How? When? How can we afford this?"

"I know Mattie, but Mr. Corbaley has worked out all the details with his attorney and banker. The money we have been saving will be used for a down payment and then we will make payments when the crops come in or when the cattle go to auction. Mattie, he told me he felt as if I were one of his sons, like we were part of the family." This statement alone meant more to Sam than anything in the world. He never remembered his father growing up. With only a mother and Uncle to raise him, he felt like he had found an extended family with the Corbaleys. Sam looked into the very perplexed face of his lovely wife and searched for an answer.

"Well, don't just stand there and look at me woman! Tell me what is on your mind. What do you think about all of this?"

Mattie's mouth was dry, so she went to the white porcelain pitcher and poured a glass of water. She sat down and tried to digest everything that her husband had just told her. *Could it really be happening? Could our dream finally come true?* She sat there for a moment, trying to be sure she did not dream all of this.

"Mattie, are you all, right? I have never seen you like this! Talk to me."

Mattie looked at Sam and smiled. "I say thank the Lord! Sam, you're a ranch owner. This is truly a Miracle! What about the Corbaleys? What can we do to assist them in this time of transition? I know it must be extremely difficult for them with everything they have gone through."

Sam picked up his wife by her tiny waist and twirled her around. When they were almost dizzy from spinning, he gave her a long passionate kiss. He wondered how one man could be so blessed in his life, to find a wife such as Mattie and now to buy the Corbaley's ranch.

"It is more than I could have ever dreamed of, and it is our future now." With a gleaming smile, he held her close to his chest. "I love you, Mattie. Thank you for being my wife." He drew her in for another passionate kiss. The thought of being a ranch owner exhilarated him, but he wished his father was there to witness his success.

It was a flurry of activity around the ranch. Everyone was manic and desperately trying to get packed up while finishing the harvest at the same time. Platt was very grateful his father made the decision with Sam to hire extra ranch hands to assist with the harvest. It would have never been harvested in time before the weather turned cold. He was pleased with the fruit of their labors and knew his father was also. It had been a bumper crop for corn and wheat this year and would bring in a nice price, as well as the herd of cattle he was sending to market. It would certainly be enough to start a new life for them in a new place, one where they would be able to breathe more easily. Platt knew his place was with his family, but he couldn't help but think of Nellie and what she must have felt when she was forced to move out west. He understood devotion to family and knew college was out of the question at this time. His place was with his family until he was able to start his own family with his love, Nellie.

The moving day came soon, maybe too soon, for it seemed no one was ready for the emotions that came with leaving the ranch. Although everyone knew it must happen, the reality of it hit them like the wind of a tornado. They were not prepared for all the hidden feelings that they had associated with their home. It was the first, and only, place that Richard and Jane had lived in after they were married. It was the home where Platt and A.L. were born and grew to be fine young men. So many memories! Jane wondered how she could leave such a sentimental part of herself behind. Similar thoughts whirled through Richard's head. He had grown up in the house and was the one brother who decided to stay and run the ranch after his parents had passed away. He always dreamed of passing it on to his own sons. This was the death of a dream for him.

"Darn Asthma! Why did it have to come along and ruin everything?" Richard blurted out before he even realized he was speaking.

Platt looked at him and then at his mother. He tried to find the right words to say but was at a loss. Platt went to his father and put his hand on his shoulder, as if to show his understanding and solidarity.

Richard looked around for his foreman. Sam sensed that the family needed to be alone, so he busied himself in the barn all day. He was distracting himself from the emotions that their departure would bring. Mr. *Corbaley* had been like the father he never knew or had. He was beyond grateful that Mr. Corbaley allowed him to fulfill his dreams and made him a ranch owner. Sam gave the boys hugs and went to shake Mrs. Corbaley's hand. She threw her hands around his neck and gave him a big hug.

"You know that you were always like one of the family to us! Take good care of Corbaley Ranch for us. Be a prosperous rancher, okay?"

They arrived at the train station with their previous lives neatly condensed into trunks. They sold their buggies, wagons, and all their furniture, except for a few family heirloom pieces that could not be parted with. Those were sent ahead on a freight wagon, and they would be at their new residence when they arrived. Platt was antsy and ready to get on the train headed for California. He would be closer to his Nellie! He missed her so terribly, his heart ached within him.

Soon they were responding to the conductor's call. Each step aboard the train was a step closer to a new adventure, a whole new world of opportunity, which would bring him closer to his Nellie. Soon the Corbaleys were on board and settled in for the long trip. Platt decided it was a good time to sit down and write Nellie a letter and tell her about the events of the past few days and how he was headed to California. He wanted to tell her about his decision to stay with his family due to his father's failing health and that college, although a grandiose idea was not to be at this time. As he began writing and reciting all the happenings and details of the last few weeks' time went by and before he realized it, his father was gently nudging his shoulder and telling him that it was time for dinner. Time seemed to have escaped him. He didn't even realize how late or how hungry he was. He joined his family at the community table and sat next to Mr. Humphries. He worked for the railroad and Platt was so fascinated by his stories. He explained how the railroad was being laid across the country and their recent difficulties with railroad bandits. He was so engrossed in the stories that he almost forgot about his dinner. That night after dinner, he spoke privately with his father.

"Father, I have a dream of working for the railroad as a deputy sheriff to help protect and keep this land safe!" His father always encouraged anything his sons wanted to do that was within reason and good sense. He felt that if his son had a desire to do something in the field of law enforcement, he must encourage it.

"Life is a journey with many twists and turns in the road. You may never know where it will lead you but remember to always enjoy the journey. Life is full of surprises! Learn to smile and say thank you." His father's little proverbs and sayings were sometimes what kept him going when things got tough. He knew he would draw on them for many more years.

The next day on the train, Richard, A.L, and Platt were sitting and mapping out their itinerary for when they arrived in Healdsburg California. Richard was going to contact his brother who lived there, in hopes that he may be able to help them get settled. Platt and A.L knew that they must get to work as soon as possible to help support the family. The sale of the ranch would help to sustain them for a time, but it would certainly not be enough to get resettled, purchase another property, and sustain the lifestyle they had all become accustomed to. When conversing about their plans, they were interrupted by Mr. Humphries.

"I was not intending to eavesdrop in on your conversation, but I will need to hire some workers when I return to California. If your sons are interested, I could use two smart young men of their caliber. If either one of you are interested, please come and see me." Platt and A.L. looked at each other, rather dumbfounded. *Could this really be working out so perfectly?*

"Mr. Humphries, my sons and I appreciate your generosity and will certainly discuss it and get back to you with their decisions."

Platt sat there with his mouth open, ready to speak but nothing came out. He deferred to his father out of respect. *How could he even "think about it"? Didn't he know this man was offering them a gold mine? Why in the world would he have reservations?* He couldn't figure it out, but he had learned to trust his father, even when he didn't understand. Platt was deep in thought when his father came to join him.

"Platt, I know you have some questions about my reservations for Mr. Humphries' offer. I know you don't understand and really, I am not so sure why myself. But I have learned to trust the voice inside and I had to go with my heart and not my head. We will have to wait and see why on this one."

"I don't understand it father! I know your brother has offered work in his store, but this opportunity sounds too good to pass up."

"Son, if things seem too good to be true, they probably are."

Platt sat and pondered his conversation with his father and thought that was true in most things, except Nellie. She was as good as she seemed, honest, funny, smart, and witty, not to mention, incredibly beautiful. She was everything any man could ever want.

Before he knew it, the train was pulling into Healdsburg, California. It was more of a rough and tough gold mining town than he was used to. He told himself he was ready for a new adventure but at this moment, he was rethinking that thought. The town was even smaller than Marshall. There was a general store and a small white church at the far end of town that he noticed as the train had pulled in. He saw a diner called "Martha's Home Cooking" and wondered how close to home cooking it really was. He was perplexed at why a town of such a small size needed 2 saloons. He would soon come to find out that the clientele that frequented such establishments were the miners and gold diggers. The streets were dirty, and the sidewalks were made of wood that made your boots echo when you walked. There was a rooming house run by a sweet gray-haired lady named Mrs. Smith. She was a widow that loved people and cooking. When her husband passed away it seemed like a logical thing for her to do with her large house. There was a hotel above the Dixie Inn Saloon. It was where most of the gamblers stayed when they came to town.

They decided to stay at Mrs. Smith's while they looked for suitable housing. Mrs. Smith was most likely in her 50's. She was short of stature and her cheeks were red. Her hair was black with streaks of gray, and she had weather beaten skin on her forehead. Otherwise, she did not look middle-aged at all, but one could tell if they looked closely that life had left its mark on Mrs. Smith. She and mama became fast friends. Platt was relieved since Mama had to leave all her family and friends to come and follow father to California. He had not really thought about her sacrifice because he was preoccupied, feeling sorry about his own.

One of Platt's first orders of business was to get a job. He wanted to save enough to buy a home for him and his future bride. He knew good and honest work would keep him busy and would make time go by faster. He had to make a good home for Nellie. Of course, getting his parents settled in was a very important priority but he was a man now and had his own personal agenda. Platt was a rancher and was used to getting up and working the land from dawn to dusk, but he knew at some point in time he would change professions. Platt was able to secure a job right away working with horses. He had always been good with animals, so this job seemed to be a perfect fit for him at this transition time. It helped him not miss Corbaley Ranch so much. Platt was working with the horses in a makeshift livery stable.

It had a wooden fence that kept the horse penned in and a makeshift awning that would protect the horses from the elements. Platt knew the set up was not going to be workable when the winter weather arrived. He knew from winters in Marshall that he needed to convince Mr. Blackhawk to build a wooden livery stable. He also knew that Mr. Blackhawk was a very frugal man. He had to convince him that it was in his own best interest to do this and not just for the benefit of the horses. Platt went to the general store and asked about lumber prices. He knew the more information he had to persuade Mr. Blackhawk, the better. He also found out the going rate for boarding a horse at a nice livery. To give the horse shelter, a good rub down, and to bed it down for the night after a long ride would cost a man a pretty penny. Once he had all his information, he went to see Mr. Blackhawk. He was very reluctant until Platt showed him how he could benefit from the proposition. He changed his mind and decided to give Platt a chance to prove himself.

He built the livery stables, board by board and nail by nail. A.L. helped him so he could get it done before winter set in. It was a fine livery stable when it was finished. People would come from all over just to see the livery stables and board their horse for the night. Mr. Blackhawk was so pleased that he gave Platt a raise. Life seemed to be going good for Platt. He had a good job that kept him busy, and he had respect from his boss and people in the town. Despite this, there was a missing element in his life. Nellie! Oh, how he missed her. He wrote to her almost every day. Her letters came every day at first, but now something was different. *Is it her Papa? Is she busy with school or is she falling out of love with me? No, I won't let myself think such a thing and yet, that thought is stuck in the back of my mind. I ache to hold her in my arms again, to feel her body pressed hard against mine! And her soft lips! I can't imagine her with someone else, someone else kissing those lips, holding her tiny frame and feeling her heart beating so fast and hard. When she was close to me it seemed like we were one person.* The very thought was driving him mad. He would have to keep himself busy to keep his mind off her for now.

Chapter Eight
Nellies New Home in California

What a dreadful place! Nellie didn't know if she would ever adjust to this new city. It was vastly different to everything she had ever known. Her very security was shattered, but she decided that she must be strong and not utter a word of complaint. After all, it was also difficult for her parents. Their world had also changed so she told herself that she must not be selfish. She pointed her chin high, and with a determination that was beyond her years, made a commitment that she would be strong.

Papa and mama seemed happy enough in their new home and papa was getting stronger all the time. California seemed to agree with him. Although everyone seemed friendly, making new friends was difficult. They couldn't compete with the lifetime friends that you grew up with and had history with. Nellie decided to be friendly but to concentrate on just one thing, her studies and graduation. The school was much smaller than in Marshall as California was still being established as a territory. Most of the towns were mining towns. Everyone was coming to California to claim their stake of land and to mine for gold. It was all new country with its share of rattlesnakes and sage brush. It was so different from her hometown in Marshall. There were much warmer temperatures and they had not yet seen the wonderful colors of the fall season. *What could be so glorious about this?* She missed all her friends and most of all, she missed Platt. She had heard from him every day and then nothing. She was beginning to wonder what had happened. She knew she could not make it in this awful existence without him! If not in person, at least in his letters. His letters were wonderful. She missed him and his letters and wondered if he had found someone else. *Had Matilda thought to comfort him, and they fell in love? What had happened and why had he not written to me?* She decided to think that he was busy with the ranch harvest and getting things ready for winter haying and such. She knew he had wanted to go off to school, but she also knew he promised to write every day. Many questions whirled through her head. She knew their love was real, but could she be wrong? She had so many questions with no real answers, only speculations.

One day after going to check the mail in town and still no letter from her beloved, she was so upset she burst out of the post office in hysterics. She failed to hold back the ocean of tears. At that very moment, she stumbled into Fredrick from the train.

"Oh, excuse me. I didn't see you. I really must be going." Nellie stumbled through her words. All she wanted was to be alone and have a good cry. Fredrick could see she was very upset.

"Nellie, are you alright? You look upset. Would you like to talk about it?"

Normally Nellie would run as fast as she could from Fredrick, but today she needed a friend to talk to. "All right, if you don't mind a few tears."

They went for a walk, and she told him all about not hearing from Platt and how important he was to her. It wasn't proper to discuss her true feelings for him as they seemed too personal to share with a stranger. She knew him from their introduction on the train and they were in the same classes at school. He wasn't a stranger, but he felt that way for Nellie. It was apparent to everyone, except Nellie, that he had a fond affection for her. He tried to offer sound advice and a shoulder for her to cry on. What he wanted to do was take her in his arms and kiss her deeply. He knew that was not his place and that he would have to settle for being a friend, but was a challenge being friends with such an extraordinary beauty. *If Platt has really let her go, then he is a fool!* After they talked, Nellie's mood improved.

"Thank you for being here today and being my friend when I desperately needed one. I don't have any real friends since moving here and I would be honored if I could call you a friend."

Frederick was speechless at first. "I would be most honored to call you a friend and since we are friends, would you accompany me to the harvest dance next week?"

"Oh Frederick, I will have to get back to you with my response. If there is another young woman you would prefer to escort, I certainly understand. Do not hesitate on my account."

"Nellie, there is no other woman I would prefer to escort. I would feel like a king if you would do me the honor of being my escort, as a friend only."

Nellie went home and discussed the offer with her parents. They gave their approval since the plan was to go as friends. They had some reservations about how it would appear, but it was not a proposal of marriage, it was merely an invitation to a dance. Nellie debated over if she should go or decline the offer. *What was Platt doing? Why has he not written to me*? She spent hours debating with herself, trying to be sure she had made the right decision. She promised to be true to Platt, but it was not as if she was courting someone else. And was it not Platt who had stopped writing? She wondered if she was looking at it from the wrong angle. Maybe something happened to Platt or his Family? How would she find out? Now she was worried. She decided to do the one thing she could do, pray. She asked God to watch over Platt and his family, wherever they were, and to give her direction in what to do about the dance. She felt at peace even though she did not know where Platt was. She knew he was okay, and he would be all right with her going to the dance because he trusted her and their love.

What to wear to the Harvest dance? Now, that was the big question. Everyone at school was busy with preparations for the biggest dance of the school year. When Nellie was going with Fredrick, which did not take long since it was a one-room school house, everyone was shocked.

"Doesn't she have a beau back home?"

Nellie decided that she was not going to let what people said bother her. They were going as friends and he, just as well, may have been her brother. She needed an escort and he had asked, so she had accepted. Frederick was not bothered at all by all the malicious gossip or rumors. In fact, some of it, he rather enjoyed. He knew in his heart that they were friends and nothing more. Although, he hoped that this dance might change her opinion of him, and she may begin to see him in a whole new light.

Nellie paced back and forth in front of the mirror. *This dress does not look right! But why should I even care? We are only friends. Why do I care?* Fredrick was more of a nuisance than a suitor and certainly not one she could give her heart to. Her heart was already taken but he was not there, and she had not heard from him in such a long time. The more she thought about it, the angrier she became and the more justified she felt. She was going and planned to fully enjoy her evening!

What troubled Nellie more than anything was why the letters had stopped coming. She wondered if something dreadful had happened to Platt or if he had changed his mind about her? She told herself that she couldn't have those thoughts and that she must keep a positive attitude. She assumed his letters must have been deterred for some other reason. She couldn't dwell on the matter anymore or she wouldn't be ready in time for the dance. To keep the look of propriety, Hattie, her longtime friend agreed to come along. Hattie came to live with the Jefferson's as a young girl with her mother Gertie their housekeeper. Gertie was not her biological mother, but the only mother Hattie had ever known. Hattie assisted her mother with the household chores, and she was always happy. She was rather shy and soft spoken but was endearing and soon found her way into the hearts of the entire Jefferson family and became best friends with Nellie.

That evening Fredrick came to escort Nellie and Hattie to the dance. Nellie came down the stairs wearing a brown two-piece dress. The top was fitted with puffy sleeves, tapered down at the wrist, and buttoned with tiny brown buttons. The skirt was straight in the front with a bustle in the back and a brown satin bow at the bottom. She had her hair twisted up on top of her head which made her look older than her years. Hattie looked lovely as well, she had a cream-colored two-piece dress with navy trim and puffy sleeves, she wore her hair twisted up on her head and had the most beautiful completion she looked beautiful. Frederick, who was spellbound not only did he have one beautiful lady to escort but two he was sure to be the envy of every boy there because all he could do was stare. She called his name to break him out of his trance. He was smitten, which was a great dilemma for Frederick. He wanted to be close to Nellie and be her friend, but how could he do that and not tell her what burned in his heart? He refused to jeopardize his friendship with Nellie, even at the risk of his own heart.

The trio had a splendid time at the dance. They laughed and danced until their feet began to hurt. They bobbed for apples, ate apple pie, and drank apple cider. Despite being amid so much excitement, Nellie was saddened when she realized just how empty her life was without Platt. Frederick was very handsome and had been a perfect gentleman in every way. She was the envy of every girl at school, but she did not love him. As much fun as they had together, they were friends and nothing more. Frederick could see the faraway look in her eyes. He thought Platt was the luckiest man on earth to have the heart of the most beautiful, witty, and smart young woman he had ever met.

"You are missing this young man of yours, Platt, are you not?"

"Oh Frederick, I did not mean to be so obvious! I was just thinking about the dance we attended when we lived in Indiana. It was a magical night! I will remember it forever. But I did not mean to ignore you! Why, without your friendship, I don't think I would have survived those first few months of being in a new town."

Friendship. That word pierced his soul. He was falling for Nellie, and he knew it. He also knew that to be near her, he would have to remain her friend. If Platt broke her heart, he would be there to pick up the pieces. But for this moment, he was her escort, and he was going to enjoy it. At the end of the dance, he drove her home and was the perfect gentleman. He walked her to the door and bid her goodnight. He took her hand gently, gave a light kiss to her hand, and thanked her for a lovely evening. It was probably the most difficult thing he had ever done. He knew he could not allow himself that much liberty with Nellie. She belonged to someone else, and he was too in love with her to risk his reaction to that much closeness. The dancing, although very enjoyable, had been torturous to him. As they swayed on the dance floor, he dreamt of taking her in his arms and kissing her. Knowing it was impossible was more torturous than he first thought.

Nellie was greeted by Mama and Papa when she returned from the dance. Nellie told them all about the grand decorations, the band, games, apple bobbing and how lovely everyone looked. She spoke of how Frederick was a perfect gentleman and a good friend. Although most would perceive it improper for a young woman to be good friends with a young gentleman, he was a Godsend to her in this transition time. She did not forget to mention that there were several young men who asked Hattie to dance but she had refused all except one, Samuel Drysdale, and they danced and danced. Nellie even saw her smile. Hattie blushed and had to laugh and admit she had a wonderful time. Mama and papa were pleased. They felt responsible for Hattie ever since her mama passed away. She was no longer an employee but a family member. Nellie excused herself and went to her room to write a letter to Platt. She gushed over the dance and told him about how much she missed him. She couldn't help but wonder why she hadn't heard from him.

Chapter Nine
Trip to San Francisco

Nellie could hardly wait for the Holiday to arrive. Although it would be the first Christmas without snow, she still loved Christmas! It meant school would be out and that much closer to graduation. She was going to be a graduate and the sum of that had not yet sunk in. But first, the holidays. Papa was feeling much better this winter and although she still had not heard from Platt, she knew there must be a reason why the letters stopped coming. She knew in her heart that he still loved her. Although Frederick was as attentive as ever, coming over whenever he could and today was no different. He sprinted up the walk as if someone's house was on fire.

"Nellie, I must talk to you at once!"

"Frederick, what is it? What is wrong?"

"Nellie, my family is going to San Francisco for the holiday."

"That is wonderful! I hope you have a wonderful time."

"No, Nellie, you don't understand. Every year I am allowed to bring a friend or two with me on holiday. I have decided to bring you since you are my best friend, what do you say?"

"Frederick, I don't think that would be proper if I accompanied you. After all, you are a young man, and I am a young woman."

"No. Of course, Hattie can accompany you. Please come! I can't imagine the holidays without you."

"Frederick, I will have to discuss this with my parents, but I would love to accompany you to San Francisco!"

Nellie ran into the house to find her parents and discuss the trip with them. They were not certain about their youngest daughter going off to San Francisco with a young man. However, Hattie would accompany her, and they just heard from their eldest daughter, Melissa, and she would be in San Francisco at that time, so they felt okay with the girls going. Still, there was something about this trip that troubled papa. He knew his youngest daughter was now a young woman and that he couldn't make all her decisions, but he had a strange feeling. He couldn't shake the feeling nor put his finger on it, so he guessed he would have to trust his daughter.

Things were buzzing in the Jefferson's house as Nellie and Hattie tried to decide what to take with them to San Francisco. They couldn't decide on which dresses to bring but they were so excited that they decided to take them all. Frederick's father told them that space was not an issue. They were taking the stage, and they could bring as much luggage as needed. Hattie was so excited she would burst into giggles when the girls would talk about being in the big city of San Francisco. Nellie wondered what it would be like to be there with Platt, but she decided not to dwell on it. This was a happy trip, and yet, her heart felt incomplete without him.

Frederick came over and told Nellie and Hattie about all the lovely restaurants and theaters there were to attend. And the holiday ball! It was the most sought-after invitation event in all of San Francisco and they were asked to accompany his family. This year Frederick hoped the young woman he escorted would return the emotions that were beginning to stir every time that he looked at her. *This is pure madness! How am I going to manage an entire holiday with Nellie? Having her nearby and knowing I cannot even hold her!* It was worth it, he assured himself. Just to see her face every day, with her large dark blue eyes and beautiful lashes. Her smile that would light up a room when she walked in it, especially when she saw something new and exciting. Not to mention her frame, she was petite with the tiniest waist. She flowed with such grace when she walked, yet she was not one of those pretentious southern bells who only pretended to be a lady, she was a real lady. Yet, Nellie was confident and outspoken and would tell you exactly what was on her mind. She was a bit high spirited and maybe that's what was so attractive about her. Most girls her age only want to find a husband, settle down, and have children. Not Nellie. It was important to her that she graduate. The more Frederick let his thoughts about Nellie carry on, the more smitten he became.

The morning of the trip, they were ready to leave for a holiday. Nellie and Hattie were so excited that they could hardly stand it. Although they were a little sad to leave mama and papa behind. Mama and papa saw them off on the stage with Frederick, Mr. and Mrs. Wickham, and their daughter, Bella, who assured them that she would watch over the girls. They gave the itinerary for their trip and then were off for their adventure in San Francisco.

Unexpected Surprise

Nellie was sure the road to San Francisco was as long as the road from Indiana. It seemed they would never arrive! She was in awe of the new and beautiful countryside, so lush and green; it looked as if it belonged on a carpet. The sun shined so brightly that it illuminated everything around it, making it appear as if you were glancing into a picture. The excitement was overwhelming and in no time at all, they were pulling into the San Francisco stagecoach station. The city was a lot larger than Nellie expected it to be. Everyone seemed to be in a hurry and there were foreigners! She had never seen a foreigner before. She did not want to stare but the men had long braided ponytails and wore sandals on their feet. They spoke in a different language. It was much faster than anything she had ever heard before. Being the proper young woman she was, she pretended she didn't notice. All the while, she wanted to stare and ask questions. She was curious as to who these peculiar people were, where they came from, and why they looked and talked so differently. Frederick saw the look on her face. He pressed his lips close to her ear and reassured her that he would explain everything later. Nellie politely smiled and continued to walk towards the hotel. She turned to Hattie and began to talk about San Francisco and what a lovely city it was. How lovely everything was decorated for Christmas! About that time, something came along the street. It was a cart without a house.

"Whatever is that?"

"That is a cable car. It runs on cables and does not require a horse or steam as a train does. It is the way of the future!"

Nellie was very impressed by both the cable car and Frederick's knowledge.

"After we are all settled in at the hotel, we can take the cable car to the theater and dinner. I am sure it will be all right with Father."

Nellie was bursting with excitement but at the same time, she felt empty. Something was missing. She wanted this trip to be memorable, one she would never forget, and all she could think about was Platt. She was angry with him, he hadn't written! She didn't know if he was dead or alive or if he had moved on to someone else, but she had a nagging feeling that things were not as they seemed.

Hattie came into the room, and they began putting their things away in the closet. The Hotel was amazing! It was grand in every way, as if entertaining royalty. The curtains were heavy red velvet with a large gold cord that tied them back in the daytime. The bed linens were also made of heavy red velvet. There were starched cotton sheets on the bed with cotton lace trim. The wash basin in the room was a large white porcelain bowl and pitcher set of the finest quality. The towels were embroidered with the Hotel initials on them. Such extravagance! She had been raised in very comfortable surroundings, but this was an extravagance, like she had never seen before.

That night for dinner Nellie had decided to wear her blue fitted suit. It had puffy sleeves and gold buttons, fitted at her tiny waist, and had a bustle in the back. She scooped her hair up on top of her head. It made her look so sophisticated, which made her fit right into the neighborhood. She wore her grandmother's broche at the neck of the blouse under her suit. She looked exquisite, like a porcelain doll. When she walked down the spiral staircase to meet Frederick and his family for dinner, Frederick's jaw fell open. After he regained his composure, he reached out his hand to help her down the stairs and complemented her on how lovely she looked. He quickly turned to assist Hattie down the stairs, who was looking equally as lovely, but did not evoke the same effect on Frederick. Oh, how he wished that she were his.

The restaurant was fancier than anything Nellie had ever been to before. They had waiters in suits with towels over their arms, asking you if you had reservations and would show you to a seat. This was a lifestyle that was totally foreign to Nellie. It was exciting yet, she wondered if it was indeed worth the cost. The food was a five-course dinner and Nellie had never seen so much food. She thought she would burst out of her dress if she ate the full meal. After dinner, there was dancing in the grand ball room attached to the restaurant. Frederick had been looking forward to this for days! To have Nellie in his arms and to himself, he could feel his pulse begin to quicken as the time approached. He pushed his chair back away from the table and reached his hand toward Nellie.

"May I have this dance please?"

Nellie nodded politely and rather shyly as she took his hand. Nellie was quite an accomplished dancer and loved to dance. Frederick was enjoying himself and found himself the envy of the other gentlemen by having the most beautiful dance partner. Hattie was asked to dance by a gentleman in the crowd and very shyly, agreed. She was a beauty with dark eyes and hair and a slim build. She always turned heads but seemed to pale in the shadows next to Nellie's beauty. They were having a wonderful time, laughing and dancing, when Nellie felt a tap on her shoulder. She turned her head and became white in the face. She gasped and thought, for a moment, she would swoon. She was standing face to face with Platt Corbaley.

"May I cut in on your dance? Please, Good Sir."

Frederick was about to say no when he saw the expression on Nellie's face.

Hattie rushed over from across the dance floor. "Platt! Where did you come from? How did you know we were here?"

Nellie stood completely still, speechless. He was the last person she expected to see in San Francisco, and she didn't have a speech prepared for this occasion. She stared at him in disbelief, not knowing if he was real or a ghost sent to haunt her thoughts and memories.

"Nellie, are you all, right?" Platt asked as Nellie regained her composure.

When she was finally able to speak, she asked to speak with him privately. He took her arm and led her over to the edge of the room.

"Where have you been Platt Corbaley? Why did you show up here in San Francisco? Why have you stopped writing? You promised!" She couldn't contain it any longer and she burst into tears.

Platt looked at her, upset because she felt as if he betrayed her. He realized she had never received letters about his father and selling the farm.

"Oh, Nellie! So much has happened. We left Indiana shortly after you did and moved to California, not far from San Francisco, in Healdsburg. I am working now, and I never made it to college. Father almost died from Asthma, and they told us we had to sell the farm and move. Nellie, I thought you had moved on and forgotten me!"

Nellie didn't know what to say. She looked into his dark piercing eyes and saw the love she had always known. She knew she was in a public establishment and must maintain the utmost propriety, yet all she wanted was to throw her arms around him and embrace him.

"Platt, this is just too much to absorb all at once! You must understand. I thought you had completely forgotten me and now you tell me all this. I know you wouldn't lie to me, but I must process all of this. I will need some time."

"Nellie, time is all we've had since we've been apart! What we need is time together."

She didn't know how to respond. She had long dreamt of this moment and now he was here, in the flesh, and she was at a loss for words.

"Platt, I need to go back to the Hotel now and think about all this. Can I see you tomorrow? Will you still be here?" Nellie asked in exasperation.

"Yes, we just arrived in San Francisco this evening and plan to be here for three days. I would absolutely love to see you tomorrow, but Nellie…." He gently took her arms to bring her face to face with him. "Know that I have not stopped thinking about you for a moment. When I told you that you had my heart and my love, I was honest. My love for you has gone stronger with each passing day!"

Nellie could feel her heart begin to beat more rapidly. She feared it would burst from her chest. "Oh Platt, I need to work all this out. You know I love you! I am just so surprised by all of this. I knew in my heart that you hadn't deserted me or found someone else."

"Nellie, I could never find someone else! What we have is special a love that few experience in a lifetime and yet, we have found each other at such a young age. We do not have to go through a lifetime looking. We are truly blessed Nellie!"

About that time, Frederick came over. "Nellie, are you all right? Is this young man bothering you?"

Platt looked puzzled at Nellie and then to Frederick. He thought that he was just someone that she was dancing with. It never entered his mind that she could have moved on with someone else and forgotten him! Nellie nervously looked at Platt, who was searching for reassurance.

"Platt, this is Frederick Wickham. He's a friend. He brought Hattie and I with him and his family to San Francisco for the Holiday. And before you ask, mama and papa did agree."

Platt, being the gentleman that he is, extended his hand forward. "Thank you for taking such extraordinary care of my Nellie."

Frederick was in shock. He never thought that he would ever meet Platt, especially not when he had plans to win Nellie's heart for himself! He told himself that he must stop his unfruitful daydreaming, regain his composure, and be able to respond appropriately.

"It is wonderful to finally meet you Mr. Corbaley. Nellie speaks of you often."

"Oh, she does? Well, she has never mentioned you in any of her letters, of those that I did receive," Platt replied with the utmost sarcasm.

"Platt, may I have a word with you in private? Will you please excuse us, Frederick? We must catch up on family news and it would be dreadfully boring for you. So, if you will excuse us."

Platt and Nellie walked towards the lobby where they could speak in a more private area. The tension between them was so thick, one could cut it with a knife. She debated what to say to him. She had waited so long to see him and now she was full of such anger, hurt, and excitement all at once. *Why was he being so rude to Frederick? The only friend I've made since the move.*

"Well ladies first. Nellie, you may go first and tell your side and ask your questions. But ask them one at a time. I really do better to answer questions one at a time." Platt looked at her with piercing eyes, in a way that no one else could, and she began to melt. She rushed into his arms and began to sob.

"Platt, where have you been and why didn't you come for me?"

"Nellie, I wrote to you every day! I don't understand why you didn't get the letters but what I must know is if you moved on to someone else?"

Nellie stepped away from his embrace. "I promised my heart to you forever. I knew we would find our way back to each other. I have never even thought about someone else!"

"But what about Frederick I can tell by the way he looks at you that he is smitten! He would love nothing more than to call you, his girl. And why are you here in San Francisco with him?"

"Platt, he is my friend, nothing more. He befriended my family on the train from Indiana and we became friends. That is all. I have always made him aware that my heart belonged to someone else, and I talked about you incessantly. For you to even think otherwise of me does not say much about our relationship!"

Nellie could feel the heat in her face as she spoke for all the months of not hearing from Platt. The frustration was pouring out like molten lava from a fiery volcano. Platt did not get angry. He knew the agony of not hearing from the one you love and the endless days of waiting and wondering what happened. You were helpless in the situation.

He looked down into Nellie's eyes. They had become the eyes of a young woman. He was more in love than he could have ever imagined.

He lowered his face close to hers and covered her lips with his. He didn't care that they were in the lobby of a restaurant. He couldn't wait one more minute to have his long-awaited kiss. Nellie didn't hesitate. She had dreamed about this moment for months but soon realized where they were.

She cleared her throat. "Platt, we are in the foyer of the restaurant!"

Platt didn't seem to realize or care. A couple walked through the restaurant and Nellie stepped back a distance, so as not to give the look of impropriety.

"Why did you do that? Nellie, are you ashamed to be near me?!"

"Never!" She took a bold step towards him. "I want you to come and meet the Wickham family."

Nellie took his arm, and they strolled back into the restaurant towards the others. Nellie introduced Platt to Frederick's family. The rest of the evening was filled with laughter and stories. Everyone appeared to have a wonderful time. Platt was the guest of honor! The Wickham's were all truly impressed by him, except Frederick. He felt very torn. He, too, was impressed by Platt and liked him very much but at the same time, he wanted to have Nellie all to himself. He knew in his heart that would never happen. He had hoped that with the magic of Christmas and the city that maybe, just maybe, she may turn her heart toward him. Then Platt showed up and ruined everything!

After dinner, Platt walked Nellie back to the hotel. It was a beautiful night for a walk and Mr. Wickham said it was all right. They laughed and talked as they walked arm in arm. Nellie realized just how much she missed him and how difficult it would be letting him go again. As they walked along the street in San Francisco, they talked about their families and how strange it was that they both ended up in California. They laughed about how it must be fate.

"No Platt, it's not fate. It's divine providence! We are soul mates and destined to be together for eternity. You must understand it was not an accident that we ran into each other."

Platt smiled and nodded in agreement. He was quiet about his faith, but he had a deep faith in God and tonight confirmed it even more. They walked for what seemed like hours, talking and talking. They could not run out of things to say. He shared how he just built the livery stable in town and was going to work on the railroad to complete the tracks in that area. He told her about the small mining community where they lived and how the boarding room lady had tasted Mama's pies and was now selling her pies in her boarding house. Papa was breathing so much better and with the sale of the farm, he had bought a piece of property closer to town. He said he had done enough farming, and it was time to take it easy. He explained how his father sold the farm to Sam and he was making monthly payments. It gave Father a monthly income and by last communication with Sam, the farm had a bumper crop this past year. As they spoke of home, Nellie realized that the people who lived in Indiana were now grown up and walking in San Francisco. It was surreal. It was like a dream; one she had dreamt about for months.

When they finally reached the hotel entrance, Nellie stood in awe. "Are you real or am I going to wake up tomorrow and find out this was all a dream?"

Platt reached down and touched the sides of her face. "Does this feel real?" He kissed her tenderly. Nellie desperately tried to regain her composure.

"Will I see you tomorrow? I never asked what your plans were." Nellie knew that a proper young woman would wait for the gentleman to approach her, but she knew she did not have a lot of time.

"I have come in town for the ball tomorrow evening. It is a major fund raiser for one of the charities that father ascribes to. He was unable to attend so he sent me instead to represent him and the family. Would you be interested in letting me be your escort?"

Nellie wondered if there would be more than one ball in San Francisco on the same night. "We have been asked to attend a ball with the Wickhams. I wonder if it is the same one."

"Nellie, there is only one major ball in San Francisco. I do believe we will be at the same event. May I see you before?"

"I am not certain of the events planned for the day and since I am their guest, I do believe I owe them the respect of abiding by their schedule."

"Of course, I can. Nellie, I love you even more for your sensitivity to others."

At that moment, Nellie felt as if her heart would burst. He kissed her goodnight, and she reluctantly went inside. She did not immediately go to her room but remained by the window. She watched until she could no longer see Platt. *Was he here or am I dreaming?*

Hattie was sitting up in bed, waiting for Nellie to get back to hear all about her evening. They laughed like two young schoolgirls. She told her all about what happened with the letters and why he had not received hers. She couldn't explain why she didn't receive his letters and it plagued her. She told Hattie that he was here to attend the Great Charity Ball.

"That's the ball we are going to!"

"I know, and I already promised Frederick that I would accompany him. This could get really complicated."

"I know! Why don't I tell Frederick that I would like him to escort me to the ball? I'll tell him that I've never had an escort and it would mean so much to me."

Nellie looked at her adoringly. She was a beautiful girl with peaches and cream skin. "You would do that for me, Hattie?"

"Oh, of course I would! You are like a sister to me. Your family took me in and gave me a home when I did not have one. I would do anything for you!" They hugged for the longest time. Hattie looked at Nellie inquisitively. "You're going to marry Mr. Platt, aren't you?"

"Hattie, I still have a few months of school left but if he would ask me this very minute, I would I know I would say yes. I have never felt like this in my life. He makes me feel a way I never thought possible! I go weak in the knees just being around him. Yes Hattie, I will marry him when he decides to ask me."

"Oh, he will Miss Nellie. Some things a girl just knows!" They both laughed.

Sleep became more difficult for Nellie that night. She was certain if she closed her eyes and went to sleep, she would awaken and find it was all a dream. She did not want to take that chance but sleep finally overtook her. She dreamt of the first dance that she and Platt ever attended. They danced and danced all night in her dream.

It was a big day! The day of the ball had arrived, and Nellie and Hattie were overwhelmed with excitement. To prepare for the event, the girls made appointments with a hairdresser. Nellie had servants assist her with dressing in the past, but she was going to an establishment where they had people doing nothing except assisting with hair platting. They were going to ride on a cable car to get there. It was like a train without an engine. It runs on a cable and rings a bell when it comes to an intersection, so as not to run into the wagons or horses. It was all so exciting! It was like a dream come true.

After breakfast, she saw Hattie ask for a moment to speak with Frederick privately. She explained the situation and asked if he would consider being her escort to the ball. Frederick was more than gracious and asked her before she could humiliate herself by asking him. She shyly agreed with a blush on her cheeks. Frederick found her very attractive at that moment. He began to engage in conversation with Hattie, a feat not easily accomplished due to her extreme shyness. After speaking to Frederick for what seemed like hours, she excused herself so that she could begin her day of preparations. She reassured him that she was looking forward to their evening.

He reached over and took her hand. "Not near as much as I am, Miss Hattie."

She rushed off to the Hotel to join Mrs. Wickham and Nellie and start getting ready for the ball. Never had they been fussed over in such a way! The woman at the Hotel came to their room and did the hair plaiting. She pinned curls up on top of Nellie's head. She looked like a princess and today, she felt like it too. The girls tried hard to act sophisticated and grown up but indulged in many moments of pure delight. Giggles spilled out with an anticipation that seemed to fill the entire room, what a wonderful day this has been being treated like a princess and now at last with hair done and even make up applied which made them look more gown up and elegant it was time for the ball gowns! These ball gowns were exquisite, they were beaded with satin and looked so grown up. Nellie's was of a deep blue with embroidered flowers and a full skirt and cinched waist band it was stunning on her with her deep blue eyes. Hattie's gown was of a deep purple which showed off her fair flawless complexion perfectly it hung to her petite frame as if it were a custom fit for her, it was finished off around the neckline with tiny pearl buttons which also ascended down the back of the gown. When these two young women ascended the staircase ascended the staircase at the hotel it was not only Plat, Frederick, the Wickhams who were in awe of the beauty of these two women but every head in the entire hotel turned to look.

Nellie and Hattie looked at each other as if something was wrong but realized all was well when Platt and Frederick both reached out their hands to the ladies and told them how lovely they looked. They all boarded the cable car to take them to the ball with the thrill of excitement in the air so thick it was almost tangible.

When they arrived at the ball Platt with Nellie on his arm he felt as if he were the luckiest man alive! The Ball was nothing like either of them had ever attended before it had a full orchestra the ball room floor was polished so brightly one could see their reflection in it. They were serving dinner, and the flat wear and table service was of china this was the most elaborate ball or dinner she had ever attended. The music was grand, and they danced and danced until their feet hurt.

The dinner was the most amazing with fresh fish, shrimp, lobster and that wonderful sourdough bread! After the dinner and more dancing Platt asked Nellie if they might have a few minutes to talk alone. She could sense that he had important matters to discuss that could not be discussed at a ball. They made their way out of the ballroom to where there was more privacy and a place where they could talk.

"Nellie, I want to know that I can see you again soon since we are both in the same state now, I mean I don't know why you did not get my letters I wrote to you every day! I have missed you more than I could even imagine was possible to miss another individual I know that it would be easy to run to another when you're lonely."

"Platt, I care about you and our love, and I know what we have is real! How can you think that I would defile our love by pursuing Frederick, or anyone else for that matter?! If what we have is real, it will last just as it has thus far." She fell into his embrace, and he held her tightly in his strong arms. That had only gotten stronger with farm work and building the livery. Platt looked down at Nellie's sweet face and became lost in her eyes. He kissed her with the softness and most tender kiss. It left Nellie weak in the knees.

"I love you, Nellie."

"And I love you, Platt." She stayed in his tender embrace, and he kissed her again.

Platt's heart was beating, near bursting through his chest. "Maybe we should join the dance."

Platt needed a distraction to help maintain his composure. The two were totally unaware that their blissful reunion had been watched. Frederick hadn't meant to spy on them but saw the interaction from the other room. He couldn't deny the feelings he had for Nellie, nor the jealousy and rage he was feeling. He was irate at the thought of Platt stealing his date on what could've been a magical night. He reminded himself that he was a gentleman, and that Platt would be gone soon enough. He would have Nellie all to himself, even if she were not truly his. He began scheming, thinking of ways to have moments alone with Nellie. He would console her from an aching heart or offer a walk to get her mind off Platt. He would be her knight in shining amour. He felt pity for Hattie. She was a very nice girl, but she wasn't Nellie Jefferson.

"Frederick." Hattie spoke softly, bringing him back to reality. "Are you all, right? You looked as if you were miles away."

"No. I was just taking a moment to rest between dances and get some refreshment. Are you having a good time this evening?"

Hattie began to blush and nodded her head. "I've never dreamed of anything as spectacular as this evening! I want to thank you. I know you wanted to escort Nellie, but she asked you to escort me."

Frederick started to speak but Hattie held up a delicate finger and continued. "This has been the best night of my life."

Frederick looked at Hattie and saw a beauty that he had never seen before. He halted in his steps, not able to take his eyes off her. He hadn't experienced anything like it before. He looked into her large blue eyes and wondered how he could've been so blinded before. He reached forth his hand to her, and she accepted it.

"Shall we walk outside for some fresh air?"

He motioned to the terrace, and she glided through the open door. He closed the door behind them and walked over to Hattie. He grabbed her face and tenderly kissed her. Hattie was stunned. She had never been kissed before and had certainly never been alone in a room with a man. She didn't know how to kiss a man and was concerned she did something wrong, but she didn't care. She had her first kiss, and it was wonderful!

"Shall we return to the ball?"

"Yes." She floated back to the ballroom.

Nellie and Platt saw her and instantly recognized the look on her face.

"Where have you been? We've been all over the ballroom looking for you! Do you know where Frederick and the Wickhams are? We danced until our feet were sore! We are going to walk back to the hotel. Can you tell them, please?"

Nellie and Platt had so much to talk about in such a short amount of time. Platt hadn't told Nellie that his stage was leaving first thing in the morning, and he wouldn't be able to see her off in the morning. He decided he wouldn't tell her and spoil the evening. He knew that another evening as perfect as this wouldn't come along for quite some time. As they strolled through the city, they saw many ships in the harbor, houses that had been built up on a hill, and all the stores and saloons. It was a mining town from the big gold rush in 1849. It was very different from Marshall. Nellie saw a new world before her but wasn't sure if she wanted to be part of the big city life. It was exciting but seemed too dangerous with saloons on every corner.

Before they knew it, they arrived at the Hotel. Platt had been dreading this moment since he first saw Nellie. He knew it would break his heart twice as much as it did the first time. He couldn't bear it, so he decided not to tell Nellie he was leaving in the morning. He would write her a letter explaining everything because it would be too painful in person. He would tell her that he was coming for her as soon as she graduated. They would never be apart again!

Nellie could sense that Platt was deep in thought. "Platt is everything all right?"

Platt didn't want to worry her. He cupped her face and kissed her forehead. "No, my love, everything is absolutely perfect." He held her close, and she could feel his heart beating. She felt so secure and so safe.

"I've had a wonderful evening! Oh Platt, I don't want it to end."

"Neither do I, my love." Platt wondered what her response would be to his departure. He looked into her beautiful eyes and kissed her with the most passionate kiss she had ever experienced. She was positive her heart would burst out of her chest.

She loved every moment she had with Platt, but sensed there was something he wanted to tell her. She decided not to spoil the evening with the possibility of an argument. She wanted to enjoy every moment. They stayed up much later than what would've been deemed proper. Soon, the dreaded time for departure had come.

"No! I don't want to lose you again, Platt! Not after these past few days, can't we just go away and marry?"

Platt looked into her pleading eyes. There was nothing he wanted more than to take Nellie as his wife and marry her! But alas, good sense gave in, and he realized that she must return home to her family and finish school.

"Nellie, my love, I want to marry you tonight more than anything in the world but we both know we must wait. I need you to make more money for us, and you need to finish school. I promise I will come for you!"

They fell into each other's embrace and kissed again. He gently pulled her away and said his goodbye. As painful as it was, they both knew putting it off any longer would make it more difficult. Platt watched as Nellie went to her room. His heart broke. He didn't know he could hurt this badly. It took every ounce of resolve not to run after her and whisk her away and marry her that very night. He knew it wasn't the right way and he must write a letter to explain everything to her. He prayed that she loved him enough to understand and forgive him for leaving without saying goodbye. His next great dilemma was who he could trust with such a great document. The logical person was Hattie, but when would he see her to give her the letter? Platt carefully curated the letter, pouring out his heart to Nellie in such a way that he was shaking after composing it. *Nellie must get this letter!* He paced the room. *How can one woman have such an effect on a person?* He adored her, everything about her.

He packed for his journey and attempted to sleep, but to no avail. His priority before leaving was making sure that Nellie received the letter. He went to the front desk of the hotel and just by happenstance, Frederick was up early and saw Platt. They greeted each other with common niceties and Platt, who was rather short on time, decided to ask Frederick. It wasn't his first choice, but he needed someone to deliver the letter to Nellie. Platt told him that she would likely be upset and would need a friend. He appreciated all Frederick had done for Nellie and what a wonderful friend he had been to her.

"Thank you for doing this for me, Frederick. I wish I could explain why I am doing it this way but trust me, it is all in the letter." Platt shook his hand and took off to catch the train back home.

Frederick stood there with the letter in hand and decided. He put the letter in his pocket and went into the hotel to have breakfast as if he had never seen Platt that morning. The ladies joined him for breakfast, along with his parents and Sister. They spoke of the ball and what a lovely time they all had. Everyone except Nellie. She scanned the hotel and restaurant and was beginning to feel confused. *That's odd! Where could Platt be? He said he would be here this morning, didn't he?* After everything, she was positive he wouldn't desert her. But where was he? Her mind was in a whirlwind. She couldn't eat and had difficulty participating in the table discussion. She excused herself from the table because the more she thought about it, the more emotional she became. Frederick followed her. Nellie inquired with the hotel clerk if Platt had checked out of his room.

"Why, yes ma'am, he checked out early this morning to catch the early train. Is there anything else I can help you with?"

Nellie was in shock and found it difficult to breathe. *How could he do this? He disappeared without even speaking to me!*

Frederick rounded the corner and could see the sheer horror on her face. He had a decision to make. *Should I give her the letter and relieve her suffering or come to her rescue?* The tug-of-war of emotions was strong. He knew what the right thing to do was and yet, he wanted Nellie to look at him the way she looked at Platt. Being rather indulged by his wealthy parents, he was used to getting what he wanted. Frederick walked over to Nellie and tried to console her. He put his hand on her shoulder.

"Nellie, are you all, right?"

She was so distraught, she melted into a puddle of tears and Frederick took advantage of the moment. He tried to offer comfort by letting her cry on his shoulder, but Nellie felt uncomfortable and pushed him away.

"Thank you. Frederick, you are a wonderful friend, but I am fine. Thank you for being here." She dried her eyes.

Frederick knew she thought of him as only a friend, but he was hopeful that would change. Seeing the look on her face made Frederick wonder if he had made the right decision by not giving her the letter. He figured he could still produce the letter and later say he forgot he had it. Or, he could go with his original plan and not give the letter to her, in hopes that she would turn her heart to him. He would be the one there to pick up the pieces. He was sure that, in time, he would win the heart of Nellie Jefferson.

Nellie excused herself. She was too upset to talk to anyone and went to her room to pack for the trip home. "How could he do this to me after everything we have been through!?" she yelled through the tears, half expecting an answer.

She decided she wouldn't give him the satisfaction of having her fall apart again. She told herself that, like Mel, she didn't need a man to complete her. But why didn't her heart feel the same? Would she ever recover from this pain in her heart? She busied herself with packing, so she had less time to think about it. When Hattie entered, she seemed to know without saying a word. She went over to Nellie and put her arms around her, and Nellie cried for what seemed like hours.

The trip home seemed endless for everyone was still a buzz with excitement about the ball, everyone except Nellie. She was polite and would enter conversation when asked otherwise, she kept to her thoughts. They drifted back to the night Platt arrived at the restaurant and how surprised she was. What a glorious time they had, just to end in such disappointment and heart break. The stage couldn't pull into home soon enough for Nellie. She debated how to tell her parents what happened without them hating Platt. After careful consideration, she decided she would keep the events of the San Francisco hidden away in her heart. She knew Hattie wouldn't say a word unless she gave her permission to do so.

Mama and papa waited anxiously at the stage for the girls, ready to hear their stories. Mama knew immediately when Nellie exited the stage that something was amiss, but Hattie and the Wickham's were abuzz with excitement. Nellie attempted to appear normal, but it was a futile attempt. Mr. Jefferson thanked Mr. Wickham for his generosity in taking his girls on holiday to San Francisco.

"It was my pleasure! They are delightful young woman and wonderful examples for my daughter. I think everyone had a grand time, especially Nellie when she ran into the nice gentleman friend of hers, Platt Corbaley. It was such a shame that she did not get to see him before he caught the first train this morning. She seemed rather upset!"

Once inside her home, Nellie went straight to her room to unpack her suitcase.

"Do you need any help with that?"

"No, thank you, I am going to unpack and then lay down. It was a long ride, and I am terribly weary." Mama understood that her daughter needed some time to herself, and she didn't want to force it.

"Very well, I will come and get you for dinner," Mama replied. Mama walked back to the parlor where she met Lester in his chair.

"Sit down, mama. I think I know what is ailing our daughter."

Mama sat down and braced herself. "I knew it was a mistake letting her go to the big city without us!"

Lester looked at his beautiful wife and saw the concern on her face. "She saw Platt while she was in San Francisco. They had an accidental meeting and rekindled their love for each other but then he had to leave on the train. She didn't get to see him before he left, and she is heartbroken. She doesn't know that we are aware of this, and we must let her tell us in her own time."

Mama didn't know what to make of everything. She had so many questions that no one could answer them besides Nellie and Platt.

"Oh! My sweet Nellie! Her heart must be breaking, and I can't even comfort her in her deepest sorrow."

"She will tell us her whole story in her own time and way. Let her work this out herself. You know she is a young woman now, having an 18th birthday coming up." Letting go was the hardest thing for a parent. He had been through it before, but this time was special. She was their baby girl. *How do let your youngest grow up into a young woman?*

"What do we say to her now? How can we act as if we know nothing?!"

"I don't know but I am puzzled. Why did he leave without saying goodbye? That is not like him at all, not after everything they have been through. It just doesn't make sense."

Mama contemplated for the longest time. "There is a missing piece to this puzzle! Lester, I know it. I need to find out what it is!"

"Now, wait a minute. This is her battle, remember, we can't fight it for her. This is a time for patience and to trust your daughter. She will come to us when she is ready."

"I know you're right, but we always want to protect our children from hurt and harm. I think it's the realization that she is grown. It's difficult to deal with."

"I know Mama, I know." Papa gave his wife a hug around the shoulders, and she put her head on him.

Nellie took her time unpacking, choosing to do it herself so she could be alone in her room with her thoughts. She tried to make sense of what happened. A life without Platt seemed void, almost not worth living. However, she was a determined young woman and had never let a man define who she was, and she certainly was not going to start now. She was determined to complete her education and then, she would find Platt and let him have a piece of her mind for leaving without saying goodbye. No one with a proper upbringing and manners would treat someone they claimed to be in love with this way! The more she thought about it, the more resolve she had. This was her plan! She was strong and she would survive. With this new determination, she became a different person. She was more focused and not as carefree as before. She had turned into a young woman.

School was back in session and Nellie was studying and bringing home exceptional marks. Her parents couldn't be prouder, but they were concerned for their daughter. Nellie refused to speak of the San Francisco trip. When Hattie would speak of it, Nellie would comment very briefly, but never a word about Platt. Her parents wondered if they should tell Nellie they were aware of what took place and harbored no ill towards Platt but decided to let her work it out on her own.

Her 18th Birthday was soon approaching on March 2nd. That meant she was officially an old maid, a spinster, but she didn't care. She had her sights set on a career, just like her sister. It had worked out well for Melissa! She was one of the only woman printers in the business and she was very successful, so why not her? She was content working towards a career and was determined to be a success! Every day she did her schoolwork with such determination and that the school master asked her to stay after class one day.

"Nellie, is everything all right?"

"Why, yes sir, did I do something wrong on an assignment?"

"No. That's just it. Nellie, your work is flawless, but you don't socialize with any of the other students. All you do is study. You may need to think about trying to balance both. It may help with adjusting to the new school."

Nellie looked at him, not knowing how to respond without being disrespectful. "Thank you for your concern but currently, all I am focused on is completing my schoolwork with good marks and graduating. However, I will heed your advice." Nellie couldn't get out of the classroom fast enough. She knew her course was set, and she had to complete it.

Nellie rushed home and was greeted at the front door by Frederick, who came over to ask her to go for a walk. She didn't want to appear rude, but ever since San Francisco there was something odd about him. It seemed like he had a secret he was withholding from her. She couldn't tell exactly what it was, but their relationship had never been the same. Hattie on the other hand, had all the time in the world for Frederick. Their relationship appeared to bloom with the start of spring flowers. Hattie had a sparkle in her eyes and Nellie knew the look, for she had experienced the same feeling just one year ago.

Nellie had been working so hard, day and night, to complete her studies that after class one day, the school master asked her to stay after class again and she worried she would receive another lecture about being more social.

"Nellie, you have done a tremendous job on your studies and have completed everything you need for graduation! After careful consideration, I have decided that you may have your diploma!"

Nellie was stunned. She stood there, looking at him, not knowing what to do or say.

"Thank you, Mr. Smithers! I have been working so unbelievably hard for so long and I can't believe it's finally here!"

"Well, it is, and you did an excellent job. Your parents will be very proud."

"Thank you, thank you!" she hollered as she sprinted out of the school towards home. She ran so fast that when she arrived home, she was completely breathless.

"What is the matter child?" Mama was perplexed by the state of her daughter.

"I did it! Mama, I graduated! I am done with high school. I did it!"

"I knew you would. After all, you have studied hard, and you are determined and brilliant. You can do anything you put your mind to." Mama hugged Nellie and they cried tears of joy. They told Papa that night at dinner, and he was excited and very proud of his daughter.

"What now, my strong independent daughter?"

Nellie knew the unfortunate time had come and she needed to tell her parents the San Francisco story. She hadn't prepared to do it now but knew it was time.

"Mama and Papa, there is a story I need to tell you. While I was in San Francisco, I ran into Platt Corbaley. We had a wonderful reunion; in fact, we fell in love all over again. It was a magical time, but then he left without saying goodbye. I don't know what happened to him or where he went. He was gone as quickly as he came. He promised he would come for me! How could he just disappear without a word? I don't understand!" The more she spoke, the angrier she became. All the anger and hurt she kept inside began to flood out in a wave of tears. It was a purging of emotions and the tears seemed endless. "How could he leave me after he said he loved me? How?!"

Papa sat quietly for a while, then spoke gently. "Nellie, we have known the whole story for quite some time. Mr. Wickham told me, but we did not want to pry or push you. We knew you would tell us when you were ready. We hold no hostility towards Platt. He had to catch an early train and couldn't bear to say goodbye again because he loves you. Didn't you get his letter? I'm sure it would have alleviated some confusion."

Papa was made aware of the letter's existence after he spoke with Mr. Wickham on the day of Nellie's return. Mr. Wickham only vaguely knew of the letter after Frederick haphazardly mentioned it by mistake.

"Letter what letter? I never received a letter! If I had, maybe what I went through these past few months would have been bearable. Who was supposed to deliver the letter to me?"

"I am not sure. It surely wasn't Hattie for if he had given it to her, she would've delivered it. I would assume it was supposed to be Frederick."

"But why would he not give me the letter? …Oh…" A light went on inside Nellie's head. "I know why." Nellie became red faced. "How could he?! I have a good mind to go over there and tell him what I think of him and if it weren't for Hattie, I would. I would never take away the chance of her finding happiness. No, I will not say anything, but I am glad to know the truth."

It was one of the toughest decisions she ever made. Every time Mattie spoke of Frederick, she felt ill. She was deeply hurt by his deceit but what she wanted more than anything was the letter. She longed to hear from Platt and wondered if they would ever be reunited. She knew she had to go on with her future but for so long, all she ever imagined was a future that included Platt. Now, she just didn't know and felt empty and hollow. As she peered out the windowpane, the rain fell gently in rhythmic beats. The sound was mesmerizing, making it easy to get lost in her thoughts. *What was Platt doing right now? What was in his future?* Nellie drifted back to when she and Platt first met, and things were simple. They knew they were in love and wanted a future together, and then, everything fell apart. *Will we ever be together as we once planned?*

Chapter Ten
Platt's New Journey

It was late today. Why was it late? He paced back and forth in front of the stagecoach office, waiting for the mail to come. He told himself he would hear from Nellie today. If he didn't, he decided it would be time to move on because, obviously, she didn't want to continue their relationship. He continued to pace back and forth, waiting impatiently. He kept reaching into his pocket to check the time, as if it would make the stage go faster. He chatted with some neighbors which helped pass the time when he noticed, out of the corner of his eye, something looked amiss over at the bank. He couldn't put his finger on it but decided to investigate. After all, he had some time to kill. He proceeded with caution. He noticed a man next to two horses that weren't at the normal hitching post. The man paced nervously in front and his eyes darted all around. It appeared to Platt that he was a lookout. Platt was unarmed but knew he must do something to intervene, or the bank would be robbed, and innocent people would be harmed.

He snuck around the back of the bank and picked up a big rock and branch that were lying on the ground. He crept slowly to the side of the building. As the lookout paced by the entrance, he quickly crept along the water trough and loosened the reins of the horse. He slapped the horse on its hindquarters, which startled both the horse and lookout. The lookout was so preoccupied by the horses running; he didn't notice that Platt was the one who loosened the reins. This gave Platt time to slip inside the bank, where he saw the bank robber with a gun aimed at the teller's head. The robber glanced over, expecting to see his partner, and met the gaze of Platt. The robber tried to maneuver, but to no avail. Platt hit him over the head with the tree branch, knocking him out. The lookout gathered his bearings and entered the bank, where he saw his partner unconscious and immediately retreated. He took off and ran out of town as fast as he could. While the robber was still unconscious, Platt and the bank teller were able to tie him up and wait for someone to notify the local sheriff. The sheriff was so impressed with Platt's quick thinking that he offered him a deputy position. Platt felt honored and it made him think deeply about his future and what he wanted to be. He had successfully built the livery and was now working for the railroad, but it all felt empty without Nellie. *Why had she not written back?*

He knew she had a stubborn streak, but this was far beyond what he had previously experienced. *Maybe our time together meant nothing to her. Did Frederick have something to do with it?* Platt greatly regretted their hasty goodbye and was infuriated that he forgot to give her his address. *How could I have been so stupid and distracted?* He knew she was in Oceanside, but that was all he knew. Without a proper address she would never receive the letter. He debated if he should try one more time to communicate with her. All she seemed to do was bring him more heartbreak but at the same time, living a life without her was unfathomable. He found himself pacing back and forth when his Father walked in.

"Platt, who are you talking to?"

Platt looked startled, as if being awakened from a dream.

"No, no one, I was just thinking to myself. I presume I was doing it out loud and didn't even realize." Platt was extremely deep in thought, causing his brow to crease in the middle.

"You look as if you have the cares of the world on your shoulders, young man."

"I just can't decide what to do next. I have completed my work here and have been offered a grand position with the railroad and an offer has come open in Washington. I know it is a new territory, but it would be an exciting adventure. I need an adventure to help clear my head of Nellie Jefferson. I want to get on with my life…or find her and see if she wants to be my bride. I can't forget her or live without her. Father, what am I to do?" He was on his knees, pleading for answers.

"Platt, you know your heart better than anyone. No one can choose for you, but I must ask you this question. If you can live without her, then do it. Go on with your life. But, if you find that your life is empty and incomplete without her, then you must find her. Tell her how you feel and make her your wife, for then, you will know you are truly soul mates."

"Thank you for your wisdom. I have a lot of thinking to do. I don't know if she'll want me if I do find her, but it is a chance I must take!"

In the morning, he felt good about his decision. He would make something of himself and then go find Nellie. He could go and homestead a place and have it waiting for them. He went down to breakfast, feeling good about his decision. He felt that if Nellie and he were meant to be, she would wait for him. Father saw the dark circles under his eyes and asked how he had slept that night before.

"Not a lot of sleeping, I am afraid. A whole lot of tossing and turning, but I do feel as if I have come to a decision that is right and good." He described his plan to his brother and Father. A.L. was so impressed; he decided that Platt wasn't going alone and that he would go with him. Father, after much discussion, began thinking about homesteading in Washington. He and Mother would come after Platt and A.L. arrived. It was a good plan with all the necessary ingredients for success, except one, Nellie. But he would have to work with what he had been given and leave the rest up to God.

The plans began to start the journey northwestward. They would need warmer clothes than they had the past winter and a lot of supplies. They needed two wagons with building supplies, food, and basic furniture. There were so many details to remember for this new adventure into the wild Midwest. A new frontier, totally unsettled, was a place for new beginnings. They were looking for a piece of the "new Americas." Platt was excited, but thinking of the unknown and unchartered area made him anxious.

"What have I gotten us into here? I mean, we can still call this whole deal off if you're feeling uncomfortable."

"Platt, we say we are men of the wild and have the mountains in our blood. Since we've moved to California, although exquisite in it beauty, we have been stifled in our mountain men routine. All kidding aside, it just feels right. All except that you have yet to mention Nellie. Boy, go find that girl! You love her and know she loves you too."

"If only it were that simple." He walked away from the wagon thinking about their conversation. Everywhere he looked, he saw her in every sunrise and sunset. When it rained, he remembered the day he found her after her accident and first knew she had his heart. When the sun would shine, he remembered their walks after school and their strolls along the riverbank. He couldn't escape it, as hard as he tried.

The last of their things were tied down in the wagon. He hoped they had thought of everything that might be needed. They packed building supplies, food, winter clothing, furs, trinkets for trading with any unfriendly person they may encounter, and of course, their guns and ammunition for protection. He thought they were ready.

"I have to stop by the general store to get a shovel before we head out," Platt called to A.L. as he rode off towards town. *Am I doing the right thing? Should I, at least, try and contact her one last time before I go? No, I will stick to the plan and make a home for us. Then I will go get Nellie. Right now, I have nothing to offer but myself and a promise of a future and she deserves more.* He was so deep in thought; he almost ran into another rider.

"Woah!" he said to his horse. "I am so sorry! I didn't see you coming." The other rider tipped his hat and rode off. Platt dismounted his horse and tied him up in front of the general store.

Westward Journey

They left Sacramento Valley, in all its beauty and all the way, Platt thought of Nellie. *Am I making the right decision? Am I doing the right thing?* He knew she still had to graduate and then he would come for her. He promised her and he would be good for his word. *But why hasn't she contacted me? Has she decided she liked Frederick better? After all, he is a wealthy young man from a well-established family, and she could have a very comfortable life with him. But it would never be the same. He could never love her like I do.*

The most difficult part of the journey was not going through California, but the Sierra Mountains. It was a treacherous journey, especially in areas that were snow packed. The brothers were very grateful to have each other. This was a journey no man would want to make alone. Once they made it through the Sierra's, they made their way into Oregon. They crossed over the Oregon Trail and wondered if they would make it to Washington alive and with their wagons intact. A.L. was a tremendous source of encouragement and companionship. Platt thought he was blessed to have A.L. as a brother and friend. A.L. was always ready for a new adventure. He was a confident man with a heart of gold. He would give you the shirt off his back without hesitation. He was not afraid of hard work, and it showed in his muscular build. Sometimes, Platt felt envious of his muscles and strength, but quickly recovered when he looked at the wonderful man his brother was. Today was one of those days when he appreciated his brother's strength. They were having a wonderful time, but anxiety hit as they approached the Columbia River. As they entered the water, they slowly crossed over and held their breath out of fear. Suddenly, one of the wagon wheels slipped off the trail, which was not nearly large enough to carry a wagon in the first place. Platt tried desperately to get control of the horses as they reared out of control with fear. He calmly spoke to the horses to try and calm them so that they didn't totally spiral out of control. He tried desperately to get the horses to move forward and bring the wagon back up on the trail, but they were not responding. The wagon dumped all their supplies in the murky water. Everything he needed to start a home for Nellie vanished in front of his eyes. He dismounted from the wagon and tried to manually lead the horses forward, but the rear wheel was stuck over the edge and was slipping on the rock. The wheel was slipping and pulling everything away from Platt, including his team of horses. A.L., who had been riding further behind on the trail, came around the corner of the mountain and saw the perilous situation. He immediately stopped his team and dismounted. He sprinted to Platt.

"Steady the horses and on my word, have them go forward!" Platt looked at him with such relief. A.L. went to the rear of the wagon and with what seemed like superhuman strength, lifted the rear of the wagon so it could get traction and move forward. Platt gasped a huge sigh of relief. He ran back and threw his arms around his brother's neck.

"What took you so long?" Platt said as he laughed and hugged his neck.

After the adrenaline died down, they realized the territory was very different than anything they had ever known. They would have to stick closer together and be more aware of their surroundings, but their journey was almost over. They both excitedly daydreamed of what it would be like. They wondered if there would there be any claims left to settle and if they had come all this way for nothing. They told themselves they had to think positively, and they would be settlers and have a wonderful new life in Washington. But Platt wondered if it would be wonderful without Nellie. He had come to prove to himself and her that he was successful, and that was what he would do.

The boys were weary of the day's events, so they decided to stop earlier than they planned to reassess and map out the rest of the course. They didn't want to miss any details and were right on course to go to the County Assessor's office to find where the unclaimed sites were located. Platt and A.L. were men of detail. They wanted to leave nothing to chance and felt like after their catastrophe, the rest would be smooth sailing. They would get a good night's sleep and tomorrow was a new day and closer to their dream. Sleep came easy for both men. Usually, one slept and the other stayed on the lookout, but they were both so exhausted that staying awake and on the watch was nearly impossible. Thus far, they hadn't had any difficulty with wild animals or unfriendly Indians, so they decided that a good night's sleep would be in order. Before they knew it, they were both in a deep sleep. Platt always welcomed sleep, for it gave him a chance to dream of Nellie and the day when they would be reunited.

Platt's sleep was abruptly interrupted by a sharp object poking him in the back. He thought it was A.L. trying to wake him, so he hollered out with his eyes still shut.

"What are you doing? Trying to wake me up, I just went to sleep!"

There it was again. It was sharper than before and this time, it was met with chanting. His eyes flew open wide, and he stared at the end of a long sharp spear, which belonged to a very angry looking Indian. Platt tried to remain calm but, on the inside, he was a bundle of nerves. His heart was pounding so loudly, he was certain it could be heard by all those around. His hands were sweating but he kept his composure as he was commanded by the Indian to stand. *A.L., where is he? What have they done to him?* Platt knew some Indian dialect and was hoping it was the correct one for this tribe. They motioned him over to a tree and as he started in that direction, they shoved him, causing him to go face first into the ground. He looked up and saw his brother standing there. His mouth was bleeding and he had bruises on his arms.

"A.L., are you all, right?" Platt's heart raced with concern for his brother and not knowing what was going to happen next.

He spoke in a low voice, as not to call attention. "I am all right. A few bruises, but no broken bones that I can tell. They came up to me when I was relieving myself and I was not prepared for hostiles. I resisted when they tried to confine me and that was where the beating commenced."

Platt looked at Brother, feeling responsible for his pain. "I should have stayed on guard duty, and this wouldn't have happened."

Al shook his head. "No brother, you're wrong. There was no way to hear them or know they were coming. They pride themselves on being able to sneak up on their victims. You would have never heard them coming. We should have been anticipating this since we were following Indian trails."

Whose fault it was didn't matter. What was of the utmost concern at this moment was what they were going to do to stay alive. Platt had studied Indian dialect in preparation for this journey, just in case they encountered Indians. Now was his chance to see if it had been beneficial.

Platt began speaking to the Indians. They were amazed that a pale faced man could speak and understand them. Platt was fortunate that the Dialect he studied was the correct one. He told them he wanted to see their chief and they meant them no harm. He explained they were settlers going to stake a claim and start a new life.

The weapons of the Indians were the bow and arrow, spear, bone dagger, and wooden amour. Platt understood that the Indians were very leery about white men since the US Government began making treaties with the Indians from 1850-1871, when a Congressional Act halted the process of the treaty making with Indian nations. An important precedent had been established with the removal of the eastern tribes, via US Indian treaties during 1820-1840. Treaties became the legal means for obtaining Indian homelands as an alternative goal.

In all, there were 389 ratified US Indian Treaties. The desire of Indian land by the white man settlers created uncontrolled momentum that would break any promise with the American Nation.

The tribe in the area was the Sinkiuses tribe, who was led by Chief Joseph Half-Sun. Understandably, they were very cautious of the white man. But Platt was not a normal white settler. He saw the Indians as a source of knowledge to learn from and he saw them as human beings that God created. After all, they were the strangers on their land, not the other way around. He determined that he would make the chief his ally. Platt figured the Chief would be a great resource of information when it came to homesteading. The Indian warriors were good to their word and took Platt and A.L. to see Chief Joseph Half-Sun. When he walked into the room, he engulfed the entire entrance with his presence. He wore leggings made of animal skins, a vest beaded with rows of colored beads, shells, and bones, and his head dress was large with massive colored feathers, precisely placed and banded at the top with brilliant-colored beads and shells. Platt began to speak to him, but the chief held up his hand, as if to silence him. Platt was very nervous, his heart beating wildly in his chest. He questioned if his request to seek a personal appearance with the chief was such a good idea. The chief motioned for them to sit, and they did as request. Platt didn't take his eyes off the chief, not wanting to miss anything. Once seated, the chief motioned for the other warriors to leave. Platt guessed he knew they were no threat to him. He looked at Platt and A.L. and spoke in English. The chief asked what they were doing on his land and where they were going. Platt was so relieved that they were not going to have their heads cut off and spoke to the chief as an old friend. He shared their plans of home steading and his hopes of their being friends and working together as neighbors. The chief sat silent, smoking his peace pipe, then he took it and passed it to Platt.

"Then we smoke peace pipe." Chief Joseph Half-Sun handed the pipe to Platt.

Platt thought of himself as a grown man but never smoked a pipe in his lifetime, let alone a peace pipe. He wasn't going to leave anything to chance, and he refused to insult his host. He accepted the pipe and puffed on it, choking a bit but maintaining a serious face. He passed it back to the chief.

"Friend," the chief exclaimed as he passed the pipe to A.L., who smoked with more finesse than his brother.

After they concluded the peace pipe ceremony, the chief spent some time talking to Platt and A.L. about the new settlers and how they were pushing his people farther and farther back from their homeland. This was why they had such a distrust of the government and the white people. Platt reassured the chief that he and his family would be true friends and they could always count on them to help. It was sincere and the chief could tell. The chief insisted they stay for dinner, for some of the warriors had returned from hunting with an elk and they were celebrating with a feast.

"We would be honored to be your guests."

The food was incredible. The maze was ground into meal to make bread, which they noted was very tasty. They roasted the meat over an open flame until it was so tender and juicy, it nearly fell from the bone. There was a spice rubbed on the meat they couldn't identify, but knew it was delicious. They took the vegetables and cooked them in the ground. It was a different way of cooking, but it was delicious. During the feast, Chief Joseph Half-Sun introduced Platt to his daughter. He wanted to offer her to him as an extension of their friendship. Chief Joseph Half-Sun's daughter was very beautiful with long braided hair, wrapped at the ends with cloth and beads. She wore a robe cut from rabbit skin and a necklace of abalone shells. She had large dark brown eyes and high cheek bones. She had an innocence in her eyes that was very alluring to any man, except Platt. Platt didn't want to offend their new friends and knew that the friendship could, at any moment, turn violent. The truth had always been his best policy and it never failed him. He hoped and prayed it would not happen at this moment.

"Chief Joseph Half-Sun, I am honored that you find me worthy of your beautiful daughter, but my heart belongs to another. Her name is Nellie Jefferson, and I am here to prove my love to her and establish a claim. Then, I am going back to marry her as I promised her. Sir, I am totally consumed with another's love, to the extent that she occupies my mind day and night. I am truly flattered but to accept your daughter's hand in marriage would be unfair."

He hoped that he said it eloquently and correctly, so as not to offend their newfound friend. He sat, searching the chief's face for a hint of what emotion he might be experiencing. It was unheard of to turn down the chief's offer of his daughter's hand in marriage. It was the same as issuing an insult and Platt sat there, contemplating what could conceivably be their doom. He felt beads of sweat drop from his forehead as he curated a plan for if things turned violent and they needed to make an escape. The Chief sat there, looking at his daughter who looked miserable and anxious. Platt wondered if anyone considered her feelings about the offer to be wed. Sweat continued to drop off his forehead as they awaited the decision of the Chief.

"So, you are making a home for your squaw, and she is not here with you and yet, you say you love this squaw? Peculiar ways of the white man, and you are refusing to marry my daughter because you love this squaw?"

Platt was not only sweating but shaking as well. "Yes sir, I am very much in love with Nellie. It is to the point where I cannot even look at another woman without thinking of her. You see, sir, we are what Nellie likes to call soul mates, kindred spirits destined to be together! She has eyes as blue as sapphires. When you investigate them, you lose yourself completely. With a woman such as that, there is no way I could accept your daughter's hand."

The chief puffed on his pipe and contemplated the situation. "I am beginning to see that the white man does things very different. Maybe, I should listen to my daughter and allow her to marry her choice, the brave warrior, Taro." He looked at his daughter and then at Taro. At first, she was confused, not knowing if she was free to run to him and not wanting to get him in trouble. She was unaware that her father even knew about her relationship with Taro and her love for him. They had been so secretive and private in their meetings. "Taro, do you wish to marry my daughter, Bright Star?"

Taro was speechless. A warrior was, never before, permitted to marry the chiefs' daughter because of love.

Taro spoke eloquently, stating the undying love and devotion he felt for Bright Star and that he promised to love her for eternity. The tribe clapped, broke into song, and danced around the campfire. There were whoops of joy, for the daughter was allowed to marry her love.

"Let us celebrate with a wedding tonight!"

The ladies rushed the bride off to make her ready for her groom. The groom was dressed in his finest headdress with beautiful colored feathers and beadwork. Platt and A.L. were impressed and thankful to be there with their new friends to witness the momentous occurrence. The chief told them he knew the new world would bring changes, but he wanted to keep the traditions of their past and culture. However, he knew when it was time to adopt some modern ideas. He thanked Platt and A.L. for giving him a new way of viewing life and love and that they were now friends for life.

"I am deeply touched by your acceptance of my brother and myself. We feel very fortunate to have found new friends and brothers." Platt extended his hand to the Chief.

The Chief took his hand and shook it, knowing they were forever knitted together in the bond of friendship. If either would ever need anything from the other, they would be able to count on each other through any circumstance.

The wedding was different from any wedding they had been to before. There was dancing, singing, and celebrating that went well into the night. Everyone was adorned in their very best attire. The men wore head dresses with colorful feathers and beaded vests. The woman wore their best and most colorful beads. There was feasting and merriment at the wedding of the Chief's daughter. The wedding feast was amazing and so full of joy and love between the newlyweds.

It was a privilege for them to be invited as guests. When the time came for them to be escorted to their teepee, the chief's daughter and new husband came over to Platt and A.L. and in broken English, thanked Platt. Platt told them he understood love and wished them a lifetime of happiness. The bride walked away, gleaming, and went into the teepee of the groom, where they were to be solitude and not disturbed for several days.

Before they said their goodbyes to Chief Joseph Half-Sun and the tribe, the Chief inquired about the route they were taking. When Platt showed him the map and explained their course, the Chief offered a different direction through Indian trails. It would be faster, and the path was well traveled by the tribes, so it was not unchartered territory. Platt and A.L. were very grateful to the Chief for imparting this information to them. It would save them several days' journey.

"Platt and A.L., my fair skin brothers, I want to give you this. Take this with you and if you come across any other tribes, tell them you are fair brothers of Chief Joseph Half-Sun, and no harm will come to you or your family." He handed Platt a long stick adorned with beads and feathers.

Platt thanked him and said they would return. They finished saying their farewells and were, once again, off to Spokane, Washington.

Platt found his thoughts turning to Nellie, in fact, it was almost all he thought of these days. She invaded his dreams and thoughts. He was consumed by her love, but not knowing if she still wanted him was tearing him apart. Despite this, he stayed determined to make something of himself, someone that Nellie would be proud to be married to.

They followed the Indian trails and were amazed at how well defined they were. The brush had been cut away from the side of the road, making travel with a wagon more manageable. They thought if they kept at that pace, they would be in Spokane before they knew it and could start working at the store. Platt had already been offered a job. A friend of the family heard of it and told Platt, knowing he was an enterprising young man with a smart head on his shoulders. The next thing Platt wanted to do was to go the claim office and stake his claim for his homestead. His father and A.L. would do the same. They would be pioneer settlers in the new frontier! The eagerness of the boys and lack of eventfulness for the remainder of the trip allowed them to make impeccable timing. They were exhausted and were kept awake by nothing else, other than pure excitement. Despite a perilous journey, they had arrived.

At the claim office, they found sites that were still available were in Badger Mountain, Douglas County. This area was totally undeveloped, and they knew they would have to clear the land start from the ground up. Platt and A.L. decided to act like the prudent businessmen they hoped to be. They decided to ride over and check out all the unclaimed stakes before deciding.

The territory was more breath taking than he ever imagined. The mountains stretched across the land, billowing snowcapped peaks touching the heavens. Laid out before it was an ocean of green lush land, rich in soil, he knew. The area was heavily wooded. There was a stream that fed directly into his prospective land, and he knew it would make irrigation much easier once crops were planted. It was the most beautiful sight! His only regret was that Nellie wasn't there to share in the momentous moment. It was almost too much to take in. Platt fell in love with the land and decided it would be where he made his claim. There was much to be done on the property, but he was more than enthusiastic to start. A.L.'s place was near Platt's and the neighboring plot was a parcel soon to be claimed by his father.

They returned to the hotel in Wenatchee and they could talk of nothing else the entire evening. It was a dream that was becoming a reality! It would take a lot of work to make the land habitable, but they were lucky enough to take residence at a nice hotel for the time being. He hoped that with hard work and determination, both of which he had in large quantities, he could make his vision a reality. He had a new life and new land, now he needed to find Mr. Mathewson. He owned the general store and promised him a job upon his arrival. First thing in the morning, he would be well on his way to making something of himself and proving to Nellie he was worthy of her love. He hoped that being a great distance away would help ease his mind from thoughts of Nellie, but no matter what he did, his thoughts always drifted back to her. While he slept, he dreamt that Nellie was there with him, and they had begun their life as husband and wife in the new territory. They were blissfully happy, running through the meadows, hand in hand, laughing and delighting…

"Platt, Platt! It's time to get up and go! You have that job to inquire about, now come on get up."

A.L. woke him from a perfect dream that was nearly impossible to shake off. But this morning, he needed to concentrate on getting the job. He would have to be strong and not think about Nellie, at least for the time being.

Platt was up and eager to get busy with the task at hand. It put him one step closer to fulfilling his dream and, at last, having his land and a home to bring Nellie to. *No! I can't keep thinking about her, not right now! But how do I put someone, my soul mate, out of my mind? Get it together! I must. I am on a mission, and it starts with this job.*

"Mr. Mathewson, I am Platt Corbaley. I am here about the job, working in the general store which we mentioned in our correspondence. I am anxious to start work as soon as you need me. I am a hard worker and not afraid of a challenge!"

"I am glad to hear you are not afraid of a challenge. Platt, to be truthful with you, since my wife died, I have been a little lost. You see, she was the one who did most of the work in the store. I just handled the feed and seed division for the farmers. She did all the organizing and the ordering and well, it is a bit of a mess since she passed on. I am holding you to your word that you're not afraid of a challenge, because I really could use someone like you son."

"Well then we best get to work!" Platt shook his hand and smiled.

Platt quickly realized what Mr. Mathewson had spoken of. The shelves were half empty and what was there wasn't properly displayed and the merchandise was unorganized. The dust was so thick; he wondered how it could have gotten so bad since his wife's passing.

"I don't mean to pry, sir, but how long did you say it had been since your wife passed?"

"Oh, it was three years ago."

Three years! That explained the buildup of dust and disorganization. He certainly had his work cut out for him. Mr. Mathewson looked at him, half expecting him to gather his hat and coat, bid him a good day, thank him for the opportunity, and leave. But, not Platt, he was there to stay.

"Where is the dusting cloth and broom? And after I do some clean up, I would like to look at the books and inventory them. I'll see what we need to order if that is agreeable with you sir?"

Mr. Mathewson was so excited that Platt wasn't leaving, he told him he could have whatever he needed. Platt went to work and worked tirelessly. He cleaned and rearranged the store in an orderly fashion, much in the way he was sure Mrs. Mathewson had done it. He followed her outline of the store and added some details of his own and before he knew it, the store was clean and thriving with business. People flocked into the store and commented on how much they liked the new look and inventory. Platt loved working with people, so he was a natural in his position. It kept him busy and content, but he still had a deep longing in his heart and soul for his sweet Nellie. Everything about her made him miss her so much that sometimes, he felt as if his heart would surely break. He welcomed the busyness of his life in Washington. The busier he was, the less time he had to dwell on Nellie. One day while working, Mr. Mathewson approached Platt.

"Platt I would like a word with you. You have done a wonderful job here and I would like to make you store manager. Now, it is only a title, but you deserve so much more than that. It's the least I can do to say thank you." Platt was very touched and moved by the promotion.

"Thank you, sir, this means a lot to me!"

Platt continued to work for Mr. Mathewson as hard as any fellow could and the store became known as one of the finest general stores in all of Wenatchee Washington.. Despite enjoying his position, Platt grew anxious, restless. He couldn't explain it, but figured he needed to get away for a few days. Since the store was doing well, he decided he would take a few days and go up to the land to work on the house. He and A.L. went out to the land regularly to work on it so it could be habitable. It had walls, a fireplace, a stove to cook on, and two bedrooms. Platt was sure it would be a very nice house once it was finished and was determined to make it a pleasant a place to live but he had to face the facts it was hardly a home it was nothing more than a shack, but he had a dream and hoped and prayed it would all come to fruition.

One day while Platt and A.L. were on their way to the property, Platt realized he had forgotten some things he needed at the general store. He quickly headed over and while he was picking up some essentials, he noticed a newspaper from Healdsburg. This, of course, drew his interest and he inquired if he might look at it. He saw in bold letters, written across the front, "Graduating Class" and a photo of his Nellie. *She had done it. She graduated, which meant she was free! She is free to be my wife!*

"YES!" he shouted and Mr. Mathewson looked at him in a very peculiar manner. He was so excited. At long last, his dream might come true! His head swam with thoughts as he began to wonder what he would do if she did not want him. After all, he hadn't heard from her after their meeting in San Francisco. What would he do if she rejected him, or worse yet, if she had taken up with someone else. Would he have to challenge the young man to a duel and fight for her honor? Or would he walk away with a sad broken heart?

The room began to spin. The clerk noticed he was looking very pale and losing his balance. He fell against the display of gardening rakes and landed on the floor, with the rake striking him on the head.

"Go get the Doctor!" Mr. Mathewson yelled to one of the other customers. "Fetch me a cool cloth and a glass of water, quickly! And give this young man some air," he ordered the clerk. Soon, Platt came around.

"What happened?" he asked as he rubbed his sore head.

"Why don't you tell us that story? You came in for supplies, saw a newspaper from Oceanside California, yelled, and then grabbed your head and passed out."

Platt told them about Nellie and how he told her he would always come for her, and that was his intention at that moment. But first, he must break the news to his brother. A.L. came into the store, concerned, since he knew Platt never took long to do anything. He saw all the commotion and rushed over to Platt, who was still lying on the floor.

"Platt, are you alright?"

Platt told him of the newspaper and that he had to go and get her. He knew it changed everything for them, but he felt this was a sign. He promised her that when she graduated, he would find her, and they would marry. He had to see if she still wanted him, or he would live his whole life wondering. A.L. understood and offered to accompany Platt, if he wanted him to.

"There could be no better brother alive on this earth than you! A.L., yes, I want you to accompany me. But, what of your position on the railroad?"

"It was coming to an end soon anyway, so I say, let's go find out if Nellie wants to come west!"

Platt pulled up in front of Mr. Mathewson's house with lightning speed. Mr. Mathewson was concerned and wondered if everything was alright. He rarely saw Platt in such a rush and after the fall in the store he was worried. When he saw Platt's face, he knew him well enough to read his expressions and know what he was seeing was excitement, not worry or fear.

"Platt, my boy, what can I do for you? I thought you might have heard from that girl of yours."

"Whatever do you mean?"

"Platt, my son, I know you well. You have to go after her. Find her and tell her how you feel, or you will never have peace in your life."

"Nellie did what she set out to do. Now, I must do what I promised. I'll find her, see if she'll forgive me and if she still loves me. If she does, I'll ask for her hand in marriage. Now, I know this will throw a curve into your plans and you'll have to find someone to replace me at the store, but I must try. In fact, I feel compelled."

Mr. Mathewson walked over to Platt and put a reassuring hand on his shoulder. "Go, Platt. Go get your love. Don't hesitate, go my son, go!"

That was all the encouragement Platt needed. He headed out to find his brother. A.L. was ready and waiting for Platt. Before he could realize what, they were doing, they were on the road to Healdsburg to find his Nellie. He was grateful to have his brother's company. It made the trip much smoother and faster to have someone to ride with. Despite A.L. being great company, questions swirled around his mind. The only way to get answers was to embrace the questions. With every mile and the closer they got to their destination, the more questions he came up with. On several occasions, he almost convinced himself to turn around and go home, but the pounding in his heart told him he must prevail.

His horse was sweating and thirsty when they finally arrived in Healdsburg. The town was small and consisted mostly of vineyards and orchards. He was amazed at how well incorporated the town was. The quaint little town had a city hall and a landscaped plaza. There was an arched bridge, and a brook was running beneath it. They planted flowers along the riverbank and there were small sapling trees, showing promise to be a great shade oak one day. The main street had offices with magnificent architect and water mains in the buildings. There was a public library where he could see Nellie sitting, studying, or reading a good book for pleasure. He could see why she had fallen in love with this town and questioned if he would be able to convince her to give it all up. He continued his surveillance of the town. It was so beautiful and green! As he continued through the town, one thing caught his eye. They had what so many other towns wanted, the long-awaited arrival of the Northwestern Pacific Railroad. He knew, from what he saw, that this town was an agricultural and mining town. But now, they were a stop on the railroad's destination map. That would make the town even more prosperous. He was quite certain of that, especially after spending time with Mr. Wickham in San Francisco.

That's who I should find! I'll confront Frederick about the letter! I'm quite certain she may have never received it. He knew he would, soon, face the truth, so the sooner, the better. He turned his buggy towards the Sheriff's office to inquire about the whereabouts of the Jefferson's. He was so engrossed in thought, he had a near miss with a gentleman crossing the street. He stopped his horse quickly and jumped down to help when he suddenly realized the man was Mr. Jefferson.

"Mr. Jefferson! I apologize! I didn't see you crossing the street. Are you alright? Are you injured in any way? Do you need a physician?" Lester was rather stunned from the near miss of a horse and buggy, but more stunned from seeing Platt.

"Platt, what are you doing here, my boy? And to answer your question, I am quite fine. I was just stunned and lost my balance. But enough about me, please tell me about you?"

Platt told Mr. Jefferson the whole story. He concluded with seeing Nellie's graduation announcement in the newspaper and wanting to find her and seek her forgiveness. He explained eloquently that he yearned to tell her he loved her and ask for her hand in marriage.

"That is quite a story, Platt. But there is no need to explain. Mr. Wickham explained about the letter when they returned from San Francisco. Although, for a long time, she was heartbroken thinking you had deserted her, but she knows the truth. She also made you a promise to graduate and that's exactly what she did."

"Where is Nellie now, Mr. Jefferson?"

"She moved to Alameda to work as a telegraph operator. She was offered the job right after graduation and she is living with her sister Dora. She hadn't been very healthy, and Nellie went to lend her assistance. She wanted to prove to herself to you that she could make something of herself."

"Do you have her address, sir?"

"Yes, I do. Come to the house. Mrs. Jefferson would love to see you and I will give it to you." He agreed and after a short visit, he was on the road to find his Nellie.

The road trip to Alameda wasn't as long as the trip to Healdsburg and before he knew it, he arrived in the quaint little town. There were lots of green trees, a general store, a restaurant, a post office, a schoolhouse, and a dress shop. It was a progressive little town with a brick town hall and a water tower. It had its own fire station, equipped with a state-of-the-art fire truck. He was busy taking in all the sites of the town, all the while trying desperately to quiet the pounding in his heart and his head. At long last, he pulled his buggy in front of the address Mr. Jefferson had given him. He knew she would most likely be at work and surprising her may not be the most advisable idea, but meeting in public could give him an advantage. She would be less likely to make a scene if she were still angry at him. He thought about their reunion for miles and miles and imagining it was near made his mouth dry and his heart rate increase. Platt took a deep breath and while walking into the building, noticed a beautiful woman walking out. He knew instantly who it was. She was busy talking to a group of women and didn't even notice him at first, but Platt was in a trance. He couldn't move, seeing her, looking more beautiful and grown up, he was spell bound. She covered her eyes to shield the sun and looked uncertain about what she was seeing. She looked again, this time, moving closer.

"Platt! Is that you?"

"Yes Nellie! Your father told me where to find you."

"Oh, Platt, what took you so long?!" She ran into his arms, right there, in the middle of the street.

Platt swept her up into his arms and held her close. Before he realized what he was doing, he pressed his lips to hers and kissed her passionately. He had forgotten how wonderful it was to hold her and kiss her. After a few moments, they came back to reality and realized they must get out of the street.

"Platt, how did you know where to find my father? Tell me, what is going on?"

Platt explained how he saw the newspaper article regarding her graduation. He also explained what happened in San Francisco. He had to ask about the letter, to know for himself. He knew what Mr. Jefferson had told him and he believed him but needed to hear it from her lips.

"Did Frederick give you my letter, the morning I had the early departure on the train?"

"No Platt, I never received a letter. I thought you had deserted me! That our time in San Francisco meant nothing to you, and when I never heard from you, I was heartbroken for months. But I recently discovered the truth. That's when I decided to move here and make something of myself and prove to you that I am worthy of your love." Platt grabbed her up in his arms.

"Worthy of my love? Whatever are you talking about? I am the one that has never been good enough for you. I never stopped loving you, not for a moment. I went to the post office every day, waiting for the mail to arrive on the stage. I always hoped that you would write and when I never heard, I decided to move out west and settle out there. It is unclaimed territory where one can stake a claim on large parcels of property. In fact, I was headed out of town when I saw the newspaper article and knew I must find you."

By this time, his heart was pounding so fast he could hardly speak. He couldn't even think about what he was doing and reached out to pull her closer. He looked deeply into her beautiful brown eyes and dropped to one knee, right there on the sidewalk.

"Nellie Jefferson, would you agree to be my bride and make me the happiest man in the world?" Nellie was so overcome with emotion. At last, this day she had dreamed of her whole life had finally come true. She started to cry, and Platt looked perplexed, not knowing what it meant.

"Oh Platt! Yes! Yes, I have waited what seemed to be an entire lifetime to hear you speak those precious words. If you will forgive me, I am inclined to take a moment and savor this sweet moment. I have longed for this. But, to answer your question, yes! Positively, yes!!"

She jumped into his arms and kissed his lips, right there on the sidewalk. They didn't care. At long last, they found each other and were going to be together! Platt told Nellie how glad he was that she agreed to marry him. She worried him at first with her long acceptance speech.

"No, I wanted to be sure you knew that I accepted your hand in marriage and was never coerced; I married you because I was madly in love with you." He pulled her close to his side and kissed her head.

"What are we going to do next, Nellie? Do you want to go out west to Washington State and homestead? A.L. is ready and waiting for us, if that is what you want. But, if we marry, we are a team. We are one and that means we make decisions together. So, what is it that you do want to do?"

Nellie was shocked by such a statement from a man. Most men do things, and the women go along with it, and that's just how it is. She knew Platt understood her temperament and how strong-willed and opinionated she could be. She loved him, even more, for that.

"Platt, we are a team and when we marry, I agree to go with you, wherever that is. You know me. I am always excited for a new adventure, or should I say, new frontier."

"Oh Nellie, that's one of the things I have so missed about you, your strong spirit. I must tell you truthfully, the trip will not be without trials and difficulties, but we will face them together and we will start a new life in a new state. I know you've had a life of privilege, and this will be completely different at first, but I promise I will provide a comfortable life as soon as possible and send for your parents to join us. What do you say?" Nellie paced around the parlor of Dora's home, as if she were giving the whole matter some great thought.

"I see you have thought this whole process through in every detail, except one. What if I say no to going out west?"

"Then we don't go. I finally have you back in my life and that is more important to me than staying home steadying in Washington. Nellie, you are my life. Without you, I will cease to exist."

Nellie stood there, rather amazed by his response. She knew beyond a shadow of a doubt that his love for her ran deep and together, they could face any hard ships life would throw their way. She knew there would be trials, after all, that seemed to be in their history. Life alone would be difficult but together, they could forge through life united in soul and purpose. Now they had to tell their parents about their upcoming marriage and journey out West.

"Nellie, your father said your sister, Dora, was not in the best of health and that was what swayed your decision in coming here. Are you alright with leaving your sister, especially since you have only been here for a short period of time? Is she healthy enough to care for herself?" Platt asked with such great concern that it made Nellie smile and then, almost burst into laughter.

"Oh, sweet Platt, Dora has been in poor health for quite some time. She manages to live a very independent life and teaches at a school. She isn't bed ridden, at least not at this time. It may be years before she needs more assistance and letting her be as independent as possible is what the Doctor ordered, but I love your concern. Now, let's look at those plans. Shall we?"

As they began their discussion, Dora came home from work. Finding her youngest sister, whom her parents had entrusted to her care, with a strange gentleman, was not the type of thing she had not expected, nor was comfortable with.

"Nellie, what are you doing with a gentleman in the house alone, with no escort? Mama and papa are going to be furious!" She picked up a large vase and planned to use it as a weapon against Platt.

"Dora, put the vase down. This is Platt. He came and found me and asked for my hand in marriage. He knew where to find me because he saw papa first. So, papa knows he is here. It's okay; you can put the vase down now."

"Oh, I am so happy to meet you, at last! All Nellie has done is speak of you. I do apologize, but a single woman can never be too careful living alone in a town. Please accept my apology." Dora stretched out her hand towards Platt.

Dora was an attractive woman. She had large eyes, like Nellie's, but hers were crystal blue. When she turned to put the vase back on the mantle, Platt noticed a limp as she walked. It was hardly noticeable in comparison to her beauty, and he wondered why a woman like her would be single. She was a few years older than Nellie, a working woman who was independent and intelligent.

Platt accepted Dora's apology and Nellie and he began explaining their future. Soon, the afternoon had passed, and it was time for Platt to go back to the Hotel for the night. They didn't want the evening to end, for fear of never seeing each other again. They had a rather eventful past, but this time, he was not boarding any train. He would meet her in the morning, and they would make plans for their future, for a brighter tomorrow.

That night, sleep did not come easily to Nellie. She couldn't decide if seeing Platt again was a dream, or if he really came for her like he promised. If it was a dream, she did not want to go to sleep. She feared she would wake, and it would all be over. She knew how silly it sounded, but they had been through so much and the thought of losing him was unbearable. When the morning sun shone through the curtains, Nellie got out of bed and was dressed in record time. She raced down the stairs and headed out to meet Platt for breakfast. But sleep did not come easy for him either. He was already at her kitchen table, talking to Dora, when she came downstairs.

"Platt, what time did you arise this morning? It's the crack of dawn, even now!"

"I told you, I'm not going anywhere, except with you by my side. Nellie, we are together forever."

"Oh Platt, I am so glad you're here!" she said as she rushed into his arms. Platt held her close and looked at her with eyes that took her breath away.

"Would you two love birds like some breakfast?" Dora asked excitedly.

"Yes, that would be wonderful. Thank you, Dora."

They ate breakfast as they discussed their plans and what the next step would be. Platt told her that he would love to take her to the judge that day to marry, he knew the proper thing was to go back to Oceanside and ask for her hand in marriage. Marrying there without her parents' blessing just wouldn't be right. After much thought and discussion, they decided that they would do just that, and do it as soon as possible. Nellie called her employer to resign her position and packed up her belongings to begin her long awaited life with Platt.

"You certainly have a lot of belongings. Nellie, how are we ever going to get them all the way out to Washington?"

"You will just have to get a bigger wagon or add another cart. There are some things a girl can't live without!"

"Oh, I now understand how things are going to be in this marriage," Platt replied as he winked at her. She looked at him as she sat down on the wagon and snuggled up close to him.

"And you're just now figuring this out?" They both laughed. They knew it was going to be a marriage of give and take, and always thinking about the other person first.

The next day, Nellie loaded up her belongings and said farewell to Dora.

"You will try and come to the wedding, won't you, Dora?"

"I will try, desperately, but it is so difficult to get coverage for my class unless the wedding is during the holidays or in the summer. Then, I will have a free schedule, but you must let me know when this blessed event will take place," Dora said her goodbyes and bombarded Nellie with hugs and kisses.

They were on their way to Oceanside to see the Jefferson's and Platt was nervous. He knew Mr. and Mrs. Jefferson liked him, well enough, but he wondered if it was enough to welcome him into the family and offer their blessing. Platt knew it would be tortured to come so far and not be able to wed his true love. Platt was deep in thought and Nellie could tell.

"Are you having second thoughts about getting married?" He spun his head around to look at her. He was in shock that she would even utter such a thing.

"What do you mean? I was having concerns that your parents would deny me the privilege and honor of being your husband," he said, with such sincerity he almost was tearful.

"Platt, my parents love you. They want us to be together but even more, they want me to be happy. I am when I'm with you. I truly love you."

Platt pulled the wagon over to the side of the road and put his arms around her. He looked down and tenderly pressed his lips to hers. It took his breath away. It left him wanting more. His blood rushed warm, and his heart was beating out of his chest. He hadn't experienced anything like this before and he knew they were in were in danger of getting carried away if he didn't stop. The longing between them was so strong; it was more than a physical desire. It was something he couldn't comprehend at that moment.

"We best be getting back on the road," said a very breathless Platt, knowing the sooner they became husband and wife, the better.

He always treated Nellie with the utmost respect and propriety, and he would continue to do so. They both knew it would be harder and harder to restrain the physical desire that burned within them so strongly. They would have to limit the times they were alone until their wedding day, which they were hopeful was not too far in the distant future. *How does one quench the desires of passion when they have been so long denied?* Platt didn't know but he knew he must find a way. If they ever gave in to the burning lust that raged within them before they were married, he knew she might resent him, or worse, lose respect for him. He couldn't risk it, not now, not after everything they had been through. They would marry quickly. He hoped Mr. Jefferson was agreeable with that.

"Platt, you are so quiet, are you alright? And, you know, we never discussed when we would depart for Washington. Don't we have to plan around the time of year?" Nellie tried to make conversation and was getting rather concerned because Platt had grown so withdrawn.

"I do apologize, Nellie. I was thinking about asking your father for your hand and if he made us wait, how it would be a very unfavorable scenario."

Nellie laughed. "Is that all that is the matter with you? I was thinking you were reconsidering and ready to turn around and leave me at my sister's. I didn't know what was wrong, but you got so quiet after we kissed. Are you sure you're alright?"

"Nellie, I love you. It's going to be alright." He put his arm around her lovingly.

Before they knew it, they were in Healdsburg and pulling up in front of Jefferson's place. It was a nice place, not nearly as large as they had in Marshall, but a large house. It had a wraparound porch with a swing and flower boxes overflowing with fresh blooms in the windows. The house was a two-story home with a parlor and a sunroom. Inside, the floors were hardwood, and the walls were painted blue in the kitchen. He had never seen blue paint like that before, just white. In the living room there was a large fireplace, although he doubted it ever got cold enough to use, it was still quite impressive.

After taking in the structure of the Jefferson home, he was, at last, ready to see Mr. Jefferson. He needed to ask him the most important question he thought a man could ever be faced with in his lifetime. His heart was pounding, and his palms were drenched with sweat. He wondered if Mr. Jefferson might have second thoughts, due to their tumultuous courtship. *Might he think him too unstable and unable to care for her?* Dark thoughts ran through his head and his stomach began to churn. If Mr. Jefferson didn't hurry, he might lose his strength and resolve.

"Platt good to see you, my boy," Mr. Jefferson said as he came around the corner.

"Yes sir, good to see you again. Mr. Jefferson, may I get right to the heart of the matter? I love your daughter. I promise to take good care of her, to love her all of my life, and do everything I can to provide the best life for her and to continue in the lifestyle she has become accustomed to. Sir, what I am, not so eloquently, asking is for Nellie's hand in marriage and your and Mrs. Jefferson's blessing on our union."

Mr. Jefferson knew, full well, what Platt's intentions were before he even gave his speech. "Yes Platt, we give you our blessing on your marriage."

"Thank you, Sir! I promise I will make her happy!" He shook his hand and ran off to find Nellie to tell her the good news.

Platt leaped out of the house and excitedly began his search for Nellie. He looked in the parlor and the living room and then, instinctively, turned in the direction of the garden. That was her favorite place to be, among the beautiful blooms of nature. Sure enough, she was looking at the flowers. She was so taken with the beauty of the rose blooms that she didn't hear Platt come up behind her.

"When would you like to start westward, Mrs. Corbaley?"

She spun around and leaped into his arms. "He said yes?!"

He nodded his head and kissed her, right there in her parents' garden. It was not as passionate as the kiss on the road, but his kisses were passionate, soft, and loving. They thought they were undetected, but mama and papa saw the whole scene unfold. They knew their little girl had given her heart away. She would be starting her own family now. Papa could sense that mama was sad and happy, all at the same time. He pulled her close for a hug.

"It's all right to let her go. Platt has always been her love and it's their time now to start their own story."

"I know. I really love Platt and he has loved Nellie for years but with those two, it seemed as if they would never be together. To have it happening now, I was not prepared."

"I know, I know." He put his arm around his wife. "You know, he wants to homestead out west in Washington and he asked that you and I join them once they are settled?"

Mama's head spun around. "No, I did not know. I may not have been so quick to give my blessing had I been given all the details before hand," she said rather sternly while looking at Lester with eyes that still brought him to his knees.

"Mama, I just learned about their plans myself. Do you really think we could have prevented this?" He motioned to the garden where they were sitting on a bench, holding hands and looking lovingly into each other's eyes."

"No, you're right. No one could prevent this kind of love. There have been several who have tried, all to no avail. Who are we to stand in the way of their happiness? So, I guess we better get busy with wedding plans," Mama said excitedly and spun off to the garden.

Platt and Nellie didn't want to wait any longer than necessary because of the need to meet the next wagon train headed to Washington. They decided not to prolong courtship, as was customary. Considering their relationship, it felt as if they had a long courtship already.

Mama and papa called Platt and Nellie into the parlor to talk about wedding plans. They were a little nervous, fearing that her parents would make them wait for the customary waiting period for the wedding. Nellie knew she could not bear the wait.

"Mama and I have talked it over and understand that you two want to go ahead and get married as soon as possible. First, we need to contact Platt's family so they can come for the wedding. Let's go down to the telegraph office and send that telegram and see when they can come."

Nellie was so excited that she jumped up and hugged her papa. "Oh! Thank you for understanding." She could not believe her own ears. She was going to marry Platt after all this time. She couldn't imagine herself with anyone else, however, the thought of being a wife made her a little uneasy. She worried she wouldn't know how to love him the way a man liked, and needed, to be loved. She had no idea if being a virgin would make this new experience pleasant or toilsome. She had so many questions and didn't know who to ask. She had these thoughts and was convinced every woman did before they married and just didn't voice them. She walked back and forth in her room, so enthralled in thought that she didn't even notice that Mama had slipped in.

"I knocked. You must not have heard me with all your pacing. Is everything alright? Nellie, are you having second thoughts about marrying Platt?"

"Oh no, mama, I love him! He is my soul mate in every aspect, except… well… I am not sure I should say."

By this time, mama had a concerned look on her face. She never considered her daughter could have been inappropriate with Platt. "Is there something you haven't told me about what has happened with Platt?"

"Oh no! Mama, how could you think such a thing about my relationship with Platt? He has been nothing but a proper gentleman! Mama, I am worried about, well, the wedding night," Nellie told her, all the time looking at the floor, making sure not to make eye contact.

"Oh, is that all it is?" Mama said laughing.

"Why are you laughing? This is a very serious matter, and I didn't know who to speak to about this. What if I can't love him enough or be a good pioneer wife? I have so many questions and not enough answers! What do I do?"

"The fact that you have worries and concerns lets me know you will be an excellent wife. None of us knew what to do, but we learned. That is the joy of true love. You grow together in every way. Relax and enjoy the journey, my daughter."

"Oh Mama, thank you for letting me speak to you! I feel much better now and more confident that I can be the kind of wife he needs. No one could love him more than I do and I promised to go where ever he goes. Now, excuse me but I must go meet Platt and go get that telegram off to his folks as soon as possible."

Nellie bounded down the stairs with a spring in her step. She was so anxious to find Platt and be on their way to the telegraph office. She found him in the kitchen, enjoying a cup of coffee with Papa. They were deep in conversation about Washington and homesteading. Platt was so excited that he jumped up and started speaking with his hands. He motioned to where the mountains and the rivers would be, drawing a picture with his hands and words. She became so engrossed in the details that she felt as if she was already there. He certainly has a way with words, she thought to herself. He was so convincing that it made her want to want to leave, that very instant, for Washington.

"Platt, are you ready to send that telegram?"

Platt jumped up from the chair and turned to face her. Once again, she took his breath away. "Why, yes, my lady. I was telling your father about Washington, and I think they may want to come and join us when we are all settled. Wouldn't that be great?"

"Oh Platt, I can't believe it. How do you always know what it is that will make me happy? I love you so much," Nellie said as she rushed into his arms and pressed a kiss to his lips, almost forgetting that her father was in the same room.

As they walked down the street, enjoying each other's presence immensely and deeply engrossed in conversation, they came upon Mattie and Frederick. They were both shocked and hadn't prepared themselves for this possibility. Mattie saw Nellie and ran to give her a hug.

"Oh! Nellie and Platt, when did you get into town? I have missed you so!"

Frederick stood there, looking at Platt, not knowing what to say or if he would bring up the letter and was heavily perspiring. Platt, being smart, decided it was better to let him wonder what he was thinking. Like when playing a card game, you can't show your hand too soon.

"Good to see you again, Mattie and Frederick. We arrived, just this afternoon," Platt said as he extended his hand towards Frederick and noticed his palm was very sweaty.

They visited for a few moments and then Nellie reassured Mattie, she would catch her up on all the news when she returned home. They sent a telegram to Richard and Jane Corbaley, telling them about their desire to wed as soon as possible and begin their journey out west. They went back home and waited anxiously to hear. Platt rented a room at the boarding house, for he felt it improper to be living under the same roof as Nellie until they were wed. He needed to avoid moments that could lead to intimacy. He had to have a resolve of steel, for his love for her was greater than a moment of passion or lust, it was based in love. One day, soon, he would love her as a man should love a woman. He had hopes that his family could come soon, and the wedding plans could be completed. She already had her dress and was anxious to wear it, and he to see her in it. There was just some unfinished business that needed to be settled and how and when to complete it was the question. Frederick: he couldn't let it go. Why hadn't he given the letter to Nellie? He understood that Frederick had feelings for Nellie, but he couldn't let it go. He thought about challenging him to a duel, but that was a little extreme. And, what if he was a better aim than he? No, he would make him sweat and play with his mind and emotions. It would be a game of wit and intrigue, which he found more fascinating than any gun slinging. He also knew that Nellie would have nothing to do with any form of violence. It was more complex now that Hattie was so in love with Frederick. Should he warn her of his true character? He truly cared for Hattie. After all, she was like a sister to Nellie, and she grew up with Platt. He wished her no ill will from anyone, especially someone like Frederick Wickham.

That night at dinner, Platt, Hattie, and Frederick joined the Jefferson family. They all tried to be cordial, but Nellie had a great deal of difficulty knowing that Frederick deliberately kept the letter from her. She was polite but decided to excuse herself early from dinner. Platt followed closely behind her.

"It's too much! Platt, I can't bear it! Knowing he withheld the letter purposefully and here he is, at my table with Hattie! I can hardly stand seeing her with him and not saying a word. I don't know how long I can continue this façade!" Nellie put her head on his chest.

He put his arm around her tiny waist and pulled her closer to him. He whispered in her ear. "It's all right, Nellie. I have a plan and he will learn his lesson."

"What exactly are you planning on doing?" He smiled and closed her mouth with a soft kiss.

The Jefferson's decided Platt and Nellie were deserving of a proper engagement party to announce their upcoming wedding. With their tumultuous courtship, they, of all people, certainly would enjoy the celebration. Mama and papa called them in and announced their plans and were met with mutual excitement. The plans were now in motion. Mama and Nellie were off to secure the town hall as the location and were delighted with the availability. Next stop was at the printers so they could send out invitations to all their friends and family. Then, off to the bakery to order a cake. It was exciting to have a facility that would only make bakery items. Nellie had to wonder if such an eccentric business would ever catch on and be able to stay in business. At first, she had concerns about diners and restaurants, but folks seem to enjoy a good meal prepared by someone else for a change. They decided on a sheet cake with butter cream frosting and simple decorations. It looked so wonderful and of course, it had to be chocolate for it was Platt's favorite. The other food would consist of roasted beef with potatoes, fried chicken, and corn on the cob. It was a feast! Mama was busy preparing food, night and day, getting all the preparations just right. Everyone they sent an invitation to be coming; they were excited beyond words! But still, no word from his family. It was beginning to worry Platt and Nellie could tell, but he never complained. He worked tirelessly, doing mundane chores to get ready for the big engagement party.

"I am a little concerned about my family, Nellie. I know they were waiting to hear from me, and I cannot understand why they haven't responded, especially about such wonderful news. Yet, in my heart, I feel they are safe." Nellie walked over to Platt and put her arm through his and her head on his chest.

"We will hear soon, I know it. Maybe something went wrong with the transmission of the telegram wire? That can happen, Platt. I know when I was working as an operator it did." She tried desperately to reassure him and yet, felt very inadequate at that moment. All she could do was be there and offer her love and understanding.

They went back to the garden where was plenty of room to work on all the decorations for the gala. While hard at work, they heard a lot of noise coming from the front of the house. Nellie became concerned and wanted to ensure her parents were all right.

"What is all that noise about?" Platt asked as they darted around the corner of the house, not knowing what they would find. To their shock and surprise, there, standing right in front of them, A.L. and Mr. and Mrs. Corbaley! Platt was so relieved to see them. He ran straight for his father's neck and hugged it, then his mother, and then his brother.

"What are you all doing here?" Platt asked.

"I received a telegram that there was going to be a wedding and I could not miss my son's wedding! Why, are you not glad to see us?" Mr. Corbaley questioned curtly.

"Oh my, yes! I…well… just didn't expect you. I expect to hear from you about when you are coming. But it doesn't matter. What matters are that you're here and safe."

"Son, I must confess, I did not mean to cause you undo anxiety. Lester knew we were coming! This was a wedding surprise."

Platt looked puzzled at the two men. They had known each other for most of their lives and had been known to pull practical jokes, but he never thought he would be a victim.

"What are you saying? Are you here for the engagement party and the wedding or is there something else you're not telling me?"

"Son, we discussed it. Your mother, brother, and I decided there was nothing keeping us in Oceanside, so we put our house up for sale and got a good price for it. We've decided to come here and be with you two until the wedding and assist with your move out west, if you would like us to."

Platt was so excited; he looked over at Nellie who was nodding her head in approval. He hollered a yelp, forgetting his gentleman training and thinking of himself back on the ranch in Indiana.

"Yes, father, that is a wonderful plan! You did catch us by surprise. We were just hoping you would make it for the wedding but this, this is the best news I've had since Nellie agreed to be my wife!"

Nellie strolled across the room to Platt and put her arm through his. "We could not be happier," Nellie added.

The Jefferson house was a flurry of activity. Everyone was hard at work completing all the arrangements for the engagement party, which was turning into quite a gala event. Mel and Dora had telegrammed that they were coming. Everything was perfect, Nellie thought. She and Platt were engaged, the Corbaley's had arrived, and her sisters were coming. That was all she really cared about, but her parents insisted on inviting other people. Some of them she had never met and didn't mean anything to her. Nonetheless, she was determined to be a gracious hostess, for that was the proper thing to do. To do anything less would be ungrateful, considering everything her parents had done for her.

The wonderful thing about living in Southern California is the weather is wonderful all year long. The days are warm, and the sky is a wonderful color of blue and is almost always adorned with wispy clouds. The sunshine in California is brighter and more beautiful than anywhere else on earth! The morning fog kept everything so green and lush it looked as if a green carpet rolled out before you. The farmers had recently found the earth rich for farming and the climate favorable for reaping a bountiful harvest. Nellie fought coming to California with her parents and now she was saddened at the thought of leaving. It was a land of so much promise. People were flooding into California from all over since the news had spread of the gold rush. Everyone wanted to stake their claim on land and mine for gold. Unfortunately, there were few with large gold strikes, but many found gold nuggets and gold dust. The little bit of success encouraged the desperate to continue with their opportunistic quest.

Mary Jefferson was in her favorite spot, in the garden, attending to her roses. She loved caring for the flowers and the roses were her pride and joy. Nellie came around the corner and saw her Mama in her rose garden and noticed how truly lovely she was. She still had her girlish figure and her hair had not a hair of gray, or a wrinkle on her face. With all the turmoil they had gone through the past year, it was amazing.

"Mama, are you ready to finalize the plans for the engagement party?" Nellie asked as she walked up to her Mama.

"Yes Nellie, let's go finish. While we are out, let's make sure we have the right dress for you."

"I have dresses that I've hardly worn. I'm sure any one of them would be fine. I am trying to conserve on my finances right now so we can save for our journey."

It was such a beautiful day; they decided to walk while they completed their errands. They talked about all the plans for the party, the upcoming wedding, and the future. They laughed and had a wonderful time together. As they walked out of the bakery shop, Mama pointed eagerly at the general store.

"Let's stop in there for a moment. There is something I want you to see!" Mama pleaded and reluctantly, Nellie agreed to join her. As they walked into the general store, Nellie was greeted by a very energetic store clerk who was giddy to see her.

"Nellie, come this way. I have something I think you will love!"

"Thank you, but I am not sure I am really in the market at this very moment for a dress. But that is exquisite! I cannot believe it is the exact dress I saw in a magazine a while back. I didn't think you stocked such frivolous items?"

"Well, we normally don't. Nellie, your mother ordered it from the picture in the magazine!" Nellie gasped. She turned to her mama and hugged her as she cried.

"Don't cry yet. Child, you are not even sure if it is going to fit," Mama said, trying to act stoic and untouched by the moment. Mama paid for the dress, and they skipped towards home. As they stepped out of the store, both enthralled in laughter at Nellie's big surprise, they ran right into a friend of Papa's, Cesar Alexander.

"Pardon me ladies, are you all, right?" He reached out to grasp mama's arm.

"Yes, thank you. We will be more careful of where we are walking in the future. We will be on our way and not take advantage of your kindness. Have a good day, sir." She nodded and took off down the street with one hand still on Nellies arm. She walked as if she were running a race.

"Slow down, please. And would you explain what just happened back there?" Nellie pleaded.

Mama looked at her daughter, knowing she could tell her anything. "I apologize. I don't know why that I react that way whenever that man is around, but he makes me uneasy. I know your father and he are friends, but he always wants to talk to me and touch me. It's probably nothing and I am overreacting. He is a very affluent man and is most likely used to woman falling all over him, but I don't care about his bank roll!"

Nellie looked at her Mama, seeing a beautiful woman, not looking near her age. She knew why Mr. Alexander couldn't keep his eyes off her, but he picked the wrong woman this time. Nellie went and hugged her mama.

"You are such a beautiful woman. It's no wonder he is always so nice to you. He just doesn't know what kind of woman you are. Now, let's take a better look at the dress."

They opened the package to reveal the most beautiful dress she had ever seen. It was a dark blue satin dress with seed pearls across the bodice and a scoop neck. It had the puffiest sleeves, which were beautifully adorned with pearl buttons. The extravagant dress had a large bustle in the back, which bustled three times and had a large ribbon sash. It was the most exquisite dress she had ever seen, and it suited her as if it were custom made. She felt like a princess in a story book. Her Mama knocked on the door and asked if she might come in and see how the dress was fitting. When she entered the room, she started to cry.

"You look more beautiful than I could have ever imagined! Do you like it?"

"Yes mama, it is the most elaborate dress I could have imagined! I do love it, but are you sure? It must have been very expensive, and I don't want you and papa to spend any more money. I am a grown woman now, about to be married!"

"Yes, but you're still my little girl. I can indulge you if I so feel inclined. This is our gift to you, Nellie."

"Oh mama, it is the most beautiful thing I have ever laid my eyes upon! I can't even imagine what it would be like, wearing such an exquisite gown." She hugged her mother's neck and began to cry. She was overwhelmed by her parents' generosity.

"Oh, come now, no time for tears." Mama too, had tears in her eyes.

As if opening presents on Christmas morning, they excitedly finished taking the rest of the dress out of the box. They unbuttoned the countless buttons, which ended up being an extremely lengthy process. At last, Nellie was able to step into the lovely gown. Once she slipped the satin over her skin, she knew her parents had spent more than they originally said on the dress. This dress was of immaculate quality, the kind that would last for years to come. Mama completed the endless buttoning and Nellie turned to look in the mirror. They gasped in unison. Nellie looked like royalty, better than the model in the catalog! This dress was certainly made for her. Nellie stood there, she gazed at her reflection in the mirror and wondered who it was she was seeing. The person staring back at her was not a girl, but a woman. She looked stunning and felt beautiful.

"I can't even describe how I feel in this dress! I feel like a princess. I know that sounds ridiculous and self-absorbed, but that's how this dress makes me feel. I am confident, beautiful, and ready to be Platt's wife."

Mama was overwhelmed herself. "I agree. You are a princess. You look so lovely but now that we know it fits, let's get it off before anything happens. I'll have it pressed before the party."

The day of the party had finally arrived. The Jefferson house was buzzing with excitement and busy with the final preparations. Hattie's mom, Gertie, was busy cooking along with another hired cook. It was to be hailed as the largest and most grand event Healdsburg had ever seen! What started out as a little intimate gathering of friends and family had fast expanded into the social event of the season! Anyone of importance was invited. Uncle Thomas even said he might attend if he could tear himself away from his duties in Washington.

Mama made sure that every detail of the event was carried out to perfection and stayed perfectly calm while doing it. She ordered the cooks in one direction and the servants in another, attending to it all with such grace. Nellie wondered how she was able to do it and if she would inherit her gift. Mama looked over and noticed Nellie staring intently.

"What are you doing, young lady? It's time for you to start getting ready now! Gertie will be along in a moment to assist you. Now, hurry up or you will be late for your own party!"

Nellie picked her skirt up and walked up the stairs, excited and nervous about the party. She loved parties but being the center of attention made her nervous. That was where Platt excelled. He loved it and she was content to be in the background. As she began to step into the magnificent dress, her fears seemed to dissipate, one by one. She never knew she could feel or look the way she did. She felt beautiful, like a woman about to take the place alongside the man she loved with all her heart. As she thought about becoming Platt's wife, she couldn't help but blush. *What will it be like being married? Will he like being around me all the time? Will my habits annoy him?* All these thoughts raced through her mind. Her thoughts always circled back to the fear of him finding her undesirable in bed. After all, she was inexperienced and really had no idea how to please a man in that way. But then, she would think about Platt and his dark piercing eyes and how he looked at her. She knew it would all be alright, for they would learn and grow together. She was sure they would both make their share of mistakes.

Tonight was not for worry or concern about the future, but for celebration. As Nellie worked on the finishing touches and put her comb in her hair, she heard a knock on the door.

"Come in," she said with a sigh of relief as she realized it was her mama.

"Oh my, sweet angel, you look exquisite! I bought them for you to wear. I thought it would complete your outfit and it would mean a lot to me if you would agree to wear it on your special night." Mama handed Nellie a broach. It had tiny seed pearls all around with a diamond in the center, resting on a blank velvet ribbon.

"Mama, this was your mother's broach. I can't take this. What if something were to happen to it? It is very valuable. I know how much it means to you," Nellie said as she started to hand it back to her mother.

"Nellie, don't you realize how important you are to me? I want you to have it. It would have made my mother very happy to see you wear it. Come on, let's finish getting you ready or you'll be late for your own party." Nellie carefully put the broach on. She looked in the mirror and then back at her mother, who gave a nod of approval.

Platt waited at the bottom of the stairs, wondering why Nellie was taking so long to get ready. He paced the floor until he heard her descend the stairs. He turned to see her, and his heart stopped for a moment. His palms became sweaty, and he found his head starting to swim. She was the most beautiful thing he had ever seen. She appeared to float down the stairs, as if she were descending on a cloud. He blinked his eyes, for he was sure he had gone to heaven, and she was an angel. He stood there, not knowing what to say. He had never seen anyone look so exquisite in his life.

"Platt, are you ready to go?"

"Yes, let's go. My, you are looking lovely this evening," Platt said to her, knowing that the compliment was not near deserving of her. She deserved so much more but at this very moment, that was all he could manage.

Nellie took Platt's arm, and they were off to the party. Nellie was overwhelmed with excitement for the party. After all, it was the most sought-after invitation in the county. The whole town would be there, in fact, anybody who was anybody would be there. This wasn't the small gathering they originally had in mind, but both were ready to embrace the party to its fullest.

When they entered the town hall, Nellie was astonished to see how beautiful everything looked! There were flowers at every table and candles around the entire building, which gave it an atmosphere of romance. Nellie was so pleased she could hardly contain herself. They had a wonderful time dancing, and the food was superb! Her mother had the cook baking for what seemed like weeks and everyone in the church group had offered to cook, so the food was the most wonderful sample of delicatessen delight. Nellie knew that the party was extravagant, and more than her parents should have done for her. She had pangs of guilt, but her mother insisted and would do nothing less for her youngest daughter. Mother reassured her that the party was a gift to her, and Platt and she wanted nothing more than to show off her daughter and soon to be son-in-law.

Besides, they had a great time. Platt knew how to work a crowd and loved to be the center of attention. But she loved that about him. He was so much like her father. She hadn't seen the similarities in their personalities before tonight, but she was always papa's girl and guessed that was one of the reasons why she loved Platt so much. She thought to herself, how strange it was to think you want something different as you grow up, but the person you're drawn to is just like your father. That was ironic to her. Or maybe not, after all, she never apologized for loving her father and would never for loving Platt.

They danced, laughed, and socialized with everyone, trying to make them feel important and that they were grateful to everyone for coming. When they called for a dance for the happy couple, Platt was all too happy to have Nellie in his arms again. He walked across the dance floor and offered his hand to Nellie. They waltzed as flawlessly as anyone had ever danced. Nellie appeared to float atop the floor, almost as if she were an angel. After the dance, everyone applauded, and everyone was invited to dance.

Mary Jefferson enjoyed the evening as much as anyone, or maybe a little more. She watched her daughter and was hit with the realization that her baby was getting married and would not be living at home any longer but instead, starting her own family. As she was deep in thought, she felt a touch on her shoulder. Thinking it to be Lester, she went to put her hand on his when she heard the voice and quickly turned her head.

"May I have this dance, mama?"

She turned her head quickly to be face to face with Alexander, the one person she did not want to see. "No thank you, Sir. I feel quite certain my husband would not approve of such a gesture."

"I just spoke with your husband. He said he loved to see you dance and gave his permission. If you would, give me the pleasure of this dance?"

Mama looked at him, closely, wondering why he would want to dance with the mother of the bride. There were so many beautiful eligible women in attendance who would love to have a dance with him.

"I don't know why you would bother dancing with me. Why don't you choose one of these lovely ladies as a dance partner?" Mama replied, rather annoyed.

"Because I want to dance with you so will you or will you not dance with me?" Alexander asked, trying to smile and not make a scene. By this time, he was feeling embarrassed, but part of him thought intently. *No, I have come this far to ask this lovely lady for a dance. By gum, she can oblige me and be polite and the lady everyone says she is.*

Mary sent a look across the dance floor to her husband and chastised him without words. Reluctantly, she took the hand that was offered to her and followed him out onto the dance floor. Papa felt badly that he put Mary in an uncomfortable situation. He could tell by the look on her face. *Mary danced with other dance partners, so why was she so uncomfortable?* He would investigate the issue further, but not until after the party. Tonight was about Nellie and Platt.

Platt and Nellie continued their dancing and greeting the guests when she turned and was faced to face with Frederick Wickham. She knew he was coming with Hattie, but her objective had been avoidance. She thought in a room full of people, the chances of running into Frederick were greatly diminished. Yet, there they were. She tightened the grip on Platt's arm and looked deep into his piercing eyes.

"Not tonight. This is not the time or place to address this."

"Nellie, you know there is nothing I can or could ever refuse you. I respect your family too much to cause any scene," Platt told her, lovingly.

Hattie looked at Nellie. "What is going on here? What did I miss? What am I not being told, Frederick?" Hattie asked frantically, while still in the sweetest voice she could manage.

"Nothing you need to concern yourself with, Hattie. It's between Platt and Frederick and they will work it out," Nellie reassured her and took her arm. "Now, let's go see what all the girls are wearing to the party! Come on, Hattie."

Nellie whisked her best friend away from a potentially flammable scene. She knew it would be best to just forget the incident. She and Platt had found each other, and Frederick and Hattie seemed happy. But it meant that Hattie was with a deceitful liar who lied to her and Platt and now was being dishonest to Hattie. This was the hardest reality for her to live with. After all, she and Platt were reunited and his scheme had failed, but could Hattie go through life with that scoundrel? Nellie struggled with what to do. The thought of Hattie getting serious, or worse, getting married to a liar was more than she could bear. *When to tell her? No, not tonight this evening is too perfect, and I won't let Frederick Wickham spoil it. This night belongs to us.* She took Platt's arm and gave it a squeeze. He seemed to get the message, for he tipped his head towards Hattie and Frederick.

"May I have this dance?" She curtsied in agreement and took his hand as he led her out to the dance floor.

They danced as if they owned the floor. He led with strength, and she followed with such grace and beauty. Every eye was on the young couple as they floated across the dance floor. Mama watched and began to get misty eyed, realizing that her baby girl would soon be a bride. As she watched the happy couple, she was reminded of the time when she was the bride. She was deeply engrossed in thought when she felt a hand on her shoulder and not knowing who it would be this time, she felt herself jump away.

"Mary, are you all, right?" a familiar voice asked her. She turned and it was the face she had loved all through the years.

"Why yes, of course darling. I was just startled, that is all." She reached up and took his hand in hers. "Aren't they the most handsome couple you've ever seen?"

"Yes, my dear, they have never looked happier. I only wish my other loves were here to share the joy of their sister," Lester said as he remembered when his daughters were small and danced around a room merrily with their father.

The dancing and merriment continued for quite some time while Lester and Mary started to give orders to get things cleaned up. The Corbaley's had a wonderful time visiting the Wickhams, as if they were long lost family. Nellie was uncertain how she felt about that, but it certainly was not the fault of the Wickham's that they had such an incorrigible son. She was completely enthralled in her thoughts. Suddenly, she was brought back to reality by a commotion that was going on over by her parents. Her thoughts ran rather sinister, and she was concerned about a duel between her father and Mr. Alexander. She hurried over to the corner, and she was instantly overwhelmed. She couldn't contain herself. Immeasurable joy leaped from her heart when she saw Melissa and Dora standing before her!

"What on earth, when did you arrive? I thought you were unable to attend?!" The questions came rolling out as fast as the tears of joy spilled out over Nellie's cheeks. Mama was delighted to have all her girls in the same room and rushed to join in on the group as they hugged.

"Alright, let's get back to the reason for the party tonight," Father said with a wink in his eyes, equally delighted to have all his girls home. "Let us raise our glasses high and have a toast to the happy couple. Platt and Nellie, my darling daughter and the man who won her heart, may you have God's Blessing on your journeys through life. May you find as much happiness in each other as I have found with my beautiful wife, to the happy couple!"

Platt reached over and kissed Nellie lightly and everyone applauded. Nellie blushed for she was not accustomed to public displays of affection.

"Now, everyone dance!" Papa announced to the crowd.

"My feet feel as if they will surely be blistered from all the dancing. I've had such a wonderful time!" Nellie said to Platt, who looked unbelievably handsome at that moment.

"Nellie, I have never been happier in all my life than I am at this very moment. The only thing that could make it more complete was if this were the wedding and not just the celebration." He had the most peculiar look on his face, as if a light was turned on and now, he could see.

"Wait just a minute! Why not now? Everyone is here, the food is made, the band is playing, and your sisters are here, and you know they must leave soon. Nellie, will you marry me right now?"

Nellie had been contemplating the same thing but had been reluctant to give it voice. "Yes! Platt, of course I will marry you! Now, the next step is finding our parents and seeing if it is agreeable to them. Let's go." She grasped his hand and pulled him away to find their parents and discuss their plans.

They found their parents visiting with each other and began to reveal what was on their hearts. Both sets of parents laughed. Nellie and Platt looked at each other, a little puzzled, wondering if someone had spiked the punch.

"We were discussing that exact thing when you walked up, but we were quite sure you would never agree to such a turn of events. We know you want a grand church wedding."

Nellie looked at her parents. "All I wanted was a small intimate affair with family and friends. I went along with this party because I knew how important it was to you. I don't need things to be fancy to make me happy. I need to be Platt's wife. That is all." She looked over and noticed a tear in her mother's eye. "Did I offend you, mama?"

"No, my dear, you understand the truly important things in life. God, family, and love are what a marriage must be based on, or it will not stand."

Papa looked at the couple, lovingly. "Let's find Reverend Nelson and ask if he would perform the ceremony. I will announce to our guests that we now have a wedding, but first, let me find your sisters and tell them." Almost instantaneously, Papa was off to take care of the details. Unfortunately, Reverend Nelson had retired for the evening and Nellie's heart began to sink.

"Do not be fearful, sweet daughter of mine. Tonight was your engagement party and that it was. It shall be tomorrow, and we'll proceed with the wedding plans while your sisters are here in town. But this time, Nellie, it will be your way. Only your friends and family members will be there. You'll have the wedding of your dreams." Mama put her hand on Nellie's face and gently touched it, as if were made of the finest porcelain.

"You always understood me so well! Mama, what ever will I do without you?"

The evening was a huge success and a memorable night. People in the county will be speaking of the event for some time to come. Melissa, Dora, and Nellie spent most of the night talking and laughing, like schoolgirls. They couldn't believe their baby sister was getting married.

Nellie awoke the next morning and couldn't believe it was the day of her wedding. It was going to be a small church wedding with their families and closest friends, not a room full of strangers and acquaintances. It would be the way she always dreamed.

It took no time at all to have everything in place. Dora and Melissa were her attendants and A.L stood up with Platt and his father. Everything was perfect, Nellie thought as she strolled down the aisle with her father to become Mrs. Corbaley. Platt's eyes watered as he saw Nellie approaching in the beautiful satin gown. Platt's face was memorable, and Nellie thought it would live with her forever. His eyes didn't leave her, even for a moment, during the ceremony.

It was a moving ceremony. When they finally said their "I do's," there was a shout of applause from the crowd. The audience cheered as Platt and Nellie kissed for the first time as husband and wife. They waited so long for this day and at last, she was Mrs. Platt Corbaley. She couldn't believe after all this time, it finally happened. They joyfully walked hand in hand back down the church aisle. They happily greeted their guests and commenced the celebration of their happy union. They had cake and punch and all the ladies generously decided to surprise them with a potluck lunch. They had a wonderful time feasting on the scrumptious display of delectable samplings.

After the guests had gone and the ladies were busy cleaning up, it was time for the new bride and groom to be off for their wedding night. She waited so long for this moment and now that it was here, she worried she wouldn't know what to do. The ceremony happened so quickly, she didn't have time to mentally prepare herself as she normally would. She felt very ill prepared, but wondered if a virgin bride would ever know what to expect.

Their parents felt they deserved a honeymoon, so they surprised the happy couple with a trip, to none other the city of their reunion, San Francisco! They would leave on tomorrow's train, but tonight they would be alone as husband and wife for the first time. The thought sent chills of terror and excitement up Nellie's spine.

Platt was as nervous as a pup. He didn't want Nellie to know but he was a virgin and was having doubts that he would be able to please his bride. He heard that it all came natural and he was counting on it. But, his overwhelming love for Nellie nearly left him weak in the knees. He tried to control his nerves, but he was lost at what to do first. He looked up and saw her exquisite beauty, with her dark hair around her shoulders and her blue eyes looking at him with such love. He couldn't comprehend it but in an instant, the answers to his questions were answered.

All their apprehensions disappeared as Platt and his skillful hands made Nellie feel things she never felt possible. She wondered if it was proper to experience such things but reminded herself she was a married woman. Nellie loved the feeling of lying next to him and decided she didn't ever want to be without him again.

Platt rolled over and gazed lovingly into her eyes. "How is Mrs. Corbaley?"

"I'm not sure. I haven't spoken to your mother today," she said with a twinkle in her eyes and a tease in her voice.

He rolled over and grabbed her up in his arms and began kissing her. She pretended to resist but they both knew neither one could.

Morning light came all too soon and it was time to get up and dressed for the train. What Nellie really wanted was to stay curled up in Platt's arms. It was where she felt safe from the outside world and felt waves of love pouring over her. It was like standing on the seashore, lapping in the waves. It engulfs you and your balance it lost, but you don't worry.

The conductor called "all aboard" just as they arrived at the station. They boarded the train and got settled in for the trip to San Francisco. It wasn't going to be a long journey, but it was a scenic route. They visited with a gentleman from San Francisco who was returning home. He was a business owner and owned a rather large import and export business. They visited with another young family, not much older than themselves, with a small child. They were a very pleasant couple. The casual conversations helped pass the time and Platt never seemed to lack for people to talk to. She loved that about her husband.

Once in San Francisco, they made their way to the hotel and soon arrived at an exquisite looking building.

"There must be some mistake! Platt, the Palace Hotel is the most exclusive Hotel in San Francisco. No one can get a reservation here! Why, Mr. Wickham said they were booked up for a year and was upset he couldn't stay here last Christmas. He also said that they only let certain people into their hotel, so I am certain we have the wrong address."

Platt looked at her and smiled. "My darling wife, my father is great friends with the man who owns this hotel. That tends to make a difference when trying to make a reservation." He reached down and kissed her lightly on the lips.

They walked into the foyer of the hotel and Nellie was in awe of all the elaborate furnishings and ornate designs. The window dressings were made of a thick maroon tapestry with gold cords and tassel hanging from the circular drapes. The floors were done in a high gloss marble stone. There was a grand dining room, breakfast dining room, a billiard room, and 755 guest rooms, which Nellie had difficulty imaging would be totally booked. As you walked into the lobby, you were met by large statues pouring out cisterns of water into a great pool. It was all so magnificent and almost too much to absorb. Platt was in awe, almost as much as his young bride. It was a magnificent place! He never dreamt of anything as grand as this and yet, there they were. They were together at last as husband and wife.

Their room had a large iron frame bed with a feather mattress that was overstuffed for extra softness. The bed linens were white and light blue with white islet lace along the edges. On the dresser sat a large porcelain pitcher and bowl set with a painting of a country scene. It was intricate and beautiful. The room was such a contrast to the extravagance they had just witnessed in the lobby, but it was inviting and comfortable.

They decided to have dinner in the grand dining room. There was only dinner apparel allowed, so it was an excuse to wear her beautiful dress from the engagement party. Platt dressed in a suit and looked incredibly dashing. Nellie was still getting used to the fact that she could dress and undress in the presence of a man and wondered if all new brides experienced this. As she was changing for their dinner reservation, Platt came over and decided to start being affectionate. She could hardly refuse her husband, after all, that wouldn't be the wifely thing to do. They were late for dinner, but it was well worth it.

The dining room was breath taking and the room seemed to go on forever. Nellie had never seen so many people before who were the "the upper" of society. The women were dressed beautifully, with jewelry hanging around their necks like ropes and ring the size of rocks. They were from a different page of society than she was. She was, by no means, from a poor family but never had she seen such a display of wealth.

Platt saw the look on her face. He took her hand and gently kissed it. "Are you alright, Nellie?" he asked softly, almost melting her heart on the spot.

"I am fine, just in awe of all this." She gestured with her hand to her surroundings, and he nodded his head.

"I understand, my love. Let's go have dinner."

They had a full orchestra playing while the guests ate. This was the most wonderful present his parents could have given them. It was an experience to remember for the rest of their lives and a story to tell their children. That was a strange, yet exciting, thought. They had been through such a tumultuous journey getting married, she couldn't even imagine having children!

After having the most wonderful five course meal, Platt looked at his bride, adoringly. "Mrs. Corbaley, would you care to join me for dancing in the grand ballroom?"

Nellie was always taken back, at first, when someone called her Mrs. Corbaley. She, almost always, began looking for his mother before realizing she was the lady in question.

She batted her eyes at him. "Why yes, kind sir. I would be delighted but first, I'll have to check with my husband."

Platt laughed and took Nellie by the waist. After a good laugh, she took his arm and they headed for the ballroom, excited to enjoy an evening of dancing in such elegance. When they arrived, they realized that although they were dressed properly for the grand ballroom dining, there was proper attire required for the ballroom. Platt was dressed in the finest suit but the ballroom for dancing required tails and the dress Nellie wore didn't meet the formal dress standards. They looked at each other, rather disappointed. Platt thought it was an injustice of snobbery. Nellie saw her husband becoming upset, so she gently took his hand in hers.

"Platt, I don't really care about dancing here. I just want to spend time with my husband." She reached up and kissed him in front of everybody. She didn't care. She loved her husband and wanted to express her feelings. This always got her in trouble. Her father always said she was pretentious and trouble was always close behind. She thought it was funny how it seemed that her greatest weaknesses were also her strengths. She looked into his eyes. "Platt, let's just go back to our room after we go for a walk and see the lights of the city. Is that all right with you?"

Platt's heart melted. "Why of course, my darling. Let's go for that walk so I can clear my head. Then, I would like to take my wife back to our room and make love to her," he whispered in her ear, and she blushed.

"Why Platt, should we speak of such things out in public?"

He looked down and her and winked. "Why yes, times are changing, and I said it for your ears only, my love."

He took her hand and put it over his arm. He escorted her out of the hotel and down the street. The lights were beautiful, and the ocean was more breathtaking than they had remembered. They walked along the pier and spoke of their upcoming trip and their new life together. They didn't notice how far they'd walked away from the hotel, but reality struck as the ocean breeze made it rather chilly outside. They scanned their surroundings and noticed several vessels that had made port. Despite being impressed by the ships, they decided to cut their walk short. The way the moonlight hit Nellie's skin made Platt insatiable with longing for her and the ships did little to curb his appetite.

They walked briskly to the hotel and barely made it to the room. There was a flurry of hands, only subsided by the complexity of Nellie's dress. It took entirely too long to unfasten the multitude of layers. They laughed so hard and collapsed on the bed next to each other.

"Is this how our marriage is going to be?" Platt asked as they burst into another fit of uncontrollable laughter.

"At least we have a good sense of humor about the trials and tribulations that have come our way. I have an idea that this is nothing compared to what is ahead of us."

They woke up the next morning and grieved as they checked out of the hotel. The wedding trip had gone far too fast, and it was time to return to Oceanside.

As they traveled, Nellie's mind wandered. She and Platt were a family now, it all sounded so strange and yet, so exciting. She thought there was nothing better than lying next to him and hearing him breathe. It made her feel safe and secure. When he touched her, she felt a tingling sensation that was difficult to explain. She thought a woman shouldn't even try to explain such things, but this love was amazing, and it had to be shared. It was too wonderful to be kept a secret. Nellie's thoughts kept her busy and before she knew it they arrived in Oceanside.

They were graciously greeted by her sweet papa, who requested they discuss plans for their future without delay. Despite being exhausted, Platt obliged. Nellie tried to engage but got distracted as she gazed at her husband. *Was a woman supposed to feel this way about a man?* She realized she had never heard anyone describe their feelings about their husband before. Women just didn't talk about such things, and she wondered why.

"Nellie, are you all, right?"

Nellie tried desperately to reengage. "Why yes, papa, of course. I am just more exhausted from our journey than I had first thought."

"Would you like to wait until tomorrow to discuss my proposition with the two of you?"

"Whatever you're inclined to think is the best course. What do you think Platt?" She looked at her handsome husband, which always made her heart rate quicken.

"Why don't we all get some rest this evening? We shall resume this conversation in the morning when we are all refreshed, if that is agreeable with you sir."

"Why yes, I agree. Let's all retire for the evening, and we shall see you at breakfast." With that, everyone went their separate ways for the evening.

"I wonder what papa wanted to talk to us about," Nellie blurted out as they entered their room.

"We could have found out if you had wanted to pursue the matter this evening. We could always go get your father, if you like. However, I have other plans for my bride," he said with a glitz in his eyes as he pulled her close and kissed her passionately.

"Whatever do you have in mind?" Nellie was quite breathless from the kiss but determined to act coy.

"Let me show you what I have been thinking about all day. I can't get my mind off you, Nellie Corbaley."

He kissed her neck and lifted the pin from her hair and watched as it cascaded down her back in a fluid dance. He unbuttoned her dress, slowly. He unfastened one button at a time, kissing her with each button. It drove her mad with desire. She wanted to tear off the rest of the buttons. The caressing and building of passion were a new realm for them and she found it quite desirable. She never thought it was possible for a woman to feel this way. It felt so right and so good.

At morning's first light, Nellie woke in Platt's arms. "It doesn't get better than this, you know," she said as she looked up at her handsome husband.

"I completely agree. Unfortunately, we need to get up and go to breakfast. We have our meeting with your father to inquire about his proposition."

Soon they were up and ready to join Mr. & Mrs. Jefferson for breakfast.

"My, you two are looking rested and fresh this morning," Mr. Jefferson said as he greeted Platt and Nellie.

It was odd for him to think of his youngest daughter as a wedded woman. She was still his baby, his little princess, not a grown-up. But nonetheless, he couldn't have chosen a better man, even if he had done it himself. Platt was a fine young man, not to mention, the young man who saved Nellie's life and his own. He owed him a debt of gratitude, but more than that, he respected him. Papa walked over to Nellie and gave her a hug. "Sleep well, my dear?"

"Why yes, the cottage has proven to be a grand accommodation. Thank you for allowing us to stay here until we can secure a place of our own." Nellie realized she had spoken, completely out of turn, without discussing the matter with her husband. After realizing her error, her face paled, and Platt looked at her with concern. "That is, if it is agreeable with you, Platt," she uttered quickly.

Platt couldn't control himself and burst out in laughter. Nellie was shocked, and then angered, and was about to say something when Platt spoke.

"Nellie, I appreciate your sensitivity to my feelings. We shall discuss our course of action together." He reached over, took her hand in his, and kissed it tenderly. "Thank you," he whispered to her as she blushed.

Papa was quick to interject. "Very well, let's discuss what I wanted to talk to you about. I know you want to go out west, and I also know that now wouldn't be the best time to go because of the weather conditions. So, I propose that you and Platt stay, and he can work on the railroad for a few months. This way, you can save for your trip and do some more planning. In the spring, when it's safe to travel, you can start your journey. We would like to come out West and join you after you get settled. With, you can stay in the cottage house as long as you like until you are ready to go. Platt, I have talked to the owner of the railroad company. He happens to be a friend of mine and he wants to meet you, if you're interested. You know, there is no fool like an old fool, so I don't want to be pushy with my plans."

Nellie and Platt looked at each other and didn't need to say a word. "We don't need time to talk about this one. We, very much, appreciate your generous offer and gladly accept."

Nellie was so happy, for this meant she would have more time with her mama and papa. She couldn't contain herself any longer and leaped into the arms of her husband and kissed him. Her parents smiled. They knew the dreams they dreamt of for their daughter were coming true. Papa burst into laughter. The young lovers looked at him with wide eyed surprise.

"What?" Nellie asked before joining in on the good humor of the moment.

"All right let's discuss the details of your living arrangement. You are welcome to live in the guest cottage, where you will have privacy and can live without worry of rent. We will have the added benefit of having you live close by. So, you see, we do have a selfish motive in our gesture."

"Mr. Jefferson, I truly appreciate your generous offer. We are truly humbled by it, but I would be remiss if I didn't say that I am uncomfortable in living here without paying our way. I am not one to take charity from anyone, not even family. I do not say that to be offensive to your offer, sir. We will pay for our board and room. It's only right since we have our own family now."

Their own family. Those words were still foreign to Papa, who was adjusting to the marital status of his youngest daughter. He knew it would take some time; after all, she was his little girl for years. *Does everyone really expect me to be completely comfortable with newlyweds within only a few days?* He loved Platt and could not have chosen anyone more perfect for his daughter, but it was hard to let loose of the reins. He knew from experience that parenthood doesn't stop when they march to the altar.

"Is that acceptable with you, sir?" Platt asked, looking at Mr. Jefferson because he had been staring off into space.

"Oh yes, Platt. Whatever you and Nellie are comfortable with but understand that my offer was made only for you and Nellie to be able to save some money for your upcoming adventure."

"I certainly appreciate your generosity. Nellie and I will discuss it and get back to you with our decision."

Nellie was soon making the cottage their first home. It was a lovely guest cottage, an A-frame building with shudders on the windows and flowers in the window boxes. It almost had the appearance of a Swiss Alps chalet. The setting of the cottage looked to be taken right out of a lovely painting, nestled amid the flowers and fruit trees with cobble stone leading up to the entrance. It was a breathtaking sight. The inside of the cottage was simple, but elegant with tasteful accessories that made it more like a home than a cottage. The bedroom had a large rice bed with an overstuffed mattress and a white lace bedspread. In the corner of the room was a cherry wood dresser with a matching nightstand. Atop it was a lovely lamp, adorned with a beautiful painting of the countryside. Next to that, a few favorite books were stacked neatly. It was very homey and inviting. The Kitchen was small, but after all, it was a guest cottage. It had a small sink and a few cupboards, painted white with a blue boarder. There was a small table and an oven with a stove top. It was everything a person could ever dream of needing to start their lives together. Even though this was only a temporary home for them, it would always be their first home. It was the first place they lived as a married couple, the place where Platt could come home to after a hard day of work and find his adoring wife waiting for him. It was a special little cottage, and it would always have a special place in their memories. She knew no matter where their journey took them and what estates they would reside in, none would be grander than this little cottage.

As she thought of her love and their new life, she felt lucky to have found such happiness in a relationship. It was ironic to her because growing up, Hattie was always the friend talking of love and marriage, and she had felt disdain for such topics. Now she only wished Hattie could indulge in the same type of love that she found in Platt. She knew Hattie was happy with Frederick, but Nellie worried about her. *Does she know what she's getting herself in for?* Nellie felt like she should tell her but the more she thought about it, the more she felt otherwise. Maybe he had changed. Maybe he was only cold and calculating with Nellie, but he really cared for Hattie. After all, Hattie was a beautiful, smart, and talented girl. She deserved to be with someone who could provide for her and care for her. Nellie wished more than anything for Hattie to find love. Not a passing fancy, but the deepest and truest love. That's what she wanted for her dearest friend.

"Oh, I hope she finds love!" she said to herself as she flopped down onto an overstuffed sate in the living room.

"Who finds love, darling?" Platt questioned as he entered the room. Nellie rose from the couch and ran into his arms. He reached down and cupped his lovely bride's face in his hands. "You are such a beauty. Why would you settle for a bloke like me?"

His face came down and their lips became one. He kissed her tenderly at first, and then more passionately. Nellie returned the passion, and the fire began to build stronger and stronger. Platt kissed her neck, down her back, and then down her chest. She groaned for more and he couldn't contain it any longer. He picked up his bride and carried her up the stairs to the bedroom, kissing her all the way up. They arrived at the bedroom, and he laid her gently on the bed. They made love that neither could have ever dreamed possible. They were both exhausted and rung with sweat as they lay next to each other.

"What do you think your parents would say about their daughter making love with her husband while there is still daylight?" Platt asked laughing.

"I would think they would be glad I am happy and so in love with the man I married."

He took her in his arms and held her close. She felt so safe and complete. Never had she ever believed a woman could feel like this and experience these emotions. She was thankful for a man who made her feel so extraordinary. She returned to reality and saw Platt was already dressed and on his way down the stairs.

"Oh, I thought we might spend more time resting and talking."

"Nellie, we were not resting and there was little talking going on. I thought I might take my beautiful bride out to dinner, unless you're too tired?" he said with a wink, and she smiled.

"And what is the reason we might be going out to dinner in the middle of the week?"

"Do I need an excuse to take my beautiful bride out to dinner?"

She lowered her eyes and looked at him intently. She felt like there was something he wasn't telling her. "Yes, my good sir, you do." She ran her finger along the side of his face and across his lips.

"You know that drives me wild for you. Nellie, how can I speak to you when you distract me so?"

She looked at him and laughed. "Distract you so? Really, Platt, you could have come up with something far more creative than that. But seriously, what is it that's so important that we must go out to eat tonight?"

"I saw Hattie today. She and Frederick are quite serious, and they asked us to have dinner with them. I know how you feel about Frederick, but Nellie please, it is not about him. Hattie misses you and she truly appears to be in love. So, please darling, we must leave old offenses in the past," Platt pleaded with Nellie.

"Why yes, of course we shall go. I have been longing to see Hattie for some time now and it would be delightful for us to catch up."

Platt heard the words but knew they weren't from the heart. Nevertheless, he accepted it with the graciousness it was offered.

Nellie chose a beautiful dress and adorned her neck with a lovely broach. She painstakingly applied her rouge and carefully piled her long hair on top of her head. When she was satisfied with her appearance, she entered the common room and announced to Platt that she was ready.

"My dear, you look exquisite as usual! All other women will pale in your presence."

"Oh Platt, if you keep speaking like that, we might not make it to the restaurant. My head shall swell from all the complements and will not fit through the door."

"I wouldn't be opposed to the idea of us staying in and not going at all." He gently kissed her lips and pulled her up against his body. "Now dear, we better go now, otherwise, we will never leave."

"Alright, we will go. I want to continue this when we return from dinner."

They arrived at the restaurant and scoured the entire place but couldn't find Hattie or Frederick anywhere.

"Did you have the right time, Platt?"

Platt's only response was to look at her with his piercing eyes as if to say, "do you really think I would confuse the arrival time?"

She knew exactly what he was thinking. "Alright, I know you didn't make the arrangements for the wrong time. Let's give them a few more minutes and if they do not arrive, we can either go home or stay and have a dinner date unless you have a better plan?"

Platt was too busy watching her talk to listen. He loved to watch the curves of her mouth as she talked, especially when she spoke with determination.

"Well? What do you wish to do?! Platt, Platt?!"

"Oh, my dear, I think that you look so beautiful this evening. I would love to take you home at this very moment, but we might as well stay and enjoy a nice meal. Maybe something happened that caused their delay."

They were barely seated when they heard a familiar sound.

"Nellie! Platt! How are the newlyweds?!"

They looked up and saw Mr. and Mrs. Wickham. "Why hello! We

are deliriously happy. Thank you for asking. And how has your family been?" Nellie asked pleasantly.

"Oh, what a young woman you are to ask how two bothersome old people are. You are every bit as lovely as everyone goes on about."

"Why, Mrs. Wickham, I don't know what to say about all this fuss and flattery. I truly was inquiring about your well-being."

"I know, Nellie, that's what is so endearing. Anyway, we are quite well. We were supposed to meet my son and Hattie here for dinner. They had something rather important they wanted to discuss, but they were dreadfully late. This is totally unlike Frederick."

"That's also why we are here but they said nothing of it being a dinner party, did they Platt?" Nellie asked and looked towards her husband.

"No, my dear, there was no mention. All Hattie said was to be here at 7:00 sharp for dinner. Now, my concern is for their welfare and to make sure that no harm has befallen either of them. Nellie and Mrs. Wickham, you two can go ahead and order, if you would care to. Mr. Wickham and I will go and look for them. We will be back soon. Are you ready, sir?"

"Yes. Nothing could keep me from looking for my only son," Mr. Wickham replied and off they went to look for the missing couple.

"I think we should go to Jefferson's and make sure that Hattie left the house and Frederick was with her. Then, we will look around town. Do you remember if he said anything about running any errands or going anywhere tonight?"

"I am afraid that I am of no use. We just arrived back in town this afternoon and to be quite honest, I haven't had a decent conversation with my son in a while."

"Well, let's commence our search. We shall keep going until we find them."

Back at the restaurant, Nellie could think of nothing but her dear friend Hattie. She didn't know what she would do if some ill fate had befallen her. She loved Hattie as a sister. They had been best friends since Hattie came to live with the Jefferson's as a little girl.

Nellie was so deep in thought, she completely ignored Mrs. Wickham. "Oh, excuse me, I was just thinking about Hattie, and I let my mind wander. I do apologize. What were you saying?"

"Oh, my dear, you must not apologize. I was just rambling. I do that, especially when I am anxious. Please, would you tell me more about Hattie? I know so little about her. I only know what Frederick has told us but when I look in her eyes, there is so much more to her. She appears to have had a great deal of pain her past."

Nellie looked at her, amazed at her perception of Hattie's soul. "Hattie is my best friend and has the dearest soul. However, I think Hattie would be the best one to ask about that. She is private about feelings, and I don't feel it's my place to speak of things that she may want to keep locked away in her heart. I hope you understand."

"Oh, my dear. I would never want you to feel uncomfortable telling me anything regarding Hattie. My only goal was to get to know her more."

"I do understand that, but I must keep Hattie's privacy and comfort in mind. More importantly, I want to know why we haven't heard back from Platt and Mr. Wickham. I hope they were able to find Hattie and Frederick. This waiting is so difficult. I can't stand it a minute longer!" Nellie said as she rose from her chair and walked toward the window of the restaurant. She looked outside at the people coming in and out of the restaurant. Mrs. Wickham walked up beside her and gingerly rubbed her arm.

"I believe they are alright, and that no ill has befallen them. I can just feel it. Call it a mother's instinct, but I do have a nagging feeling that things are not as they should be. Let's go back and have some tea while we wait for the men to return. Maybe Hattie and Frederick will show up after all." They had some tea and talked as Platt and Mr. Wickham finally returned.

"We have been all over and found no sight of them. However, when we went back to Jefferson's and into Hattie's room, we found a letter addressed to us. Nellie, you had better read this." He handed the letter to her. Nellie looked at her husband and saw a look she was not accustomed to seeing, one of great concerns. She nervously unfolded the letter and began to read it.

"My dearest Sister Nellie and Platt,

I know that Frederick and I asked you two to join us for dinner, for we have some exciting news to share with you. After much discussion, we have decided to marry. Since both of my parents are gone and your parents just had the expense of your wedding, I couldn't ask them to assist financially. They have been better to me than anyone could dream of, taking me as one of their own children and never treating me as an indentured servant. I shared with Frederick what happened to my parents and he and I felt this was a better plan. In short, we have eloped, despite our plans of sharing our engagement with you and the Wickhams tonight. Please, my dear Nellie, do not hate me but only wish me happiness. I don't know what I would do without your blessing. I truly love him and want to make him happy. I'll write to you as soon as we have decided where we will live. Frederick is so well educated and smart. He has had several jobs offers and I know we will make a decision soon. We will let you all know just as soon as we are settled. I can't believe I am marrying such a wonderful man! I truly love him. Nellie, please grant me your blessing.

With all our love,
Hattie and Frederick"

Nellie sat there with the letter in her hand, staring into Platt's face, searching for something that could give her a sense of what she had just read. She wanted to rant and rave about the anger she felt but out of respect for Mrs. and Mr. Wickham, she refrained. Before she could utter a word, she saw Mrs. Wickham was crimson red. She feverishly fanned her face. Then, just as quickly as she went red, she went as white as a sheet.

"Come now, I am not feeling too well. I think we should be going. In fact, I feel as if I might swoon."

Just as she spoke, before anyone could get to her side to assist her, she fell to the floor. As her body collapsed, she struck her head on a chair which caused a large gash in the side of her scalp. Blood streamed out of the wound like water from a river. Nellie was in awe of how much blood poured out of Mrs. Wickham. But what surprised her even more was the fluidity of her husband's response. Platt knew exactly what to do and controlled the entire situation. He commanded the crowd, telling a man to get a doctor, asking another for a towel to stop the bleeding, and trying to keep everyone calm. He had Nellie stay with Mrs. Wickham and apply constant pressure to her head, to control the bleeding. Platt comforted the patrons in the restaurant and assured them the situation was well under control. The manager of the restaurant came out and spoke to Mr. Wickham and offered to do whatever he could.

Soon, the doctor arrived and was at Mrs. Wickham's side. He reached into his bag and pulled out a bottle of ammonia-smelling salt. He put it up to her nose and she moved her head slightly, as if starting to come around. He held it under her nose again and she moved her head from side to side and awoke.

"Oh my, what am I doing on the floor? And where is Frederick? Oh, now I remember." She rubbed her sore head. "He ran off and got married to that girl without our blessing, without us being present! What was he thinking? This is not typical behavior for my son! My boy is a good boy. It had to be that girl! How could he break a mother's heart like this?" She began to wail out of frustration.

"Now, don't get yourself upset. I'll need to take you to the office so I can suture that cut on your head. Then, you need to go home and get some rest," Doc said assuredly.

"But do you have a suture for the hole in my heart?!" Mrs. Wickham asked in desperation.

"I am afraid not. That will have to heal on its own with a lot of time, forgiveness, and love. You're the one who decides if you're going to hang on to the anger and keep the wound festering or not. If you do, it will destroy you while they live their lives. The decision is yours."

Mr. Wickham helped Mrs. Wickham to her feet. Platt jumped in to help and while unsteady, she walked out of the restaurant and over to Doc's office. Platt and Nellie decided they had enough excitement for one night and after making sure that Mrs. Wickham was in capable hands, they returned to their honeymoon cottage.

"Platt, I feel we must tell Mama and Papa about what has happened. They'll be expecting Hattie to come home and will be quite worried if they do not know. Will you come with me? I am feeling a bit weary and you're much better at this than I."

"Of course I will come with you, my darling. With all the excitement of the evening, I didn't take into account how all this was affecting you. Please forgive me. Are you feeling strong enough to go tonight or should we wait until morning?"

Nellie looked into his piercing eyes and all she saw was love. "No, I am alright. I'm just feeling very tired and my stomach is a little nauseated. It must be all the excitement. Let's go now and get it over with. Waiting will only be more torture. Shall we go?" She gestured toward her parents' house.

Nellie wondered how they would take the news. Would they be

angry? She had no idea what their response would be and her anxiety soared. They arrived at the door and Nellie's palms perspired as she looked at Platt.

"How am I going to tell them?" she asked with pure fright in her voice.

"We tell them the facts and the truth, no dramatization, just the facts. It will be alright, I promise." Platt guided his wife to the door and Nellie knocked quietly. Before Nellie could prepare herself, Papa answered the door.

"Platt, Nellie, come in. What are you two doing out this evening?"

"Oh Papa, we have news about Hattie and must speak with you and mama at once!"

Papa knew from the look on her face the situation was serious. He excused himself and went to go get mama.

"Alright, what is the emergency that can't wait until morning?" Mama asked as she came down the stairs in her dressing gown.

Nellie couldn't contain herself any longer. "Hattie, she is gone! She ran off to get married to Frederick and didn't even have the decency to come and talk to you first. I can't believe after everything you have done for her, she repays you by running off with that that scoundrel, Frederick!" Nellie said as she burst into sobs. "I should have been there for her. Maybe if I wasn't so consumed with myself, I could have foreseen this and warned her about what a monster he really is! What have I done to my friend, my dearest friend?"

Platt came over to console her, not knowing exactly what to say. He had never seen Nellie quite so emotional. She was outspoken and opinionated, but not usually given to tears this easily. Papa and mama looked at each other and then, Papa spoke.

"Nellie, my dear, you must realize that Hattie has a life of her own to discover and we cannot stand in her way. Hattie must have had a good reason for doing what she did. She has always had a good head on her shoulders and if she eloped, she must have thought it through and decided it was the best course of action for her and Frederick. You have to let her go and know that she has a life to live and deserves a chance at happiness. Of course, we feel disappointed that she didn't tell us herself, but her letter explained everything."

Nellie stopped crying and looked at her papa. "Letter?! What letter? You mean you both knew and did not tell me? How could you do that to me?" Nellie asked, searching her father's face for some comfort or explanation.

"Nellie, we just received the letter today and she asked that we not say anything to you. She wanted to explain herself to you and Platt. Of course, we thought she would do it in person, but this is the way she wanted, and we must respect that. Now, as for you, I think you have had enough excitement and need to retire for the night. We will discuss this further later." Papa embraced Nellie in a fatherly hug.

"Alright, we can discuss this further in the morning. I just feel so empty inside, as if I have lost my best friend forever."

Platt came over and embraced her tenderly. "It's all right Nellie. You still have me, always." He bent over and kissed her gently on the cheek.

"Good night and sleep peacefully. We shall talk more in the morning." Papa walked them to the door.

In the morning, Nellie awoke to a cheerful bird's song outside her window. Her stomach and head were spinning a bit. If only she could get beyond this feeling of desertion she felt at Hattie's abrupt elopement. Hattie was like a sister to her and now that tie was severed now that she was a Wickham. She felt frustrated and defenseless. She wanted to find her friend and bring her back home, but she decided to lay her thoughts aside for now. She had to get started on her daily chores. She arrived at her parents' house to begin the day and was quickly greeted by her mother.

"Heaven's sake, child you are looking pale this morning! Come on in and let's see what is ailing you."

"I don't know what has come over me. I was okay last night and now I cannot maneuver this morning without getting ill. Do you think I need to go see the Doc?"

Her mother looked at her. She knew exactly what was wrong with her daughter, but would wait and see what the Doctor's diagnosis was. "I will take you to see the Doctor if you feel you need to go."

"No. I think I will wait and see if it is just a sour stomach. I am sure that it will pass and I'll feel better after I eat something."

"Well, sit down and rest for a while. I will make you some peppermint tea and you can rest. You've had a lot of activity lately and I know it has been upsetting to you. Now, let me have Maude, our new housekeeper and maid, make you some breakfast."

Nellie sat there, sheepishly picking at her breakfast. She had no appetite and wasn't sure if it was from the nausea or the events of the past few days. She couldn't bring herself to eat.

"I feel I should go looking for Hattie, to make sure she is alright. I can't stand not knowing if she is alright and where she is. Mama, I don't trust Frederick at all. He is not a very honest man, not like Platt or papa. He is a spoiled and indulged man who is used to getting what he wants, when he wants it. I hope I am not out of line, but I hope he didn't take up with Hattie to get back at me for rejecting him and exposing his true character. I know that is an ugly thing to say, but I can't get this nagging thought out of my mind that he is going to end up hurting her. Mama, am I wrong in thinking this?"

"Nellie, you have to believe in Hattie and her choices. I know you have concerns of Frederick's character, but you have to trust in Hattie. You have known her for far too long and been through too much together to have a breech in your relationship. Remember, you must have faith in Hattie."

Nellie nodded her head in agreement, but she missed her friend. She knew she would see her again someday, she could sense it, but it didn't ease the emptiness she had in her heart. She felt, in the very pit of her stomach, that things were not as wonderful as she had tried to make them sound in her letter. The more she thought about it, the more she thought she might be responsible if something dreadful were to happen to Hattie. Before she knew it, tears were pouring out of her eyes, like ponds overflowing after a spring time rain.

"Nellie, whatever is the matter?" Mama asked as she sat down next to her and put an arm around her shoulder.

"What if something dreadful happens to Hattie? I'll feel it is my entire fault! I was too involved in my own life, with the wedding and the honeymoon. I was not spending time with her. I was too self-absorbed and thoughtless. Mama, I couldn't bear it if something terrible happened to her!"

"There, there Nellie. First of all, if something were to happen, it wouldn't be your fault. You are not the master of their destiny or anyone else's, not even your own. My daughter, God hold's our lives in his hands. We do not make up the rules. He knows and directs our lives as a sovereign god. So, trust in that and do not feel guilty for things that are completely out of your hand," Mama said as she comforted her Daughter.

Nellie was a passionate person, but not one usually to give into emotion. This outburst even surprised her. "Mama, I don't know what is wrong with me. I think I am just tired from everything that has happened recently. I will be alright when I get settled. In fact, I should be getting back to the cottage and putting some more things away and arranged before the day gets away from me. Thank you for breakfast and most of all, for understanding. I am so very fortunate to have a wonderful mother like you," Nellie said as she gave her a mama an affectionate hug.

"Nellie, why don't you let Maude help you with the cottage She is so fast with her work around here, that I fear she gets bored. It would give me great pleasure to have her help you, especially in light of your feeling so poorly this morning."

Nellie wondered what Platt would think. He was a very proud man and was already having difficulty swallowing his pride and accepting the offer to live in the cottage. She wasn't sure what his reaction would be, but she was so tired. She felt as if she couldn't put one foot in front of the other, so she accepted the gracious offer of help, just this once.

"Alright, I will let Maude help me get settled, but not too much and only because I am so tired. I just do not have the energy today. I will do the rest myself tomorrow after I have rested. Hopefully that this touch of influenza, or whatever it is, will be gone and I'll be back to my old self."

"Very well then, now go on home and rest. I will send Maude over shortly. Do you want me to take you to see the Doctor?"

"No Mama, I am fine but thank you for the offer." Nellie excused herself and left out the back door that led down to the cottage. *Why am I so tired? I always have an overabundance of energy and now I am so tired and nauseous.* She was beginning to get concerned that maybe something horrific was happening to her. She decided she wouldn't jump to conclusions. After all, she had no other symptoms. She would wait and see what happened for surely, all of it would resolve after a day or two.

That evening Platt came home and saw the house was spotless and dinner was in the oven, smelling mighty good. He asked Nellie what she had been up to during the day and if she had been slaving away all day.

"I am sorry to disappoint you, my sweet husband, but I was not feeling well today and mother offered Maude's services. But, it was for today only so don't become accustomed to the exquisite meals."

At first, Platt was not sure of how he felt about his mother-in-law's maid doing his housework and cooking, but the smell of the food and the look on his wife's face made his pride take a back seat.

"Well, since Maude went to all this work, I think that it is only befitting that we are not rude and eat all of this delicious food. Here, let me help you to the table and then we can partake in this scrumptious meal."

Nellie was so pleased that Platt's pride was not wounded and he handled it graciously, as he always seemed to. After dinner, they shared about their day and Platt was so anxious to tell Nellie his exciting news. Earlier that day, he found out today about the departure date of the wagon train out west. They would finally be on the road to seeing their dream of being settlers come true. Nellie shared his enthusiasm and they talked and talked about what they would need to take with them while they were traveling and getting established. It was going to be a new way of life for them, but Nellie but was ready for a new adventure.

When Platt spoke of the new Washington territory and home steading, his eyes would begin to dance. He would get so excited that he would talk with his hands in grand motions, gesturing the high mountains and the great rivers. He spoke adoringly of the beauty of the country where you could backpack in the wilderness to hunt deer, elk, moose, and even bear.

Nellie knew their lives would never be the same and found herself anxious to start the journey. Nellie was excited and yet, knew that all the niceties and luxuries she had grown up with would cease to exist. For now, she would appreciate everything and prepare for their new world adventure.

That night, Nellie was feeling much better and felt confident that it was nothing more than a virus or a bad case of nerves that had ailed her. She was relieved and glad to be in the arms of the man she loved. That seemed to be the cure for almost anything that ailed her. Platt smiled and looked at her, caught with the beauty of the woman that took the breath right out of his lungs. He caressed her back and began to gently kiss her up her neck. They met in a passionate kiss that led to undressing. Nellie was being loved by the most handsome and wonderful man in the world, and she loved every minute of it.

That night after lovemaking, Nellie laid in Platt's arms. They spoke of their new adventure and Platt told Nellie how pleased he was that she was so agreeable. He knew what an adjustment it would be for her, leaving her life in California and her family behind. Nellie propped herself up on her elbows so she could look intently into Platt's piercing eyes.

"Platt, don't you know by now that you are my family? Wherever you go, I am going because we are together forever."

Platt pulled her into a deep passionate kiss. "I love you so much, Nellie."

The next morning, Nellie woke to find Platt had already gone to work. She felt queasy so she decided to eat something but didn't feel better after breakfast. She busied herself with chores around the cottage but truth be known, there was little to do since Maude lent her assistance. She decided it was a good time to make a list of things they would need to take with them on their journey out west. Before she knew it, she spent half the day working on it. There was going to be much more to this adventure than she first imagined. *Oh! Platt is never going to let me take all this with us! We will never get it all there in a wagon.* She figured they would have to take only what was really necessary to start a new life. For the rest, they would do without or acquire there once get settled. *What would this new land be like? Would there be any other settlers there? Would a town be far away?* These questions ran through her mind and she did not want to bother Platt with them, as this might signal to him that she was not in agreement about going on this adventure. She certainly was but at the same time, she could not help but be apprehensive of the unknown.

If only she could start to feel better. The nagging nausea, bouts of vomiting, and the smell of food was more than she could tolerate on some days. She endured it but told herself if it persisted, she would make an appointment with the Doctor.

After studying her list until she was almost cross-eyed, she decided to go over and visit her mama. They went down town for some shopping and walked for miles to enjoy the beautiful sunny day. After spending a lovely afternoon with her mama, she went home to start dinner for her husband. He would be coming home hungry after working all day on the railroad. Platt came home that evening, bursting with enthusiasm over the new routes that the railroad was planning to run. Some of the new routes would go all the way to Washington. He was so excited for the adventure of making the move in a covered wagon, but he almost considered making it as far as they could by train and completing the journey by wagon.

"Nellie, what do you think of that possibility?"

She looked at him, thinking carefully about what the proper response would be. Her heart was pounding so hard, she thought it might burst through her chest. She wanted to yell from the mountain tops that she desperately wanted to go by train. At the same time, she did not want deprive her husband from his adventure. It was something he had been planning and dreaming about for so long.

"Platt, let's wait and see where the routes run. When we are closer to the departure date, I will give you a more definitive answer, if that is acceptable to you. I know how much you have been looking forward to this whole adventure."

Knowing that Nellie was willing to endure hardship all for the sake of his dream, made him love her all the more. He kissed her lovingly. Nellie smiled and leaned against his strong chest, loving the warmth and security she felt when she was there. She never realized how wonderful it would be being married. It was far beyond what she ever imagined.

The next morning, Nellie decided there was no time like the present to plan their moving details. Since Nellie loved to organize, it seemed like a perfect to use of her time. *What do you take when you move across country and start a new life?* She thought it shouldn't be so foreign to her since her family had relocated just a few years prior, but that was different. They had their belongings sent by train and wagon freight. This was entirely different and she wanted to take everything with her, but she went about selecting the items that were necessities. She selected items such as bedding, linens, cookware, and winter clothing. She hadn't had to use her thick coats since she lived in Indiana and was uncertain of how harsh the winters would be. All the frivolity she had become accustomed to though out her life would soon vanish. She knew the first few years would be the most adventurous of her life and she was getting more and more excited about it.

She'd gotten carried away with her project and totally forgot about eating breakfast. It was now past lunch and she was well into the organizing stage. She stood up and became so dizzy and nauseated that she passed out. As she fell to the floor, Nellie hit her head on the edge of the table, causing a rather large laceration. She laid on the cold ground, bleeding profusely and with no one the wiser to her circumstance.

Mama had gone into town that morning and hadn't heard from Nellie all day. She wanted to show her the new dress she purchased from the General Store, for they had just received a new shipment of dresses. She was excited to tell Nellie the news, but thought about waiting until the following day as not to disturb her. Mama decided she would visit and went over to the cottage. She knocked on the door but there was no answer. How strange, mama thought to herself. She knew Nellie was home but thought she was taking a nap and didn't want to disturb her. She began to walk back to the main house and as she passed the window, she saw a pair of feet lying on the floor. Mama knew something was wrong so she tried to open the front door but it was locked. Mama ran to the back of the house and gasped a sigh of relief as she realized the back door was unlocked. She burst through the door and frantically yelled Nellie's name. She rushed into the dining room and saw Nellie lying on the floor with a pool of blood around her head. She ran to Nellie's side and scooped her head up into her lap.

"Nellie, wake up! Please wake up, my child," she pleaded with her daughter as she gently put her head down. She ran over to the sink and got a towel. She held it tightly against the laceration to try and stop the bleeding. Once the bleeding began to subside, she found a pillow for her head and tightly tied the towel around her to act as a make shift bandage. She carefully placed Nellie's head on the pillow and ran as fast as she could to her house.

She explained the situation to Maude and begged her to find the doctor. Maude had never moved so quickly and was out of the house in seconds. Mama returned to Nellie's side with a cool rag to clean up the blood from her face. After what felt like an eternity, Maude returned, practically dragging the doctor with her.

Doc bent down on his knees and examined Nellie. He took some smelling salts out of his bag and held them under her nose and she began to come around. Doc quickly realized she would require stitches. The gash was big and quite deep but fortunately, it was in her hair line and the scar would likely never show once healed. Doc warned Nellie that sutures were incredibly painful and they usually put patients under anesthesia for such a procedure. However, because she suffered a head injury and no one was privy as to what caused the syncope episode, he had no choice but to do it without anesthesia. He gave Nellie a clean cloth and told her to bite on it as he did the sutures. He knew putting needles into damaged tissue would be nearly intolerable. Despite Nellie being brave and enduring the pain, Doc noticed tears streaming down her cheek as he carefully sutured her head. He repeatedly asked how she was doing and she would always reply, "Oh, I am just fine." Once Doc had her sutured up and bandaged, he switched his focus to the cause of her injury.

"Now tell me, young lady, what happened today?"

Nellie, still holding her aching head, sat there and pondered. "Well sir, I am not certain. I was trying to organize our things and prioritize what would be necessary for our new adventure. I had been working on it for several hours when I realized I hadn't eaten all day. That's when I stood up to get something to eat and the next thing I knew, mama was here picking me up off the floor. I honestly don't remember anything else."

Doc looked at her, puzzled. "Have you ever had an episode like this before?" Nellie thought for a moment and looked at her mother.

"No never before," Mama said quietly and Nellie nodded.

"Have you felt nauseated, extremely fatigued, and emotional recently?"

"Yes, I have! Do you know what is wrong with me? I thought it was because of all the pressure I have been under as of lately. Getting married, my best friend leaving, and now, preparing for an adventure has been a lot to handle."

"Come to my office tomorrow morning with your husband and I will examine you further. For now, you, my dear, are to stay in bed and let everybody else wait on you hand and foot. I will leave some pain medication, but I only want you take it if it's unbearable until I can examine you further. Very well then, tomorrow it is. Now, if you have any problems, you let me know." With a tip of his hat, he was off and out the door."

Mama ran after the Doctor. "Thank you so very much for coming so quickly and taking such superior care of our Nellie. We are truly grateful," Mama said as she shook his hand. Mama walked back to the living room, where she had left her daughter who was now trying to make her way to the kitchen.

"What on earth are you doing, child? Did you not just hear the doctor's orders?" In a rare occurrence, mama raised her voice to Nellie."

"I am going to start dinner for my husband, who will be home soon and deserves to have his supper waiting for him." She paused briefly. "Oh mama! If he knows what is wrong with me, why wouldn't he tell me now?"

"Because, he is not certain and until he is, he doesn't want to give a diagnosis. Now, don't worry and please lay back down on the sofa. We will have dinner brought over to you tonight. I have Maude making enough for you and Platt, so please, just lie down and be a good patient."

Nellie managed to take a nap she but when she woke up her, head was pounding. The doctor told her to only take the medication if absolutely necessary. What kind of Doctor tells a patient with an injury such a thing? She thought to herself. She was deep in thought when she heard her husband bursting through the door.

"Nellie, where are you? You're never going to believe what happened down at the railroad today! It was the—" He stopped mid-sentence as he saw his wife with a large bandage around her head. His heart stopped. "Nellie! What in blazes happened?" he asked as he rushed to her side.

Nellie proceeded to recall what she could remember about the events of the afternoon.

"Darling, how is the pain?" Platt stroked her head, gently, as to not cause any further pain.

"Platt, the doctor needs both of us to be at the office tomorrow. Can you come?"

"Of course I will be there, just let me know what time. You are the most important thing in the world to me," he said as he bent over and kissed her gently.

Mama had taken leave back to the main house. She was on her way back to the cottage when she saw Platt was home. She knocked on the door.

"Come in, this is your house."

Mama responded quickly. "Nonsense, it is your home for now and I respect that. Anyway, I am here with the supper Maude made for the two of you. I will set it on the kitchen table. I knew Nellie was in no shape to cook tonight, so we had Maude make extra. I do hope she feels like eating by now. I will leave you two alone for now, good night."

"Thank you for your thoughtfulness," Platt called out after her and she waved in response.

After they finished the wonderful dinner Maude prepared, they retired for the evening. Platt held Nellie close. She had a stressful day and he was concerned about the doctor's visit the next day. The night was spent trying to reassure her and letting her rest in his arms. The next morning, Nellie was up earlier than normal. She didn't sleep well due to the pain in her head and her concern of what the Doctor would say. Platt woke to find Nellie up and busy in the kitchen making him breakfast.

"Are you sure you should be up, doing all this after yesterday? But, I must admit, it does smell delightful." He pressed a gentle kiss to her cheek.

"I feel much better today and besides, I can't let a little thing like this get me down. I have so much to do before we leave," she said with a smile as she brought Platt's breakfast to the table.

Nellie sat down with a cup of tea and toast and began going over her organization plan with Platt. She talked incessantly when she was nervous or excited and Platt listened intently. He smiled as he saw the excitement in her eyes grow with each detail. They talked, for what seemed like hours, when Platt looked at his pocket watch and interrupted.

"My dear, it's time for us to head to the Doctor's office."

Nellie sat impatiently in the waiting room. Platt held her hand and gently stroked her palm to try and comfort her. After waiting for what seemed like a century, Nellie's name was called. The doctor took them back to the examination room. He removed the bandages and checked the suture line for any signs of infection. After being satisfied with the condition of the wound, he wanted to examine her more thoroughly to try and diagnose why she fainted. He drew some blood and completed his examination. He asked her to get dressed and to join him and Platt in his office to discuss his findings. She got dressed in record time. She desperately wanted to find out why she had been feeling so ill. She thought, maybe, he would diagnose her with anemia or diabetes. She prayed, whatever the diagnosis was, would not affect their plans for their westward adventure. Nellie joined the two at the doctor's desk.

"Well, I think I can say for certain what the diagnosis is, even without looking at the blood under a microscope. Nellie, you are approximately 8 weeks pregnant. This will put your delivery date at, approximately, the first or second week of November. That explains everything, the nausea, the fainting, and the loss of appetite. You two are going to be parents. Now, when was your last menstrual cycle?"

Nellie looked dumbfounded. It was a lot to take in all at once. She didn't know what to say, so she just sat for a moment. "It was a week before the wedding and nothing since. But, how can this be? We have been careful."

"Not careful enough, but you two will be wonderful parents. You do want children, don't you?"

"Yes, we do," they answered in unison.

"Doctor, are you sure? Not that I am questioning you, but are you positive that we are going to be parents, that I am going to be a father?"

"I've brought many babies into this world and yes, I am very sure you two are prospective parents. It will be a few months before the baby is born. You have plenty of time to get moved and settled out west. Nellie, you are in excellent health and I have no concerns about your trip. We will continue to monitor you and the baby until you go."

Nellie hadn't even thought about the possibility of pregnancy. She glanced at Platt, wondering what his thoughts were. She wondered if he would be upset and was reluctant to make eye contact with him. She stared at the floor for the longest time. Finally, she looked up at Platt, whose face adorned the biggest smile she had ever seen.

"Platt," she said quietly as she looked at him with worried eyes.

He reached over and kissed her. "Nellie we are going to be parents! Thank you! Thank you, Doc! This is the best news we could have heard. I was a little shocked at first, but this is wonderful news." He shook Doc's hand firmly.

He took his wife's arm and led her to door. "Isn't that great, Nellie? We will be parents! It will be the most special baby ever born. We have to tell our parents! How should we do it? Should we invite them over for a dinner party and tell everyone the news? No, maybe that would be too much for you right now. I don't want to put extra work on you. I know some folks keep this kind of news quiet, but I think we should shout it from the highest mountain top. I am so thrilled at the thought of being a father! I know you will be an excellent mother. Oh Nellie, our lives are perfect, aren't they?"

Nellie was relieved to see how ecstatic Platt was. It made the news even more special. It was a moment to savor and cherish forever. They walked home, hand in hand, and admired the beautiful day. The sun seemed to shine a little brighter and the sky looked a little bluer. Despite being near delirium with happiness, Nellie couldn't help but worry about the trip. The pregnancy changes everything, she thought. She didn't want to ruin the atmosphere of the moment, so she decided to wait to discuss their options.

"Nellie, what do you want to do? We could meet our parents at the diner, or have them over for cake and coffee?" Platt asked excitedly.

Nellie snapped back to reality. "I am sorry, my dear. I'm afraid I wasn't listening. My mind was stuck on a multitude of details and this is just so much to absorb at once. Whichever is fine with me. Although, we would have more privacy to talk at home so to answer your question, I think dessert and coffee is the best option. I will make my lemon pound cake. Both of our parents really enjoy it. Well, I better get started."

She looked at him with a sparkle in her eyes that was so magnificent, he was uncertain if he had ever seen such beauty before. He wrapped his arms around her tiny waist and patted her stomach as he kissed her neck.

"Now, don't be starting that or I'll never get the pound cake made."

Nellie found herself in a fit of laughter as she recalled Platt's face when the doctor told them the news. He went from a ghostly white to crimson red in a matter of seconds. She smiled incessantly as she carefully measured and mixed the ingredients. Before the cake was finished baking, Platt returned home after extending an invitation to their parents, careful not to give way to any hints of their surprise.

"Darling, are you feeling alright?"

She looked at him sternly. "Platt, neither of us are going to make it through this pregnancy if you don't stop hovering over me. I will tell you if I am feeling poorly. There may be days that I am too tired to do anything, but I will always let you know. I appreciate you caring and being a wonderful expectant father, but Platt, I am not the first woman to be with child. I do not wish to be rude, but you do understand, don't you?"

Platt walked over to her and spoke softly. "But Nellie, you're my wife and this is our first baby. I am just elated with this news and I want your pregnancy to go off without a hitch." He lowered his head and kissed her.

"I understand my dear." She paused briefly. "Is everyone coming over for coffee and cake? Were you able to speak with them?"

"Oh yes, our parents, I spoke with them."

Nellie bit the corner of her lip, which she always did when she was nervous. "And? Are they coming?"

Yes, my dear. They are, indeed, coming over for cake and coffee at about 7:00 p.m. Is that acceptable with you?" He winked at her and smiled playfully.

"Very acceptable."

Nellie and Platt busied themselves with preparations and just as they finished their chores, the first guests arrived. To no surprise, her parents arrived early. After all, they only had to walk across the garden to the cottage.

"Welcome! Come in and make yourselves at home, after all, it is your home."

"Well, what is the big announcement you invited us here for?"

Nellie nervously looked at her and wondered what Platt had told them. "Can't we invite our families over for cake and coffee just because we want to see you?"

Before anyone could give an answer, there was a knock on the door. Platt jumped up to get it and welcomed his family in. Nellie was a gracious hostess and served everyone their share of cake and coffee.

"Well son, what's the big announcement you brought us all together for tonight?"

Platt stood with Nellie's hand in his. "It appears that we are not able to prolong the inevitable. Without further ado, Nellie and I invited you here tonight to inform you of the diagnosis and prognosis that the doctor gave Nellie today."

Everyone's faces grew grim with concern. "What is it, Platt?" Mary Jefferson asked in desperation.

"I am elated to announce that we will be parents in a few short months! Nellie is with child!" But, the reaction was not quite what he expected.

"Platt, we already knew that. We thought you were going to tell us about a change in plans for your trip."

Platt and Nellie just stood there, confused as ever. "Now, how could you have known? We just found out a few hours ago?" Everyone laughed but Platt and Nellie. "What? Please tell me, what is so funny? I must have missed the punch line."

"Darling, you are not the first woman to be pregnant. You had all the symptoms. We just needed an official diagnosis. It's all right, Nellie. A lot of women do not realize they are with child at first. But, isn't this wonderful A baby?!"

The rest of the evening was spent in talk about babies and the wonderful miracle of a child. Not much was mentioned about the move out west and yet, Nellie knew it must be addressed and soon. But not tonight, tonight was for celebration of a life yet to be born.

Nellie found that she had fewer days of nausea and her strength was increasing as the fatigue was decreasing with each passing day. She began to notice her waistline increasing. She was still able to wear all her own clothes, for which she was thankful for, but she knew that her body didn't look the same.

She was excited about being pregnant and starting a family, and yet, she felt she hadn't had the time to plan and prepare. There was so much to be done in such a short time. There was still the unanswered question about how they were going to move, by train or by wagon. They hadn't finished that discussion, but she knew it must be addressed and soon. She decided that evening at dinner, she would talk to Platt about it.

When Platt came home from work that evening, he was bustling with news about an attempted robbery down at the railroad. He excitedly depicted how he was involved in bringing the robbers to justice. He was so excited he could hardly contain himself with enthusiasm.

"I never realized how much of a thrill it could be to be a part of bringing someone to justice! I was not fearful. It was so natural to me, Nellie, like I had done it all my life. Well, what do you think?"

Nellie could see the enthusiasm in his face and she knew it was in his blood. After all, his father had been a circuit judge in Marshall, Indiana and he always had a love for the law and justice. "Platt, I can see you're unharmed, which is my first concern. I know your passion for the law and seeing that it is obeyed. Just promise me one thing that you will always come home to me and you can chase all the outlaws you want." Nellie walked into his waiting arms and embraced him. Platt couldn't resist and kissed her passionately. He carried her off to the bedroom and laid her on the bed. He looked at the woman carrying his child and thought she had a glow about her. He stared at her in amazement.

"Is everything alright?" Nellie asked after he had been staring for some time.

"Everything is better than alright. Nellie, it is perfect." He cherished her more in that moment than he ever thought humanly possible.

Platt knew that decisions must be made soon regarding the move out west and he needed to set the ball in motion. He knew the entire trip was entirely out of the question, especially now, with Nellie in her delicate condition. Her health was to be considered with the greatest of care. After all, she was carrying their future son or daughter. The thought of it overwhelmed him with joy. He would make his little family proud and be a good provider, just as his father was and his brothers are for their families. He refused to be the disappointment in the family tree. And with that determination, he decided to make the plans to move out west. His mind embraced every detail as his wife sleep peacefully next to him.

The next evening he arrived home from work and was so excited, he could hardly contain himself. He wanted to appear nonchalant, so he came into the house acting as if it had been just another day at the railroad track. Nellie asked about his day and they spoke briefly and when Platt could no longer keep himself composed, he interjected.

"Nellie, those men I helped capture the other day, well, there was a bounty on their heads. The sheriff came to see me today and gave me this." Platt shoved a handful of bills towards her.

"Platt, I don't know what to say and I am afraid to ask how much is here. It looks like a great amount! What are you going to do with it?"

Platt looked at her, half in disbelief in what he just heard. "Nellie, darling, do you not know by now that whatever I have is ours? I do have a dream of what we can do with this money, but I wanted to talk it over first. I am not a dictator. We are a team and we make these family decisions together, not independent of each other."

Nellie felt a little embarrassed. "What is it that you have in mind? Let's discuss it."

Platt divulged his plan to use the money for the move. The money he earned would cover the expense of the train and it would be much more comfortable for her to travel. The more he talked, the closer Nellie was to packing her bag and leaving that very night. After discussing their plans for most of the evening, Platt looked at Nellie earnestly.

"Darling, we may need to move up our departure date, if we are to be there before the baby arrives. That way we have time to build a house and get settled for the winter. What do you think?"

Nellie's heart fully trusted in his wisdom. "Whatever you think is a good time line for us, but we need to remember that A.L. is planning on making this move with us. If we are changing plans we need to let him know."

Platt had been so engrossed in everything that was going on in his own little world, he hadn't given a second thought to his brother. He had always been there for him and was so agreeable; he just assumed that A.L. would go along with whatever he planned. But, Nellie was right. He must be considerate and speak with him.

The next morning, Platt was out of bed at dawn and hurried over to his parent's home. A.L. was excited to hear that Platt and Nellie were still planning on making the move. The more they spoke about moving and pioneering, the more excited they both became.

"I wish we could go today!" A.L. said with such enthusiasm that it almost surprised Platt.

"So do I, but it will be here before you know it. In fact, if you look at the calendar, we are only weeks away and there is still so much to get done before we depart. Are you positive you haven't had a change of heart and still want to go on this adventure with us?"

A.L. looked at him rather puzzled, since he was the one doing all the pushing on this adventure. To appease his brother, he stood up and put his hand on his shoulder with a firm grasp. "Platt, I haven't been this sure about anything in a long time. I am with you all the way, no matter what we encounter along the way." He gave him a brotherly hug. "Now, let's go get ready!"

The time that Nellie was dreading as endless days of boredom while waiting for their move, had suddenly changed into days filled with packing and organization. She struggled with what would go with them on the train, the wagon train, and what would be saved to use later to set up the house. Previously, she never had to think beyond what dress she would wear to the next big event. Now, she was thinking about the new addition to the Corbaley household and planning to take things that a new baby might need. She was the youngest daughter and had no idea about caring for a new baby. She wondered how she would do it without a maid or her own mother. But, she knew no matter what, she would love the child. It was the product of her and Platt, so it had to be the most wonderful child who ever lived. She loved it already and she was sure she was beginning to feel it move inside her stomach. As she was deep in thought about her precious baby, she found herself rubbing her stomach and talking to it, as if it could hear her. There was a sudden knock at the door and Nellie was brought back to reality.

She opened the door and was elated. "Mama, do come in!"

"No, I am not staying and neither are you. My dear, get your hat and bag. We are going shopping! You are getting too large for your clothes and you need maternity clothes if you're going to make it through this pregnancy. So, come along and let's go find you something more matronly to wear."

Nellie went to get her bag and thought to herself, do I really look that big and awful? Or, was this just mother's way of trying to help out.

"Do I really need new clothes, mama?"

Mama could see her daughter was having a difficult time with having to transition to maternity clothes. "Darling, it is a very natural process. As the baby grows, so does your waist line. It's normal. Why, it happened to me all three times! It was the worst with you, I believe. I gained weight, but I lost it all after you were born. It was a small price to pay to have been blessed with such a perfect daughter."

They shopped at all the stores in town and bought material for Maude to make her some new frocks. It was one more thing Nellie could mark off her list of things to do before the move. After a long day of shopping, Nellie was surprised to have a knock at the door again.

"Mama, you didn't want to go on another shopping trip, did you?" Nellie asked with a smile on her face.

"Nellie, I was speaking with father and we would like to take you and Platt to dinner or have you two over to the house, which ever you prefer. We have something we want to discuss with you."

"That sounds serious. Mama, is everything all right?"

"It is more than all right. My dear, just let me know as soon as possible so I can have Maude start dinner preparations, or hold on them, whichever is the case."

"Alright, let me be so bold and make the decision for both of us, since Platt is working, and say we come over to your house for dinner. Platt does enjoy Maude's cooking."

"Alright then, dinner tonight, shall we say 7:00?"

"Perfect, we shall see you tonight."

What on earth could be so important that they want to call a family dinner? Maybe it's about the name of their first grandchild and they want naming rights! She had no idea what it could be, but what she did know was their shopping trip cost her a whole day of packing and organizing. She needed make the most of the time she had left in the day and get started.

Platt came home and Nellie greeted him at the door with a kiss and hugs.

"Alright, you either did something very good or something very bad. Which is it?"

"Platt, what makes you think I did either? Maybe I just wanted to greet my handsome husband with a kiss. And, my parents have invited us to dinner. Mama said she needed to talk to us about something with grave importance. Also, mama took me shopping for new maternity clothes today."

Nellie said the last part rather speedily because she knew it bothered Platt when her mother spent money on her. Now that she was married, it made him feel like he was not providing for her in the manner she was accustomed to and it made him feel inadequate. Nellie reassured Platt that he was anything but inadequate in every area of their lives. Platt looked at her, perplexed, but in the interest of not wanting to start a quarrel that he was positive he would lose, he kept quiet.

"Well darling, show me what you got on your shopping trip."

Nellie showed him her new wardrobe and Platt was, surprisingly, thankful to his mother-in-law for taking her.

"We are expected for dinner at 7:00. Is that alright with you?"

Platt nodded in agreement as he went off to the bedroom to change. Nellie decided to make use of their time and discuss the trip.

"Platt, I have most of the trunks organized and know which ones will go on the train and which ones will serve as storage for our house keeping items. But, it's the baby I am not sure about. I don't know what I am going to need for the baby!" she said with exasperation and concern on her face.

Platt spoke gingerly. "Nellie, the baby won't need a lot at first, just a cradle, some diapers, clothes, and lots of love. Don't fret. I know you will be an excellent mother." He kissed her forehead.

Nellie looked at him and smiled. She knew he was going to be a wonderful father. There was no doubt, for he had already proved himself to be a superior husband. Some days, she thought it was surely a dream and at any given moment, she would awaken. She was so thankful he wasn't a dream, but very real and every bit as wonderful. She continued to admire him as they walked toward her parent's home.

"Nellie, we are here. Shall we knock? My love, are you feeling alright? You're acting rather peculiar this evening. Is it from the head injury? Is everything okay with the baby?"

"No, I am fine. I was just letting my mind wander. I do apologize. Yes, by all means, let's find out what my parents have to tell us."

Nellie reached up to knock when Platt, who had been looking at his beautiful wife, became overcome with sentiment. He grasped her arm, pulled her close, and kissed her passionately. It was more passionate than he had intended, and it left them both breathless.

"Well, what ever brought that on?"

Platt tried desperately to recover. "I could resist your beauty and charm no longer." He smiled and kissed her again, this time lightly, and they both laughed. They laughed so loudly they didn't even need to knock. Maude opened the door within seconds.

"Mr. Platt and Ms. Nellie, won't you please come in and join the others in the parlor?"

"Others? Who on earth could she be referring to? Platt, do you know anything about this?"

"Remember Nellie, you are the one who informed me about this meeting tonight. I am totally unaware of what is going on, but there is no time like the present to find out. Let's go," Platt said as he ushered his wife into the parlor.

They were greeted by not only both sets of their parents, but A.L. and Platt's older brother, William.

"Well, what do we owe the pleasure of everyone's company? Has anyone expired or won a great gold strike? If that is the case, please remember me as your most devoted sibling or child." Platt said with a wink and a smile, as he always seemed to do. Everyone laughed in unison.

Richard Corbaley stood up and shook his head. "No, I am afraid it is not near as glamorous as all of that. The reason we called you here tonight is because we know you three, Platt, Nellie and A.L., are planning an adventure out West. We know this is a new adventure and a new start but with the addition to your family and being so far away from home as you're starting a new family, we would like to join you on your new adventure. But, only if that is agreeable with the two of you. I know Mary wants to be with Nellie when she goes through delivery, especially since it is your first child. It is just plain exciting, even at our age! What do you two think?! Now, you don't have to give us an answer right away. You can think about it and if you decide you do not want us there, we will not be offended. We all know what it is like to be young and wanting to be independent."

Platt and Nellie looked at each other, not needing to say a word. They knew what the other was thinking, from just a glance. This had been their dream for so long but lately, they had some major concerns. This was the answer they had been searching for.

"Yes!" they said in unison.

Everyone was so excited and spoke incessantly. Platt and Nellie decided to listen and let the group have their fun.

After a while, Richard looked at Platt. "Son, what do you and Nellie think about all of this? What do you have planned?"

Platt looked at Nellie, who nodded at him in approval. Platt excitedly explained his meticulous plan. He told everyone their time table for leaving and how they were going to travel by train as far as possible, then take a wagon the rest of the way. I diligently mapped out the course and the time table for departure."

"I am thrilled that Mr. & Mrs. Jefferson will be joining us. My suggestion is that we make sure we will have adequate housing accommodations in advance. You do understand this is uncharted territory that is vast, untamed, and unsettled? It is no place for the weak of heart."

After careful deliberation, the decision was made that Jane would stay in California with their other son until proper accommodations could be made for her in the new country. She and Richard felt good about their decision, knowing the path they must blaze was not an easy one. She could see the excitement in Richard's face as he spoke of the unchartered land. She knew it would be difficult being apart but knew it was for the best. She wondered what the new land would be like, and was excited for when she was able to make the journey.

Chapter Eleven
Westward Hoe

The day they had dreamed of for so long was, at last, here. They were ready to board the train and start their move out west, to their new land of opportunity.

"Is everyone ready to board the train? Is there anything we might have forgotten? Mary can bring anything forgotten with her in a month, when she joins us. So, let's get boarded and say our goodbyes. The train is about to pull away from the station."

Nellie struggled with saying goodbye to her parents. She knew it wouldn't be long until her mama joined her and it would go by quickly, yet, she had a strange feeling she couldn't shake. She goodbye to her papa and hugged his neck for the longest time. She didn't ever want to let go.

"There, little Nellie, it's not like we will never see each other again. Time will go fast and we will be reunited," he said as tears streamed down his cheeks.

It was difficult letting go of his little girl, but she was grown and would soon be a Mother. *How did this happen? Where had the time gone? It all happened too quickly.* Lester loved Platt, but the realization that she replaced him with someone else hurt, even though he was happy for her. He knew he would always be her father, but things would never be the same. Yet, he knew things were as they were supposed to be, he just never imagined how difficult saying goodbye would be. They finished hugging and they were both in tears. Nellie boarded the train just before it pulled out of station.

"I will miss you both so much, but we will see each other soon!"

She waved from the back of the train until they were no longer visible. She turned and burst into tears, burying herself in Platt's chest. He held her close and let her cry. He knew that words would fall short in easing the pain. He was not immune to the feeling she was experiencing and wanted to comfort her. This was the first time she had been such a distance from her folks. After she wept, she felt better and was ready to begin their journey.

"Platt, I know I am very emotional, but I can't escape this feeling I have that today may be the last time I see my father. I know it's silly and probably from all the excitement of the journey and being pregnant, but I wanted you to know." Nellie laid her head against his chest. It felt like the safest place in the world to be.

Platt lifted her chin to face him. "Nellie, I don't think that you're ridiculous. Whatever you're feeling, I want to know and experience it with you. That's part of being married. I don't discount what you're feeling about your father, but maybe it's because this is the first time you've had a major life changing event without your father being a direct influence. Either way, I am here now and always will be for you, my love." He reached down and kissed her tenderly. She laid her head back on his chest, feeling more confident and safe.

Platt was so excited, he felt like a child in a candy store. He took out his maps and studied the routes and mountain terrains, in hopes there would be no surprises. As he studied the maps, he couldn't help but keep his mind from wondering to his beautiful wife and, soon to be, mother of their child. *What would he be like? No, it's too early to assume it's a boy! Will I be a good father? Nellie will be an excellent mother! There is no doubt. I will have to teach him how to hunt and fish! I will do it, just as my father taught me.*

"Aren't you tired of studying those maps?" Nellie asked as she realized he was looking outside and not at the maps in his hands.

"No, I was just day dreaming, I guess. Maybe, I will take a nap in our berth. Would you like to join me?" he asked with a wink in his eyes.

"Why, Mr. Corbaley, it is the middle of the day."

"I know, my dear." He took his wife by the hand and led her to their berth.

Platt sat straight up in bed, looking around the room with wild eyes. He scanned every corner as his heart pounded in his chest. He looked out the window and realized they slept all night and completely missed dinner. *Why had no one from our family knocked on the door to wake us? Why is it so quiet on the train? Something is most definitely wrong, I can sense it!*

He gently nudged Nellie. "My dear, get up and get dressed quickly. We slept through the evening and now it is morning. Aside from that,

I have a strange feeling that something is wrong on the train, now hurry! Don't ask a lot of questions, just hurry please," Platt pleaded.

Nellie had never seen him quite so serious and acted with lightning speed. In an attempt to lighten the mood, he made a comment as to why she didn't always get ready that fast.

"Nellie, you wait here while I look around and see what is going on. It may be nothing, but I have a feeling in my gut and I've learned to trust it. I'll be back, but I want you to hide here under the bed. That way if anyone comes in, they won't likely find you. Do you still have the pistol your father gave you when you moved out?"

Nellie looked at him and knew he was serious. He was dead set against her using a gun. He always said that a lady shouldn't carry and hand gun.

"Oh course, I do. It's in the case. I thought we might need it to defend ourselves against wild animals when we got to our homestead."

"Well, we might need to defend ourselves against a two legged wild animal, I am afraid. Wait! Do you feel that? The train has stopped. I have to go but I promise, I will return. Lock this door."

He snuck down the hall of train back, against the wall with his gun in hand. He crept along the wall of the train, not seeing anything, which made his heart beat more rapidly. *Had everyone been taken off the train and held captive or worse yet, killed?!* He told himself he couldn't allow his mind to think such things and must concentrate on what he was doing. The element of surprise was his greatest weapon. He continued slowly along the corridor until he reached the dining car. To his great relief, he saw that everyone from the train was gathered there. He looked closer and his heart exploded as he saw three shady looking outlaws with guns drawn and scarves over their faces. He noticed the conductor was lying on the floor in a pool of blood. Platt figured he must have been reluctant to cooperate, so they shot him as an example to the train guests. Platt cased the layout of the room and where the outlaws were stationed. He needed a flawless plan if he was going to overtake them. The men were obviously killers and there was three of them and one of him. But, he had the element of surprise on his side and he was a very patient fellow. He positioned himself out of their sight to wait for the right moment. It wasn't long before two of the men wanted something to eat. This left one man in the main dining car, guarding the passengers. Platt was hiding in the kitchen and needed to move, or he would surely be seen. He carefully moved to the other side of the kitchen, which made him less inconspicuous, but hidden and well positioned to watch everything the two men did while in the kitchen.

Platt watched them, for what seemed like ages. He thought they had to be the slowest sandwich makers he had ever seen. The men finished assembling the sandwiches and their only focus was on their stomachs as they began feasting. It was to Platt's advantage that the men were hungry. He was able to creep along the length on the kitchen without being detected. He calculated his approach and carefully closed in on the man closest to him. With all of his strength, he pounded over his head with a cast iron skillet. Before the other outlaw could process what was happening, Platt gave him a powerful strike to the face. Hearing several loud thuds from the kitchen, the third outlaw grew concerned.

"Is everything alright in there? Now, hurry up! I am hungry."

Platt knew if he didn't answer, the outlaw would become suspicious. He tried to muffle his voice as he hollered back that everything was alright and they would be out in a minute.

"You sound funny! Are you sure everything is alright?"

"Yes! I just had some sandwich in my mouth, that's all," Platt said, desperately hoping to convince him.

Platt returned his attention to the unconscious outlaws on the floor. He used some cords from the curtains in the hallway to tie them up and pulled their bodies into the cooler. By now, the third outlaw had exhausted his patience and decided to see what was going on in the kitchen. He backed into the kitchen, still keeping a gun on the passengers. About halfway to the kitchen, he had a sneaking suspicion that something wasn't right. He decided to take a hostage with him into the kitchen as collateral, just in case. He was very suspicious that things weren't going according to plan. He poked his head into the kitchen and it put him in the perfect line of fire for Platt. He delivered an immense blow with the skillet. His strike was dead on and it knocked him out cold. The passengers began to cheer and cry and many rushed over to thank Platt as they wept.

"Now, don't everyone make a fuss. Can someone help me tie him up? Please, before he comes to!" Platt pleaded.

His father and A.L. rushed to his side with tears in their eyes. "We thought we were done for! We were scared, but not hopeless. I knew if you woke up, you would save us!"

Platt just smiled and shook his head. There was so much excitement and so people crowding around him, he quickly became lost in the chaos.

"Where is Nellie?" a voice from the crowd asked.

Platt returned to reality immediately. "Nellie I have to go get her. I left her under the bed hiding!"

His father laughed. "Well, what are you waiting for? Go get her! We will finish up here." Platt sprinted to their berth. "Nellie, Nellie, are you alright?" he asked as he burst through the door.

Nellie popped her head out from under the bed. "Platt! I'm so glad you are alright! I was worried sick. What happened? Oh, please tell me!"

"Oh, it was nothing really, just some outlaws holding everyone at gunpoint. I was able to take all three out, without one single shot fired!"

Nellie's eyes widened. "What do you mean, you took them out? Where was everyone else? What happened? Ugh! This is why I can't stand being left behind."

"I will tell it all to you over lunch. It's too late for breakfast. Come on, let's go see father and make sure the conductor was tended to."

Nellie didn't know exactly what happened, but she did know Platt was a hero. She could barely believe it. He captured outlaws! She was so proud of him and thankful he made it out alive and unscathed.

The conductor's assistant was able to take the place of his injured superior, so that the train could continue its route. They made an unplanned stop to drop off the outlaws at the closest jail on their route. The conductor was in stable condition, but he needed to be taken to a hospital. They didn't have a physician on board, so they made do with a nurse and a few people who were familiar with medical practices. They did the best they could to stabilize him until they could get him to a professional. They arrived at the hospital and the doctor attended to him quickly, deciding at once that he needed surgery for the bullet wound. The doctor advised the group that the conductor would make a full recovery and have no lasting ailments. Platt and Nellie looked at each other, relived that the situation had a pleasant outcome. They were ready to get back on the train and resume their journey, hopefully without any drama.

While waiting for the train to depart, all anyone could speak of was outlaw incident. Platt was constantly approached with questions and asked mercilessly to retell the story. He was tired of talking about it. He wanted to forget it and focus on homesteading and building their first home. Platt was a man of foresight and planning. He scoured over plans he sketched out on papers for their first home. He knew it would be rustic a log cabin. Not knowing the lay of the land, he wondered how long it would take to clear the land and start the structure of the house. There were so many details with so many unanswered questions. He felt like he bit off more than he bargained for. He comforted himself with the idea that if things didn't work out, he wouldn't hesitate to return to California.

Chapter Twelve
Dora

Back in California, Lester and Mary were busy getting things arranged for their move. Mary would move out first, and then Lester. He needed extra time to finish up his business dealings. They had been spending a lot of time in Alameda with Dora. As of late, her health appeared to be failing. Unlike her family, she had no desire to venture out to the new territory. She was content with her life as she knew it, although she would miss her youngest sister Nellie. Lester and Mary struggled with the thought of leaving Dora, for fear that she would not live much longer.

"I know they are grown, but what if they need us? God forbid, but what if Dora gets worse? You know she has been terribly ill lately. It wouldn't be like it is now where we can see her within a few hours. I know we said we would move out west to help Nellie and Platt, and you know I miss my girl and with the new baby coming, but what do we do?" Mary threw her hands up in the air in a helpless gesture. Lester was already ahead of her, laying out a plan if the situation were to arise and their plans needed to be changed.

"Mary, I have been thinking. Nellie is going to need you, especially after the baby comes. She won't have anyone except for Platt, and he will be out trying to make a living for them and building their new home. She will need her mother. As for Dora, we will have to take it one day at a time and see how her health is. I'm uncertain how long it will take me to conclude my business here and sell our home, so in the meantime, I'll stay behind and tend to Dora."

Mary smiled at Lester and knew it was the right thing to do. Yet, she had the strangest feeling that she couldn't shake, one of impending doom or disaster. She would try and forget it and concentrate on the matter at hand, preparing for the move. After completing her preparations in Healdsburg, she made a trip to see Dora for the last time before her departure. The last time she saw Dora; she looked so pale and was terribly fatigued. It saddened her heart terribly.

Mary Jefferson arrived in Alameda and found her Daughter at the school, finishing grading papers. She noticed the instant she walked into the classroom that Dora was moving slowly and her limp was more pronounced. What was most shocking was her pale, almost white, translucent skin. She looked ghostly. Mary gasped in horror.

"Dora, darling, you need to sit down and let me take a look at you! Oh my, you're looking so pale! We are getting you in to see the doctor immediately."

Dora sat down, feeling too weak to argue and rather relieved to have someone to help. She decided it was best not to argue, although, she had every intention of doing so at first.

"Alright mama, we will call the Doctor and make an appointment first thing in the morning. I got someone to cover my class when I heard you were coming, so we could spend some time together. Mama, would you mind if we just went straight home? I am feeling so tired tonight."

"Oh, of course we can. Let's go now."

Dora made a cozy home for herself. It was very inviting, which was perfect as Dora loved to entertain her friends and to cook. Since she was alone and had no one to cook for, it was always grand when she had company. She would prepare extravagant meals, for almost any occasion. Mama realized just how bad things were when she arrived at Dora's home. The normally immaculate abode was unkempt and disheveled, and there wasn't much more than crumbs in her pantry. She became extra concerned when Dora asked her if she could cook for them that evening. Mama decided she had to intervene.

"Dora, why don't you stay with us for a few days? You don't have to make it an extended stay, just until you regain some of your strength."

Dora loved to visit her parents but she also loved her freedom and would normally never entertain the thought of missing class for any reason. Dora took a while and pondered over the idea. She was so weak and tired. She couldn't fathom the trip to her parent's home. However, she was enticed by the thought of her parents waiting on her, feasting on Maude's cooking, not having to grade papers, cleaning house, or any of her other responsibilities. She decided to telegraph the school master and tell him she would not be in all week. Her parents were rather surprised that she agreed to stay, but delighted. Mama made arrangements for them to travel home the next morning.

Mama and Dora sat out, for what was a rather uneventful expedition. Dora slept for most of their travels. She was delighted to be reunited with her papa and for a moment, her pain seemed to subside. As promised, Maude concocted a restaurant worthy dinner. Dora was exhausted but couldn't pass up the delicious smelling food. She joined her parents and enjoyed a few bites before excusing herself for bed.

Mama tried to wake Dora for breakfast. She had difficulty waking her and became very concerned. She sent papa for the doctor, and begged him to act with utmost urgency. The doctor came and examined Dora. After stabilizing her, he drew some blood and returned to his office to look at it under the microscope. He prescribed some medicine to help relieve her fever, fluids, and best rest and advised he would return after running the blood test. Mama was all too pleased to have the opportunity to dote on her daughter, despite not being thrilled over the circumstance.

They received word from the doctor that he wanted to see them in his office, and they left without haste. They arrived and were quickly seated. Dora, mama, and papa anxiously awaited the doctor's diagnosis. After what felt like an eternity, the doctor came in with a look of concern on his face.

"I am sorry to tell you this, but it appears that Dora's symptoms of weakness, headache, fevers, along with her blood test results, indicate she has what is called Leukemia. It is a relatively new disease, first discovered in 1827. They are having some good results with Mustard patches, it is worth a try. Now, you may want to talk this over and get back with me about your plans." He quietly left the room.

They were numb. Nobody knew what to say or how to say it. After sitting in dead silence, for what seemed an eternity, papa spoke.

"Dora, I want you move home, permanently. Well, at least for now, until you are better. And Mary, I want you to continue with the plan and go to Washington to be with Nellie."

Mama started to protest, but before she could say a word.

"Mama, no arguments, pleases. Nellie and Platt will need you and we can't let her down. I will stay here with Dora until she is feeling better and all the business dealings are tended to. Then, I will join you. I know this isn't what we envisioned for our children, but we must be strong and work together." Papa continued to pace around the parlor.

Dora sat on the santé, feeling so weak but more than anything, she felt helpless. She was out of control, and it was a feeling she did not relish.

"Lester, I need to speak with you in the other room," Mama said with dark eyes. She was holding back a fierce and violent storm of words. They went to the back porch where they could speak.

"How could you just make decisions that affect all of our lives, without even consulting with me? How do you expect me to leave Dora when she needs me? We don't know what course this illness will take, how sick she will be, and how quickly it will progress. I just can't fathom the thought of leaving her and God forbid, something terrible happens. I wouldn't be here for her! Do you see my frustration? How do we make a decision like this? I don't know."

Dora had been listening, undetected by her parents. She chimed in. "No mama, no one is going to take care of me, at least not for a long time. I am feeling stronger and am going back to my students, which is what I live for. You can't disappoint Nellie and Platt. They will need you and you will go as planned. That is all there is to it. Papa is close by to help me with Dr. Appointments, but I have to get back to my normal schedule as soon as possible. I am making arrangements for Papa to take me home tomorrow. This is the best course of action, for all concerned. My mind is made up on the matter and there will be no more discussion. I have been an independent spinster thus far, and I can't think of any reason to break tradition."

Mama and Papa were left speechless after her impassioned speech. "Alright, then we shall make arrangements for you to go back home, as long as we can help with your house work and meals. You'll have to allow us to take you the doctors' appointments, so we can always be aware of your condition."

Dora was deep in thought as she paced. "Alright, but I don't need someone to live with me. Some assistance with meals and house work would be appreciated. Now, I am going to the house to retire for the evening. With all this excitement, I am feeling a bit fatigued and would appreciate Maude's assistance in helping me pack, if that would be agreeable."

Dora awoke to a beautiful morning for the trip back home. She was excited about getting back to her pupils. She knew if she concentrated on the children's lives, her own life would be much easier to cope with. Her heart raced with excitement at the thought of seeing the faces of her children. Mama decided to accompany Papa on the trip.

Despite her mother's protectiveness, Dora was glad she had come. She enjoyed spending time with her parents, although now that she had a diagnosis, they seemed to have forgotten that she was a grown woman with a life of her own. She understood and appreciated the love and concern, even though it was suffocating when one is used to living alone and independent.

The trip went by quickly and before she knew it, she was at her little house. It had never looked so good to Dora. She was overwhelmed with emotion, which surprised her. She'd always kept her emotions in check and under control, especially since her heart had been broken so badly. She wondered why it was happening to her and why now. She was young and doing what she loved. She felt as if she was making a difference in the lives of children. She thought it was just so unfair! But who was she to question the providence of God, and maybe the treatments would work. She told herself she wouldn't give into self-pity. She smiled at her parents.

"Home never looked so good! Come in and we shall get you settled before I go over to the school house and speak with the school master about resuming my position. Mama, what are all these flowers all over the porch? Did you tell anyone I was ill? They thought I was vacation! Who did this, and why?" Dora bent over and picked up a bouquet of flowers. She read the note attached to it.

"My darling Dora,

I know I have no right to seek a meeting with you, but I cannot forget you! Please forgive me.

All my love,
Charles."

She stood there with tears streaming down her face. Her parents were speechless, wondering who this gentleman was that would write such a bold note to their daughter. And why was Dora crying? Dora quickly had regained her composure and took a few moments as she looked at the stunned faces of her parents.

"I imagine you have a lot of questions. Why don't we go inside and I'll tell you the sad story." She marched through the path of flowers left by Charles. Mama and papa were more confused at the quick recovery of Dora. After everything from the buggy was deposited in the appropriate rooms, Dora sat her parents sit down began her story.

"I know you have a lot of questions. I know I should have spoken of Charles but after we agreed not to see each other anymore, it seemed pointless and honestly, much too painful to speak of. His name is Charles Cummings the III. I met him at a fundraiser for the school. At first, I thought he must be one of the parents, but he was the uncle of one of my students. He was visiting from San Francisco. You see, he is a very successful businessman. He was charming and so refined. He took me to the finest restaurants and all the waiters knew him by name and we always had the best table. We went to San Francisco and the Opera House. It was like a dream! But then, he would come here and be content to be in a small town and go on picnics, a walk in the park, or a ride in the country. I fell in love with him, yes, I fell in love. I felt as if I had met someone who I was truly suited for. He asked me to marry him, but it was not without a price. I would've had to quit my job and be a socialite wife. I loved Charles, but that is not my life. My life is here, teaching, living in a small town. I knew if I asked him to quit his job and move here with me, he just might do it. But eventually, he would resent me so I ended it and rejected his proposal of marriage. I was heart sick for months. I cried myself to sleep every night. The loneliness I felt for him was overwhelming, but what helped me get through it was my faith in God and my students. Going to school every day made my problems seemed to fade in the distance. I've never stopped loving Charles. I love him with my whole heart but I don't think it's the right time to rekindle a romance. I should have told you, but Nellie and Platt were getting married and I didn't want to steal from their moment. Well, I guess now you know the whole story and if you'll excuse me, I am quite exhausted. I am going to retire to my room and rest for a bit before dinner."

"Why, of course. Dora, would you like some tea? Is there anything we can get for you?"

Dora started up the stairs, then turned and looked back at her parents. They looked as if they'd seen a ghost. "Honestly, I am alright, but a cup of tea would be lovely. Thank you," Dora said with a smile as she continued up the flight of stairs.

Once in her room, Dora had time to think and sort through all the confusion of the past few days. Her diagnosis was enough to deal with and it was too much to come back to all the flowers from Charles. She longed to be held in his arms again and feel his heart beat as she laid her head on his chest. She still loved him, but couldn't allow him back into her heart. She knew she was much too weak to deal with another broken heart. She needed to stay focused on her teaching. She decided, first thing in the morning, she was going back to the school house to see the school master. Whatever time she had left would be totally dedicated to her students, for they deserved the best she had to offer.

Dora hadn't realized she drifted into sleep but she awoke and realized she had slept the entire afternoon evening and night, for it was now the next day. She had never slept so long before. The fatigue was a little worrisome to Dora, but she dismissed it as trip and emotional exhaustion. She got dressed in one of her favorite dresses, one that always made her feel good. She came downstairs and was surprised to find both her parents, with breakfast on the table. Mama had had made it and she wondered if her mother even remembered how to cook after having a cook for so many years.

"My, what a surprise this is. Mama, you don't have to wait on me and do all the cooking. I am feeling stronger and can certainly do the cooking for you. After all, you're a guest in my home."

"No, we are family and are here to help you. Don't you fuss, just sit down and eat. I needed an opportunity to brush up on my cooking skills. Now, I am not guaranteeing the taste, but it will be hot and hopefully, pleasing."

The breakfast was amazing! She had made hot biscuits, bacon, griddle cakes, fresh squeezed orange juice, and served it with some fresh fruit. They ate until they felt like gluttons.

"Mama thank you for a marvelous breakfast. You can leave the dishes and I will attend to them later, but I must be off to the school house. I will see you both later!" She grabbed her wrap and headed for the door.

"You have a wonderful day! Dora, don't you be concerned about the dishes or the house. I am arranging for a housekeeper and cook, as we agreed. So, you go on and don't worry about a thing. Papa and I will handle everything"

They were being so wonderful to her to help her out. She hated to admit it, but she really needed the help. The closer she got to the school, the more excited Dora became. She could hardly wait! Her heart began to beat faster and harder in her chest and before she knew it, she was standing outside the school master's office.

"Is he in, Mrs. Jenkins?"

"Why yes, Ms. Jefferson, he is. He will be so glad to see you. We all are glad to have you back!"

Dora opened the door with exuberance. "Good morning School Master Connor!"

She came to a complete stand still as she found herself, face to face, with Charles. She felt the color drain from her face and her heart beat rapidly. She knew this day may come, but she thought she would have time to prepare herself. The room began spinning and Dora swooned. Charles rushed to her side and grabbed her up in arms.

Within a few moments, Dora aroused. "Charles? What are you doing here?"

"Well, I heard that there might be a vacant teaching position here at the school and I decided to apply. I am sure I never mentioned it, but before I was a business man, I was a professor at University. I've been missing it as of late and when I heard of the opportunity, I decided it would afford me the pleasure of living closer to my Sister and her children, and the chance to be able to see you again."

Dora looked at him, still half dazed, and then she began to get angry. "What job vacancy? As you can see, the position is no longer available. I am back and ready to teach, so you can head on back to San Francisco! I am sorry your trip was for nothing." She said as coldly as she could manage, despite wanting to run straight into his arms.

"Well, that is not completely true." School Master Connor interjected.

"What are you talking about? If I am not being replaced and I know Miss Watkins hasn't resigned, that only leaves you sir! I know this school is your life, so please, do explain."

"Dora, my wife and I have just learned that we are going to grandparents. Our daughter and her husband are moving to Washington, much like your sister. We want to be closer to her and be there for our grandchildren and watch them grow. I have a job offer at a small school in Washington, so we are going. When I received word of this young man with such credentials that was interested in our school, I just knew it was meant to be. I was going to introduce you, but I can see that you already know each other. Maybe, I should leave the two of you alone to get reacquainted. You know, Dora, the two of you will be working closely and for the sake of the children, it is imperative that there be no friction between the staff."

"Of course, sir, I understand perfectly. You have my word I will behave in an utmost professional manner at all times. Now, if you will excuse me, I would like to check on my class room before I leave."

"Let me escort you, so I might go over the new curriculum with you. We have much to discuss," Charles said eagerly.

Dora didn't agree or disagree. She began walking toward her classroom. She was overjoyed to see all the children. They saw her and came running to hug her.

"I will be back tomorrow! Now, get back to class. I can't wait to hear about all you've learned while I've been gone."

Very obediently, the children went back to their seats. Seeing the children, for even a few moments, lifted her spirits and put a big smile on Dora's face.

"You really love those children. Dora, you have the gift of teaching, and not one that every teacher possesses. May we go for a walk, or for lunch, and talk? There is so much I need to tell you, my heart is bursting and school is not the time or place."

"Very well, we can have lunch and talk, for there is much you need to know, as well."

They walked and talked, rather light hearted, almost as if time had never stopped for them. It was the strangest feeling and they both sensed it. They talked for a long time about his business in San Francisco and he wanted to know all about Platt and Nellie. But finally, the conversation turned back to them, which she had been dreading.

"I know after everything that has happened and what I put you through that I don't deserve a second chance. You, of all the people I know, deserve a chance at happiness. I can't promise I won't make mistakes, but I can promise that I'll always be here and I'll always love you. I must admit, I've imagined seeing you again in my mind for months and never did it go the way that today did. Dora, life without you has been miserable! You are my soul mate in every way and I want to be with you. I can't stand another moment without you! Please reconsider and marry me?"

"Charles, you say you're here for the teaching position now, but what if your business needs you? I can't move to San Francisco and well, something else has come up and I just can't talk about it right now. I don't want to jeopardize my teaching position, especially with you as the new school master. I just can't talk to you about it! Although I wish it were different, but I can't even entertain these fanciful thoughts. So please, just respect my decision and don't ask any questions, please."

"Dora, whatever you're going through, we can go through it together. I'm not going anywhere this time. This is a promise you can count on."

Dora wanted to believe him, more than anything. She loved him dearly but with her diagnosis of Leukemia, it would be a cruel thing to agree to marry. He would thank her for sparing him the grief someday, she knew he would.

They spent the rest of afternoon talking and walking around the town. Dora found she fatigued more quickly than she had preciously. It was frustrating to Dora, who was a very active woman, normally. It amazed Dora how she quickly she allowed Charles back into her life and how comfortable they both were with each other. It was as if no time had passed at all.

"Would you be free to join my parents and myself for dinner this evening?"

She felt it not improper, in light of the fact he had just pledged his love for her and she enjoyed every minute she could be with him. She wondered if she was she wrong in her decision not to tell him about her prognosis. She figured time would tell, but tonight she had the opportunity to see him again and that was all that mattered. They said their goodbyes until the evening.

Dora came bursting through the door, humming and smiling. Her parents recognized the look from their youngest daughter, but were wise enough not to say too much. They sat back and wait to listen.

"Mama, I wanted to let you know I have invited Charles to dine with us this evening. We had the most glorious afternoon! We had lunch at the café and then we walked and talked all afternoon. I didn't want the day to end, so I asked him to come to dinner so he could meet you two. Please be nice to him, I love him. I will not marry him, because of my disease, but I have decided to take every moment of happiness I am given as a gift. So please, be happy for me and try and understand this!" Dora pleaded.

"Of course, we will be polite and kind to him. Dora, we want you to experience love and happiness, but don't you think he deserves to know the truth about you?" Papa asked.

She said nothing. She just looked out the window and wished the circumstances were different. *No, this is not fair! I'm happy and made peace with my lot in life. Now Charles comes back into it, why now? Why at all? How can I make anyone understand this without sounding so selfish?*

"No Papa, I know I need to tell him but I also know that when I do, he won't want anything more to do with me. So, let me enjoy these few moments of pure bliss, before the dream is over. Papa, I promise I will tell him, I will!"

Papa was shocked by how vulnerable she was. "Of course, my darling daughter, whatever you feel is best. I do feel that you need to do it sooner, rather than later. It is only fair to both of you."

Dora acknowledged her father's response and went upstairs to rest before dinner. All the excitement of the day had worn more on her than she realized. She woke from her nap and felt amazingly refreshed and ready for the evening. She found herself with a sense of anticipation at the thought of spending time with Charles. It left her breathless and with her heart racing. Her palms were sweating and mouth was dry. As she tried to sort through all her thoughts, she heard papa announce that Charles had arrived. She descended the staircase, looking as beautiful as an angel. Her hair cascaded down her shoulders and back. She looked like a goddess floating down the stairs, and it left Charles speechless.

"So good of you come to dinner this evening."

Charles was speechless for a few moments. "Yes, thank you for having me. Mr. and Mrs. Jefferson, it's truly an honor to finally meet you! Dora has spoken so highly of you."

They sat for dinner and had a wonderful time. Mama and papa found they really liked Charles. He was smart, witty, and well-traveled. There was nothing about him they didn't like and the fact that he was in love with Dora, was written all over him. They had a very pleasant time and after dinner, Charles and Dora excused themselves for a walk. Dora went for her wrap and papa cornered her.

He sternly whispered, "Dora, he is in love with you and he deserves to know! Trust him with the truth. Please tell him." Papa kissed her forehead. Dora nodded her head and smiled as she left.

They enjoyed their time alone, walking hand in hand.

"Dora, your parents are wonderful! You are blessed to have parents such as them. Dora, you know that I love you and I know you feel the same. So please, tell me why won't you marry me? It can't be because your parents don't like me! For the love of Pete, please tell me why!"

Dora could stand it no longer. She took a deep breath. "Charles, can we go over and sit down on the park bench? I'll tell you the whole story." Dora looked at him and saw the concern in his eyes. "Charles, what I am going to tell you must not change my teaching position, is that understood?"

"Nothing will change your teaching position, unless you decide you want to change it."

"Alright then, I was not going to tell you about this, but my father persuaded me to be completely truthful with you about everything, and that includes my health. You see, Charles, when I was visiting my parents, I was in actuality seeing a Physician. I haven't been feeling well as of lately and wouldn't you know it, I have a disease. It's a cancer of the blood, called Leukemia. As of now, there is no cure. There are a few new treatments, but no cure. So, do you see why I can't marry you? If you get up and leave right now, I will certainly understand. It is a lot to deal with. That is why I cannot marry you. Do you understand?" She got up and began walking off.

"Where are you going?" Charles reached and pulled her close to himself. "I am not going anywhere. How could you even think that? Do you really have such little faith in my love for you? I am here for the duration!"

He pressed a passionate kiss to her lips and she melted into his embrace. She knew this was where she belonged.

"We will find another doctor! Maybe, they have will have a cure for this disease, or at least the newest treatment! I just can't lose you again, Dora. Not now and not so soon," Charles whispered into her hair.

She stayed in his embrace for a long time. She felt so safe and secure there, she felt she could stay forever. At the end of the evening, they sadly said their goodnights. Charles took Dora in his arms and kissed her again, this time more passionately and deeply.

"Please reconsider and marry me, Dora. I love you and will be there to take care of you. I want to be with you, no matter how long that will be," Charles pleaded.

Dora looked up into his pleading eyes, wanting more than anything to say yes. Her heart was beating so hard, she felt as if it would burst. She held Charles hands and looked into his eyes, as difficult as it was.

"Charles, you have no idea of how debilitating this disease process will be. I have made up my mind. I will not burden a husband with this, nor, will I leave him a widower. As much as I may love you, it is because of this fact that I cannot say yes to you. Please try and understand."

Charles scratched his head. He didn't say anything for several minutes. Finally, he picked up his hat and spoke. "I will see you tomorrow. You need to get some rest." He kissed her lightly and was off.

Dora sat there, trying to decipher what just transpired between them. With his quick departure, she felt justified in her decision. She went back the house and up to her room. She lay down, but sleep did not come easy. She couldn't stop thinking about Charles. She couldn't help but wonder if she ruined her last chance at love? There were so many questions with no answers. Eventually, the fatigue from the disease overtook her and she was fast asleep.

In the morning, she was nervous about having to see Charles, but she decided she would act professionally. Dora walked into the classroom and the children came rushing around her. They hugged and greeted her. It was the best reception she'd ever had in her life. She quickly regained her composure and told her students how much the warm greetings had meant to her, but they needed to start class. They were in the middle of class when there was a knock on the door and Charles walked in.

"Good morning, children. I wanted to make sure you were having a good day and not giving Miss Jefferson any trouble."

The children all laughed. He certainly had a way with the children, she would give him that. Dora took a deep breath and smiled at Charles, who looked at her with a spark in his eye. Charles stayed until it was time to dismiss the children for lunch. The children vacated the room for and Dora sat down to eat her own lunch. She looked up and saw that Charles was still there.

"Is there something you need, or would you like to share my lunch with me?"

He stayed silent, while smiling widely.

"Are you alright?" she asked, feeling rather uncomfortable.

Finally, he emerged from his trance. "Dora, I only need you. I know we have a lot to talk about, but I am not going anywhere. In fact, I want you to know I am here for you day and night, for whatever you want or need. I know you said no to marriage and as much as I don't understand it, I respect your decision. But, please, allow me the privilege of being with you and loving you, as long as that may be. I know that is a lot to absorb for a lunch time discussion, but don't say a word. Think about it and I will see you after school. I'll be taking you to dinner, no argument." He left the classroom, turning back to poke his head in and wink at her.

Dora tried desperately to process everything Charles just said. Part of her was relieved that he still loved her and wanted to be by her side through this illness, but part of her was so confused. So much had happened in the past week, but now, but she felt like she knew what to do. Her thoughts were interrupted by the school bell and her children came flooding back in.

That night, Charles showed up at Dora's house to take her to dinner. "Are you ready to go my dear?" he asked with a large grin on his face.

"Yes, I am. Where we are going?"

Charles looked at her and shook his finger. "Dora, it is permissible to be surprised once in a while. I will let you know what you need to know, in due time." Charles reached down and kissed her cheek. She smiled and took his arm as they left for the evening. They drove past the diner. Dora was puzzled. It was a small town with few restaurants to choose from.

"Where are we going tonight, Charles?"

"No, no, all things come in good time, my dear. Tonight will be a night of suspense and surprises. At least, I am hoping it all happens as I have it planned." He kissed her cheek softly.

Dora's mind was a whirl with what he could be up to. Before she had too much time to ponder all the scenarios, they pulled up to a house. *Whose house was it?* Her curiosity peaked. It was a very nice house made of wood, with a beautiful garden in the front and a white picket fence. It had a front porch with a rocking chair and looked as if it came out of a picture. Blue gingham curtains hung from the windows, giving it a darling cottage look. *Who could live in such an idyllic house?*

"Well, here we are. Shall we go in?" Charles helped her down from the buggy and pointed the way towards the door. He offered his arm as they walked up the cobble stone path. Charles opened the front door to a darling house. It had an overstuffed chair and a sate, a wooden buffet, and a beautiful porcelain pitcher and bowl set on top of it. The Kitchen was charming with wooden cupboards and a white painted table. It was so quaint and beautiful. She was quickly drawn to a wonderful aroma.

"Who lives in this darling home? And who is the cook that made this delicious food?"

"I am guilty, on both counts," Charles said with a smile and a wink in his eyes. Dora gave him a doubting look. "No, seriously, I am telling you the truth. I own this house. My mother and sister are the decorators, so I can't take credit for that. But, I am the cook, so why don't we eat?"

They moved towards the table and he pulled the chair out for her. They excitedly sat down to enjoy the scrumptious meal.

"You see, my dear, my mother thought it was her duty to raise future husbands. She taught my brother and me how to cook and clean. We are not accomplished, by any means, but we can survive in the kitchen, and even cook for a beautiful lady. Now, are you going to look at it or eat?"

Dora looked at him, rather surprised, and then laughed. They both laughed and enjoyed a wonderful meal, and even more enjoyable company. After dinner, they made their way to the living room for coffee and cake.

"Dora, don't you see? I can take care of you. I am well capable of cooking for you and caring for you. Won't you let me be there for you? I love you Dora and if you will not agree to be my wife, at least, let me be by your side, for whatever time we have. I want to spend it together. We enjoy each other's company and make each laugh. Dora, I am not going anywhere. So, what do you say? Can we be together?" Charles pleaded as he reached for Dora.

"Charles, are you sure you're ready for what lies ahead?"

"Yes, Dora, I have thought this through and I am here for you, forever."

Charles looked at her with love in his eyes, serious, almost sternly. It was a look she had never seen before. Dora looked intently at him, searching his eyes for sincerity and finding what she needed.

"Charles, you are aware that this illness is not an attractive one? It can make one weak and emancipated? Are you certain you are ready to make this journey with me?"

Dora kept constant eye contact with Charles, so she could detect any hint of reluctance. She needed to know for sure that he wouldn't run away. All she saw was an overwhelming look of love. It was more than she ever dreamed of and, a part of her, didn't know what to do with it. Charles picked her up around the waist and held her close. He pressed his lips against hers in a kiss that lasted several minutes.

"Does that answer your question?" he asked.

Dora rested her head against his chest. "Yes. Charles, I want you. If it is for day or a year, I want you to be by my side."

Charles got up, swung her around, and they both laughed.

"Let's go tell your folks about our decision!" Charles said excitedly. He could hardly contain himself.

"They may have already turned in for the night, but we can go by the house and see if you can't wait until tomorrow."

They quickly left his house and made their way over to Dora's house. They were delighted to see the lights still on, which meant they had not turned in yet. Dora went in first to make sure her parents were presentable to receive quests. She found them sitting up, papa reading and mama working on a baby quilt for Nellie and Platt's anticipated new child. They looked surprised when they saw Dora come through the door so early in the evening. They saw Charles standing giddily by the door.

"Come on in and have a seat while I put on a pot of coffee. The two of you can tell us what has put these silly grins on your faces tonight."

"How did you know we had something important to tell you?"

"First of all, you are home early and both of you are here. Secondly, you both have a look on your face that says you will, most certainly, burst from sheer excitement." Papa nodded and laughed.

"When did you become so clairvoyant and all knowing?" Dora asked playfully.

"Oh, that comes from having three daughters. So, come on, out with the news."

Dora and Charles went on to tell to them all that had transpired that evening. Mama was so overwhelmed, she started to weep.

"Mama, what is the matter?"

"I am so glad that you and Charles found love in each other. However, I am not completely comfortable with the prospect of being so far away from you in your time of need. I don't think we have exhausted every possibility or scenario at this time. We have more discussing to do before we commit to a plan. But, with that being said, we are thrilled for you two. So come, let's talk about your plans."

They all sat down and had coffee and cake. They were all so excited, none of them could think of sleeping. They were just so thankful it was Friday night and there would be no school the next day. After hours of discussion, they came to the decision that Mary needed to go out west to help Nellie and Platt with the new baby. Papa would as stay behind as planned for as long as Dora needed him. It would give him time to wind up all his business before he joined them in Washington. It was the only solution they could all agree upon and made sense to everyone. It was a bitter sweet decision with all the unanswered questions about Dora's health and it weighed on Mama.

Dora and Charles spent every waking moment together. They were inseparable when they weren't teaching classes. Charles was true to his word in standing by her side at all times. The love they shared was unique, and seemed to grow deeper and stronger daily. To watch it blossom was an almost magical experience. They were so enamored with each other that they hardly even noticed that mama was making plans to head out west. Papa was spending his time between Healdsburg and coming to visit as often as could. Mama was spending her time preparing for the big move out west. She organized what would need to go with her and what household items would be left for Papa. She had lists for everything. The woman loved to organize!

Dora found she had more strength than she imagined and was certain that the doctors must have made a mistake with her diagnosis. But maybe, it was due to the altered mental state that being completely in love can cause. Dora and Charles were blissfully in love. Everyone that they came in contact with them noticed it. They worked very hard to be discreet and not let anyone be aware of their relationship at the school, but some things were hard to disguise. Neither of them had ever imagined they could be so happy and they accepted every day as a gift. They had no guarantee of how many days they would have together, so they made the agreement not to argue and love each other passionately.

Mama was soon packed and ready for her big adventure out west. She and Papa came in town to see Dora and Charles before the departure. They were amazed at how good Dora looked. She didn't appear pale or fatigued. In fact, her facial expression seemed to glow with a peaches and cream complexion, giving her the appearance of health and vitality. They were delighted she was so happy and her teaching assignment was not too taxing on her health. They knew Charles was watching over her and had her on an abbreviated schedule. Anytime she started feeling or looking tired, she was off her feet and not allowed to teach. It was infuriating to Dora at times, but she knew it was for her own good and Charles did it out of love. She found it was rather nice to have someone care so much about how she was feeling. She knew that town people were likely talking about the school teacher and the school master, who were seen keeping company entirely too often. She didn't care now that her days were numbered. Dora was deliriously happy and wasn't going to let idle gossip ruin it. They were too in love to bother with such things, always bearing in their minds that they had no guarantee on how long their time would be together.

Each day, Charles would bring flowers to Dora. Some days, it was a bouquet of wild flowers he picked on the way to school, and other days, he would purchase them from the local merchant. Most days, he went out to his picture perfect back yard and picked roses and daisies. Those were Dora's favorites and he made sure they were growing in the garden when he purchased the house. They went on walks daily, but on the days when Dora was feeling fatigued, they would spend their time in Charles' lovely garden. The fresh air and scenery was medicinal.

The doctors were amazed at her condition. The disease wasn't progressing nearly as fast as they anticipated and they credited her happiness to that. When Mama heard from the doctors, she knew it was alright to go. Up until that report, she had reservations and was ready to change her mind if Dora's condition had worsened. But, everything looked favorable for mama to go forward with her adventure out west. Yet, something was nagging at mama. Something wasn't quite right something, but she couldn't put her finger on it. She thought, maybe, it was because she and Lester were going to be separated for such a long time. They hadn't ever been separated, except for when Papa was in the hospital or when he would be away on business trips. She figured that must be what was bothering her and tried to put it out of her head.

One morning, Dora was having a good day and felt strong and full of energy. She wanted to go to the seaside and see the ocean. Charles couldn't refuse her request, so off they went. They brought a picnic basket and planned on staying at a hotel for the evening. Dora was so excited. She loved the ocean and felt like a child as she felt the ocean breeze against her face and saw the waves crash against the rocks. She buried her toes in the sand and collected shells as she walked along the coastline. Charles watched her walk and noticed her losing momentum. Dora was beginning to look very tired.

"Dora, do you think it's time to return to the specialist?"

"My darling, Charles, I told you it wouldn't always be pretty. I could go back and see the Doctor, but I don't know if he'll offer any hope. There is no cure, so let's just enjoy every moment, shall we?"

Charles agreed and held her close, yet, he felt very concerned. He'd found the love of his love and wasn't ready to lose her. They still had so much to do and they needed more time. Charles was deep in thought as they strolled along the beach.

"Dora, I know we said we wouldn't get married, but I want to be your husband more than anything. Please reconsider," Charles pleaded.

Dora thought for a while before answering. "Charles, you are the most wonderful man in the world. I feel so blessed to I know your love, but Charles, I can't do that to you. To leave you a widow would be selfish and unfair! But, I can promise you that as long as I live, I will love you completely."

Charles was not pleased by her answer. "Alright, we will save this discussion for a later time. Shall we have some seafood for dinner? What do you think about that?"

They had a delightful dinner and were walking back towards the inn when Dora looked at Charles. "Alright, but it will be between you, I, and God. I don't want anyone else involved, just us. I will agree before God to be your wife, but it is to stay our secret. Not that I am ashamed, but I prefer it to be intimate and quiet. Do you agree to these terms?"

He could hardly believe what he was hearing. "Yes, of course! But, do you not intend on telling your parents, or making it legal with a judge?"

"No, this is just between us. So, are you agreeable or not?"

Charles swept her off her feet and into his arms. He gave her a kiss so passionate; it left her weak in the knees and barely able to speak.

"I'll take that as a yes."

"Yes, yes, if that is the only way I can have you, then so be it."

That night, they stood on the shore of the ocean and pledged their undying love before God and each other. It may not have been traditional, but it made them happier than they could have ever imagined.

When they returned home, Dora decided to decrease her work load to just a few days a week. Charles wanted her to stop teaching all together, but he knew that seeing the children was a good dose of medicine for Dora. She wanted to be with the children every day possible. Charles arranged for a substitute teacher, who was able to teach the class any time Dora felt poorly. They tried desperately to keep her condition hidden, to avoid upsetting the children and their families. That was Dora's wish and Charles did everything he could to fulfill it. But, living in small community, news travels fast and the families soon found out. They were incredibly supportive and offered to bring meals over and help Dora clean her house. It was the most wonderful outpouring of love. Women would show up with entire meals prepared and be willing to clean her house. There was always someone available to run errands for Dora. She felt so spoiled and pampered. Charles and Dora made jokes that they felt like celebrities with all the attention.

Mama and papa came down to see Dora before mama's departure out west. They were so pleased at Dora's health. She seemed to glow with joy and contentment, which they'd never seen before in Dora. They had dinner together and afterwards, Dora and Mama took advantage of their time together and went for a stroll. They caught each other up on all the latest news and more importantly, mama wanted to know what was putting such a wonderful glow on her face.

"Mama, I am very happy to be teaching and to be with Charles. It has been the best medicine that I could have found!"

Mama looked at her, not quite convinced of her answer. She decided not to pry but knew that Dora had a secret she was keeping close to her heart. She respected her daughter enough not to insist, although, she was curious. Instead, knowing their time was very short, she wanted to enjoy the moment. They walked and laughed at the funny stories Dora told about the children at school. Dora began to fatigue and mama could tell, immediately.

"Why don't we sit here and rest before we go back to your house?"

Dora nodded in agreement. They sat in silence for a few moments before Dora blurted out, "We said our vows!"

Mama's head spun around so fast, she was sure she snapped it. "What did you say?"

"We said our vows, Charles and I! It wasn't before a preacher, or anyone for that matter, but before God and us. We pledged our unending love and committed ourselves to each other. We said we wouldn't tell anyone but mama, I just couldn't keep that secret from you! We know it isn't a legally binding marriage, but it feels real to us and honestly, that is all that really matters. Don't you think?" Dora sought approval from mama's face.

Mama was perplexed by the idea of a pseudo marriage, she'd never heard of such a thing before. Then again, if it was what was keeping Dora, happy then it must not be so wrong.

"Dora, you and Charles are obviously in love and beyond happy. So, if this is what you feel you must do, then I am supportive. Please be sure to relish every moment and regard it as sacred. Make happy memories for Charles to remember. I want you to know that even though I'll be a long way off in Washington, I will always right here in your heart." She then reached out and touched Dora's heart.

Dora and Mama hugged each other and cried, knowing that this was a moment they would cherish forever. After they recovered, they finished their walk back to the house and found Charles and papa waiting. The time they had together seemed to go by far too quickly and before they knew it, the time had arrived for mama and papa to leave. Mama tried to remain stoic, but she was falling apart. She knew this farewell may be their last but, she wouldn't allow herself to dwell on it. She pretended as if they were headed home and would be back to see her in a few weeks. This way, she could manage to get through the farewell. Mama tried to fixate on anything that would distract herself from reality.

"Now, where has your Papa gone? He knows we are leaving! I thought he was right in front of me?" She put her hand on her petite hip and furrowed her brow.

Dora looked around and shrugged her shoulders. "I am sure he will be along any moment. Mama, they may not have had the horses ready at the stable? Would you like to come back inside and wait?"

Mama tapped her foot impatiently. She wasn't one usually gave to impatience, but today her emotions were far too volatile and she wanted to get on the road before she broke down. Shortly, Papa came around the corner in a new carriage. It had plush cushioned seats and elegant fringe adorning the top the canopy.

"Whatever are you doing with this? What was wrong with our other buggy? Where is it?" She ran her hands over the luxurious fabric of the cushions and thought they would be much more comfortable than the seats from the other buggy.

"I traded the old buggy in for this new one. It is the newest in the line of Surrey buggies! Mama, you know I only want the very best for you." Papa reached out and touched her face.

"But, you will be leaving to go out west soon? What are you going to do with it then?"

Papa looked at Dora and Charles, and then at Mama. "No need to worry, my darling. All of those details have been worked out. Charles and Dora will take the buggy when I leave. I have thought of everything! So now, shall we make our way home in comfort?" Papa ushered Mama into the buggy, after one last farewell hug to Dora and Charles.

"Now, will you write me when you arrive at Nellie and Platt's? And, please, let me know when I am an Aunt! Send a telegram! I'll need to know as soon as possible. I love you both."

Mama looked concerned as she waved good-bye. Dora knew exactly what she was thinking.

"Mama, I will contact you as soon as we have any news from the doctor. So, please, go in peace and feel confident! We will let you know as soon as we know anything. Rest assured, mama, I am in good hands." Dora pointed to Charles.

Mama laughed and waved as they drove off out of town. Still, she couldn't shake the ominous feeling she had. She knew Dora's prognosis was hopeful with the new arsenic treatment the doctors were starting. They had some patients show great improvement with the new treatment, but she was well read and knew that not all of the patients had improved. Dora's chances weren't that great, but they were hopeful. But, it wasn't just Dora that was bothering her. It was something else, she just couldn't pinpoint it. The feeling of impending doom wasn't a feeling she embraced, but she tried to focus on the time she had left with her husband.

"Is everything alright, mama?" Papa could read her like a book after so many years. Mama looked at him and saw the young man she'd fallen in love with many years ago. She was a blessed woman, indeed.

"No dear, I am fine. I was just caught up in my thoughts of Dora and Nellie. Thank goodness Mel is doing so well!" Mama said and they laughed.

Before they knew it, they were back home in Oceanside. Home for now, at least, but everything was changing so fast. Nellie and Platt were on their way out west and should be arriving soon. She and Lester would be Grandparents, very soon! Dora with her new diagnosed illness and love in her life, everything was moving so fast. She knew nothing would ever be the same again.

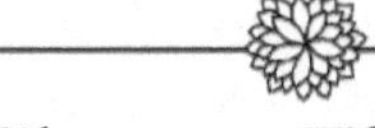

Chapter Thirteen
Wagon Train

Nellie, Platt, A.L. and Richard Corbaley had nearly completed their train portion of the voyage and were ready to transition onto the wagon train. They were joining a group of settlers going to Washington, for Platt felt it was wiser and safer to travel in a group. He was grateful that the longest part of the journey had been by train. The train would take them as far as the tracks were laid and if his calculations were correct, the train tracks would end in Baker City, Oregon. It wouldn't be too long of a journey to Washington from there. He arranged for a wagon to be ready for them once they arrived in Oregon, but there were so many details to be dealt with and he wanted everything to run smoothly.

Platt found Nellie sitting in a box car seat, working on a baby quilt. He looked out the window and admired the beautiful mountains. What a beautiful land they were going to, he thought. He knew Nellie had concerns about the rustic conditions in which they would be living in upon arrival, but he had confidence that their conditions would not stay rustic for long. He looked at his wife, adoringly. She was so courageous to join him on the journey to a new uncharted land. Nellie looked up at him and smiled sweetly.

"Do you need me for something, dear?"

Platt sat down next to her and began to pour out his heart. He told her all his concerns and that he wondered if he made the right decision. He breathed a sigh of relief.

"That must have been building up in you for quite some time."

He stood up and looked at her, confused by her response.

"Platt, please sit down. Did you not feel this was the right thing to do when we made the decision? And did we not discuss all the difficulties and trials we could face along the way?"

"Yes, of course, we did but…"

She interjected, "Well, from where I am sitting, I would say that we are in this journey together and that is how we will see it to the end. We are committed to a new and better life for our child. I believe in you Platt and I admire your passion for this venture. So, I think the matter is closed for discussion, unless there is something else you wanted to discuss?"

The remainder of their train ride concluded quickly and before they knew it, they were in Baker City, Oregon. Mr. Watkins was the foreman of the wagon train and when they met up with him, he was already organizing the departure for the next day. There wouldn't be a lot of time allotted to obtain all the necessary supplies they would need for the journey. Nellie and Platt went to the general store to find food staples and other basic items they would need. They tried to stockpile enough to last them up to 6 months. They were hoping this would last the trip and for a little while once they arrived in Washington. Richard Corbaley and A.L. made a trip to the hard goods store to get the equipment needed to build their dream home. They returned with shovels, ropes, lanterns, hammers, nails, and a plethora of other items.

The wagon they would use was about five feet wide and ten feet long, and covered with a canvas top. It didn't take long to completely fill the wagons. With the trunks from the train, supplies they bought, and what they brought in barrels, they were loaded to the maximum capacity. Nellie wondered if there would be room for her and Platt, but he assured her he made room for her to lie down and rest during the journey. Platt was anxious to start their journey, but the sooner they started, the sooner they arrived and could begin their lives together.

They found the only hotel in town and secured rooms and settled in for the night. They woke up early the next morning and made one last stop at the general store. They bought a few luxuries, such as butter and eggs, because they knew it would be a while before they could secure chickens. Platt purchased a cow and planned to pull it behind the wagon. He knew it would be a tough journey for the cow, but thought it would be nice to have fresh milk along the journey and a constant supply of dairy when they arrived.

They met with the other settlers, who were just as excited and anxious. There were a few single men and several couples. Most had children and were looking for a better way of life for their families. Nellie was relieved to see there were woman around her age. She met a woman named Sally Smithson. She, her husband, and son were going to settle near Platt and her. She was a lovely woman, probably in her late 20's. While the men spoke of the route and all the plans for the journey, Nellie took the opportunity to visit with her new friend. Nellie found out she had married her school sweetheart and they'd lived out East. Her son was seven years old and thought himself a man already. They talked and talked for hours.

"I am so grateful to have another woman to talk to! Now, don't misunderstand me. I love my husband but sometimes you need a woman to talk to, and especially with the baby on the way. I am so grateful we met!"

Sally looked at Nellie, rather peculiarly. "Baby you are expecting a baby?"

Nellie detected a sudden changed in her attitude, but thought she must be imaging it.

"Our baby is expected in November."

"I am so very excited for you! I was just taken back that one would embark on such an adventure while in your delicate condition."

Nellie thought for a moment before answering. "My husband and I are excited about building a home in a new state and welcoming our new baby into it. With you being a mother, I'm sure you can understand how exciting that is. And, I did want to thank you for your concern of my condition, but I assure you, I am well bodied and will always have my husband near for help."

Sally nodded her head. "Yes, of course. I understand."

Sally got up and said her good byes. She knew they would be friends and was pleased to have the company.

All the wagons had their place in line and the families were eager to begin the journey. Nellie looked out and there were wagons for as far as she could see. Being in a wagon train was more exciting than Nellie first thought and the first day of travel went incredibly smooth. There were no problems or misadventures. They had made good time and thus far, everyone seemed in good spirits. One advantage of the wagon train was the cook the wagon master hired. He cooked for the entire group, morning and night. Everyone could contribute to the meal if they elected to, but it was chef's responsibility. This allowed the travelers to focus on the journey and other duties that must be attended to, without the worry of their next meal.

At the end of the first night, they devoured a hearty dinner and Nellie began tending to the livestock and horses. Sally approached

Nellie and before she had the chance to greet her, Sally was deep in monologue.

"Nellie, I must apologize to you about our earlier conversation. I believe I offended you, and well, I must explain why I reacted when you told me you were with child. You see, my husband and I have recently lost a baby girl. She wasn't more than a few months old. I went to check on her one morning and she had passed in the night. She was gone! I tried to wake her, but to no avail. She looked so peaceful, like she was having a beautiful dream. I felt so guilty! I should have checked on her during the night. She'd never slept that long before, but I was so tired. I slept all night and when I woke in the morning and realized she hadn't stirred, I knew something was wrong. It was the worst feeling, as if someone had gone into my chest and ripped out my beating heart. The pain was unbearable." Sally took a deep breath and a long pause. "That was when then we decided to come out west and start over. So please, forgive the way I reacted to your news about the baby. Maybe, we can still be friends?"

Nellie reached out and touched her arm. "Sally thank you for telling me your story. I do appreciate it and hold no ill will. So, why don't we put this behind us and have a fresh start? I know I'm going to need a friend on this crazy adventure." They hugged and were thrilled at the budding friendship.

The next day, everything seemed to be going great. The train was ready to depart on time, they continued to make good time, and on top of that, the weather was most favorable for traveling. The first issue arose around midday as they began the climb up the side of the mountain. There had been several wagon trains that made the journey before them, so it wasn't uncharted territory. Nonetheless, Nellie had concerns about the wagons and their weight going over the winding roads and trails along the mountain. Overall, the day was pleasant and the warmth of the sun shining made Nellie tired. As they stopped for a break, she decided to lay down in the back and rest. Platt was concerned, knowing that Nellie was not one to complain or give in to fatigue. Nellie saw the look on his face and reached out.

"I am alright, Platt. The sun was just making me a little sleepy, so I am going to rest for a while. I promise, the baby and I are alright." She saw the relief in his eyes.

It wasn't long before the wagon train was back in procession upon the trail. The path seemed much more winding and narrower than it had when Platt and A.L. traveled previously. Nellie rested and it gave Platt time to think through the plans for their new residence. He had many plans for the cabin they would live in while he built their dream home, but their forever home was his real focus. It would be large, to accommodate all the children they eventually would have to fill it. He had dreams of building a horse farm with corals filled with wild horses on their acreage.

As they approached the Columbia River, Platt noticed the road narrowed severely and he was dangerously close to the edge. It required all his strength and concentration to keep his wagon on the road. He was grateful for a good team of horses who responded to his commands so well. Just as he was starting to relax, a snake slithered out in front of his horse and spooked it. The horse reared up, causing the rear wheel of the wagon to slip off the road.

"Woah!" he called and tried desperately to control the horse, all while trying not to lose control of the wagon and get back up on the road. All the excitement awoke Nellie and she instantly realized what was going on. She quickly shifted her weight to the opposite side of the wagon. Platt used all his might in his attempt to regain control of the wagon and horses. Other wagons quickly saw what was happening and jumped into action. They grabbed and pulled at the wagon's side, trying to get it back on the trail without losing any freight. Platt's thoughts shifted to Nellie and it gave him the extra adrenaline he needed. He gave loud commands and was able to bring the team back under control. Once the horses were calm, the men were able to pull the wheel back up on the trail, with no major damage. Once Platt knew the situation was under control, he flew off the front seat and jumped in the back of the wagon.

"Nellie, please tell me you are unharmed?" He held her tightly to his chest and she felt his heart pounding. "Nellie, I was so scared! I thought I was going to lose you." A tear escaped from his eyes.

"I was afraid too, but I had every confidence in you, my darling. I knew you would protect me. I never doubted you for a moment!"

Overwhelmed with emotion, Platt couldn't resist and drew her in for a passionate kiss. Neither cared who was watching. They were the only people in the world at that moment. After the long embrace and regaining their equilibrium, the wagon master decided it was time to stop for the night. Platt was relieved to set up camp for the night and digest the events of the day.

That night as they ate dinner, Nellie couldn't bring herself to eat. Platt noticed and was very concerned.

"Nellie, are you sure you're alright? It's not like you to not eat your dinner. Is the baby okay? I am so concerned for both of you. I don't know what I would do if anything happened to you! Please, tell me you're going to be alright," Platt pleaded.

Nellie saw the worry on his face. "Platt, I assure you, I am fine. All the excitement has taken my appetite away. I promise you, it will return. I will be back to eating everything within sight in no time. So please, do not worry." She stroked the side of his face.

"Alright, but you have to promise that if there is any change in your condition, you will let me know at once," Nellie agreed.

They were exhausted and turned in early that evening to get rested up for the next day's travels. The next day proved to be a profitable travel day. They made up for the lost time from the day before. Platt was thankful for every good day they had, but he knew they would soon enter Indian Territory. He was on constant watch for any friendly's that might be sneaking around. He was fortunate to strike up a good relationship with Chief Joseph half son and his tribe, but there were many other tribes around. He was doubtful he could be that lucky twice. The day's journey was uneventful and they all sighed a breath of relief, as they were another day closer to their destination. They had settled in for the night when Platt was aroused by A.L.

"Platt, come quick! I think we have visitors." He motioned for him to come, trying not to wake Nellie. Platt slipped out quietly and joined his brother and father, as well as a few other men.

"What is going on?"

"Mr. Martin heard some noises over by the horses after we stopped for the night. No one has seen anyone, but you know Indians are sneaky. The horses are jumpy. I just don't have a good feeling about this."

Platt knew the native people well enough to know that if they were that close and wanted to attack, they would have already done such. If they were there, they were most likely watching to see if they were friendly or not.

"I propose that we take shifts, standing watch throughout the night. We can work in two's. That way, no one will be left alone and four eyes are always better than two. What do you all say?" Platt asked. The men unanimously agreed on the plan.

"Well then, A.L. and I will take the first shift and then in 2 hours, Martin and Smitherson will go next and so on. Is that agreeable?" The men nodded and returned to their wagons to rest before it was their turn to stand watch.

"Why did you agree for us to be on the first shift?" A.L. questioned his brother.

"A.L., I am sorry but if it's Chief Joseph's tribe out there, I want to have a chance to speak to them before anyone has a chance to act rashly. Also, if we go first then I can get back to bed before Nellie realizes I am gone. That way, she won't worry."

"I know you worry about her and the baby all the time, but you aren't giving her enough credit. She probably knows you're gone from the bed and will be up looking for you before long."

"I hope you're wrong on that one, brother." He gave his brother a pat on the back.

They began their patrol of the camp. Nothing looked suspicious, and they were grateful for that. They continued walking and checked all corners of the camp, as well as the horses. Out of nowhere, they heard the sound of cattle and other livestock in distress. They rushed over and were met by the sound of high-pitched yells. Indians rushed toward them with tomahawks and they instantly drew their guns. Platt looked closer and lowered his weapon. He yelled something in an Indian language. He spoke slowly and calmly to the Indians until they were all congregated around him. A familiar face broke through the crowd and took Platt into a strong embrace. Platt looked at everyone and observed countless faces, wrought with confusion and concern. He explained to the settlers that the man by his side was the soldier who married the chief's daughter. He went into detail and told of how the chief wanted him to marry his daughter, but he wasn't able to, due to his love for Nellie. He assured the crowd that the Indians were not their enemies, but their friends.

Not everyone was eager to embrace the new found friends, but for those who were willing, it was the beginning of a wonderful partnership. Platt was smart enough to know his Indian allies knew the land better than anyone and would be an asset in every way. They knew the proper crops to plants at certain times and where the fertile ground was. Best of all, they knew the best places to hunt buffalo, deer, elk, and turkeys. They were, undoubtedly, master hunters. There was much to learn from his friends and Platt was genuinely intrigued by the culture and enjoyed the company of the tribal people. There were many settlers who didn't share his view, but that didn't stop him from entering into friendship.

The trails were narrow as they traveled up and over the mountains, but Platt was grateful for the assistance from their friends. Knowing that they were inching closer and closer to their new home, made the trip go by expeditiously. Platt observed how the Indian woman and children never complained and walked most of the way on their journey. Some rode on horses, but most walked and carried their children on their backs. Nellie noticed one woman in particular. She was very beautiful and young, with dark black braided hair. She had an infant child, a boy, Nellie thought. She carried him in a wrap and he seldom cried or made noise. Nellie often wondered if it was alright. Nellie wanted to make friends with her. She knew neighbors would be scarce once settled, and having someone around with childbearing experience made her feel more comfortable. She was reluctant to approach her because of the language barrier, but decided to try, nonetheless.

"Hello, my name is Nellie Corbaley. I am with the wagon train and would like to make your acquaintance. Now, I know you may not understand me, but…"

The woman interjected, "What part did you think I wouldn't understand your unusual name or that you wanted to be friends?"

Nellie stood with her mouth open, not sure of what to say. "You speak English?"

"Yes. I studied at Yale University. My father is Chief Joseph and he wanted his only daughter to be educated. He sent me away to go to school, but I didn't finish. I came home, fell in love, and didn't return to school. I know your husband, Platt. I will be forever grateful to him, for he convinced my father to allow me to marry my true love. I am so glad to meet you, his true love. He spoke so highly of you, and now I've met you and see what he spoke of."

"So, you are the chief's daughter, the one that Platt almost married before we were reunited? He told me the story. I am so glad to meet you! Why don't you and your child come to our wagon and ride along with us? We shall get better acquainted!"

The women couldn't stop talking. They laughed, talked, and found they had more in common than they could have ever imagined. As it turned out, she was a midwife and studied medicine at the university.

Nellie sighed a great sigh of relief, knowing she had help nearby if needed.

The next day, they arose to the most glorious sunrise. Platt knew it was going to be a remarkable day! Everyone was hopeful to make good time, as the weather was favorable and the entire team was in good health. The Indian guides were immensely helpful in leading everyone safely over the trails. With their guidance, the group shaved numerous days off their trip. Platt was feeling quite good about the day. Nellie, on the other hand, felt like she couldn't bear to go much longer on the journey. The days seemed infinite and she felt like they would never arrive at their destination. Not to mention, the discomfort of the wagon. In her condition, it was near unbearable. She was determined not to complain and bit her tongue on several occasions but today, she was tired. Her body was growing larger and more uncomfortable every day.

The day went on and Nellie was uncommonly quiet. Platt could bear it no longer and broke the silence. Nellie feared that if she spoke, she would burst into tears. She knew the journey had worn on Platt and to unload her stored up emotions on him when he was so vulnerable, didn't seem fair. She responded in her typical manner.

"Platt, I am fine, but a bit fatigued from the ride. My back side, I must confess, is more than tired of riding on the buck board. I will be all too happy to arrive at our new home but other than that, I am doing well. I think I shall ride in the back of the wagon today on the pallet. I didn't sleep well last night, so I'll join you after I rest."

Nellie didn't want to add any more stress or tension to their eventful trip with her complaints. Her wish was to sleep and rest until they arrived.

"Nellie, wake up, you have to see this! Quick, Nellie, come here!" Platt yelled frantically.

Nellie was in a deep sleep and was startled by the commotion. "What is it? Platt, what in the world could be so important and cause such a great urgency?" Nellie asked, feeling a bit testy.

She poked her head through the opening in the wagon and immediately knew what the excitement was about. Never before had she seen anything so beautiful. The snowcapped mountains were huge and in the distance was a huge waterfall. The mountains were lush and covered with an abundance of trees. The sky was a deep, beautiful blue and looked like it came off an artist's canvas. She'd seen mountains in Indiana, but they were nowhere near as breathtaking. She was speechless for a moment.

"Nellie, we are home. What do you think?"

"Platt, I've never seen anything more lovely. It's truly breathtaking. Now, where did you say we were home steading?"

He feared she would be disappointed after enduring such a treacherous journey. "Nellie, remember when I said you could design any house you wanted and I would build it for you? Please, keep that in mind when I show you our homestead. What is there now is not indicative of what is to come."

Nellie sensed his uneasiness and had a strange churning in her stomach. "Platt, our home is wherever we are together. That is what makes it a home. Whatever the condition, we will fix it up and make it ours, until we have opportunity to build our dream home. The most important thing in the world is that we are starting our lives together. Let's celebrate that victory and the rest will fall into place." She smiled sweetly.

Platt was overwhelmed by her response. He picked her up off the ground and swung her around before realizing he was swinging around his pregnant wife. He quickly regained his composure and put her down. Nellie laughed. She loved when her husband had those momentary lapses of composure. Life with Platt was a continual journey of unexpected twists and turns, and she didn't want to miss a single moment of it.

"So, where is our new home? Are you going to show me or do I have to beg A.L. for directions?" Nellie asked with her hands on her hips.

"Alright, but remember to keep an open mind and thinking about all the plans we'll have for the new home and…"

"Alright, alright, you make it sound as if it were no more than a stable with a door attached." Nellie saw the look on his face and became more anxious. "Let's not put off the inevitable. Take me to our new home. Platt, would you please?"

He knew he couldn't put if off any longer and started up the Badger Mountain Trail. The trail was full of dense pine trees and the lush green of the mountainside was unlike anything they had ever witnessed. They watched wild mustangs run free, as if they owned the entire territory. He came to a complete stop and stayed silent.

Nellie became impatient. "Platt, what are you doing? Are we ever going to arrive at our cabin?"

"My love, we will be there soon. all good things to those who wait."

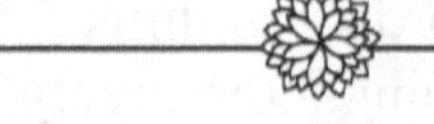

Chapter Fourteen
The New Home

"Alright, you can open your eyes and look. But remember, this is only temporary."

Nellie took her hands off her eyes and was awestruck at the nature surrounding their little cabin. There was a lush green pasture that she imagined would, soon, be full of young calves. She envisioned them running in the meadows, kicking up their heels glad to be free. She looked to the left of the mountains and saw a roaring waterfall in the distance. There were trees everywhere she looked! They were so beautiful and the smell of pine was heavy. She was convinced it was the most amazing place for their new home. She spun around, trying to take it all in.

"I know why you fell in love with this place. It's breathtaking!" She wrapped her arms around his neck.

"So, you don't mind the small cabin we will all have to share for this first winter?" He searched her face for clues.

"No. We are family and it will be close quarters, but we will make it our home. So, let's take a closer look at this cabin."

Richard Corbaley spoke to all of them. "We need to give thanks to the Lord for our safe keeping on the journey and to bless our new homes."

They bowed their heads and gave thanks for their safe arrival. Although their journey had been anything but smooth, they'd finally arrived and were ready for the next stage of their lives.

As they looked inside the cabin, Nellie could see why Platt had concerns. There was one large room, which would be the living room, a kitchen, a small bedroom, and a small loft. It was in bad repair with boards falling off, holes in the wall, and a missing door. Nellie wasn't sure if the stove worked, but was hopeful. The cupboards that once held doors only held hanging boards and dirt was caked everywhere she looked. She pulled her sleeves up and started commanding orders of what needed to be done. She got busy and the men jumped into action, like soldiers in an army.

It seemed like it took forever to get the cabin clean, but with everyone working together, the transformation was truly an amazing sight. The men made repairs to the floors, walls, cupboards and doors. They didn't have a large enough piece of wood to replace the back door, so they hung a large blanket to keep the weather and animals out. That night they sat for dinner and were all exhausted, but grateful for a new place to raise their family. They slept well that night but the next day, Platt was up early. Nellie was still in bed and questioned where he was going so early in the morning. He reassured her not to worry and that he was taking the mules up the mountain to start getting logs for their new home.

"You're going by yourself into mountains that you are unfamiliar with? I don't think that is wise."

"Don't worry, Nellie, I am going with him," A.L.'s voice boomed from the other room.

"There, you see, I am not by myself. We won't be gone too long. Don't fret, my love. Please, rest today. I fear you worked far too hard yesterday. Take good care of our child." He kissed her stomach gently.

She decided to stay in bed for a few more minutes and before she knew it, Platt was shaking her shoulders, asking her if she was alright.

"Oh, did you decide not to go?"

He looked at her and laughed. "We just returned from the mountains. It is afternoon. Nellie, are you feeling alright?"

"Of course, I am alright. I guess I was more tired than I'd realized. I need to get up and get you some lunch."

She was in the kitchen in no time, feeling rested for the first time in weeks. Platt, A.L., and their father sat at the table, setting up a schedule for getting logs from the mountains. They excitedly went to gather logs after devouring their lunch. Nellie stayed busy cleaning and trying to make the cabin a welcoming home for their new addition. In the back of her mind, she thought of her mother, who would be arriving in the near future. She didn't want her mother to fret about her living conditions. She'd been privileged to grow up with more than she could ever need and knew if her mother cast eyes on their meager cabin in its present form, she would grab her up and haul her back to California. She wasn't about to let that happen. She dove in with all the strength and vigor she could muster and cleaned. The wood floor that had been covered with inches of dirt, now shined like marble stone. She put out a few of their nicest pieces, which might have looked out of place in a run-down cabin with a curtain door made out of a buffalo hyde but she was determined to make her cabin a cute and welcoming home.

Platt, his father, and A.L. worked feverishly to build a barn and a corral for the cows and horses as soon as possible. With the winter weather just around the corner, they needed to make arrangements for the livestock they had and plan for the animals they would accumulate as they continued building their ranch. Platt was so pleased with their work and came into the cabin dog tired. Despite being exhausted, he was so appreciative of the hard work Nellie poured into their humble home.

"Nellie, the place looks wonderful! I almost turned around and went back out, for I was certain I'd gone into the wrong house. Are you certain you should have done all this by yourself? A woman in your condition needs to be resting," he said with concern.

"Woman in my condition you talk as if I were the first woman to ever be with child! Really, Platt, I'm quite capable of running a house and carrying a child at this same time?" she said with indignation.

"Darling, you know I never meant to insult you. My first concern is for you, always."

She smiled up into his dark piercing eyes that she loved so much and he took her into his arms. There was no place she loved more. They slept well that night and, in the morning, Platt was up early to begin another day of pioneer life. Nellie continued to unpack and arrange the house as best as she could. She knew she must get all the baby's items ready, so she pulled out the cradle. It had been her cradle and her parents couldn't bear to part with it, so they kept it and now she was preparing to use it for her and Platt's baby. She wondered what it would be like, dashing and smart like his father, or would it be a girl and look like her? She wondered about the child she carried and worried about the birth. There were no doctors out here that would be there to help when the baby came. She'd been so busy with the move, she never stopped to think about those details.

The days were filled with so much excitement and they were so busy getting settled, it seemed there was never any time to relax and enjoy the grandeur of the land. One day, Nellie decided to go to the Indian village and visit her friend. Platt was hesitant about her going and insisted that he stop his work and accompany her. They embarked together to the Indian village. The morning greeted them with brisk wind from the north and clouds that threatened snow. They were thankful that the Indian trails made traveling much more accessible and safer. They talked the entire trip and enjoyed each other's company, for they both knew times like this would be scarce in the upcoming future.

They arrived at the Indian Village and Chief Joseph was delighted to see them and discuss how Platt and his tribe could work together. They went off to talk and Nellie looked for the chief's daughter, Yellow Rose. She was brimming with questions about home births and knew she could alleviate her doubts and fears. She walked, deep in thought with all the things she had to remember to ask. She heard her name and turned to see her friend running towards her.

"Nellie, it's so good to see you again! What brings you to our village today?"

They walked back toward her teepee and chatted like long lost friends. Yellow Rose laid her hand on Nellie's bulging abdomen.

"I see. It is not long before your child makes their appearance. It is growing restless in your womb. You need to prepare for your little one. When she begins to move less, the time is upon you."

Nellie shared her concerns about giving birth at home and not having a doctor close by. Yellow Rose alleviated her fears and reassured Nellie that she was a short trip away. She told her when she starts into labor, they could come get her if she had any hint of trouble and she would be right there. It was just what she needed to put her mind at ease.

Platt found her and said they needed to head back before the snow started. They bid their friends farewell and headed down Badger Mountain. They arrived just in time. Just as they made it home, the snow began. The snow and wind blew violently and they were thankful their cabin was cozy with a good fireplace. They were quickly burning through the firewood they chopped, and knew what they had would never be enough to last throughout the winter. They hoped the storm would blow over quickly and give them time to stockpile their lumber inventory.

As soon as the storm passed, A.L. and Platt knew they had to make their way up the mountain to collect more logs. They needed more firewood and to make a door before the full winter was upon them. It was important to get a head start on chopping down trees for their new cabins. They had three homes to build, which translated into a lot of lumber and as many logs as they could get down the mountain before the snow began, the better. It was grueling manual labor, but the thought of building their own home and ranch propelled them forward. They made the decision to work until they obtained enough logs for one house at a time. They would work together to complete one, and then move on to the next one. It was a daunting task, but working together made it doable.

As Platt worked in the mountains, Nellie kept herself busy. She wanted to make their little cabin as homey as possible. It was proving to be a large challenge, as the cabin was lacking basics structures such as a door! But, knowing it was temporary made it bearable. With that thought in mind, she jumped into a cleaning frenzy. She scrubbed the walls, floors, windows, and the oven. She even hand washed the rugs and bedding. As Nellie took the last of the laundry off the clothes line, she looked around and was amazed at everything she'd accomplished that day. She began working on dinner, for she knew the men would be home soon. She looked out of the kitchen window and noticed dark clouds gathering and was concerned.

She sang as she was cooked, hoping that would take her mind off the weather outside and that the men weren't home yet. She finished dinner and there was no one but her to eat it. She waited and began to pace. Patience wasn't her strong suite. She took out a book to read but she couldn't concentrate, so she took out a sewing she was working on for the baby. The nightdress had tiny cross stitching and was labor intensive, but she didn't care. She wanted her child to have this garment made with stitches of love. She was deep in thought of her child as she stitched and was interrupted by a loud sound. It was the men coming down the mountain from their logging trip. They laughed as they came into the cabin and all stopped short as they looked around and noticed how cleanly the cabin was. Platt took off his boots at the door.

"Well, Nellie, it looks like you've been very busy today?"

"I don't know what happened today. I had an extra amount of energy today, so I cleaned and cleaned. Oh, dinner is ready! There is turkey in the oven, the one you shot the other day, potatoes, and there is apple pie in the oven. I made it from apples I picked from the tree in the yard. Now, sit down and eat. You must be starved. I hope you enjoy it!"

"Are you sure you should have done all of this today, being so close to your due date?"

"I don't know. I felt wonderful today and there were things that needed to be done. After all, I'm not sick! Women have babies every day! I'll be just fine."

"But, my wife doesn't have a baby every day. Don't you understand my concern for you?" Platt walked over to her and patted her bulging abdomen.

"So, are we going to eat, or not?" Al asked with a smile.

"Yes, of course we are. Why don't you all get washed up and I'll put dinner on the table."

A.L. loved Nellie and was so happy for his brother. He loved her pioneer spirit and how she didn't complain, although the cabin was definitely not what she had been previously accustomed to. It made him, all the more, endeared to her.

They sat down for dinner and recalled the events of the day and plans for the new cabins. They hoped to get enough logs before the harsh winter began, so they could start building their cabins as soon as spring came. Nellie enjoyed hearing about their adventures, but had great respect for the mountains and knew the dangers they faced daily. She also knew the weather wouldn't stay pleasant for much longer and working through the winter brought its own share of challenges. She would have to trust that the men would be careful and take proper precautions as they worked.

Sometimes, Nellie would close her eyes and dream about their new home. She imagined where the table would go, where they would put the crib, and where the rocking chair would be placed. She wanted it by a window so she could rock their new baby while looking out at the scenic mountains. She sometimes wondered how all of it would come together. The ranch, cattle, the new homes, and the baby, it seemed like more than anyone could possibly accomplish. She was so grateful for A.L. and Richards help. Every day, she saw how important family was and realized how blessed she was to be blazing the new frontier as a pioneer woman.

The next morning, Platt prepared to go up the mountain and get another load of logs. He looked over at his sleeping wife and was grateful to see her resting. She had a restless and uncomfortable night and he was worried about her. He was thankful the pregnancy would be over soon and she would be more comfortable. He looked at her and knew he made the right decision to bring her to the unsettled land with him. He reached over and kissed her head before he left for the day.

The day brought a brisk morning, but no threat of inclement weather. The sun poked its head over the mountains, casting a hue of purple across the land. It was breathtaking and the men appreciated the view as they worked tirelessly.

It made Platt uneasy to leave Nellie while he was so far up the mountain with her due date approaching quickly. Father would often stay behind to be there, just in case. Nellie protested that she was able to take care of herself, but knew it fell on deaf ears when it came to Platt. She would never admit it, but the days were more pleasant when Richard stayed behind. She found that some days, even menial tasks were becoming too difficult. No matter how tired, she always tried her best to cook for the men. She found that she was a pretty decent cook. She was grateful she spent so much time in the kitchen with Gerte as a child. She feared what her cooking would be without that time. Thinking about her childhood made her miss her mother more than she ever anticipated. She longed for the day when her mother joined them and could help them with their baby. Nellie made the startling realization that she knew nothing about raising a child. She hoped she could be a great mother, like her own. She had every confidence that Platt would be a tremendous father. But, they would take one day at a time and trust God to help them be the best parents they could be.

Chapter Fifteen
The Arrival of Baby Ida Mae

Early that morning, Nellie tried desperately, to no avail, to get comfortable. After much tossing and turning, she decided it was no use and she would get up and take the uninterrupted moments to write a letter to mamma and papa. She was concerned about Dora and wondered why she hadn't heard from her or about her from her parents. She sat on the edge of the bed and looked down at her impressive stomach. She wondered how much bigger it would become. She thought, surely, there was no more room for the child to grow. She placed her hand on her stomach and enjoyed the dance of her unborn child.

By the time Platt woke, Nellie already had breakfast on the table. It was a delicious looking spread with biscuits, corncakes, and fruit.

"Nellie, what is all of this? I told you to rest today and not to get up early. I certainly appreciate this amazing breakfast, but darling, you outdid yourself."

"Sit down and eat before it gets cold. I made extra biscuits, so you can take them up in the mountains with you. I don't know what came over me. I couldn't sleep so I decided to get up and start breakfast. After this, I have some cleaning and laundry to do. I have some apples from the tree, so I might make a pie later. I just have a burst of energy. I have to keep busy!"

Platt looked at his beautiful wife and smiled. He heard from other man, whose wives had given birth, say this burst of energy meant it wouldn't be long until their child made their appearance into the world. The thought of bringing a child into the unsettled land was a little unnerving, yet, he knew they would have a good life once they were able to finish the cabin and ranch for his family.

The men returned after a hard day's work and they all enjoyed a wonderful meal together. They laughed and sang songs after dinner, and then Nellie read in a book. After a lovely evening, they turned in for the night and were fast asleep. They hadn't been asleep for very long, when Nellie woke with a searing pain. She lay in bed, not wanting to disturb Platt. She thought it was a sour stomach from something she ate, but the pain didn't go away or lessen in severity. She stood up and a gush of fluid released from her. It startled her and she hollered as she grabbed her abdomen. Platt woke and was startled to see Nellie doubled over and panting.

"Nellie, oh my, are you alright?" It scared him to see her in such pain and he felt helpless.

"Nellie, what can I do? Please, tell me what to do!" he pleaded.

"Platt, the baby is coming! I've lost my fluid and have labor pains. I have a terrible feeling that something isn't right! Please check and see."

He'd helped deliver livestock, but this was totally different. When Nellie had labor pains, Platt instructed her to push and let her squeeze his hand as hard as she needed. After a period of pushing with no child, Platt knew Nellie was in trouble. His child needed more help and assistance than he could offer. He woke his father and A.L. and had them stay with Nellie. He jumped on his horse and rode like the wind to the closest town to get help and save his wife and child! He finally found a doctor's house and knocked wildly on the door, but had no response. He wouldn't take no for an answer. He kept knocking and after a while, a small older woman in a night dress and bonnet opened the door.

"I need the doctor! My wife is having trouble giving birth. Please, tell me where he is so I can get him!"

"I am so sorry, young man. The doctor has gone out of town. There is scarlet fever over in the next county and he is here treating those folks. I am truly sorry." She closed the door.

Platt knew he had to move quickly to save his wife and child. "The Indian village! That girl is a midwife. I am going to fine her!"

He rode faster than he'd ever rode before! He knew he must get to Yellow Rose soon, so she could save Nellie. Platt flew into the village and frantically shouted. Luckily for Platt, Chief Joseph was awake and immediately approached him.

"What brings you out in the night? What is wrong, my friend?"

Platt could barely catch his breath, but told him that he needed his daughter to assist Nellie and she was having birthing complications. Chief summoned for Yellow Rose, without delay, and told her to get her bag and be off to help Nellie. Yellow Rose mounted her horse and followed Platt. They arrived at the cabin in record time.

Wildfire saw Nellie and knew exactly what to do. Nellie was damp from perspiration and becoming very weak. Yellow Rose attended to Nellie and could see the concern Platt had for her, so she asked him to heat some hot water. Yellow Rose birthed a few mothers with babies in the same condition, so she knew she must maneuver the baby to get it out. The baby lay cross ways in the birth canal and it was impossible for Nellie to deliver the baby if it stayed in this position. She had Nellie lie on her left side with her leg pulled up, as she was hoping this would convince this baby to turn over and come down the birth canal. Nellie put on a brave face, for she was determined not to be one of those women who screamed their way through child birth? Yellow Rose used the water Platt warmed to sterilize the rags and used cool water to bath Nellie's brow. With every contraction, the sweat pooled on her forehead and she knew she was getting weaker. She would rest between contractions, but it seemed as soon as one would subside, another would come with more intensity. Yellow Rose knew it was getting serious. She'd heard about a surgical procedure some doctors were performing on difficult deliveries, but she'd never done it and didn't want to experiment on her friend. The contractions grew closer and the child still wasn't progressing down the birth canal. Finally, with one last attempt, she moved Nellie into a squatting position. She was uncomfortable, but all of the sudden, Nellie felt the overwhelming urge to push. She groaned and screamed, for what seemed like an eternity to Platt. The baby still wouldn't move, so Yellow Rose had Nellie get on all fours. Nellie looked at her with a strange look, but was too weak to argue. Yellow Rose was getting nervous, for she'd never had a baby take this long. She knew she must deliver the baby soon, before both Nellie and baby were in jeopardy. She laid her down again and tried to force the baby down. Nellie pushed some more and finally, Yellow Rose could see the head begin to crown. She had Nellie roll on her back and took two last pushes. Those in the other room, who had been praying for them, heard a beautiful cry. On November 11, 1883, Ida Mae Corbaley made her appearance into the world. She had ten fingers and ten toes, and was perfect in every way. Yellow Rose came out and told Platt he was the father to a beautiful baby girl and Nellie and baby were doing well. Platt didn't hesitate and ran to the other room. He saw the most beautiful sight. It was beyond anything he could have imagined. He stood in a trance. He couldn't speak for a while, for he was too overcome with emotion.

"Nellie, how are you and the baby?" Platt asked so softly, she could barely hear him.

"Platt, I want to introduce you to your daughter, Ida Mae. Would you care to hold her?"

He looked in awe and nodded yes. He sat on the bed next to Nellie and held their daughter in his arms. At first, he was afraid he might break her. He was so in love with this tiny bundle of joy and was so gentle with her.

They thanked Yellow Rose for her assistance. A.L. and father volunteered to take her back to her home, after being introduced to their granddaughter and niece. Before they left, Yellow Rose gave Nellie strict instructions to take it easy for a few days. Yellow Rose said she'd be back in a few days to check on them and make sure she was alright. Nellie thanked her and hugged her repeatedly. As she rode home that morning, Yellow Rose thought there was nothing more wonderful than helping to bring a life into the world. She smiled the whole way home.

Autumn in Badger Mountain

Nellie had just finished feeding Ida Mae when she went to lay the baby down. She found that, suddenly, she was not alone. She was in a room filled with Indians. They'd just entered through the buck skin door. She asked them if they needed Platt, but they were curious and wanted to see the first white child born in the territory. Nellie happily obliged them. She picked Ida Mae up and was very proud to show her off. She'd heard talk from some of the travelers from the wagon train that weren't Indian friendly, but her experiences had thus far been favorable. In fact, if it hadn't been for Yellow Rose, she wouldn't have their precious child. Platt always had a friendly relationship with the Indians, and Nellie was glad to continue it. Platt came home and the Indians were still there. He was excited to tell them he had been blessed that morning and shoot three deer. He had plans to go to their village that day to see if they could us one of the deer for meat. They gladly took the deer and left after giving Platt a gracious thank you.

"I sent a telegram to your mother this morning. I looked at the house for your parents in town and it looks as if it will be completed very soon, maybe within two weeks. So before they arrive, it will be ready for them. They won't have to stay here in this crowded cabin."

Nellie was overwhelmed with the thought of her mother being here. She needed someone to talk to and share her concerns about raising their child. She started to cry.

"Nellie, my darling, are you alright? Did you not want your Mother to come?"

"No, I think I'm just tired being up at night with the baby. I am so thrilled about my mother coming. You going to all the trouble to send the telegram and check on her house in town means so much to me."

Platt held Nellie in his arms and let her cry as he comforted her. He loved her so much and wanted her to be happy in this new life on the frontier. The settler life didn't come without its share of challenges and trials. Their first winter was a cold one with a lot of ice, which made log hauling more difficult. But, everyday Platt, A.L., and father would trek up Badger Mountain to cut down logs and bring them down the mountainside. It turned out to be more of a project than Platt had bargained for, but none the less, every day was a new adventure on the mountain. One morning, after the men had left for the day, Nellie was home and came face to face with a young Indian warrior in her living room. Nellie's heart began to beat wildly and she scooped up her baby into her arms. She regained her composure and cleared her throat.

"What do you want?"

The warrior didn't know the English language. Nellie tried as hard as she could to stay calm. They motioned to some food and it appeared they were hungry. With the weather conditions, it had been difficult for some to get meat to feed their families. Platt and A.L. had been blessed in their recent hunting trips and were able to shoot several deer. Nellie gathered a large amount of meat, potatoes, and some fresh baked pies. She felt it was the least she could do to repay them for the kindness they had shown towards them. She gave him the food and he nodded his head, as if to say thank you. Then, he started making a grunting noise. She soon made sense of it, and realized he was asking for a blanket. So, she gave him a blanket and he nodded. He was gone as quickly and quietly as he came. After he left, she sat down and found she was shaking. She clutched her baby close to her bosom and looked down at her sweet idyllic face. She had slept through the entire ordeal and Nellie was so thankful. Nellie relayed the story to Platt that evening and he was very upset. He made the decision that Nellie and Ida would not be left alone ever again.

"I can't have anything happen to my wife or child," he spoke firmly that evening at dinner. Father and A.L. agreed that this was uncharted territory and no undue risk should be taken.

"Does anyone want my opinion on this?" Nellie questioned.

"No. The decision has been made. I can't put my wife and child at risk. Soon enough, your mother will be here and you and Ida will have someone to visit with."

Nellie crossed her arms and walked across the room. She knew he was right, but they were harmless Indians. Platt being friends with Chief Joseph was reassuring, but she wondered what to do if an unfriendly showed up. She couldn't escape her thoughts and knew in her heart he was right, but she would wait to tell him that.

Chapter Sixteen
MOTHER'S MOVE

"Will you get the door, darling?" Mother asked father and he was pleased to do it.

"Telegram!" the man shouted at the door.

"Oh yes, thank you young man! Here is your tip."

He turned toward Mary with a delighted smile. "Oh Mother, the baby has arrived! It's a girl named Ida Mae Corbaley! Platt also said our house in Waterville will be ready for occupancy by the time you arrive. Oh Mother, isn't this the most wonderful news? We are Grandparents!"

She began to cry. In this moment, all her cares and troubles were forgotten. "Our precious daughter and son-in law have given us the greatest gift!"

They spent hours notifying Mel and Dora to tell them they were now aunts. Mel was ecstatic to have a little one to spoil! Dora was excited but when they spoke with her, they could tell she was getting weaker. Father yearned for the pioneer country and a new beginning with his family, but he knew he couldn't leave Dora while she was so ill. Father knew Mary was a strong woman and she would be alright on the trip out west. He knew it wasn't an easy decision, but it was the right one.

Mary stayed busy with preparations for the trip. She had to get things packed, send things ahead on the train, and leave things for father so he would be comfortable while staying back. She was excited to see Nellie and Platt and to meet her first grandchild, but the thought of being separated from her husband and the likelihood she would never see Dora again was plaguing her. She tried not to think about it and imagined what Ida Mae looked like. As anxious as Mary was to get to Nellie and Platt, she had the strangest feeling of dread that she just couldn't shake. She was a strong woman and had a deep faith to see her through anything, yet, she couldn't get past this feeling. In an effort to distract herself, she busied herself with preparations.

Father rose early on the morning of Mary's departure. He sat by the fire, drinking his tea and reading. Mary arose awhile later and readied herself for the journey. She entered the room and father was deep in thought. He didn't raise his head, but spoke to her.

"Mary, you are the love of my life and I will miss you more than I can comprehend. I know this is what we agreed upon, but I didn't think it would be so difficult."

Mary fell into his big embrace. He held her, not wanting to ever let go.

Once settled on the train, she pulled out a needle work dress she was making for Ida Mae. She had such anticipation of holding her, rocking her, and reading her stories. She couldn't wait to tell her stories about her Mother when she was a little girl and lived in Indiana.

The trip was extremely, for which she was very grateful! She was thankful the railroad was much more completed and now, connected much closer to Waterville. She was glad for the time on the train. It allowed her to work on a porcelain head doll for Ida Mae. As she stitched the doll together, she couldn't help but wonder about Nellie. The new pioneer lifestyle was so foreign to Nellie, she wondered how she was adjusting. She would assess the situation once she arrived and see their beautiful baby girl. So, for now, she would leave it in God's mighty hands.

The next day, Mary was amazed at how refreshed she felt. She was pleasantly surprised at the luxurious accommodations on the train! The breakfast was a delicious spread of pastries, teas, and coffee. It was delightful! After eating, Mary went back to her berth to work on her sewing. She wanted to finish the doll before she arrived, because she knew it would be a flurry of activity once she was there. She wondered what she was getting herself into. As Mary carefully sewed the doll, she looked out the window and noticed the enormous and majestic mountains. She grew up in the mountains, but she never remembered them looking like that. She enjoyed the beautiful view as she lovingly sewed the doll for Ida Mae.

"There," she said to herself, proudly.

She finished the last stitch and Olive, the doll, was finished. She had dark wavy hair and her body was stuffed with cotton, so she could be hugged. Her feet and hands were made out of porcelain and she was adorned with a beautiful blue dress. Mary hoped the doll would be loved by her granddaughter, and maybe even her daughters. She hoped they would know the doll was stitched with love by their grandmother, Mary Jefferson.

She'd been so busy with Dora, father, and getting everything packed up and ready for this move, she hadn't had time for the luxury of reading. Now, since she was captive to a berth, she took advantage of the past time she enjoyed so much. Before long, she found herself drifting off to sleep. She dreamt about arriving in Washington and it was such a joyous occasion. It was so real and vibrant in color, it was if she was there already. She startled as she was woke by the train attendant.

"My lady, I apologize for waking you. I came to get you for dinner since you didn't make it to the dining car."

"Oh, I was so exhausted. I decided to rest and I must have dosed off. I had a dream and it was glorious! Oh, look at me rambling on, please forgive me."

The young steward reassured her not to worry. Mary quickly readied herself and made her way to the dining car. All through dinner, Mary couldn't get the dream off her mind. She developed the overwhelming urgency to write to Papa and check on Dora's condition. Maybe she was just over tired. Either way, she missed him and wanted to write him. That night, Mary retired early, knowing she was almost at the end of her journey to Washington.

Mother Arrival

"Platt, please hurry! I don't want to miss the stage," Nellie pleaded.

She hurried to get Ida Mae ready and looking as beautiful as a baby could be. Before they knew it, they were on their way to pick up mother. They arrived at the stage early and Nellie was relieved. She could finally catch her breath and make sure she was presentable and Ida Mae looked her best, before being introduced to her grandmother.

"Nellie, the stage is coming!" Platt said with utmost excitement.

The stage rounded the corner into the station. Nellie was so excited to see her mother. Her heart pounded and she felt like a child on Christmas morning. One by one, the passengers dismounted from the stage and then, at last, there she was. Nellie almost forgot how lovely she was.

"Nellie and Platt!" Mother dismounted the stage and waved at them. "My, how good it is to see you again! Let me see this precious granddaughter of mine!"

Mother was helplessly in love with Ida Mae, despite only knowing her for a few moments. Ida Mae cooed and laughed as they played together. Platt helped with the luggage and trunks mother brought along on her journey.

"Mother Jefferson, your house appears to be coming along and is near finished. It's at a point where you can move in, get settled, and unpack all your trunks and crates. I believe you will like your new home. I know you are accustomed to a large house with a servant quarters, but this house is large and has two stories. It's right in the middle of town, Waterville Washington close to the general store and the new dress shop. I believe you will be happy there," Platt said contently.

"I am sure I'll love it. Especially, since I'll be close to my family and this precious baby girl."

Nellie hugged her Mother. She asked questions incessantly. She wanted to know about her father, Mel, and specifically, Dora. She wanted to prepare her mother to see their home. It certainly wasn't what she grew up in, but it was what they had for now. More importantly, they needed to get mother settled in her home. They arrived at the house after a short while. Mother walked from room to room and didn't say anything for a long while. Platt and Nellie were nervous and felt she wasn't pleased. Then, she spoke.

"Well, we won't have as much room as we had before, but this is adequate. It will do nicely! I'll just have to see where everything will fit." She turned to face Platt. "Thank you for all your hard work in finding this house for us. And of course, thank you for taking such good care of my daughter and granddaughter."

"You're welcome. It was my pleasure to find this spot for you. But really, it was Nellie who told the workers exactly what you liked."

Mary looked over at her youngest daughter, who was all grown up and now, a wife and mother. It was hard to absorb. "Thank you, Nellie. I guess, I still have difficulty remembering just how capable you truly are."

Mother asked Platt and Nellie how their house was coming along.

"Well, we are bringing logs down every day. We've started building the house and are trying to get enough logs to have it framed before the snow flies. If we get it framed, the rest can be done inside, even in the cold weather."

"It sounds to me like you are settling in and making great progress! This, certainly, is a beautiful country. I can see why you fell in love with it."

It would take some time and work to get everything unpacked and her house set up, but time was something Mary had an abundance of now. Mary worked tirelessly to get her belongings put in the perfect place and at the end of the day, she was extremely tired from the trip and unpacking. Despite the fatigue, she decided to sit down and write a letter to papa.

Dearest Lester,

I hope this finds you well and your business affairs will be wrapped up soon, so you can join me in our new home. Nellie and Platt seem to be adjusting to pioneer life well. Our Granddaughter is the most beautiful baby! Nellie says she sleeps and eats well, and seldom cries. They are fortunate to have such a wonderful baby for their first child.

The mountains here are majestic and the open wilderness is stunning to behold. Platt is working hard, with the help of his father and A.L. on their new home. It will be a log cabin with a large barn and corral for the wild mustangs he is planning on rounding up. Our house is a two story wood house. It's very spacious, with plenty of room for all our belongings. The township is small, but more settler families are coming to this area daily. It is really growing!

It has been a long day, but I wanted to write to you as soon as I was unpacked enough to find my parchment and pen. I am looking forward to the day we are reunited. Please send my love to Dora and Mel.
Love,

Mary

After completing the letter, Mary had the strangest feeling that something wasn't right. She didn't know what, but she just knew. She tried to ignore her thoughts and turned in for the night.

Mary woke the next morning, much later than she was accustomed to. She readied herself and was excited to start her chores. Mary wondered where to begin.

"I'll take it one room at a time. I better get started," Mary said to herself.

Mary worked tirelessly throughout the day, and was surprised at how much she was able to accomplish. It was beginning to look like a home and not an empty house. Her curiosity spiked as she heard a knock at the door. She wasn't expecting visitors. She opened the door to a wonderful surprise awaiting her! Nellie and Ida Mae came to visit. Mary was overjoyed to have the company.

"Mother, the house is looking wonderful! You've always had a special way of decorating and know just how to make your house look perfect!"

Nellie laughed. "Our home is nothing as nice as this one. It doesn't even have a door. A hide hangs there, for now. But, I remind myself this is only temporary. Platt is working very hard to get the logs down the mountain. It's a little overwhelming at times, but I can't let on to Platt. He is doing the best he can. I agreed to come out west and be a pioneer woman, so I can't complain. I'm thankful every day we have a beautiful baby girl and a roof over our heads. I wanted to let you know, Platt was approached by the settlers and asked to be a sheriff. He said he would think about it and talk it over with me, but I really think he'll take the position."

They visited and were both so glad to be together. Mother caught Nellie up on Dora's condition and the status of her father's business dealings.

"My, so much has happened in such a short time!" Nellie exclaimed.

Time passed, far too quickly, and it was time for her to head back to their home. Nellie felt so blessed to have her mother back. Ida Mae seemed to love her grandmother, even after only being acquainted for a short while. She made it back to their homestead and knew there would be hungry men coming down the mountain soon. She got busy and started dinner. She loved cooking and keeping house. It greatly pleased her when she made meals the men devoured and enjoyed. There were a few meals that were simply inedible, but she told herself practice makes perfect.

Chapter Seventeen
The First Winter

The first winter was one they would not soon forget. Every day, except Sunday, the men headed up the mountains to cut down logs. They agreed the first completed cabin should be Platt and Nellies. Since there were three of them, they needed the home more urgently. They went logging every day the weather allowed. In total, they chopped and hauled 591 logs for Platt's home. Some days, they would stop the logging and hunt for deer. Platt was a skilled hunter and almost always came home with deer.

Early January, snow began to fall in large flakes. Despite leaving early due to the inclement weather, Platt returned from the mountains with two large deer. Sometime after Platt returned, there was a knock on the door. It was Mitchel, a fellow settler. He explained that he and his neighbor, John Borowman had gone out hunting and became separated and Borrowman did not return. He hadn't seen him since that time. The men immediately left to look for him in the mountains. They were so vast and uninhabited, a man could be hurt and calling for help, but there would be no one for miles to hear him. It could become a serious situation quickly. The men looked tirelessly, but to no avail. Borrowman was found days later. He became disoriented while hunting and tried to look for Mitchel, but could not find him. He stumbled upon an old miner's cabin and stayed there to be protected from the elements. The next day, he started out walking in the direction of what he thought was home. He found a logging road marker he was familiar with and continued walking. He kept walking until a logger found him stumbling, and helped reunite him with his family.

January moved into February and real progress was being made on Platt and Nellie's home. Baby Ida Mae got bigger by the day and was such an agreeable child. She ate and slept perfectly, and became more aware of her surroundings every day. She loved her mom but when her daddy walked into the room, she cooed incessantly. It melted his heart and Nellie was grateful to witness it.

Nellie couldn't believe the day was coming, at last. They were moving into their new home, with windows and a door! It had a big kitchen, a magnificent bedroom, and windows everywhere. To her, it was a palace, one built with love! They moved their stove into the kitchen, then the trunks, and later, they moved the rest of the furniture. They set up the cradle and Nellie was busy putting things on the shelves Platt, A.L., and father built. She put emphasis on arranging her kitchen, as that was the heart of the home where meals were shared with family. Nellie was ecstatic to finally get settled in. It was even more special that the house was the built with love and by their own hands.

February 23rd 1885 had finally arrived. It was he day they officially moved into their new home. Nellie stood outside and looked at the house they built together. She knew it would hold years of memories and happiness as they blazed the pioneer life together. The move had not been easy, even though most of the work in preparation was done from before because they did not have the room to unpack their belongings from California. Nellie was glad to be in her new home, but knew the men had much work ahead of them. As soon as their home was finished, the men began to build a home for father and then AL.

One day as Platt and A.L. worked in the barn, the county assessor came to collect. Platt reminded him the county assessment taxes were not due for several months, per the pioneer settlement law. The assessor said the city government wasn't what they had hoped for and the sheriff was crooked. They asked Platt if he would run for Marshall. His initial response was to say no, as he had a monumental workload ahead of him and his first priority was to his family. He thanked the assessor and told him he would discuss it with his wife and let him know their decision.

It seemed in no time at all, Platt and A.L. were able to finish the other two houses. It was rewarding work and the men had utmost satisfaction as the day finally came for each to move into own home.

Spring began to make its annual debut and it was a different beauty than Indiana or California had been. Platt and Nellie stood at their front porch and looked out at the beautiful mountains. They felt as if they were finally home. Nellie was so grateful they had been brave enough to make the journey into this unchartered country. She could only wonder what new adventures awaited them in this new land.

About the Author

I am a wife, mother, grandmother and a retired pediatric nurse. I love to bake, craft, sew, read, write most of all spending time with my family and friends. I made my home in Texas with my husband and our two dogs Cocoa and Jax. (our rescue dog)